L O V E ' S
M A N S I O N

LOVE'S MANSION

Paul West

RANDOM HOUSE

NEW YORK

Library of Congress Cataloging-in-Publication Data
West, Paul
Love's mansion/Paul West.—1st ed.
p. cm.
ISBN 0-394-58734-0
I. Title.
PR6073.E766L68   1992   813'.54—dc20   92-6804

Manufactured in the United States of America
2 4 6 8 9 7 5 3
First Edition

Book design by J. K. Lambert

To MNW *and* AMW

In Loving Memory

Love's mansion has so many rooms.

Diane Ackerman, "At Belingshausen,
the Russian Base, Antarctica," from
Jaguar of Sweet Laughter

Contents

I

LEXINGTON

Pianos Don't
Explode

HOW IN A village free of fog could the boy and the girl have never met? Who had been keeping them from each other, in the cause of what decorum or delay? Her breath sweetened by violet cachous, Hildred Fitzalan toddled off to hear and nod pleasedly at the bells, taken to them by Kathleen Kent, who made her livelihood escorting well-to-do children on outings, in her plaid toilet bag a wet washcloth and some extra hankies freshly starched, as well as a compass and whistle for emergencies. Kathleen was a provident protectress, with a much-bitten lower lip, the badge of all she wanted to get off her chest but saved for later, at home on Southgate. She was everyone's Kath: nanny, guardian, sentry, guide, retainer, scout, and here in her charge today was the little Fitzalan who doted on bells, who seemed to hear them all the time anyway and marched deliberately toward the church only to gain some kind of amplified corroboration—perhaps a bulge of pressure in the air as the two of them neared the door.

ONCE AGAIN trying to retrieve his mother's girlhood from the penumbra of Kathleen Kent, Clive Moxon shivered at what he had long been trying to do. Each time he came from the States to visit his mother, he quizzed her about the old days, before he was born, before Hildred his mother married, before she even got to know Harry his father and they became good friends. Each summer he would ask her and she would respond, and he spent the rest of his year trying to flesh her out as child, girl, adolescent; he who had no more seen Kath Kent as a teenager than he had seen his mother as a girl. What urged him on in this he could not be sure, but he was a novelist, perhaps not a busy enough one, and in some peculiar zone of his brain, an anachronistic nursery no doubt, he longed to have his mother's and father's childhood to set alongside his own: three lost children regained against the heave of time that had taken his father, allowed him his mother as far as ninety-four, and pushed himself well into middle age. He wanted to break the laws of succession and forgetfulness, bringing those two back: his father through his mother's memories, his mother the same way. He would embellish the record with tender augments whipped up as he swam laps, shoveled snow, stood in line at the post office, and waited in airports with his customary two skim milks, one straw, on the seat beside him—as if escorting *them* to a distant destination.

Year after year he pieced it together, preferring to exclude himself, at least until he was born, checking some of it with his mother who, with every visit, varied her tale, although with no desire to confuse him. He worked into the fabric of her smallness her every particular, and thanked God for the diligence of human memory.

WHAT HIS MOTHER and Kath Kent at last stood near, their breath briefly held, was not the big bells up in the belfry, marooned among windows with Gothic points and open slats, bragging and bullying, but little handbells rung on leather straps. She saw some half-dozen men standing between the altar and the pews lazily plying their forearms to make a sound that made her flinch and wish for other bells, those from a baby's harness, a Christmas tree, a cat's neck.

The small boy next to her had a high color and hair black as that of the blackest dogs. He appeared not to flinch at all, not even during moments of emphasis when the handbells didn't so much chime as yelp and stop, their clappers quelled by a finger thrust into the bell's mouth. He seemed not to hear, as if he found her more interesting than the bells. Then he half grinned at her as if they two (and the other children) were trespassers in that vaulted chill where the noise of pigeons filtered down from on high. It was a meeting wordless and unintended, at the close of a century in which entertainment remained humble and untechnical and people strolled for miles to hear handbells, or the church organist of a nearby parish, or just to watch larks ascending.

The boy saw an ample, resolute mouth, a gray-green eye hue he had never seen before, and brown hair wrapped in too many ribbons. Older and taller than he, she "was musical"; he knew the phrase and wondered if, frail as her wrists looked, she had come there to ring a handbell or two, or sing in the intervals of ringing. They said nothing, not with Kathleen Kent standing so close, her head hidden in a dark-brown hive of the tightest curls, but it amounted to their first tryst. Courtesy of the campanology club, to visit which, during a performance, was a "treat" for her, whereas for him it was an escape. He would walk through one passage, cross a path, trot through the graveyard, and enter the church, where sometimes, up in the belfry, his father let him help mend ropes, rolling the new knots with his bare boy's feet. There were other mysteries of the church, too, which his father controlled; but for her it was just another temple of music: a mere extension of Chopin. They would encounter each other again here, they both knew that, and one word would lead to another, certainly before they were dead and brought back in here in flower-strewn boxes. To say hello to her he yodeled once, tossing his voice to the belfry for the echo, which she answered by extending one hand and playing a rippling chord in midair. The pianist and her swain had met.

For days afterward, Harry tried to imagine what her life was like. Were there really piano stools among the well-to-do? What did the well-to-do *do?* Did the girl play for people or only to herself? Had she been born able to do it, the way a robin or a thrush sings? Did she wash her hands first? What if the piano keys were dusty? Did she go to school? Not his, or he would have seen her in the playground. Was there another school, where piano players went? There was, and it was called Ruthin College, only a few hundred yards from his own, but in a different dimension, where the girl learned grammar, read Alfred, Lord Tennyson and Matthew Arnold, and studied Elocution so that she would be well-spoken whenever music failed. As for her, his yodel had made her wonder if he came from Switzerland or some northern mountainous area, where he tended sheep or goats. She wanted to play piano (pianoforte was the correct word, she knew) while he yodeled, wondering how it would sound. His jersey was torn, but his mind was whole and shone when you spoke to it without talking down. She had no idea, then, that his parents had daringly named him Hereward, after Hereward the Wake, who defended the Fen country against Norman invaders. The attempt at grandeur or myth had collapsed into Herry, which had fast become Harry, as commonplace a name as a boy could have. She, named Hildreth, had fast become Hilly, and would soon learn that "Sam" was the self-applied nickname of anyone put upon.

In this matter of naming they came together, both sets of parents having been influenced by the local parson, who wanted to bring old Anglo-Saxon names back into currency. So this once-Roman village in the Byron–D.H. Lawrence country had people walking around in it who, at a pinch or during a thunderclap, would answer if called upon to such names as Wulfric, Aelfric, Athelstan, Wenhaver, Winifried, and Hroswitha, which readily enough had lapsed into Rick or Rich, Alf, Stan, Wendy, Winny, and Rosy, the ancient heroic legacy lost beneath a chummy surface that put paid to anything outlandish.

Harry and Hilly, almost vanishing into extreme informality, made anonymous by similarity, wandered into life together, little occupied by their names' ancestry, more intent upon what force had lured them together and taught their eyes the trick of mutual smiling even when they had no idea of what to talk about beyond My dad's a butcher (hers), My dad's down the pit. Harry wore boots whose laces dangled, whereas Hilly wore button-up boots fastened with a special hook. They met often enough at the handbell ringing or, until shooed away when the organist came to practice, in an otherwise empty church, and Harry and Hilly felt they had been rolled up in some big melodic blanket she called Always-Bach.

Hilly could come to see Harry only when accompanied by Kath Kent, whom Hilly's parents thought prophylactic. When Kath was not around, she recruited her two elder brothers, Thurman and George, who in turn brought to the church (or the river bridge down the slope behind it) Edith, who had a lovely voice in the making. The two had one girlfriend between them. She sang for them both, with German strain for Thurman, in a manner more French for George. Truly she sang for everyone who would listen, her gift being unquenchable and unshy. But Harry had never heard Hilly play, not until they arranged for him to pass by Number 7 Market Street, next to the fly-loud meatshop entrance, and listen at six o'clock as she tapped her way through scales, Bach, Chopin, and something by Sir Hubert Parry. Harry always tried to whistle some of the tunes while going away, but he found them hard to memorize, even to pick out, and so made a vague whistling as he left, an honorable sound of leaking air, even as he tried to come to terms with the mystery of it, of her, whose nimble hands knew something without having learned it, whose lilting tunes at once set Edith off into a small girl's coloratura, the two of them leaving the three boys behind in a swill of dumbfounded admiration. Boys were for baffling, that was all. Girls were angels in disguise, tuneful phantoms who sang pure notes to purify the thoughts of boys.

The five became a little gang, with Harry the only one from the wrong side of the tracks, and he learning fast to cross. Then Hilly took to bringing her third brother, little Douglas, the weaker and paler for having been born so late. Douglas cried. But not Harry, ruddy of face and quiet of tongue. His own mother was producing a child a year and the tiny house on Church Row was filling with siblings he would rather have done without. Hilly's mother, on the other hand, was not: Douglas would be the very last. Harry, the first, and Douglas became firm friends; indeed, Harry delighted in this well-to-do clique, in their big Great Dane called Ben, who came romping with them through Reresby Woods, and watched them like a shaggy superintendent when they built leaf houses, climbed trees, paddled in the stream among the minnows or plunged their arms deep into Woody Nook spring. Nobody at home missed Harry anyway, and he began to wonder which family he belonged to, graft that he was. To a father who chipped coal from the bowels of the earth and came home ebony, needing to soak in the big tin bath in front of the kitchen fire with the tots trying to climb in beside him, he preferred one who bought sheep, pigs, and cows, then brought them home to slaughter, this done with a humane killer and a long stout rope that, with a dozen volunteers on its other end, tugged the doomed animal's head low. There was more color, more drama, to the abattoir, although he could see that coal and blood had much in common. So: He belonged to two families that required a great deal of washing. Not that Hilly's brothers were destined for the trade of slaughter. No fear, they said. They were going to be metallurgists, George and Douglas certainly, Thurman just perhaps. Harry, in his mind, added steel to blood and coal, supposing that if he mingled with enough children he would run into lead, honey, gold, and acid. It was one way of discovering the world.

It was to Hilly, pianist and reciter, however, that he clung the most, dreaming her into a magical creature who one day soon would go to London to take an especially hard examination. It was for her that dusty, taciturn men visited her parents' home, *to tune* the piano (although you never, he understood, said the last bit). *To choon.* That was how you said it. When they had gone, she played all the better and felt mighty important, a monopolist of vibration, a queen of yet another ivory coast. He too, he told her, would soon be taking an examination to see if he was clever enough for the grammar school her brothers went to, and then (if he passed) the great circle of their lives would be complete, for Edith went to school with Hilly. It was as if some enormous multicolored web were heaving into view past the horizon, with petals and jewels threaded into it, all theirs for the plucking: the promised life, the life to come that some parents prated of, not his.

Most of all, he liked Hilly's telling him that the music she played, or even that of the handbell players, was a pale imitation of another music with which the world was full, although few might hear it. The church said it was there, though she trusted parsons little and looked to her mother, whom she believed much more.

"It comes from?" He couldn't finish.

"Up there, you," she said. "In the sky, if you like, although it's under the golf links too, and in the dams, the rivers, the woods. It's *inside* you, silly."

In that case, then, it was down in the mines, in the pit, and it ran through the blood of the slaughtered cows, sheep, pigs, of her father, and it would resound along the steel of George and Douglas. He felt for the first time, at the hands of this prodigy who played piano, in touch with things worth being alive for—all the fuss of being born, of getting sick, of getting up early every morning, of going to school. What he read about at school enthralled him (history and battles, for instance), but this was different, this vast armada of light and color that sailed up to your bedroom window, full of Chopin and Bach that only she could hear as they should be played. He fell into the web of guileless adulation, at last a member of something that wasn't a family.

HARRY ADORED to concentrate on his school lessons, most of all the Wars of the Roses and anything to do with Napoleon. He found he could do this at the same time as he pondered Hilly's words about what lay beyond things they could see and hear; almost as if they were dogs hearing what only dogs could hear. He, however, was not a musician, and he sometimes got it wrong, telling her that he could see clowns and acrobats in midair, sticking their forefingers, in the corners of their mouths and pulling down to make a grimace. He saw waterspouts too, plagues of locusts and stampeding buffalo. That, she told him, was imagination, not (she said sternly) to be confused with the other stuff coming through from the angels or from God, or simply from amassed human memories of all the dead, including those killed in mining accidents and never brought to the surface. Entombed. There was music in the air, she said: a crude way of putting it, but it was as well to get things straight at the outset. Then, Harry told her, if it kept coming through, who needed pianists to play it? We need pianists, she said, to keep its confidence up, to make it feel worthwhile; and then he said it must be like lightning, at which she giggled, telling him he had no *method* (her mother's word). No, he admitted it, but he was anxious to learn, to hear, to hear.

Harry thought he was getting the point, but he could never be sure. Perhaps he was; millions of grown-ups had died gibbering in the attempt, losing faith in their Creator as they did so. What should a small boy know of such things beyond the fact that, when you needed to cheer yourself up, you were able to do so? No, she said, tenderly instructive, it's like a current, a chorus, not interrupting the music you play. It was like the sky against which someone was a cloud. He dimly knew then that it was a background/foreground problem suitable for musical professionals only, though similar to what he had heard through some ricochet about the Boer War and the African veldt. At dusk your eyes played tricks and you failed to see what was out there while seeing what was not.

Was it the same just before dawn, too? He half knew, having at an early age tried to imagine what his father's life was like, slotted at that early hour into a foot-high cavity in the coal, chopping away sideways as if to embed himself horizontally deeper. This image had made him choke and cough, which his father presumably never did; but Harry knew the century was over in which they sent boys up chimneys to sweep, and bottom-naked too; so they would not be sending children down the mines either, as long as there was a good supply of older men who didn't mind getting caked with coal dust and, indeed, regarded it as a veneer of honor and courage.

His mind kept going back to what Hilly had told him. He knew she couldn't quite get it into words, and she certainly couldn't play it because she wasn't playing her own music, but Chopin and Always-Bach. One day perhaps she would write something and then he would know. In the meantime he would have to make do with an approximation that went like this: All minds think more than they need to, than they need to in order to speak, for example; so some of this excess sometimes got through as music or electricity. It was an Over-Soul that he and Hilly were thinking of, or something such.

She knew music was a domain, a kingdom, not something shut away in a cupboard to be opened when company came and they wanted a little rondo. Not that. It was what her sense of melody splashed about in, but she wasn't going to tell Harry something sloppy. It was what roamed through her mind as she was falling asleep, making her want to get up and write it down it was so beautiful, having come out of intrinsic nowhere; but she was always too late, it came too fast, it wouldn't wait, it was too spread out and ample, like all the gold and gossamer cloaks from an enormous hunt ball. Hilly had made contact with the natural lyricism of the mind, with its steady surplus, when it did not celebrate anything at all but merely exercised its golden mental throat, as when Edith sang by the river bridge, alone.

One Saturday, after all the pomp and warnings of the living room (be a good boy, don't climb on things, don't touch anything, don't tap with your heels), Hilly took Harry upstairs to the music room; and he suddenly realized the sound he had heard in Market Street had been falling down on him, a shower. What a fancy room this was, full of fire irons, gilt-bound books, paintings of oxen and horses, rugs he sank into. There stood the piano, a grand, with a vase of daffodils atop it, like something that had grown upward from the lid. Might not a heavy-handed player spill the water? Look, she told him, cranking up the lid of the piano stool, revealing big blue volumes of Chopin, Liszt, and Always-Bach, nodding at him to lift them, and then together they adjusted the first one into place on the music rack, flipping up the two brass sprigs that held the pages back.

She did not play, though, she just wanted him to see the piano at its best, and she was not allowed to raise the big palette-shaped lid, either. She motioned him to sit on the piano stool and try to decipher the music, and he laughed, said something about metal-ur-gy (spaced thus). It was not for him, but he loved the sounds. "Play, please," he said. "It'll be better hearing in here than out there in the street." Off she went, making him wonder how hands so small could master so many keys; she played fast and with much brio, transporting him again into that enormous, vivid hinterland she had told him about, giving him the same complete, heart-stopping dream and, after a few minutes more of Chopin, making him wonder why humans did anything else with their lives when this flood of delicacy might be had for a little elbow grease and some memory work. He decided to be a pianist too. Well, in his next life, if he was asked. He had other things to do with the present one, but he would for ever, in both this life and the next, be a listener, a dreamer at the keyboard, lifted or lofted to that abyss called music, though it deserved a better name, one that told of its coming-from-within quality. Hilly said it came from all over the world, but Harry had begun to think it came up like a spring within you, and never ran dry.

She showed him the metronome then, letting him alter the beat and rest his finger just beyond the wedge-shaped weight's farthest reach. When, he wondered, would the Chooners come back. She had told him of the odd, discordant noises they made, as if pulling out of the piano all its bad behavior, after which it played angelically. She made him play, showed him middle C, and held his fingers, telling him to crook them upward. He had hands as small as hers and she told him he was not cut out for the laboring life.

"Soft jobs for you, Harry," she whispered, for once wrong, "you'll see." Then she played to demonstrate the two pedals, allowing him to intrude a foot, bootless, and hold down the sustaining pedal for a few minutes, only to make such a drum of the room that her mother shouted to them from the stairwell. "Not so much pedal, Hildred, or that boy will have to go home." The whole idea of a room consecrated to music moved him. He knew there were rooms elsewhere devoted to billiards and smoking, but he wondered if there were rooms devoted to, oh, history, or metallurgy, or warfare. Deep in his being he groped for some principle of suitability, aware that life was a race in which much got wasted unless for each worthwhile thing a room was created, and it would be against the law to do anything else in there. Two rooms up and two down, he saw, breached all the laws, especially when half the family had to eat on the couch since the table was too small. Here he was, accustomed to seeing everything piled on top of everything else, and she was revealing to him a world *laid out,* spread out, with a flat place for everything; so many places, in fact, that you could not see most of them unless you went up a tree.

How glad he was he had friends to play with, creatures from another dimension, each with a bedroom to himself (Hilly, too), who treated him not as a pet or a beggar, but as one of themselves. The soft-job brigade he called them, in his fits of mellow resentment, just the sort of folk the king would appoint to kill animals. When there was a war, though, it was the likes of him who did the killing while the soft-job brigade stayed at home and lived off the fat of the land. Once he became a grammar-school boy he would think differently, he knew, not that he wanted to study metals or languages or even music; but he might become an engineer or an accountant, he could see that far—there was no coal in his future. When he went home that Saturday, music coursing through him, the routines of a different life were tugging at his mind.

The instant he walked in, his harassed mother contrived to fit a beef sandwich into his mouth before he could even speak. She would sit at the door, sandwiches piled on a big oval plate crazed with tiny hatchings, and hand food up to the face as it entered. She oversalted the beef, but she sliced it so thin that Harry could almost see through it. When the children cried, she sliced little ovals and put them on their eyes, making them lie still for this special treatment, as if cold beef were a panacea; but the meat in his sandwich was cooked; Harry had heard about cold beef, raw, as good for the eyes and for bruises, whereas beef cooked he knew nothing about. He just ate it when plied with it and wondered how she kept the bread so moist. Then he thought he saw: It was not the bread but the beef, which was moist with tears. The beef was one of the things that made his home a home. He felt his heart lift up, awkward and lurching, as if there were nothing but joy in his life. Would he always feel like this? You felt joyful when you wanted to; it came from within like Hilly's music, and had nothing to do with coal, blood, metal, or God or Jesus, and certainly not with his parents. Happy to be alive, he let the sense of joy work its way through him, warming and calming. He knew he was going to be all right as soon as he grew up.

At the same time he tried to fit things into one world, as a little holist might; he also tried not to make up his mind too soon. He yearned for what went on at 7 Market Street, where Hilly's brothers let him use their chemical balance, playing with milligram weights and tiny pans, or allowed him to put on the pierrot hats and striped drawers they used for charades. He preferred that other life, not its plumage so much as its surplus: there were always too many things to play with, or, if not to play with, then to work at. The boys had slide rules, protractors, compasses, thin wooden triangles with perfect angles cut into them, and there were paint brushes and sets of watercolors for the asking. Hilly, using thick broad nibs, penned with oil paints on rectangles of canvas, making birds and flowers to which, like God, she signed her name.

ONE DAY, when it was "allowed," in other words when Harry and Hilly could have the music room to themselves for an entire afternoon, Harry opened up his book of military pictures, a book lent him by Miss Lindisfarne, who taught miscellaneously in all classes, from Kindergarten to Top, like a badly distributed polymath. One day he would have to hand the book back, but by then, he hoped, Miss Lindisfarne would not want it, and would have had a new one sent to her from the shop in Sheffield he had never seen. Hilly told him it smelled like a dairy, somehow creamy and luxurious, as if, she mused, leather and blancmange and eau de cologne and pencil shavings and fresh-baked bread had been mixed together and made newly marvelous. She often went off like that, tempting his just as lyrical but more hesitant mind to follow. She always seemed to know what was behind things, what was concealed, and each week the out-of-sight improved, for having been thought about so intensely. Coming to know her had instilled in him an almost equal yet derivative capacity for savoring what was beyond the next hill.

For now, it was enough to counter her musical and visionary offerings with his own vignettes of martial splendor, which meant mainly carnage, a fact he chose to overlook, arguing with himself to good effect that, if there was enough pageantry (he did not know the word), then the bloodletting got somehow transfigured (another word he didn't know). He had many concepts he could not articulate, though Hilly had vowed to coach him, a process she sometimes also called poshing him up, making him not quite a parrot in a cage, but in some way a captive creature filched from the common folk and destined to be *made over;* like a barbarian being baptized, even if he moaned and fretted during the deed.

"We're going to toff you up," she told him the day he brought his book of military pictures with his finger stuck into it; he had walked raptly like that all the way, numbing the finger as he walked, wondering how you could judge the right degree of clamp so that when you arrived you didn't have to suck the finger like a baby to bring feeling back.

"No, you're not," he whispered, afraid of the music room's echo, "you're going to leave me alone, like a dead dog."

"We know what to do with dead dogs here." She laughed. "The butcher's is the ugliest shop in the street. We make dog pies and feed them to pigs. There."

Harry was only ten to her fourteen, but he was beginning to like this sense of being a trespasser. He had known for some years there were places he must not go, especially in the woods, where pellets from Fab Ashley's shotgun would come after him if he strayed into certain enclosures marked with a white fence, barbed wire, and faded warnings. What on earth could be in those locked decrepit sheds? He now preferred the music room to almost anywhere else, although he wanted to inspect the slaughterhouse. The shop he had been in, liking best the tiny rapiers that pinned name and price tags to the joints of meat on which, in summer, flies strutted with a no doubt comparable sense of trespass. As for Hilly, she enjoyed the feeling of being in charge, of putting the apt but cautious Harry through his paces; he grimaced, he faltered, he sometimes beat a retreat, but he always got the hang of things eventually, mincing as a tutored bird. She began to feel she owned him, had even created him, a rough diamond she had finessed. At first he had shivered with nerves, fumbling his thumbs, blinking as if to clear some foreign body from each eye, and licking his lips before he spoke. Then he said little. He was soaking up the ambience of the well-to-do, marveling at the aroma of Irish stout (although all bottles were hidden before he arrived), the almost constant smell of a joint's roasting, the big and leaky bottle of eau de cologne in the outdoor toilet that was so close to the house it nearly qualified as indoors. In the winter it reeked of paraffin from the heater kept within to prevent the pipes from freezing. Something like a big doily fell over him whenever he addressed her parents: the portly butcher with the plump mustache and the languid swagger; the gaunt stern woman with the cane, forever fussing the shawl about her shoulders. It was an embroidered atmosphere concealing the eyesore that he was, except to the daughter, already so many years older than he and so socially adroit, so eager to (he felt) adopt him, convert him into a proper little gentleman.

"You'll go to the grammar school," she said.

"I'll never pass," he sighed, "not me."

"What if they ask all history questions, then? About famous battles? You'll gobble it up, won't you?"

If he was nervous here, on Market Street, what on earth would he be like confronted with *questions* on which his life depended, which was to say having Hilly and her brothers as his friends, for boyhood, for ever. Was there not another way in, through one of those little doors cut into big doors to admit a cat or a dog, hinged at the top by a provident, caring family? That was how he would prefer to enter the grammar school, not with his spelling and counting in question and the dreaded "composition" lasting a whole hour—*Write about your hobbies or a place you would like to visit.* Could he, when the day came, work Lieutenant-Colonel Henry Clay, Jr., done by Currier in 1847, and the *Attack on the Tuileries, 10 August 1792,* into everything? He could write about his wonderings: the sort of thing he talked to Hilly about. How he longed to be just another of those boys who sauntered home in green blazers, green-and-black ties and green shirts, gray socks with green stripes, caps like the tops knocked off boiled eggs and dyed green, a black bull's-eye imprinted on top for birds to aim white lime at. Not to be especially clever, or even promising: just one of the gang, thumping girls (except Hilly) and tying doorknobs together with rope before knocking at the same time on both doors. If that was the heroic life he would take it, and then forget where he came from.

For ever after, Hilly would seat him in a good light, then hand him one of the big blue books in which all the Bach was printed; when he looked at the pages he would see tadpoles frozen in drill postures against thinly delineated fences, five lines to a fence. Then she would change the pages into music, like a conjurer. He wondered what he could conjure up that would be half as good. He would show them a slice of beef cut so thin it allowed enough light through to read a page of music by; but you had to have inside your head the special reel, the spinning top, the gyroscope, whatever it was, that *let* you read music. You had to have trained hands, like Hilly's sombered by fat and blood from the shop counter, but tempered by having been dipped repeatedly into hot Irish stout and held over the paraffin lamp to dry. His refined self lifted its eyelids and liked all it saw, the wonderful thing being that her family did not need half of what it owned. They had too much of everything—one too many of him, for example, who was a cross between a pet and a little bathtub boat.

When he went home, it was as if he were nobody, just something to be slotted in place and left for the night lest he got in the way of the others. He heard his father gasping, his mother squealing, the chamber pot chinking against the metal of the bed frame, and then the enormous fruitful silence before one of the other children woke and wailed. Baby Nora or baby Raymond.

"Yes," he told Hilly with amateur fervor, "I'm going to write about battles whatever they ask."

"You do, my lad, and they'll make you a general."

Closing his mind's eye to the future and its written ordeals, he stared at her candid, heavy-featured face, at the gray-green eyes that seemed to suck up light and send it out again made sharper and more searching. Her hair, brushed hard, still tended to curl and stray, much like his own; each morning his mother wet his and then sealed it shut with the palm of her hand, as if to keep unwanted matter from seeping into his outsize skull. Hilly planted a kiss on his brow, then urged him downstairs.

THERE WAS already a small, untidy crowd in the back yard, there to watch the killing. Inside, the doomed cow made round, awful pleas as they slipped the noose over its horns and drew it tight about the neck. The other end of the rope now appeared in the yard, slipped over the slaughterhouse door, and all took a two-handed grip and began to haul. After about a minute of hard work, in which Harry but not Hilly joined, Jim Webster waved to them to stop, and Harry raced forward to see what they had accomplished. He wished he hadn't. The cow's head was on the wet concrete floor, firm against the wall and the iron ring through which the rope slid. The rest of it held an ungainly steep crouch, forced down at one end, but bucking to be free at the other. Nothing, Harry thought, should be manhandled like that, turned into a wheelbarrow of flesh, its nose the wheel. Mooing almost without pause now, the cow slipped and skidded with its two hind legs, befouling itself at the same time and managing to swivel its body round through some twenty degrees: a technical escape, but not good enough. The humane killer cracked, sent its steel tube deep into the brain, and the cow slumped, its rear legs folded up, and it became quite still, down without any need to fall. Faster than Harry could say it in words, Jim Webster and Gerald White cut its throat and sent blood coursing through the runnel to the outside drain. Moments ago it had been nourishing the cow, and now it ran away to nowhere it could be recovered from; Harry blinked, suddenly aware that he knew something about saving the blood for puddings and such things. Why were they wasting it today? Next they raised the cow on chains and slit its belly open, broke its legs, and hauled the big cumulus clouds of its innards down to the floor, where they bulged and flopped while being hosed. They were several times bigger than he was and still looked full of life, full of sloppy grass. The empty hulk swayed in the center of the slaughterhouse, the head already amputated and ready to stew, with flies landing on the slowly browning suet. Two big sheep would have gone into the carcass, Harry thought, and into each of those sheep a single calf—it sounded like one of those songs he had to learn and sing at school. Now Gerald White began sawing downward until there were two halves of the cow, each dangling from an enormous hook, and Harry wondered if they ever caught diseases, the cows, or if the killing-men caught diseases from the cows, or, indeed, if the boys who helped pull the rope caught anything from that. Staring in at the blood and the beeves, inhaling the dank, moldering smell of innards, he began to wonder that the slaughterhouse was only a few yards from the music room. He heard an ungainly clatter accompanied by a fibrous splash and saw that the cow's entire skin, with hooves attached but somehow no legs, had been thrown into the corner of the slaughterhouse like a set of wet oilskins, for—for, yes he told himself, for once using his brains, *leather*. This was how people got shoes.

"You've seen it before, haven't you?" Hilly was talking at him in that airy, possessive way of hers.

"Not all of it. I never looked before."

"Well, now you know. I'm sick of it. Pigs, cows, sheep, calves. It goes on all the time, and the yard's full of noise."

"I'd rather not see it again," he said.

"Sometimes," she told him with boisterous disdain, "they grab hold of little lads and pull their heads down to the ring. Then they butcher them. There's many a family feasts Sundays on a joint of Little Lad, done to a turn, you know, with a nice helping of Yorkshire pudding on the side and some roast potatoes."

Harry felt his entire torso contract, not with fear or shame, but just with nearness. He had to move away, back off from the carnage, into the arena or aroma of music, to the idea of which he homed clean-handedly, Hilly his guide. His father had told him about men crushed under whole seams of coal in the mines. The world was a bloody place, yet "bloody" was a dirty word, one for which he got spanked or had his ears boxed if he said or even mouthed it. He ached to watch, but he yearned to flee—to his books of war, of all things, perhaps because the din and smoke and blood were shut off from him; he had never been to a zoo, but had heard about zoos, and he thought his picture books were a bit like that: stirring but not sickening. Besides, above the chromatics of the martial inferno flew the colors of honor. What country had the cow died for? The answer was obvious, but there was a difference between keeping the enemy at bay and filling the Sunday-dinner plate. Wasn't there? Hilly agreed, but, having inflicted butchering on him, wanted to be rid of him for the day. She had to practice, she said. He could find his own way home.

Dismissed, he vowed never to haul on the slaughterhouse rope again. Why was it that animals in there, with no rope in sight, at some point began their dreadful clamoring, night and day, as if they scented the executioner? On they moaned as if trying to deter the one who came and slipped the rope over their horns. The sheep bleated and the pigs squealed, but they manhandled them through into the slaughter-house. Or they came right from a van into the slaughterhouse door and had their throats cut before they knew where they were.

Cows had escaped, he knew, barging out into the street or career-ing through back gardens and smashing greenhouses until lassoed and brought back gibbering. Hilly had seen a lot of killing, he could tell; her father had bought the big upstairs piano with the meat: ivory for sirloin, flank, and tail. Those big unwieldy books of music came from sausages. They did not humane-kill calves, they smacked them on the head with a sledgehammer and sometimes just slit the throats of sheep and pigs, barbering the pigs after, with scalding water and scrapers. Were the sheep shorn before arriving? Wouldn't the wool be stained with blood otherwise? But didn't it matter if the cows' skins were stained? He saw, faintly, an entire procession of skinned cattle hobbling up the yard, their haunches bright as bacon in the prismatic sunlight of the end of the world.

He wanted to throw up, but more than that, he felt panic, suddenly deciding he was ready for girls. He was what local people called a lad-lass, what Hilly said was nesh, in other words, tenderhearted, shy, wincing, easily hurt, never to be trusted not to cry. He did not feel guilty, but he felt out of place. When other small boys hurrahed at the crack of the killer, the first gush of blood, the glistening tumble from on high of all those intestines, as if they had just come to terms with their own frailty, he wanted to go in and release the head, stanch the wound, hose down the whole floor, and then lead the animal gently back into the fields where, shuddering and complaining, it subsided onto a divan of uncut grass. All the way home, past the china shop, the sweetshop, the White Hart that smelled of beer and smoke, he hungered for a reconciliation with the slaughter on which niceness based itself.

ALL OF A sudden Clive's telescope quivered, and his idolized mother became a serious, austere girl standing on a footstool emblazoned with fleurs-de-lis, and in her hands, hugged against her plain white pinafore, a green birdcage with a yellow parrot inside. Or she was holding against her cheek a rabbit she had just taken from its hutch. Or with a token whip (the kind she struck tops with) she was riding her brother Thurman on the rug, pulling at the bit between his teeth (a pencil with two strands of wool running from it). Misbehaving, she was tipping Smethwick's Cathartic Pills by the dozen from an oval-shaped box into her nightly bath. Or—Clive told himself there were no *ors*; she was doing *all* these things, one on top of the other—building herself into a whirligig of graciousness, in which feeding her doll a rusk was compatible with winding a paper snake around her arm to cast a spell.

This was the world denied Clive's father: A world in which people did more because they had more stuff on hand. He, Harry Moxon, had never rolled a hoop, worn a necklace of clover, made a daisy chain, played cat's cradle or blown a wish on a dandelion. It was as if he had never lived, not quite; he marveled at the plenty to which Hilly and her brothers brought so much energy, and not as if they had been told to do it, or how to do it, but as if it came naturally, out of nowhere. Their parents read their children's minds in their sleep, and willed unusual feats from them, far beyond his capacity, he was sure, although if they ever got to armies and battles he might give them a hard time. To each his toy, he thought. Hilly always appeared to him among her apparatus, an elf of perpetual motion, but she also soared toward him, especially when he was trying to sleep, a bonny girl with pink-painted cheeks posing for a die-cut portrait of the ideal daughter, every curl honed, the outline of her body masked by pastel bows, her runny places (six or seven, he judged) not so much dabbed as sent away, dispatched as uncouth for the surrounding overgrowth of roses, ribbons, butterflies, pansies, lockets, teething rings, and tiny watering cans. He had seen a picture of someone else and kept fitting her face and shoulders into it, thus making her the queen of all the pretty, wholesome stuff she posed among. Actually, the picture was a stove-pipe cover, used to seal and beautify a pipe during summer, but so grandiose it quite obliterated what it hid, even the memory of it, so the entire household went hunting in November for the stovepipe: *It was here, wasn't it?* The cover was a permanent carapace and the young child adorning it immortal, at least if beauty had any rights at all.

Clive winced when Harry winced, each forcing into being a not quite accurate rendition of Hilly: Clive presuming but adoring, Harry reeling away from life into a Pre-Raphaelite sycophancy. In this skewed kaleidoscope, Harry his father was younger than Clive was now. Hilly saw her middle-aged son dreaming of someone or other, unaware of the childhood he kept guessing at and then foisting on her.

Of one thing Harry was sure: The roses around her, tightly wound, would unfurl enough to sheet a bed, and he was just as sure that roses themselves had about them something secret and calamitous. Harry tried to tell Hilly some of this, but she wanted no accounts of the iconography in which she simpered. She had a mysticism of her own, unconnected with the ruffles and flounces her mother thought appro-

priate to virgin girlhood. In other words, to reach Hilly, Harry had
to cut through both the trappings of a Victorian bourgeois upbringing
and Hilly's robust, clever sense of self. She might be trafficked with,
or signaled to, but she was not easily exposed; only when she was
intent upon him with that uncoiled yearning of hers, when she
seemed to mind-read and invite him all in one, could he reach her in
an intimate way. It was as if she were royal, or promised elsewhere,
and he still had not become used to how she made him feel: keen and
ravished, but also a chump pitching his cap toward what he could not
have, in his grimy fist a wad of merit cards filched from school, for
punctuality, diligent attention, penmanship, good conduct, obedience, courage, and spelling.

What a paragon. Who needed anything but his own unblemished
reputation? In posh homes, he'd heard, mothers handed out these
cards, signed, to their children, sometimes imprinted "National Bank
of Merit, Four Shares for Deportment." When the child had twenty-
five, say, a new pet would follow, or an appealingly painted toy. Or
even a model airplane kit from France, such as Harry had watched
George cutting out and putting together, leaning over his shoulder as
George breathed hard and began to grow hot. It had been an "Aéroplane Monoplan du Système dit *Antoinette.*" In French the plan told
any francophone youth that all the pieces had been scrupulously
verified; if the pieces were assembled with care in the order indicated,
the result would be "perfect." With penknife blade whetted outside
on the flat gray stone on which Jim and Gerald, the butchering
assistants, sharpened their sticking- and dressing-knives, George had
cut the pieces, trimmed them with straight-bladed nail scissors, and
then pushed the tabs into the slots. The entire monoplane was gray
blue and pale brown: to Harry uninspiring and stodgy, yet miraculous
in that it evoked a world still deemed impossible. The model would
not fly, but it sat levitatingly on mantelpieces next to landbound cars
cast in lead.

Harry doted on the kits, and sometimes George or Thurman gave him the leftovers, the sheets from which the parts had been cut free, which gave Harry an odd feeling of, well, since this was a butcher's house, receiving offal donated as a gesture to the poor. What he wanted, but never had until Hilly stole for him an "Aéroplane Biplan du Type Wright (Imagerie D'Epinal, No. 1378, Pellerin"), was the intact, gleaming sheet with, strewn about it in no particular order or design, an arm, a wheel, a propeller, like seeds split and flattened, now to be meshed together with stinking fish glue. Damp warped the planes, though, and it was better to varnish them if you could, though the varnish warped them in a different way. Whatever a boy did, these planes never ended up perfect, in spite of what the legend on the cardboard said, not until Hilly, as if she had invented fretwork, suggested that they paste the cardboard to thin wood from cigar boxes, and then saw around the outlines. Some chunky models came from this procedure, with Harry helping as the wobbly clamp, screwed to the side of a table, slid this way and that. Eventually, however, with all of them hanging on to the vee or the wood while one of them sawed, the planes began to come out right like the dead arising. Harry kept the *Antoinette* plan under his pillow, which had no pillowcase, imagining the veer and flaunt of the assembled model tossed into a fierce wind off Yarnall Bank, the steep land behind his home. Other images lorded it in his dreams, from the toy rabbit that clicked into view from the heart of a green cabbage to the gingerbread jigsaw puzzle that you made difficult to do by eating pieces at random as you worked.

"You have so much," he told Hilly. "It isn't fair."

"It would be unfairer still, wouldn't it," she scolded him, "if we didn't let you come and play. Hush. Kiss me on the nose and think pink cheeks."

—

NOW THAT, Clive thought even as he eavesdropped the encounter into being, was the limit. Had his mother really been so tart, so caustic a little scold? She was almost telling Harry that, although he couldn't tweak the stiff upper lip, or tug the whiskers of the patrician's mustache, he could if he wanted sniff the dirty laundry. Well, almost. He resolved to make his similes more accurate. It was no use improvising the libretto of nostalgia only to begin getting things wrong, not because he didn't know (he would never know), but because he wasn't coming up with fine enough plausibilities to convince himself. He squirmed for his father, coming from so little, aiming so high like someone blinded by the sun continuing to ascend, lured higher by the sound of a violin or piano, but then he warmed to his mother; Hilly's generosity of spirit countered her smart tongue, and Harry knew this from the first, dealing with her as if what she said came from her own mother, whereas what she played came from heaven, ushered down by special permission. Harry was a judicious infatuate, which in a small boy amounted to huge emotional savvy. To him a good-night kiss was never short or merely perfunctory; it was a pledge renewed, and made golden again through wordless tenderness.

Beyond the novelty of Hilly's life with her three brothers, and the majesty of holy music, there was a future in which people sat demurely eating aboard trains that belched, camels knelt and straightened up again according to human whim, and sportsmen perched in beach chairs at the far end of the strand and shot at little birds called sandsnipes so adept at dodging that it sometimes took an hour to knock one down. "Out there," as he thought of the back of beyond, were India rubber, revolvers, and ice made with sulfuric acid. You reached it all when you were fifteen, maybe twenty-one, but only after tremendous hardships in the colonies, and redemption in crowded tabernacles of prayer and hymn.

It had even been said, according to George and Thurman, that the next war would be fought on bicycles, which would replace cavalry. Harry thought he saw hundreds of cyclists riding abreast, each with a rapid-firing gun mounted on the handlebars, and he could hardly wait to be big enough to go. For now, he hovered in futurity's anteroom, confident that, if he kept his mind on the minor things talked about or pictured in Hilly's world, he would come into his own not only as a rough boy among nice children, but also as some-one attuned to marvels, novelties, prodigies, soon to be unveiled. So he took with forward-looking seriousness the New Easy Lawn Mower, the Mexican Hammock with Braided Edges, the gigantic vermilion grandifloras thrust into Viennese glass epergnes in the Fitza-lans' front hallway. One shred of this plenty was enough to make him different; he had only to flash it, and the world would *know* he was different, had had something to do with folk of quality.

In a word, he was a metaphysical snob, but thoroughly forgivable in that he saw social distinction not as something brought about by human beings but as something as natural as an oak tree: a given. Hilly took her privileges without a thought, though glad to share them, especially with Harry, whom she had identified as having silk in his disposition. They had a habit, when not in public, of hooking their little fingers together and standing looking into each other's eyes (hers the greener) until blinking brought on tears. What they saw "in each other" in this special way they did not know, but the vibration of its magic possessed them again and again. It might, Clive thought, have felt like little needly corn flies that homed in on eyes, nose, mouth, hair, nipping and pricking; but it was not, it was reciprocity truly ineffable, a sort of magnified trust lauding itself in the ambit of innocence. It thrived, serious and indelible, in the presence of such undignified things as seedsmen's catalogues, hanging ferneries with nine pots, and covered brick doorsteps. The here and now was merely a training chapel for the hereafter and its angel-ringed firmament.

Hilly and Harry had tapped the glorious before they knew what it was, and staring remained their homage.

For the moment, Harry dreaded the day when Hilly, as planned, went away to London to play recitals under the stern eyes of Mrs. Barnaby Wainfan, a judge's widow. At about the same time, Harry would have to go to the examination room to do his sums and write his essay, to see if he was bright enough to join George, Thurman, and Douglas at the grammar school. Parting loomed, and loneliness licked its chops. Hilly wanted Harry to hear her play her best, under the pressure that drove her to fanatical perfection and a state of expressive bliss she found it hard to come down from, while he longed to have her there to tell all about it: What he wrote and what he got wrong.

There was no parting, however, no scene of the two being torn asunder. Hilly's mother and Mrs. Barnaby Wainfan made her practice at the pianoforte, and brush up her manners as well. Off she went in the Fitzalan cart, tugged by a groaning horse who had to pull Wainfan and Gerald the driver too. Halfway, at a nontown called Intake, Hilly and her escort made a short rest stop at the St. Agnes Retreat for Young Gentlewomen, a place Hilly and her fellow schoolgirls would enter with a hoot, taking there a smelly dump with cries of mock dismay, and then giggling their way out again, having ruptured the pondlike calm of the retreat, the smell behind them that of (as they helplessly agreed) a dead donkey. Today, though, with Mrs. Barnaby Wainfan on the other side of the partition removing layer after layer of clothing, Hilly did her piece with solitary decorum and had to wait in the vestibule. On they went toward the train station, the bustle, the whistles, the shuddering jolt of punctual departure. Two days later, Harry chewed on the brand-new pen provided (almost a mapping pen, he thought; it was so narrow), and chose his topic from the two that confronted him: Holidays *or* Happiness. He chose the latter and wondered if he must at all costs omit holidays from his view of happiness. It took him a while to get started, but then he let go in earnest, wondering if those who would read his effort were happy themselves or hoping to get a hint on how to be so.

I am most happy when a friend of mine plays the piano, which is when soldiers with cutlasses come flashing out of the dark and the smoke puthers all over. The crashes of battle are loud. Some of the horses have big bottoms at least until they get cut and pieces fall off. The ground is littered with rifles that have dropped. This is only a dream of course and what I like best is riding a cock horse and turning the pages of the music as my friend plays. Sometimes we march in step together with our flag the Union Jack between us. Or we make a big carrot from yellow crepe paper and fasten it with a hairpin. It is as long as my leg. At other times we play at statues with a little sprig of grapes held up in our hands. It is not sissy at all. Or we play French cricket when your legs are the stumps and you have to defend them against the bowler. Sometimes I make models of cardboard, aeroplanes and cars and airships. They do not fly but this does not bother me much. One day they will. I could go on about my happiness. It does not end when I stop writing. But we have to. I have enjoyed it and I am looking forward to the next test. The end. H. Moxon.

He had done this without much pausing, suddenly aghast at how things came out of the pen's nib, as if it had been loaded beforehand. When his two sheets of prose had gone, he felt a pang of devastation; he had no copy, and he had not memorized it. Surely, if it had been any good, he would have an exact memory of it. What had he written? He had no idea beyond the piano, the war, the cardboard kits. Happiness was no doubt something quite different, put together in a glass vase from flowers and peppermint. What if he had written something *girlish?* Would they call him a lad-lass and refuse to let him in? No, he had written nothing lad-lasslike; indeed, he had been heroic and honest. That was enough, Harry.

Clive nodded at the accuracy of his impersonation, or so he saw it; writing for Harry he found his mind a sudden erudite blaze of love as his father's copperplate handwriting came back to him, neat as the knot in his necktie, the bows above his shoes, the long narrow links at a right angle to the cuff holes in the shirt. His father read a map like a genius, much as Hilly scanned a page of Brahms. Clive came from meticulous people, and he was proud to be sitting here with Hilly on the occasion of happiness renewed.

Try as he did, Harry could not get Hilly's recitals into the right order; at least what went into them. Did she receive the medal first, and play because of it, all excited? Or did she march on to the stage, bow, and then play, with the medal coming last? She was there because she had won a medal. Was it a medal for winning medals? Perhaps they let her take a rest, drink some water from a fancy crystal glass, and gave her the medal then. They could always send it to her in the post; a tiny box would do, although tiny boxes with valuable contents had a bad habit of getting lost. Just possibly she got a medal to begin with, one halfway through, and then, for a rousing send-off, one at the end, a mighty medal you could strike as if it were a gong. "Always-Bach," she told him when he asked what she would be playing. This Bach, whose music he had heard and found clockwork-like, must be well in with God Almighty. Was that because his music was more churchgoing than anybody else's? There had been lots of Bachs, she told him, and they all made up music. The Bach family must have been like the Moxons, he thought: a new baby every year in the same-size house. If there were boys, playing or listening, he wondered if she would be talking to them: boys who hadn't needed to write essays on happiness in order to get where they were going. She was bound to prefer them to him, just as (he thought) she preferred her brothers to almost anyone. In a way he felt her music was his, in that certain playings of it had been addressed to him, and him only; a public concert was a profanation, almost, and he began to loathe the name of London, all the railways that led there, all the pianos in London, the medal-giving music teachers, the Mrs. Barnaby Wainfans, those cruel specialists in separation who, not having enjoyed their own lives, insisted on destroying those of others. He knew that when Hilly returned she would have changed into someone snooty and stuck-up, insisting on being called Hildred, or even *Miss Hildred*, and he would spend the rest of his days picking up her gloves and hankies, opening doors, closing windows, fishing Always-Bach out of the piano stool, holding the flashlight when the light began to fail.

He tried to make his mind behave, but images of unattainable suavity haunted him and made him tremble with unexpressed fear. This was what happened to those who stayed behind, like those left out of the Ark: You grew up into a bigger nobody, pronounced in Exington as *nobdy,* as if the principle of self-effacement extended to the very letters in the word. Soon they would be saying, if they could, *Nbdy,* and that would be that.

HE FORCED his mind back to the essay on happiness, wondering why he had said so little, suddenly aware of the heroic distance between thought and penmanship; how long it took to think things out, then set them down, which proved it was not natural. Better to hum ideas, or keep them to yourself. He wondered vaguely if there was any way of finding out what other people long ago had done about *their* essays on happiness; then, with a buoyant giggle, he realized that reading was the answer. Of course. And no doubt some of the pieces Hilly played were about happiness also. They sounded like it, especially when she pushed down the sustaining pedal he called Loud. Was it quicker, then, to set things to music? It looked laborious to write out, but perhaps they did it fast after long practice, like those monks in the Old Ages. . . . The thought dribbled away as he wondered if those old monks making their handwriting pretty, like plumbers squeezing colored fluxes into the gaps in pipes, were writing music straight out, or if they were only writing essays about happiness, and enjoying it so much it felt like music, which gave them even more to write about. To illuminate: That was a word he didn't know a month ago, and here it was for ever, a bolt of magic, handy for all kinds of light. He wondered if young boys could apply to be monks, illuminating until they dropped dead, their finger ends raw with color, and their eyelids too, from constantly rubbing their eyes as they worked. He could see how anyone's appearance might change from getting on them what they worked in, like the miner his coal dust, like his father, whom they all scrubbed after a day underground. He, Harry, would prefer paint or chalk all over him, and he felt a sudden pang: Once the monk had applied his colors, finished his task, he never got to keep the result, but had to leave it there in the big fat book for all to see. That meant, he thought, the monks wouldn't do their best work in the monastery, but at home, for themselves alone. Then he remembered that the monks lived in the monastery, that it was their only home, so they were no doubt always illuminating at their very best. Had God created the best world He could? This sort of question applied to everything. Was there a better world else-where, prettier and more colorful? If so, where? He had an inkling that not just painting, but music and dancing, were part of the other world that Hilly knew about. Harry wanted to have the various pieces of this paradise brought together and made permanent, as you did with a jigsaw puzzle so hard you knew you would never solve it again, so you glued it together, burying the faint chance of overwhelming delight in the tame certainty that it would never cheat you anew. He wondered.

Feeling alert today, he managed to see himself in the grammar school's gray-and-green uniform. Boys walking around clad in it had a different look, as if they had come from America or South Africa and had been made in a secret factory out of brass alloys and horses' hooves, then to be wrapped in fabrics he saw stretched across the sky without even knowing their names were muslin and serge twill, crinkled piqué and the heavy silk lace known as quipure, and surah and foulard and bouclé Cheviot suiting. They were outlandish, these boys within the pale, but his sense of what the world contained was richer far than his notion of happiness even, or of love, such as he felt for Hilly, to his smoldering mind a rapacious, deviant flush-inducing dizziness and movable headaches. Only Hilly had ever told him anything, and his mind was gearing up for the next five million things, whether the names of fabrics or those of composers, monks, or inventors.

Harry felt inappropriate in the world and yearned to run for cover, which meant getting into grammar-school togs as soon as possible or going underground like a naked ferret, especially when Hilly donned a white taffeta blouse trimmed with lilies of the valley, an even whiter taffeta skirt, and a small-brimmed white panama hat, simply for tennis at a place called Stead's Field, where the net drooped between two rusty stanchions. She wore chamois-leather gloves to keep her hands from blistering. They made him play, but he fled, feeling roughly overclad in boots and jersey, wondering why boys should have to subject themselves to the flimsy discipline of taffeta, cambric, and black bombazine.

He liked Hilly best when her hands were naked and she played music, not tennis, and he wondered why she complained that, good as she was, her hands were too small, her fingers too short, requiring her to "bridge" certain chords that long-fingered geniuses such as Liszt had played with contemptuous ease. His own fingers were no longer than hers, and he thought they might play cooperative duets, seated side by side on the piano stool. If the polish was recent, they could see themselves mirrored in the panels.

NOW CLIVE began to track them both in their different places: Hilly, as the puce-faced examiner commanded her to play the next piece and hurrumphed to remind her that the human voice would be an instrument long after the piano disappeared; Harry, as he was called out from class to go and see the head teacher. Hilly knew how she would play the Bach; she had always played it well, mainly because it gave her no problems with reach. Her hands could be themselves. "I like," said the head teacher, whose curly gray hair reminded Harry of a certain dog, "to see a boy who is clever and can show it. You will be going to the grammar school. Good boy. You will need books and uniform, of course." Gazing sideways, Hilly saw the examiner's face contort with mute exasperation, but she was playing well, playing it for Harry, who perhaps did not realize that she was taking examinations as well as giving recitals. She envisioned him sneaking out to hear the handbells, feeling his hand waft loose and lonely in the evening wind. Harry was back in class with a jubilant smirk, looking at them all for one of the last times, off soon to school with George, Thurman, and Douglas. For the first time in his life he was a celebrity for girls to hug and boys to thump. He was the only one who had passed. Hilly, however, had played the wrong piece; it should have been the Bach, of course, but there was no problem, she at once began to play it, upset and trembling, yet still full of perky self-esteem.

The examiner had gone, though, as if relieved to find something to hate her for, yet unable to look her in the face or hear out the superlative Bach she went on playing for lack of anything else to do. At last the supervisor stopped her, patted her on the back, and ushered her into the presence of Mrs. Barnaby Wainfan. Hilly crumbled now, unable to explain, sensing that her recitals were a thing of the past, like the gold medal she had been aiming for. Imagine: to be failed for playing pieces in the wrong order. All in her that loved art and hated routine rebelled in hot, scalding tears. Mrs. Wainfan got her back, tugging and hauling, to the bed-and-breakfast and spoke to her sternly. Failure or not, the prodigy would still have to play the Mothers' Union concert tomorrow. Hilly knew she was doomed now to wrap beef in her father's shop, fetch and carry for her brothers, at best teach grammar at a local school. Had her teeth fallen out, or her hands fallen off, she would have been pleased; any maiming would have done, whatever the pain.

Seething with well-preserved rage, Clive wondered at his own volatility. It was an old and tepid story. The Bach had indeed slowed his mother's career, though without its having anything to do with music. He wanted, even now, to break into that accursed college of music and choke its patrons, its teachers, its examiners; he wanted to melt down its medals into one ungainly ingot to be thrust down the throat of Matyas Whoeveritwas, the examiner, long dumped into an early grave along with his never-played symphonies and his pastiches of Brahms. Nowadays, he thought, several phone calls and some irate letters would have put the matter right; but back then, in 1910, aspirants were humbler, aspiration itself was a canker on the beanstalk of privilege and fame, and anyone not from London, even if backed by the haughty contralto of a Mrs. Barnaby Wainfan, knew much more about his or her place than about vacating it. Hildred, his mother, had gone soaring off into emptiness because her finger slipped, her mind out of sheer headlong jubilation had skidded slightly. An examiner had thrown his version of a fit and stormed away from the scene of the music's beauty. Fool, Clive raged, an inward animal ready to kill on his mother's behalf. If only someone had complained, even to the police, say, or the Royal Family. If only someone had started the ball of complaint rolling, even if it took years to put things right. But Hilly came home to wear her silent, terminal scar, no longer so pleased with herself and doomed, as she put it, to become a provincial when she might have been important. It was as if she had done something shocking, like losing her virginity under the railway arches in darkest Whitechapel. As her father said, she had handed over a parcel of steak instead of lamb. But no one listened to him, notorious as he was for unsimulated sympathy. He was too kind to have any brains, they said, and he was always giving money away; but his mind was a serene analytical casement in which, confronted with unbleeding beeves, he smelled heather and peppermint. He consoled Hilly while her mother fumed, and Clive played and re-played the awful scenes in his mind's eye, wishing to have intervened before he was born, hot to bring his mother a solace Harry could not provide.

Whose was the insult, whose the injury? Harry's mother had been told how much the school uniform would cost and what its component parts were: cap, socks, short gray trousers, school ties, school shirts, school scarf, school raincoat. On and on in unfathomable superplus as if the list included also a motor car, six white dogs, a couple of retainers with flags and trumpets, a sedan chair, a ceremonial balloon, and a horse for riding home on. She could not pay, this child-worn, anxious, uninitiated wisp of a woman with smooth damp pastry-making hands. Each week they spent everything. In all their minds, the notion of a scholarship surfaced and then sank: A scholarship covered fees for tuition, that was all, and in those days (Clive winced at how glad he was he hadn't been a boy then) no school would relent about uniform, any more than the Navy would. Boys arriving at eight in the morning minus the school tie were thrashed and sent home, denied math and grammar, foreign ports and the story of the empire and its builders. Harry, *tout court,* was one of the unwashed, never mind how frank, how felicitous his prose style. Again, 1910 being 1910, no one thought to borrow or to beg, even though something as advanced in taste as the Post-Impressionist Exhibition was going on in London.

It was either have it provided or not go, though the Fitzalans might have offered money if asked; but they *had* to be asked. After all, only a childish friendship linked the two families, and Hilly's mother already saw the school affair as a way to banish the Moxon boy from her children's lives.

Having discovered vicissitude, Hilly and Harry began to talk more, hardly aware how much they already had in common. Both having come down a peg or two, as the unkindly said, they considered schemes for getting to London and acquiring ten pounds. Stealing they dismissed as too dangerous. Pawning the Fitzalan household goods a bit at a time they decided was hardly worth the trouble. They decided to go from door to door, she playing the triangle, he singing hymns, uncannily aware of the power of pathos.

"How about begging?" Harry said, almost in tears, but with his nails jammed into his palms to explain why.

"It would take weeks," she said, nonetheless impressed by his willingness to cry. They began one bright morning, knocking and telling a tale about money for lost puppies until Gerald White, sent to track them down, took their money, gave them a florin of his own, then took Hilly home, sending Harry on his way with a dusting flat-hander to his rear. Whenever Hilly and Harry met, they exchanged the look of loss. She told her father, begging for Harry, but he referred her to her mother, unwilling to rock the unstable family boat. *If only he had,* Clive told himself with the fervor of a vow. If only. His father would have become an historian, maybe a newspaperman; but Exington had its laws about mingling and giving, and Harry was to be stopped in his tracks every bit as much as Hilly. Why, Clive mourned, didn't they pass the hat around at school? The teachers?

Having, as he thought, written a good essay and achieved a good result, Harry felt energized, even if he was going nowhere after all. He wanted to go, anywhere, but there was nowhere to go, even though he heard about P'u-i, the three-year-old who in 1908 had perched himself on China's Dragon Throne, like a pea on a meadow. Some boys had all the luck. Perhaps you had to be three; any older, and you were too late. If he stayed put, and kept on writing good essays, Harry would end up with something splendid after all; someone august would come along with a golden pointer and say, This is the very boy. We need him in China. And Harry would be off, never to return: tireless, famous, a little plump. Hilly would have joined him in China, after having played the right piece for the examiners and able to travel now with the thick, rustling certificate rolled up inside a napkin ring. He thought of subjects to write about, from the Union Jack and the Mustache to Country Life and the Shape of Cows. Some of these he actually wrote for his teachers, and then they gave him that pitying, uplifted look, thanking their stars that their own parents had had the wherewithal. He had all the characteristics of a superfluous boy, a nuisance man.

What puzzled Harry most, however, was the way the Fitzalan children never seemed to lack for fabrics, from veils to blazers, from cummerbunds to tennis aprons, and all for playing in, whereas he couldn't find a blazer or a cap to fit himself into, simply to go to school. He half-expected Hilly some day to hand over a bundle of discarded school outfits that would see him through the next seven years or so; but she never did, although her mother, had she been of such a mind, could easily have done it. Harry could have been a true Joseph in cast-off coats. In fact, Hilly's mother, not eager to encourage the Moxon boy, gave her boys' cast-offs to the Salvation Army and the Band of Hope.

STEAMING with belated anger about his father's virtual loss of a life, Clive juggled energy and nakedness, the two things his father had, and tried to follow him through the years from 1910 to 1914. All he found was a youth whose command of English and copperplate hand augured a career in letters, even if only filing them and leaving behind him row on row of exquisitely emblazoned folders named Plumbing, Accounts Past Due, and Compound Interest. Things like that: dry indices to someone else's profit. Hilly retook the examination and sailed through, although she played with less than her usual flamboyance, worried that the lettering at the top of the page would melt and rearrange itself; Bach would turn into Chopin and the examiner would storm out again. Had he been anyone important, Hilly knew, he would not have been examining in the first place, whereas all beginners had to be examinees: There was no other way to begin to climb the Niagara of musical fame.

Harry developed a chronic desire to be examined again and again, even if he failed every time; he wanted to be tested so that he might prove himself at almost anything, clad in a white sheet as a ghost, making ghoulish sounds; or wrapped in bulbous rubber folds to advertise pneumatic tires; or crammed between two boards, plastered with gaudy advertising, to make him a "sandwich man," Turner's Ice Cream on his front, Izal Soap on his back. All he needed was an outfit, he sometimes told himself, perhaps a commissionaire's uniform in which to huff and puff, fawn and bow, keeping the ruffians out of some big lacquered hotel. Or a postman's. Or that of the man who took and punched your tickets on a train. Whatever it was to be, it would be kind of military, he knew. Such was the way his imagination leaned, but he was too young, even though he lay full length on the floor within the wet outline left by the tub in which his father had bathed, and did his best to lengthen himself. A charcoal mustache aged him almost enough, he thought, and brushing his hair back hard and greasing it into place with lard gave him just a touch of receding hairline. Patting flour into his hair to gray it, he got some in his eye and spluttered, wondering if wet eyes made you seem older, or blackened teeth, or a nose reddened with oxblood boot polish. He was resourceful, but immutably young, and his voice, unlike the voices of the Fitzalan trio, had not broken. He was willing to limp, to pretend to cough up blood, to cut lines of worry across his brow with a potato knife, to stoop, to stammer—but he knew none of this mummery would ever convince those who ran the world, handing out palms and laurel wreaths, ribbons and medals.

CLIVE FELT the rage in him climb and fall as he lived out those years of his father's. Hilly soothed Harry, of course, but frustration coarsened him as her brothers moved ahead from one grade to another, George and Douglas surpassing Thurrie, all three leaving Harry behind to breathe their exhaust. They all five, plus Edith, played heartily, and they saw how Harry adored dressing-up games. Out of doors he had a good eye, could hit and place a ball, and he loved to take a high catch with the sun in his eyes and the wind almost blowing him over. Safe hands he had, and a mean, lunging foot displayed when he introduced them to a game their mother looked upon as vulgar: Kick-Can, simple as it sounds. Hilly pruned and groomed his English, and Clive winced with awe as his mind murmured That makes two of us. Over the years, Harry belonged less and less to the folk he came from, and they knew it, all those brothers and sisters, sensing the eldest had turned snooty even if he didn't go to the grammar school. To some boys, though none of his brothers, he was a grammar-school toady and had to battle his detractors in many a fight. He knew he was almost doomed, whereas other boys knew they were not only doomed but enjoying the best years of their lives on the lip of the slippery slope. Harry spent more and more time at the Fitzalans', going home only to sleep and get his ration of Mother's roast beef.

The Fitzalan house was his grammar school, and Hilly was his wizard; he could imagine no other kind of life, and to the end of his days would be her pendent swain, honoring a superior code of living with nothing so blatant as a tug at his forelock, but with measured, mellow assent. The brothers even lent him cricket and tennis clothes, so he felt he had the glad trappings of an aristocracy without ever having the baleful privilege of wearing the garb in which they went to work—in other words, to study. It pained him to belong so incompletely, to be some fraction of an imposter, both welcome and *de trop*. It would make anyone limp or hunch, he thought, or develop a squint, a lisp. He was Mister Facing Both Ways; he could be kicked in the ass both back and front, not for lack of math, grammar, or geography, but for lacking something spun in the mills of Wigan, a few miles north of Exington, where the mystery happened and the blazers came out buttonless, the socks with the dark-green stripe woven in, the ties with the shuntling silky weave going clean across the slant of the stripes. Had he known the word and the concept, he would have called it immigrational magic. He felt that, in being denied, he was being exposed, and he took to blackening the covered parts of his body with soot, to conceal himself if his clothes ever fell off.

Among the terms of abuse his father endured, "lad-lass" was perhaps the worst, implying, Clive surmised, effete androgyny: Harry liked classical music, a stuck-up girl, a swank gang from what was essentially the other side of the tracks, the track being the single-track railroad known as the Penny Engine Line, a leftover from the Industrial Revolution, overgrown with dandelions and nettles. It might have been different if the word had signified esteem for female qualities, such as candor or peace-making; it did not, and though Harry knew that refinement was effete, it was what he hankered for. But he

knew, too, that adolescence was by no means over. There were many
bloodied noses to come, together with other derisive formulae, from
Pittlebum to Jamrag. Harry fought well, having developed a slate-
hard jab that set his tormentors up for a solid right. He could usually
despatch two of them, but a third was always trouble, often managing
to thwack him a low blow before fleeing. After about a year, they all
began to leave him alone: He was heavier, his reach was longer, and
he boxed them with his small fists as if inspired, his eyes wide open
to perfect his focus. He also learned, from George, to heave at their
faces with his elbows in simple follow-up lethal to the eye. He
thought of Robin Hood and the merry men of Sherwood, wishing
he had a staff to beat his enemies with, or even a broomstick. He bled
easily but had learned from Thurrie how to duck, which was odd
because Thurrie was the burliest Fitzalan and took a punch without
flinching. When Thurrie struck back, appalling injury followed, and
many a mother had appeared at the Fitzalans' back door, pleading for
money with which to buy bandages and iodine, pleading for steak for
the black eye. Ben the dog usually sped them on their way, Thurrie
or his father crying "Shoo!"

Harry's problem was social, not pugilistic. Having sensed greatness
or at least difference in himself, he knew he would have to go off to
Australia or Canada lest he founder in the mines or the iron-and-steel
works, the grocer's shops or the tart-aromaed cobbler's. All he wanted
was to be old enough to go; but how leave a Hilly? Perhaps he should
aspire to become a butcher's boy, as Gerald White had been all his life,
and leave it at that; admiring in blue-and-white striped apron the
bubbles of fat on his hands, blood on his collar and shoes.

Would it be enough to be near her, that and nothing else, like
someone in love with a statue, knowing love's language but having
had his tongue cut out long ago? Harry had hugged Hilly, kissed her,
fondled her bulges in almost complete innocence, but he had only the
merest idea of what was coming. Others desired her. Girls developed

sooner than boys. She was four years older, speeding along the curve from skinny pal to buxom girl, from playmate to sweetheart, even as he watched, powerless to halt flesh or light or the gradual onset of youths talking airily of Mozart and horses, banks and books. Harry wanted to fence them off until he was older: old enough, and he would tackle them one by one, wielding a rolling pin or a walking stick. How could he fight both them and the subtle hierarchy of algebra, German, Latin, and galvanometers as well? They were not as bright as Hilly's brothers, these suitors; knowledge had come to them as rain lands on ducks, but they had it, they had an edge, and all Harry could do was smash their services at tennis played in the rectory garden or Stead's Field, or brain them at cricket by bowling fast at their heads, which he did, with almost as much success as at tennis. Gathering up his meager forces, he became quite a contender, dreading the wrench that would come when school shot him out and he refused to do what was expected of him as a lapdog menial.

"If I was older," he told Hilly, "I'd propose."

"Then don't ever grow up."

"I know I come from muck."

"Muck is brass," she said, citing local wisdom.

"Honest as houses."

"You're not so bad," Hilly said. "It's *music* for me, love, not *lads*. My mother wants a maid, see."

"Then you won't be walking out with the likes of Charley Jones."

"Only to his funeral. Don't you think you ought to grow up first before you start talking about proposals?"

"I will," Harry muttered, "if you'll all give me time."

"Catch me up," she said in a whisper.

"Can't."

"You will. You're one of us anyway."

But Harry in the bliss of his adoration knew he was not. Even with his mouth full of flowers, in a white blazer with cream flannels, and a silk tie popped into his heartspoon, he would never pass muster, not even with a cheroot in his mouth and a monocle making his eyelids sore. Even the long wavy hair she loved to stroke was dead.

Hilly was humoring him, hoping he'd clear off; that must be it, he thought. The magic time was over. It had only been a game, a preamble, what they called a warm-up. He was being instructed in knowing his place, slightly below the sheep and above the lamb. Yes, Clive told himself, agonizing for the little boy who would become his father, it is not the vastness of space that terrifies us, nor its vacuum silence, but the preposterous off chance that it was *thought* into being, tainted with the malefic; some are born to suffer, to stand on hot stones while peering into a mirror that reflects the velvet-and-auburn paradise behind them. It just depends on whether or not you were born looking into a mirror or with your feet on fire. Could he tell that the effort the universe required of him would have paralyzed Robin Hood? Cap, blazer, and tie would have made a king of him in a trice.

AND SO came the day on which Harry, choked to the brim with love coming to birth, nonetheless began to make his move away, in a set of cold echoing rooms where young men volunteered and faked their ages in order to be smothered in red-white-and-blue. Turn to the right and cough, they said, and he did, aghast that they wanted to inspect his genitals. Why? To see if they bounced or if they shrank from the chill in there? He bent over. He opened wide. He read the eye chart, thinking *how easy*. He watched the round rubber hammer tap his knee below the cap and the little reflex kick that followed, urged by a goblin from behind. Did they really care what kind of a body he brought them? So long as they stopped the kaiser, affably known as Kaiser Bill, all would be well, and Exington would be safe. He was half-expecting to see George and Douglas join him, but they were already en route to a career in metals, essential to the war effort at home, and only Thurrie enlisted with him, destined, he hoped, to be a cook, whereas Harry wanted to shoot the Boche and fight a manly war. Then they gave him a list of what to bring with him: It was rather longer than the list supplied by the grammar school, and he suddenly wondered if it wasn't easier to get into grammar school after all.

He would take the train from Reresby south to Derby and then he mustered into his regiment, the Sherwood Foresters, of course. It was like moving centuries away or joining a new cricket team, expecting any moment, from behind a barbed-wired wall or the steaming flank of a horse, the king himself, in pale-brown field-marshal's uniform. The king's charger had a sky-blue plume beneath its head, but he seemed to have no weapon. Perhaps his sword was concealed within his tunic. In a flash Harry had defended him from the marauding Huns as they swept across the grass; he held his sword horizontal as the Huns arrived, beheading them one after the other as they ran into the blade. It was a slight dream, but an effective overture. For a moment there was even a trumpeter sounding something, either the call to rally or that to retreat, perhaps only to emphasize how Harry held his ground, shivering in his underwear, telling Huns to turn to the right and cough.

When he got his uniform, it scratched his neck and rubbed it raw. The boots blistered his feet, but they shone, and he kept white things white with Blanco (spit on a cake of chalk) and black things black with Cherry Blossom boot polish. What had the recruiting sergeant told him? "Off you go, lad. Come back tomorrow if you're any older." Next day came the king's shilling plus almost twice that amount for ration money. It was an easy life, this; they fed you, just like his mother, before you'd done anything. Now he rushed along with the others from blankets on the floor of the barracks to something called Gunfire at the cookhouse: a mug of tea served in a soup plate, into which he had to dip his muzzle like a dog. In the bell tent at night he and twenty-one others lay like the spokes of a wheel, all feet aimed at the center pole, and he wondered if there were some punishment that consisted of having your head next to all those feet.

Equipped at first with a dummy rifle, he yearned for the real thing, wanting to flaunt his prowess on the firing range. The tea, those in the know said, was spiked with jalap, which kept them all trotting to the latrine, even during physical training from 6:00 A.M. to 7:00 A.M. Somewhere inside him he felt the contrary emotion of wanting to receive letters from Hilly without having to write any, as if he had gone beyond the world of stamps, envelopes, and sealing wax. All *that* was flimsy and fancy compared to the puttees he had to wind around his calves, from his ankle to his knees: khaki leg bandages like those used in the Indian Army. The overlap had to be smooth and parallel, though some untutored sense of geometry told him that, if the puttees made a helix as they went up his legs, the edges could never be parallel, even if his leg extended all the way to heaven. Some of the rules they were supposed to live and die by were for the book alone. If only he had heard Clive cheering him on for posing questions all the time, for arguing with corporals about his puttees and the chores that came his way, from dumping urinal tubs to peeling potatoes. It was worse than being back in the Endowed School in Exington, where you could go home to your own bed after work was done. He missed Hilly's music; walking through the woods with her and her brothers, whom he now thought of as civilians; but he convinced himself that, never mind how stultifying and unheroic a recruit's life was, it was an appropriate prelude to feats of monstrous valor with rifle or machine gun. Without deceiving himself, he knew that something wondrous had taken place: He belonged to a vast, intricate organization that saved him from falling through space from the level of schools to that of butcher-boy, and from that of butcher-boy to that of one who lounged on Market Street, at the Cross, against the railing, where Northgate, Southgate, and Market Street met, and where long ago ancient conquering Romans had made water in the dust. That was as low as you could get in Exington; unless you were a miner on the way home, in which event a lean at the Cross was allowed, provided it didn't last too long while the bathwater at home cooled and the plate of dinner dried.

True, his uniform was a poor fit, a rough and spiky fabric. Not for him the smooth collar of the senior officers, or tinkling spurs on tan riding boots that gleamed, or the monocle that caught the sun and sometimes reflected a narrow scalding ray against the cheek of the soldier being stared at. A raw recruit might hope, though, to have as many initials as some of the officers. Before dozing off, he would wonder what Capt. A.L.D.G.M. Jethro, B.A., stood for; the man was festooned with frippery from another world. Algernon Lochinvar Dalby Goldsworthy Montague, he thought; more elaborate by far and much more inherited than a mere Moxon, only two syllables between him and death. The officers were so exquisitely spoken he decided they were going to humiliate the Germans into defeat merely by exposing them to all those diphthongs.

Harry was convinced that Hilly was almost completely occupied with her sturdy brass-bound rosewood writing box, while Hilly, for her part, had made up her mind that all Harry cared about was getting his hands on a Prussian flag-bearer's gorget from Imperial Germany. Backed with green cloth and spray-painted black, this gorget was a small metal shield of crescent shape, originally protective and part of the helmet. A black Prussian eagle trapped thereon seemed to be trying to escape the gilt in which it had been embedded. Or perhaps (she mutated the image, happy so long as it did not bring her the flames and fury of war) there was a gilt flaming grenade between crossed flags. If she thought of him as a thing, he was invulnerable; if he thought of *her* as one, she wouldn't miss him too much. It was a sublime way of protecting each other at a distance. It was the semi-irrelevance of the writing box, the gorget, that made them useful, their remoteness from what either truly cared about. In fact, Hilly heard her music as Harry heard it, forcing herself to an unsophisticated low, while he, marveling at how the sergeants and sergeants major barked without getting hoarse, could easily see the gorgets he admired as useful clobber in the Fitzalans' dressing-up games. Harry and Hilly kept trying to impersonalize each other, for all the world as if two devout toast-eaters tried to console themselves when apart by thinking only of the fork's hot tines and nothing more. The hot metal brought them together again, crouching in front of the fire on a smoky autumn afternoon, the plate of crumpets set between them, the butter in the shade their bodies cast while leaning forward to tend to the toasting: One to hold the fork, the other to test the slowly darkening hue of the floury disk.

For Harry, the war was a big celebration, of what he never knew: A churning uproar of unknown dimensions rushed through his head, as if someone who had loved too much had lost all power to care and had begun that monstrous, ravening hoot to proclaim to the world what lack of love was like. He hardly knew he thought this, but his childlike apprehension of hell was full of tremors and shudders that told him something he adored at home had ceased. Except for the excepts: He stood a better-than-average chance of not being shot—he was too small a target for any but superlative marksmen; alive, he liked to mimic officers who held golden cigarette cases over the mouths of the severely wounded to see breath blur the sheen (Harry tested himself with shined-up tin plate); and because the Germans used enormous mirrors for observation purposes, perched on their earthworks, he found himself with an easy target, and when he hit the glass it sundered far and wide, spectacular if the sun had been shining into it.

Without warning, he was rushed away to something called the Blue Blind Factory, a huge billet where they taught him to fire and maintain a Vickers machine gun. The good eye he had had with bat and ball, and for catching and throwing, stood him in good stead now, and he excelled. Taught how to fill the water jacket that cooled the Vickers gun, and a score of more intricate things, he went back into action. He quietly told himself that this would be something to write about when he at last got into grammar school, a hardened campaigner who had welcomed even the occasional capricious order to polish his buttons while in the trenches; there in that Sargasso sea of mud, policed by rats and stacked with its own unique harvest of corpses, sometimes ten feet high, constantly blown up only to resettle into different heaps until the next bombardment—as if some loose cannon were casting *I Ching* with human sticks. He saw that many soldiers, when shot, would fall with their fixed bayonets sticking into the mud, holding them up for a while at about forty-five degrees until they sank lower and lower like strict sentries fainting. He had never seen ballet, but he had heard about it from the Fitzalans, and he wondered if this kind of gracefulness was what drew people to the theater to ooh and aah.

Dead horses full of gas exploded and left the air rancid. The horror was not human at all, but came from God or Satan and duly went back. Aloof in his uncomprehending way, Harry did not realize his mind had been numbed almost as soon as he arrived. This was just as well since, between his young hands, he now had a machine that killed at enormous speed. Right across the parallel white ridges made by troops digging trenches out of chalk, he fired and fired, or, as one of the five-man team, watered and cleaned and adjusted. What he loved most about the Vickers was the way the water in the gun's jacket boiled into a steam that passed through a soft tube into a canvas bucket, where it became water all over again, ready for second use. He had discovered a complete, sealed system, and, Lord be praised, there was never rising steam to give their position away to the observant enemy with the big hungry mirrors.

ATTUNING HIMSELF to his young father in the act of inventing a stoicism to survive by, Clive shook his head in order to move from 1914 to 1990. My God, I'm only fifty-five. He told himself that those manmade ridges of chalk, bulging here and there, were ridges of cocaine awaiting the addict's sniff. Did they never blow away or become sodden with rain? His father always spoke of them as if they were permanent, with a few spectral trees growing among them to remind nations of what a landscape used to be. Harry would soon be promoted to lance corporal, he knew, having heard the war stories a hundred times, hardly ever from his mother, who shrank from the way his father, and some of his cronies from the village, had seemed to enjoy war as a supreme game. At home, boys collected lead piping and melted it down over an open fire, then poured molten lead into the cavities on the side of building bricks to make lead ingots. At war, they collected spent bullets and pressed their cap badges into the mud, making a mold in which badges of silvery lead came to birth: small, inert miracles to marvel at while the howitzers and *Minenwerfers* growled. At night they attached a pipe to the muzzle of the Vickers to curb and quell the sparks; the only person who could state their position was one toward whom the red-hot rounds were already speeding. Harry found this just, and hoped whoever it was would dodge aside in time: *just* in time. At criminal speed he had ascended from the humble role of reserve and gun carrier to ammunition supply and so to belt feeder and leader. He knew that, if they ever had to defend a crater very close to other craters held by the enemy, each of them would have to fill out a postcard addressed to his next of kin, saying "I am quite well," which meant that he would probably be dead within half a day.

The craters came from exploded mines planted by teams of miners who, sometimes, when the earth partitions between them broke, fought hand-to-hand with shovels underground until the tunnels fell in on them. Why any crater was worth defending, Harry never found out, but he gathered it was more a matter of honor than of clear-cut victory. The important thing was to have fought, and died, for something worthless; it was all in the mind; it was courage stripped of its appropriate occasion and its pragmatic baubles. Those who defended a crater stood near the rim, facing outward, and dug their toes in as far as they could, so as not to slide down the funnel-shaped mudhole into the sump at the bottom; but bombs landed behind them, so they tried to rig sandbags against their backs to keep the shrapnel off.

HARRY remembered the process by which he had been plucked from the Sherwood Foresters and transferred to the Royal Machine Gun Corps. Was the word for it *seconded,* said with the accent on the middle syllable? It had been as if he had been told to give up bow and arrow, Lincoln green, stout staff, all the far-fetched trumpery of pastoral scuffling, and join the war now being staged between industrial nations. With the shift to the RMGC went some of his craving innocence, although it meant only the same chance of being killed; having the gun meant he would take more of the Hun with him, that was all. When the *Minenwerfer* landed, it destroyed impartially: boys and men, officers and privates, Sherwood Foresters and machine gunners. Now came the first onset of the twitch that never ends: in the hands, the knuckles, the wrists, even as he balled up his hands into sweet fists he could not use; that way, only the wrists trembled or, rather, they were all he could see in the act of shaking. You dug a hole, then a Minie landed on top of you and buried you down deep. You had stopped breathing long before anyone found you, though some had been known to have been blown skyward, only to land in a standing position so convincing that whoever was handing around bully beef and biscuits served up breakfast to the dead. There were no fires to make tea with, so it was a dry, cold repast, followed, if the smoke allowed, by a quiet look at the cards that came in packages of cigarettes. These cards depicted the badges of various army divisions, the faces of senior officers, the colors of battle standards; wadded together by a rubber band and stuck in the pocket in front of your heart, they might absorb the impact of a bullet. Fifty cards would slow it up, a hundred might block it altogether. But who ever had that many? Who survived long enough to acquire the complete set? Sodden with sweat and sometimes blood, the cards stuck together, and Harry had given up trying to pry them apart. It was like peeling some old scab away from his own body. Most of the cards ended up as inadequate toilet paper, fit for a quick scrape at the backside during a lull. Nobody squatted for long, not in the same place, even if the distance between squats was only a foot or two within the haven of the latrine trench.

Because there was no water, there was no shaving, which made his face itch, but not with a pain worse than that of young soldiers with false teeth—dental hygiene being nothing then—trying to chew hard-tack biscuits. Usually what food there was reached the front jumbled up in one sack: tea leaves, crumbled cheese, and rotten beef all came out together by the handful, a carnal sawdust best thrown to the winds to seed trees of death. Tinned plum or apple jam survived its journey to the front line, although there was more sugar in it than fruit, he thought: Tickler's, the brand name, after a year become an almost soothing neutral sludge they missed when, from Australia, Melon and Honey or Pineapple or Quince Conserves began arriving. The more resolute palates mixed the tea, cheese, and beef with their jam, calling it Tweedsmuir or Feldspar, and these names seemed to Harry to have a certain military splendor.

Out of the line, as when removed from the Hohenzollern Redoubt to one of the villages near Béthune, he was able to concentrate on delousing himself, unable to resist the notion that Hilly could dispatch them faster with a fusillade of Always-Bach. He would apply a lighted candle to himself and hear the lice pop, or he would scrape them from the seams of his pants, the creases in his woolly underwear (that chafed him cruelly), and then drop them into a tin can held over the flame. The *pop* or *phut* would be the same, and the blot of blood on skin or can bottom. This they called chatting, although he had tried to keep that word in reserve for Sunday mornings when, perhaps out of loneliness, two machine guns began to talk to each other, one German, one "ours," each mimicking the cadence and rhythm of the other in short bursts, aiming at nothing and wasting bullets.

He loved to hear the stern cry from the battalion cookhouse: "Roll up for dip, lads!", which meant you could go off to where pink rindy bulbous bacon was frying in long pans big enough to hold a baby and lay a slice of bread deep into simmering grease that, if you then dipped your bread into the thick mahogany tea mixed with condensed milk, floated on the surface like see-through scabs. The smell of dead pig and rancid caramel became forever linked to Sunday mornings; and, in turn, the smell of those Sunday mornings to time out of the line, among the French, who were as amazed to find live soldiers in their midst as the soldiers were to find people going about their ordinary business not far from the grotesque slagheaps of the inferno. This was where Harry learned to smoke, and to roll cigarettes from shag and tea leaves in a square of brown wrapping paper.

Unable to tell the lurches in his stomach from the convulsions of fear, he noticed hands, arms, of the dead sticking out and moving as the sludge moved with each explosion, and he tried to conceal each with an empty sandbag, so much so that he became nested in a cavity of sacking and, with some degree of equanimity, leaned against pieces of body that stuck out. If this was the process called blooding, akin to that of wiping the young hunter's face with the blood from the dead fox's tail, he accepted the word, the stance it required, wondering how many schoolboys, *youths,* would have the adaptability for this, the tutored nerve that said what you could not see could not blind you.

Names that remained the same in peace as in uproar astounded him, even though he never knew how to pronounce them. They had a festive, raffish sound: Festubert, Givenchy, Auchy-les-Mines, Cuinchy, Loos, Hulluch, and Neuve-Chapelle, with Armentières to the north (recalling the song that went "Mademoiselle from Armentières,/*Parlez-vous, parlez-vous?*''); and he sometimes, at least in the treacherous domain of pronunciation, mixed them up, creating Festency and Givtubert, like a huge crumpling map, knowing what was there but, in some fit of escapism, defying the birds, the compasses, the signposts laid like wounded at the roadside, aimed half skyward, half into the ground.

HOW DID HE, Clive, say it when Hildred his mother looked at him quizzically, murmuring "Now what?" He answered with what had almost become a tender formula: "I'm thinking about Daddy during the Great War: what he went through because he volunteered." She always shook her head, still unable to face the details, and looked away to the big birch tree that tossed beyond the window, unaware that he was reliving them both in her very presence, separating them and then in a frenzy of adoration bringing them together star-crossed and disjointed after so many years. He blinked the wet away and resumed consumption of his father in a foreign field.

He tried to imagine Hilly imagining how the war was: the noise, the flashes, the rats, the bully beef, the mud, the sandbags, the French lace and the executions for cowardice, the incessant curse words and the filled latrines beginning to leak into the main trenches during rain. No, she was not thinking of such things; she had the gift of wholesome loneliness and no doubt envisioned war as cherry orchards, chiming bells, and soft paintable sunsets. Were there warm baths in Hilly's imagination? There was music, martial perhaps, but slithering out of the top of the universe to grace and sway the men in tin helmets, urging them to gentleness: always to surrender; to turn the other cheek; to aim into the sky and not at the others on the ground; to disobey, be tried, be shot, rather than—what? Have all the pianos in Christendom explode. Something as devilish as that.

She sent him cakes and cigarettes, some bars of chocolate, knowing these last would make him homesick for the chocolate machines that, for a penny slid in, would make a thin wafer clatter down from a steel brow into the little drawer beneath. He would come home to chocolate, she thought. Or so Clive surmised, finding his mother cannily remote in that time of his father's trial by hellfire. She ached and, at the piano, prayed even as she played scales, up and down, only half-minded, fleeing what obsessed her.

It was now that Harry, chosen to be Number One in the gun team and therefore obliged to carry the tripod, began to wonder about human speech in that flooded wasteland. The more he learned of trench argot, the less he understood—the words never seemed to recur. *Pozzy* was jam, *shackles* was soup made from rancid leftovers, *burgoo* was porridge, and *spotted dog* was currant pudding. He learned a word as fast as he did just to keep abreast of the appalling, and that was that; he tried to forget it, knowing it would never serve him again. Or at least that was how he felt, tuned in by his future son Clive, journeying to his father-to-be through aerial corridors, prompted by his father's confessional memories of poring over the table with map spread out and little pins stuck here and there: one for Festubert, one for Givenchy. Clive ached with yearning for the young warrior already so expert in the ways of mechanized war that he kept the spare lock for the gun in his pants pocket to keep it warm in December but every half-hour whipped it out and fixed it into the gun, carefully adjusting the cold one into his pocket. Had he not done this, the oil would have frozen.

Harry's voice became higher and weaker, even as a corporal giving orders. He had become a corporal because the other soldiers eligible had been killed, so he knew his own time was short. Boots marching on cobbles in the night were often a prelude to executions; the salvo of intimidated rifle fire usually followed in five minutes, and somebody else's boy bit the dust for cowardice or for having caught VD and hidden himself away to suffer. One day he received a revolver on a lanyard, easier to wield than the rifle that sometimes stopped him from moving up and down a trench, wedging him there while he sank into the mud. Soon the mud became so deep they were also issued with thigh-length rubber boots, which worked well until you got into water deeper than they were high. Then you were moored for target practice until a couple of those not waterlogged tilted you sideways and heaved you out.

Clive's father's voice had always risen when mentioning such matters; his face had flushed and his immaculately manicured hands had hovered over the map as if supervising an incantation. He had been through hell, he admitted, but he had never lived so intensely since. Between sixteen and twenty he had grown up some twenty years, apart from wondering helplessly about the red-light districts in Béthune and other villages, wondering why, amidst the carnage, he had no sexual desires at all, certainly not for the antiquated madams and their wartorn women of the evening. He would go and linger; a sexual life postponed too long would never start. All the come, he had heard, eventually drained back into the hollow in your spine if not called into service. That was what a bachelor was, like a spinster; he had heard these words in church and recoiled, sensing something deathly and clammy. Bachelor and spinster were what they called you if you hung on too long, but he could not for the life of him, like the other men in the brothels' waiting rooms, take out his organ and caress it, patting it and appraising it as if it were a small puppy, silent and obsequious, its head aimed blindly at the ceiling above which sat the floor where it all happened. The beds creaked, the plaster fell, the sounds came through like dismembered music; and then the clients bumped downstairs, a bit sheepish and clumsy, tapping their uniforms, flicking their thumbs against the corners of their mouths, their eyes newly sunken after the magic of the upstairs crones had taken away the best of them. No, he could never do that with a total stranger, or with someone he knew well either, such as Hilly. He was doomed. So he remained an experienced accompanist aroused by the familiar lewd spectacle, but, as the others teased him, pure.

When he did it, it would have to be the equivalent of war: something as profoundly shattering as that, with all ancillary parts of his being dragged red-raw into the onset. Just as his taste buds yearned for condensed milk and bacon grease, his thigh craved the cool line of the spare lock, and his sodden feet wriggled their way toward some unattainable zone of dryness in his boots. It was a war, he knew, of preposterous lopsidedness, in which exhausted men tried to balance themselves for a seven-kilometer walk from trench to trench along floating duckboards, their minds on a few raisins squashed together with rat bristles. Their feet and legs were pickled, rats would pillage their packs while they slept the sleep of the done-in, and they returned bearing the dead aloft like ghosts walking a series of tightropes with stretchers in between them. Not bantamweight, said a boxer among them, but phantomweight.

Eventually Harry threw away the war souvenirs he was going to lug home to Blighty: the spent rounds, the spike from a Prussian helmet, the snapped bayonet, the mud-encrusted flag-bearer's gorget that had made a *clink* sound against his boot. The ideal souvenir, he now knew in that December of 1915, was a small bag full of mud that reeked of sulfur and rotting feet. Nothing else would quite do. Neither he nor his team got leave, not even for Christmas, which meant that war had conquered the calendar and would thenceforth heed only its own loathsome festivities.

MANY a time Clive had fought alongside his father, knowing that ever after Harry would have to be described as a warrior, a soldier, a veteran. Other occupations would supervene, but these would be only so many diversions; his father's adolescence had been epic, heroic, and he belonged from then onward to the small band that never said but knew, sometimes even clasping hands over a pint of beer as the dreadful clamor, the stench and wire came back to them on the crest of a death-dealing wave they themselves had repelled with their bare hands, thus hoisting themselves up to the level of Aeneas and Odysseus, King Alfred or Hereward the Wake, halting the Saxons and the belligerent Prussians like a tide of vermin; and without becoming so inhuman in the act as to grow an extra leg, turn green overnight, or develop saber teeth after a week of it. As his father had often said, only about one in twenty came back, as far as Exington went anyway, so these men had more than an inkling of supernatural good luck: They had heard the gods rattling dice and had stood their ground waiting for their number to come up, and it had not, while thousands died around them, mown down, buried under mudslides, drowned in craters, squassated by concussion—killed by almost anything that was not a puff or a quiver.

Machine-gun practice became even stricter now, and had to be done blindfolded, which was more enthralling, Harry thought, than doing it in the dark, as if the gun were his woman, his mind on the slice or pleat between her legs. It was all right in the dark, wasn't it?, because it was something disgraceful by Fitzalan standards, to be sure. Clive caught his father in the act of being prudish and smiled, telling himself sex was much more than merely plunging, just as the novel was much more than a morass of faintly consecutive sociology, the scurviest pseudoscience of all. Had his father, he wondered, ever used the thousands he'd killed as a fillip to lust, thought about them in grisly detail during the act merely to prolong "relations"? The thought almost made him gag, so he knew he was still not hard-boiled enough to see snot in a raindrop, to think scabs dropping from the nostrils as beautiful as bees.

Whipping boy of memory that he was, Clive played another game here in the anteroom of the past, turning a red-hot cauldron into an effigy of filial love, seizing his mother before time did, refloating their uncanny childhood like someone adept at bringing bachelors and spinsters together; almost as if, like a preacher manqué, he read out the bans of engaged couples in church, urging everyone to come forward now who saw some impediment to the union other than the son who wrote everything down and squeezed their love to make it linger for ever. He tried to stay calm, taking deep breaths, but the fibrillation had begun, and all his habitual maneuvers—loud coughs, "bearing down" so as to reset the vagus nerve, splashing cold water on his wrists—failed to work. It was hours to his next dose of quinaglute, so it wasn't the lack of medication that had started the atria jiggling, it was the matter in hand, it was all this ranging back and forth in the time that belonged to others. He was reading them, inventing after their example, as if both Hilly and Harry were literature, unable to fight the presumptive inroads of the reader's mind. The temptation was to give them a lovelier life than they had had, but the chore was to record their happiness, between body soil and intelligent anguish. He had to make a good job of this, or he would never be able to remember them without lethal guilt.

UP TO THEN, Harry's military life had been fairly uncomplicated, and Clive fixed on it as a relief from trying to plumb his mother's condition at the same time—how she coped mentally, in enormous shuddering secrecy, while Harry trudged from crater to crater, trench to trench. In the early spring of 1916, his life became more complex because, as he judged it, he was more successful. He had become a sergeant, not least because his mustache had at last begun to assert itself in obedience to some private fluid that had finally begun to flow, no doubt on account of terror. One night, as he peered over the rim of a crater, he heard a fidgeting in front of him and thought it the sound of a big rat; but the sound became heavier, more deliberate, and there rose from out of the night the figure of an English officer complete with monocle, swagger stick, and shooting stick, upon which he managed to sit for a while, in full view, before it sank gradually into the mud. He then tugged it free, folded the twin seat halves back together, and climbed up into the machine-gun position where five slept while Harry watched.

"Peaceful night, sergeant."

"Sir." Who ever disagreed? There was always an uproar out here. The only way of remaining safe was to have a mother animal following you around to eat up your feces as you went about your duties, lest predators find you.

"Certainly is. Just checking. I'm called Intelligence Addendum, see. Lone wolf scouting for cubs. Captain Rees-Cardus at your service. This is my last leg, so to speak. A quick shufti, and I'll be off to cocoa and ham sandwiches."

Shufti, Harry knew, was an imported word—Arabic—for look, as *bint* was woman, and the Hindi word *charp* meant sleep. Officers talked this way, as if in retaliation to cockney rhyming slang (which also baffled Harry) and the thick, contorted vowels of the Sherwood Foresters. This officer, this dandy, smelled too good, as if newly unwrapped, and by the semilight of the moon Harry noticed his white collar: unique in that all other officers he'd seen wore collars of khaki. Besides, the white made him too good a target.

"The password, then, sir," Harry said, determined to start the meeting on the correct foot. "If you please."

If this popinjay didn't know it, Harry was going to shoot him, firing squad or not.

"Passwords we don't use, sergeant, we IA blokes."

"It's 'White Heather,' isn't it?" Harry said, lying.

"For all I know," Captain Rees-Cardus said, "it's Aunt Fanny's Knickers. Don't worry, my lad, we don't need to be that punctilious. It's just the two of us, no Huns in view."

Don't you know, Harry was thinking of a way of telling him, this gun here could blast you to smithereens? I am going to do it if you keep on giving me that blarney. The password, or what you deserve, blathering and fooling about in no-man's-land in the middle of the night.

"Have you a medal?" The exquisitely modulated voice came from miles away.

"Have I a medal?"

"To show."

"No, sir," Harry muttered. "No medal."

"Then," the captain said, "we'll have to get you one," thus starting a train of thought unknown to Harry until that moment. Did the man have a handful of medals to pin on the deserving brave during the night? Was he some kind of good samaritan who trod the mud only to cheer men up and get them dreaming grandiose dreams of heroism, leave, and reward? Harry felt his resolve weakening, knowing he would have to use his revolver as the captain had come too close, was within the machine-gun's arc of travel. The others were awake now, not moving where they lay with backs against the sacking-shrouded wall of mud. They saw an officer and hated him, but no more than that, whereas Harry, primed for intruders, saw a German going through the motions in a white collar.

Turning away, Harry unsnapped the holster of his revolver and seized the butt, ready for action as he wheeled to confront the bizarre captain, who was there no longer, dissolved or sucked aside. In a sudden fury Harry opened up on the machine gun, bathing the mud in lead, shooting as wildly as he ever had, knowing the fake officer was out there somewhere, a prime target in his white collar, a little skim of moon cruising above the pocked land. Harry stopped firing. He knew better, but his mind went on pursuing the idea of a medal. What did you get a medal for? It would never clink until he had two. He would hardly gain one from a German, but it would have been a wonderful joke if this bogus officer had managed to award German medals during the night to soldiers who, the instant dawn came, put them on with insomniac pride and marched back to their billet, degraded, made ridiculous, traitors even. That was what they called propaganda. Germans had been to Oxford to learn the lingo, and now they were popping up all over France and Germany, specially trained in the argot of cricket, beer, and tobacco. Sometimes, as sergeant, Harry went out on patrol when his own officer checked the four or five gun positions in his charge; Harry vouched for the officer, and they both knew the password. Surely it would have been possible for the spy, Captain von Kaiserstein, as Harry now called him after he had melted into the night, to have lain a yard or two away, and picked up the password. But the password would have been spoken only when an officer arrived to inspect: a long wait. Germans were always willing to go to endless trouble. It could have worked, Harry was sure. Von Kaiserstein could have said Bubble and Squeak and shot them all in the back from where he lay pretending to snooze. Harry wondered how long the von Kaiwerteins survived, and how much useful information they amassed, how many innocent soldiers they left dead behind them.

Out here in the trenches it was a poor, disgusting life, not half as good as leaning against the fence at the Cross in Exington, but on a not-too-noisy, moonlit night in France it gave you uncanny privileges over others: the right to blow their brains out, or to let them off. It was amazing to be so powerful at sixteen, pseudoseventeen, with no one in sight to correct or advise you, only God Almighty watching one of his new-created prepare to cold-skull yet another Hun. Was it of this that he would prate in after years? Of the phantom Captain von Kaiserstein, neither shooting nor shot, unless one of those random rounds discharged into the night had found him after all and maimed him in the monocle, shot the white collar to shreds, clipped his balls?

Would I, Harry asked himself, fancy a job like that, even as an officer, scrambling about in the sludge, well disguised except for the collar, talking fancy German to the Huns and wondering which of them would eventually twig it that I wasn't a Hun after all, but a Sherwood Forester detached to the Machine Gun Corps? By then I'd have become a captain too, but when would that be? Not until the war was over. Think of all the education you would have to have to do a job like that. And the courage. He was heartily glad he had not shot the captain, with his revolver anyway, and in a tender way he wished him well, as if the captain had been one of the more edifying animals: not a rat, but a ferret, a badger, a fox. Perhaps, already, he was sipping schnapps and looking at dirty pictures held up in front of him by a batman even as the earth trembled around them and the stench of cordite, mingled with that of rotting meat and incinerated sacking, became intolerable. Harry's dream of promoted autonomy died when he got an order to mix Vaseline with the water in the cooling jackets lest it freeze. He did as he was told, thankful he knew the password, yet all the same feeling in his rear end the knife-edged pucker that evinced a fear as private as cancer. His day would come. How long a war would it be? What, after five or ten years of peace, would a sergeant have become?

He could not answer that, although he knew he was not going to be a metallurgist like George and Douglas. Metals meant little to him, but wood did, so he might become a carpenter, a joiner, from bookshelf to coffin. Already he knew he was not among the brutal sergeants, of whom he had seen many; soldiers came to him with all kinds of problems, men older than he, as if he ran some kind of children's crusading service for seniors. They wanted leave, mail, food, liquor, sleep, sex, most of all the intimate, conclusive reassurance that they were not going to be among the dead. Harry told them all they would survive, for different reasons, certainly for some time to come, and then they would have to ask someone else. Seers only saw so far, and not to the end of the war. More music would have soothed them, he thought, and not the pompous blurts of brass bands, but what Hilly played, larding their sleepless nights with the presence of the amateur god whose war it was.

He had given up trying to poke the filth from under his fingernails or trim the dead bleached skin from the soles of his feet. He let his body take its course, became used to the ancient reek of it, and began to murmur magical words to himself merely to focus his mind: *shufti, bint, charp,* like a tourist getting ready for an excursion, hoping to have acquired enough words in time to create the design of his life abroad, certainly extended beyond sleep, death, and women.

He not only murmured words, filched from officers and spies; he began to chant under his breath, into his hands, the kind of music monks made, which he had first heard in Béthune in a still-functioning monastery: a sound both disciplined and lax, calling the soul to rigor even as it invited it to sprawl. Knowing no Latin, he made up his own language, discovering how to extend one sound for half a minute, reaching no one within earshot, but tanking up his spirit with it, making its monotony into something like prayer. Was this from Hilly? He doubted it; the noise he made—a scurrying huskiness on the brink of syllabification—came from pagan sources: the chunter of those who otherwise ate earth, who shrank still from masticating flesh and were full of gas from too many vegetables and whose ears, while keen, were cued to process rather than event. Harry seemed, to others, as the spring persisted cold, to be blowing into his hands to warm them; but he was really chanting, and gradually learned to vary in pitch and impetus, a litany of the human mind, or soul, or spirit (he used all three words to himself interchangeably), emancipated from cause and effect, from space and time, but cached beneath God's eyelid, in a safe but thunderous place like the belfry of all belfries, where an old ally of his, the hunchback of Notre Dame, a good ogre, had lingered, deaf, deformed, but open-hearted as a corpse with its chest smashed in.

The war was changing, Harry knew. It used to be that he could tell, roughly, what was happening from day to day. There used to be events, clear as stitches made in flesh, and there were names to attach events to. Now the war lurched from one process to another, then back, and you had to surrender your mind to it, go numb and blank, forget your name, become a mote swimming across a shaft of putrid sunlight—as if this were all your life were going to amount to henceforth. Clive understood how Harry had felt, even if he was inventing it. Surely Harry had never used such words or come out with such hypersensitive findings: an observant man, but, even as a sergeant, not yet gifted with the sheer indefatigability of eye that brought a thousand nuances into the métier of slaughter. All right! Clive knew his successive calibrations of Harry's war more or less matched how his father watched other things: a crop, a son, a soccer team.

To Harry, the war was lumbering and smothering, no longer an affair of locales but a huge infestation blighting the map; and the old sense men had that they were individuals fighting for a cause gave way to something fouler: The war was using them, bunching them up, wiping them out in groups, even if, in some weird particulars, it was improving. When he first arrived in France, a gas mask, so-called, was a pad of cotton wrapped in muslin. When the warning came of a gas attack, he was supposed to urinate on the pad and clamp it over his mouth and nose. Many a farmer called to the colors said they would all be safer face down in a cowshed. Now the drill was different. The helmet had refined itself into a flannel bag drenched in some chemical, with a slice of mica for a window. This, he thought, was what the new century had come to; who could want better than this? He meant not having to inhale your own urine. He saluted the sybilline gods of progress and yearned for his next plate of egg with *pommes de terre frites,* and his glass of coarse, tangy *vin blanc,* which he said as *vanblonk,* and that was that. They laughed and served him; even such an oaf, a yokel, might help to save *La France.*

All winter he had rubbed whale oil into his feet, with little thought about the whale, hoping to fend off trench foot, which caused the feet to dissolve from the combination of cold and wet. Thurrie, whom Harry never saw during the war, was already suffering from it badly enough to be taken out of the lines.

Harry's mind was on something else. Without in any way wishing to shirk his portion of daily bombardment, he had begun to think about his medal, or rather his decoration. The infiltrating Hun, if such he had been, had made a valid point: someone singled out for valor, or for having been in the hem of its penumbra's edge, would perhaps be given assignments of less foolhardy risk. The only snag was that to save your life you had to risk it first, and in the company of reliable witnesses who survived to testify. This meant that Harry had to find a reckless young subaltern, preferably one who had been a doughty sportsman at rugger or rowing, who saw the war as one huge game and counted not the cost. Another snag was that machine-gunning, apart from the standard trek to the crater or the redoubt, was static soldiering: The Hun came to you; you did not dash out toward him, gun firing. Your eyes poured with dread. The entire thing, Harry decided, would have to be worked out with more than military prudence. He would have to ask around, hunting a von Kaiserstein among the British.

Taken out of the line with a miserable cough that would have given his position away in seconds, he found himself billeted with a farmer who plied him with milk that gave him something to cough up all the more. It prolonged his leave, and got him into the nearby officers' mess, where he found a gramophone he was allowed to use, passing up Chopin and Gounod for a recording of monks chanting in Latin, which so soothed and reprieved him that he began to wear the record out, to the amusement of some junior officers who joined in the chant, unsteadily, and told him he could keep the record if he could find a place to play it. What he did was make a little leather sling with which to hang the record behind the bookcase, monopolizing the grave animadversions of Eastertide Antiphons, Masses of Day and Midnight, Offices for the Dead, Vespers and Compline, and *Grandes Heures Liturgiques,* scarcely knowing what he was listening to, and guiltily acknowledging that this was not Hilly's music, even though they had first met in the presence of bells. The chanting spoke to the part of him dulled and stilled by war, agitating once again the palette of his soul, not so much uplifting him as making him reach. There were complaints that the officers' mess had become less merry than it used to be. Who was playing all that sepulchral, churchy, monkish music? The record should be found and smashed, but Harry had outthought them. They, ironically enough, had all studied the music's language at school; Latin was a part of their earlier life, a hurdle over which to trot into Oxford and Cambridge. Where to hide the record, then? What kind of sandwich to make of it? Hilly would have set it firmly between the pages of a big, impenetrable music book and remembered never to sit on it, or stamp. There were no books here, however, although, out in the lobby on the big mahogany table where officers left cards, there was a book as big as the Beethoven ones. This was how Harry came to steal the visitors' book from the officers' mess, with which to flank his Gregorian chants, wondering, after his reprieve, when the next gramophone would come to light, and if the record would survive.

It was a French record, not out of style so much as scratched into surfhood. Noisy or not, it seemed to Harry just the right mix of entreaty and bliss, just the right fusion of self-denial with panic, of urgent flight with stiff-upper-lip. Indeed, it was soldiers' music without being a march. The monks sang denudedly, their voices their one and only instrument, never sounding out of breath, and now and then achieving such exquisite falsetto effects he surmised they had shrunken back to boyhood, their knees entering the stone flags they knelt upon. He imagined the scene: all of them in rough sackcloth, feet bare, hoods loose and ample, their mouths finely rounding and tapering like the tube ends of certain sea animals. That they knelt in a trench of their own, he did not doubt. They were offering what Clive knew his father saw as remote and suave, giving thanks for having to think very little. He formed his mouth to the alien words as, once again, he made the mess Gregorian and tried to loft his thoughts, from gas masks and machine guns and grease-dipped bacon to something worth dying for.

—

AT THIS imagined moment, Clive thought, and he had mulled it over many times, basing his guesses on the few hints Harry had given him, Harry at sixteen was on the verge of religious conversion, not to lights and tunes, rugs and chalices, but to something like a breathing space, when the universe or its smaller factory, Earth, stopped, and for five minutes there was no dying, no wounding, no gunfire, no onslaught. That was all Harry hoped for: a stop, so that everyone could catch a breath. He knew he had already had enough of muddling through slaughter, taking and retaking ground that was merely symbolic, and he would have been glad to have been kidnapped by some enterprising monastery that had a press gang of its own, snapping up mystagogical sad-eyed children in sergeant's uniforms and making them over into little postulants. He waited, but only the colonel came and gave him a tongue-lashing for presuming to take over the officers' mess; the colonel had been to Spinkhill, a Catholic school, and he let the music continue at a lower level, pausing at the door to nod at the monks' effusions as if commending bugles. "A brisk march next, if you please, Sergeant, please. And smart about it, there's a good fellow." Harry's hands shook as he changed to a sharper needle, put on "Colonel Bogey," and slid the plainchant—snug between the pages of the visitors' book—behind the bookcase, caching harmony in thought.

Thus the tender, wounded side of him found a niche.

Even before being obliged to desist, however, he had picked up something about this music, not entirely gladly, but with troubled reverence. Sometimes the monks sang a word such as *gloria,* which he managed to discern in the chant, in three notes, sometimes in as many as twelve. He liked the chanting most when they sang the maximum number, but trembled when he first recognized the melismatic, in which the chanters sang as many as they fancied, thus making a single word into a spiral staircase of patterned plenty. What an idea, he thought: You might start with the first word and never get to the second, because you had managed to fit note after note into the syllable.

Dimly he acknowledged infinity, not as something colorful or lovely, but only as indefinite voicefulness, half thinking that wars would never continue if they sang an uncountable number of notes in the first bang. All it took was a little will, a habit, and a voice, and a word. He attempted his own name, Harry, then, as a melismatic yodel.

FROM THAT stuporous war, Hilly knew he would come home
coarsened; war to her was not so much a bloodbath as a degrader,
returning men to the habits of their ancestors, lowering their standards
of behavior, shifting them from Bach to Sousa. So she expected Harry
to come back spitting into the gutter, wiping his nose on his sleeve,
cutting his potatoes with his fork, holding his cup with both hands,
walking on the wrong side of her. This was her mother in her, of
course, the ultimate argument against Church Row, where he came
from, and never mind how skillful his father was in the mending of
bell-ropes, how delicate and crumbly his mother's pastry emerged
from her damp, inert hands. After the militarizing of Harry would
come his pacifying, the gradual new-honing of his manners, the
detoxification of his mind, which Hilly would attempt with coaxing,
music, and a diet short on beef. It never occurred to her that, in the
extreme convulsions of war, he might have discovered in himself a
register of gentleness by which to live ever after. How could the dogs
of war convert him into a peaceable puppy? He would never forget
how to site and fire the Vickers gun, but he had learned how to make
his brain lie down and sleep. In fact, after the trenches, he would
become (and remain) a compulsive washer; but he would also become
a little more a Caliban, wild not in the controllable fashion of her

brothers, whose rough-hewn decorum always came to heel when Papa Fitzalan smacked his cane on the dining-room table.

Misreading the future, as she was bound to (how many sweethearts in how many wars had she had?), Hilly planned all the wrong things, electing to break down his vulgar ways once again, as if she were going to refind him in the orbit of Kath Kent at the bell-ringing. Seeking to retrieve him a second time, she risked going right past him; in her bustling zeal, she risked missing the soft side of him that had come into play and curled in upon itself under the flag of melismatics. He was going to remain for ever a man who heard a million tones in a single syllable, who, commencing to say or sing an *Ave,* did not get beyond the first syllable.

Had Hilly been with him, she would have schooled him in the finesse of plainchant; she had perfect pitch and understood the palpability of the uttered, as well as the tact you could insinuate through pausing. It was uncanny—not to her, for she was a spontaneous natural, but to her brothers: She read her Tennyson as if he had written music, and she read the score of Bach as if he were writing verse. She got at least a double value from what she floated her mind toward, as unselfconscious in this as Harry in his sudden fixation on the Gregorian. It was important to them both to have this inward pastoral, inasmuch as each had a harsh countervailing pain to cope with—hers the butchering, the serving, the delivering, while his was the war. In this way they subtracted something of themselves from the cruel objects of immediate attention. And they did so with warm, almost explosive egoism, like doves flushed off the nest, dreaming of fluff while breaking sharply upward to whatever might be there. They were departure children, anchored hard in the mundane and the customary, but given to exultation beyond the norm.

Hilly tried to hate what she loved, so they wouldn't bring her so much pain; she even came up with an imaginary girl, Phyllis Tine, who hated both music and the idea of love for a young soldier. Harry was nowhere near this pitch of clever caricature, and found the objects of his hatred ready made, pouring sulfur and soot upon him daily as he squelched around, sometimes dreaming he was holding on to the Vickers to keep himself from sinking, except that it, too, was sinking.

HAD THE TWO of them been able to meet at this point, Clive decided, Hilly might have taught Harry a little wit and he might have strengthened her acceptance of horrors. As it was, she became more and more mentally ingenious, while George and Douglas calculated themselves to death as civilians and Harry became the compleat soldier.

So: Harry could soothe himself with his chants, and he could fight with appalling zest. He wanted to kill the war, and the war was made up of Huns; therefore he fired longer than he should have, he spent more and more ammunition each week, determined now to do more than prove himself. He had decided to excel. Although he was never unafraid, he saw the war go by him with insouciant cynicism, if anything a younger man than when he enlisted, because less cowed, less out of place. He was changing, but he could not define the gradations or the drift of the process. He knew only that he had been superbly trained by accident while on the job. He fulfilled what a sergeant was for.

Then it all began to happen as he had envisioned it. This time the officer was not a German intruder, a fake, but a hearty, nonshaving young lieutenant from Warwickshire, Clive Hastilow, who at once informed him that he preferred sergeants around him with at least a military medal. Harry missed the faint, intentional Shakespearean echo in Hastilow's first speech to him, but he recognized the promotional maneuver in the man's proposal to make a sortie into no-man's-land that very night and, as Hastilow put it, "almost come a cropper, with a lot of bangs, eh, and some blood splashed about."

Harry's body shrank, but his mind stood erect, knowing this was how an aspirant became a tower of strength. He could not have done it by himself, because a witness was imperative, especially one of officer rank, whose word no one would ever doubt.

Out they went, armed to the teeth, hurled grenades into an empty crater, daubed themselves with mud and some blood from a nearby German corpse, and headed back, firing their revolvers at random behind them into the indefinite sky. Suddenly Harry found himself running back alone; at least it felt like running, but through that sludge it was more a series of giddily recovered falls. Hastilow was nowhere in sight, nor was he crying for help. Had he run ahead? No, he was slower than Harry and, anyway, had wanted to be seen covering Harry's return. Back Harry went, feeling with his feet, until he found his benefactor, shot through the back of the head by some randomly firing German, shooting for lack of something else to do, or inflamed by Harry and Hastilow's advance into no-man's-land. The firing stopped. Harry dragged Hastilow behind him for a while, then pushed him forward feet-first on the smooth mud, almost like a toboggan run, until he could use the password, Pawnshop Ticket, and be received into the front trench; he gasped and spat, his chest heaving, his heart split in two. They dragged the officer home. Harry told his story to the captain, gulping hot cocoa between phrases, but there were no witnesses to his having beaten off a German patrol, to his having shot two of them point-blank, as well as wounding their officer, who had a white collar and a monocle. These details impressed the captain, but only enough to make him write them down; it was as if Harry had got an officer killed, and he discerned in the candlelit faces before him an ever-so-reluctant wish that it had been Hastilow who had brought *him* back dead.

"An informal patrol, eh? A bit of skylarking." The captain seemed to be writing these very words down as he spoke, but Harry saw numbers and some straight lines.

"None of that, sir. Just having a look."

"A look at nothing?"

"Never that, sir. We'd never have bothered."

"You ran into a routine patrol."

"Didn't I say so, sir?"

The captain yawned and, with a wholly different attitude, changing his tone from inquisitorial to bantering, said: "Sergeant Moxon, don't you detect in all this a tiny stink of a put-up job? An officer procuring a decoration for a noncommissioned officer? I grant you, I'm not against a bit of morale-building accidentally on purpose, but manufactured heroism is something I'd prefer to do without. Is there anything else you'd rather say? Anything you'd like to add?" Mother of God, Harry thought, they are going to shoot me whatever I say. I should have left him out there for somebody else to find. I'll always be a liar now. Then he spoke, feeling shrunken, his lips rigid, automatic as a regimental mascot. "Sorry, sir, nothing to add. We ran into some Huns. I'm damned lucky to be alive."

"Don't you," the captain resumed, newly interested, "find that very odd? That you escaped. They let you go?"

Harry thought fast. "My guess, sir, is that Lieutenant Hastilow was shot by a random sniper, not by anyone in the patrol. After I fired they scattered, sir." It was almost good enough. Who, he wondered, if it had ever happened, would have been the more surprised, the more belligerent: the German patrol or he and his lieutenant?

"Noted," the captain said. "Wipe yourself off, sergeant, you're all bloodied up. Not wounded?"

"No, sir. That'll come later, no doubt."

"But in the meantime you're willing to help us to win the war. Thank you. You may go." Harry toppled out of the room made of mud and headed for the latrine, his mind on fire.

Harry was convinced that he had now discovered honor and how it made the difference between officers and men. Had Hastilow survived, he would have told the truth and accepted the blame. For having lied, even in a semiheroic way, Harry knew he was going to suffer for years; something had drifted away into the air that would never come back. Its loss made him no better than a spy like von Kaiserstein. The best thing now was to head back to no-man's-land and get himself shot. Sometimes, surely, the truth seemed unlikely. What harm had he done? Hastilow was permanently dead, and Harry was a permanent liar—he would still be a good soldier, though, a good one at shooting. A quick "recce," meaning reconnaissance, was all they two had attempted: nothing ambitious, and it had all been Hastilow's idea. Surely nobody thought that Harry had killed the lieutenant, though to a hostile mind things might look that way. One officer killed was bad luck. Two killed was bad planning. Three looked like ambition. Well, he decided, no medal from this bleeder, meaning the captain, although the man had seemed to have a wry sense of humor, sarcastic as a pregnant zebra, joshing him about helping to win the war, the stuck-up sod. Harry began to wonder about officers, and what their mothers did with them when they were babies.

THE WOUNDED, as often as not, had been pinned to the soil with bayonets through their calves or hands. Several soldiers met a Belgian youth carrying a bucket of German eyes. Lighted cigarettes were found slid into the nostrils of bound and gagged civilians and left to go out in their own time. Harry felt he had spent half his time succoring the wounded and the maimed and (a new category to him) the newly maimed wounded or the newly wounded maimed. The other half he spent sleeping or, when only half asleep, mowing down the enemy. Yet he endured and, fixing his mind on postwar images of rural cordiality, prevailed over a blood storm of ripped-out tongues, children whose hands had been severed because they had clung to their parents. He looked away, able to note in passing that the Uhlans had the device of a skull and crossbones on their shakos; almost amused to learn that two German officers, after looting a house in Visé, signed a paper directing that the house be spared, pinned it to the front door, and then burned the whole thing down.

What a mix he came to know! To curry favor with the invaders, local officials staged *"fêtes nocturnes"* in the town squares, with bonfires, cheese, and hot wine, during which everyone Belgian clapped hands and haltingly sang *"Hoch le Kaiser."* One German corporal came away from a village with a bedsheet full of cigars and pipes, evidently intending to set up as a tobacconist later on. One German officer, dead of a shot through the jaw, had a sword with a golden handle and carried a card saying he was Count Fritz von Bülow. To set a house on fire, the Germans plastered its walls with inflammable pastilles, an inch in diameter, which ignited if rubbed. Clive asked Harry, once upon a time, which came first, the rub or the application, but he refused to say, and no doubt didn't know.

On he went, to his tiny son; on he had gone, recounting how he had to learn to say to himself, This is the place where such things happen. There could be such a place. On he went, telling how the regular corps of incendiaries had the word *Gibraltar* on the left sleeves of their tunics. Those assigned to the slaughter of civilians wore a small black feather about two inches long on the side of their helmets. Now and then an unburned house bore a placard that said in German, "Good People," so the *Belgians* burned it down. If your wound hurt, he said, you dressed it with Iode Tinctura, then applied the blue bandage, which was the field dressing always applied first.

He needed every flash of nonhomicidal color. His mind had filled and burst with the image of the mayor cut in half and put into two sacks; the farmer nailed across the empty doorway of his farmhouse door; the mutilated priest upside down in the fly-loud earth-and-ashes of the latrine; the babbling peasants who roamed the roads without ears, lips, noses; the ten-year-old boy (who made Clive blanch) hanged with cord from the ceiling lamp. Harry told about the German bayonet; on being withdrawn, it inflicted a tearing wound with its sawlike reverse. Never did it occur to Clive that Harry had invented any of this. Some of it was hearsay, some his own witness. Some of it came from the ongoing fund of outrage stories told one another by British and Belgian troops. He told everything as if he had seen it with his own eyes and, for sanity, had drifted into several degrees of removal.

As he gazed at his mother's patient, tolerant face, she wondering what he was thinking but hardly ever asking, Clive recovered little fragments of Harry-talk: about the ingrown toenails that plagued him, the blisters that came and bled. He once daubed a red cross on his handkerchief and left it, weighted down with four balls of mud, on the chest of a wounded comrade, hoping to give the murderous Uhlans a moment's pause. "Wasn't your handkerchief khaki?" Clive had asked. "Not white?" Harry blustered as if found out. "The cross was still red." He once met a Belgian civilian whose name was *Oui,* and he had seen grossly converted butcher's shops in Belgium with human limbs on the hooks dangling from the window rail. Clive himself, inspired yet tormented, had later on found out for himself, in the *White Paper on German Outrages* (1915), about the child in the window at Rebaix, to whom all the soldiers waved. She never waved back, so it was supposed she was a doll until they saw she was a strangled child, propped up to face outward. At one time Harry and a hundred others had run into a force of Germans who marched forward behind a screen of children all being made to sing the "Brabançonne." Harry and the rest had to fire at an upward trajectory, above the children's heads. "They'd have done better," Harry had said, "to advance behind grown-ups."

Was that, Clive wondered, what *he* was doing? Advancing behind his father's memories: primed with horrors so the world would never frighten him? His father had both seen and invented the Medusa's head, as in the story of how Uhlans had done a bayonet-cesarean on a woman six months pregnant, after which they beheaded her husband and stuffed his head into her emptied belly. Had the top of Harry's head shivered and lifted when he first heard that? In the end he and Harry had defeated the Uhlans with multicolored flags attached to sewing pins filched from Hilly's biscuit tin of cottons and needles, known in the family as Fingal's Cave. Once, against untrodden dunes bristling with spear grass, not far from the sea, and entranced by a sky so blue it seemed to have substance in it (Harry's words), Harry and his gun crew had sat still for three weeks, awaiting an invader who never came. By the end of the second week, they had begun to sunbathe in two-hour shifts and to sleep the proper number of hours. Their only diet was bully beef and fresh water fetched from a deserted villa only a hundred yards away. He would never again be so happy.

He strolled from the dunes to the villa to eat alone on a balcony that faced Holland and its Hook. By sheer good luck he found a gramophone, on which he could play his Gregorian chants, still intact in the stolen signing-in book. He stalked about the dusty rooms, picking up toys and tools, writing his name on the distempered walls and unfurling his arm to the full tumult of the voices, knowing that some special providence had sent him here to sit out the war in a life purged of smoke and rabble, to fish, pat a grazing horse, or just scoop sand with his palm. Only a mistake in orders had sent them there in the first place, and only a correction, brought by a panic-ridden motor cyclist, pulled them out. Harry had wanted to kill the messenger and stay put, but some vestigial sense of honor broke into his trance. The image of that place never left him, as if it had been some deliciously alert death, and in after years he embellished it until even to him it became intolerably sweet and he reverted to the horrors as if they were normal. Grape arbors, roses, and carnations relieved the blank of the whitewashed walls, he said. The blossoms there were of apple and pear and plum, but also of apricot, nectarine, and pineapple. Clive had blinked, but he never interrupted, and Harry droned on about beaches of smooth stones pink, white, or ocher. He had seen it all.

Clive sometimes wondered if Harry had ever existed, or if he was some allegorical hedonist whose son wore his medals for him to keep him brave. The faint clink and the starched whisper of two folded-over ribbons told Clive he was only a voyeur in magical terrain.

"Fire," Harry said, in the imperative, and Clive did duty for him as best he could, still not sure what a "parados" was, but pressing his thumbs against each other, in full view of his mother, until the nails drained white around a tiny pink isthmus halfway down, and up into the air Clive went again, past the black crown of Harry's hair, conjured by his zeal. Daddy, Dad, Da', D'.

It had taken Clive a long time to grasp the core of his father's teaching; well, if not teaching, his hints about solace. Several times Harry had told Clive, at seventeen, to settle down and light his pipe if ever he should feel rotten about life. Clive, the formerly assiduous listener at his father's knee, but now immersed in Symbolist poetry, had wondered at the allusion, sure that the life of a bright freshman could never be that bad. He failed to realize that his father's words came to him from the ground-zero of atrocity, where according to Harry the warm bowl of a pipe was equally valid. Harry was the stoic whispering from the bloodbath, devising images too extreme for the son to use, yet aware that Clive the ten-year-old was the perfect recipient, as if bloodshed were a new language, a literature even; whereas that son, stretched out into an adolescent reader of Plato and Kant, missed the point. Perhaps Harry had meant to overarmor him, teaching him how to withstand atrocity when all he would have to cope with would be rebuff. It was typical of Harry to overcompensate, but he knew all the temptations of hope and how fast they caught fire.

WHO, Clive wondered, first thought up his father's next expedition into no-man's-land? Was it the officer who went with him: ruddyfaced, auburn-haired Urqhart, with the jactitating laugh and the busy hands, the ever-cheerful, the fast strider? Or had that never happened except in his father's head, or in the heads of his gun team, eager for another exploit to talk about over a steaming tin of tea or a hunk of bread drowned in bacon fat? Who made the truth of the war? Who told the lies? Again by night, Harry had gone out, loaded with grenades, except that this time the officer had tripped into a shell-hole and drowned, despite Harry's boldest efforts in the dark, stripping off all his webbing and fastening it together to form a lifeline. Urqhart was never seen again, not even as a corpse, and Harry began to get some old-fashioned looks. In theory at least, he carved two notches on the stock of his revolver, having despatched two expensive men of good breeding without being in the least damaged himself, although, each time, liberally smeared with mud. There was actually a third time, sponsored by a sardonic, tubby major and, as far as eyebrows went, something of a prodigy—they were thick as woolly caterpillars and met above his nose.

"Any sergeant," this worthy thundered to his colonel, "who can polish off two of my officers deserves a bloody gong anyway. I'll sniff him out, sir. Let me take the bugger out into no-man's-land. I'll see what he gets up to. It's just conceivable that he's some type of anarchist feller having his own private war in the middle of the Great one. Sir, I'll tell him we are going to look for death. The first twitchy move he makes, I'll ventilate his skull. Dammit, sir, it would be a novelty to have Sergeant Moxon brought back dead by a live officer."

"Pound him, Willie, pound him." The colonel was ex-artillery.

Out the pair of them went, Harry somewhat abashed: no medal was worth all this, and, besides, their announced mission—to take a prisoner—was foolish. There was nobody there. The Germans had retreated, which was why the area was a good one in which to test this particular sergeant for homicidal tendencies. Cool, expanding, settling slowly, the flare unnerved Harry, who almost froze, at last falling untidily to the ground, a motion that made the major reach for his revolver, which in turn made Harry reach for his. He almost shot the major then and there out of sheer intimidation, but he worked on a grin instead, the grin of the old campaigner almost caught out in a flinch.

"All right, sergeant?"

"Sah."

"Over there, see?" Nothing in that chromatic sump.

"Nothing, sir."

"Go and see, about twenty yards." Harry shuffled off on his front, almost porpoising over the mud, wishing he had used his revolver, but mustering a fragment of Gregorian chant and his few words of Latin—*amen, ave, dominus*—to get him through the crawl. The first bullet missed by a yard, but the second grazed his cheek, and he almost at once tossed a grenade forward, in the wrong direction, then one behind him, realizing his mistake. Well done, Harry, because the first grenade startled the major enough to keep him from firing a third time, and the second grenade blew him apart. Harry's work with the ball when playing with the Fitzalan children had finally paid off: He knew how to lob. Two hours later he made his way in, huskily rendering up the password, Rudyard Kipling, and dragging the major's remains behind him on a couple of webbing belts fastened together. This time he made no attempt at explanation, just motioned at the sliced-up beeves that were once a major and pulled a bitter face, all rictus and disgust. No, I'm not hurt, he told them. He was out front, reconnoitering. The shell passed over him. Here he was again, the born survivor, bringing back his load: the officer-killer, the patron saint of no-man's-land, just conceivably a man who had vowed to kill a dozen officers before he met the firing squad. In a war it was possible, given enough murk and mud, enough confusion, to accomplish something so devious. It had been done before, but mostly in the heat or wincing fidget of battle.

"He's wiped out half my staff," the colonel whined.

"Thousands of *them* too," somebody said.

"Half my staff," the colonel said. "I'm all for giving the bugger a medal just to calm him down. You'd think he was shooting ducks. It's not his fault, I'm sure. He wouldn't dare. My God, I want him out of here."

Away Harry went, to another machine-gun team, to polish off someone else's officers before the war ended (there were two more years to go). Wherever he went, with his officers'-mess calling book enclosing his record of the Gregorian chant, he met with nothing but courtesy, especially from officers, who refused to accompany him anywhere, whereas the other ranks, so-called, thought of him as a hero, a man likely to become prime minister or something, one who understood like a lion in a zoo how the led felt about their leaders. As for Harry, he no longer cared whom he killed; they were all, the Germans and the Allies, getting his goat, wasting his life, mocking him with dreams that would never bear fruit. He longed for music.

OF LATE, Hilly had been devoting herself to resonance, crouching and listening to the after-music of her piano; she was trying to establish the relationship of what she had played to what lingered on, thrumming, quivering, elongating and diminishing. It was erratic, she decided. It did not leave you as you played it; instead, it gathered up and fell into the bottom of the piano, sounded but stricken, and only after you had ceased striking the hammers against the strings did the music get up to its feet, hunch its shoulders, and slouch away, at last dismissed. Perhaps some music was left in there for ever, doomed to malinger in the vicinity of rosewood and furniture polish. Her former view of music as flinging itself forth, on and on into the vault of heaven, had begun to give way to a more muddled version, in which some music leapt ahead of the player, some came out as required, and the rest was music that settled there, down into the grain of the wood, coating the wire of the strings and making them ever after resonate in a tinily different way. The world of music was more complex than she had ever dreamed, less under control, less of a program. Music was more like people, then, not really pinned down in the notation, but merely suggested there, free to bounce about, hide, and emerge in deceitful disguise.

Some heirlooms had recently arrived from Huddersfield, from a branch of the Fitzalan family now defunct: a Belleek Neptune-pattern tea service, with an extraordinary mother-of-pearl glaze fashioned in Ireland; a Portobello cow creamer with a little milkmaid hunched on her stool in front of the huge, tempting udder, her fingers busy at the downward tweak; a tiny Venus de Milo transcribed and shrunken by pantograph, done in the blond fake marble known as Statuary Parian, which, her mother told her, was heat-resistant; but who, Hilly wondered, was going to throw the naughty naked Venus into the fire? What attracted her most of all was a larger piece, a bust called "Phrenology" executed by L. N. Fowler: a triumph of Staffordshire blue and white, not flow-blue as defective ceramics of this type were called (the blue had run and flowed into the glaze or the once-fired biscuit). This bust, trimmed with something close to the Reckett "bluing" with which her mother's maids did the wash, appealed to Hilly for the genial expression on its face. A self-sufficient Roman, but with small, trim features suggesting the gentlest resignation. The blank, oval eyes stared straight ahead, but the lids drooped from some kind of stone fatigue. The head was hairless, of course, so that L. N. Fowler's divisions and labels might be applied.

Hilly read the various labels, from the word Language applied in a gentle curve beneath the left eye to the fan-shaped eye patch affixed above the upper lid, defining areas from right to left as Form, Size, Weight, Colour, Order, and Calculus. Surely, she thought, the brain isn't that clearly cut up, like a cow. Here it seemed to be, with huge areas given over to Literary and Intuitive (the latter below the former), Causality and Ideality.

As she rotated the head on its velvet diamond at the shiny kitchen table, she felt she was turning Harry this way and that from bullets, making him scan the landscape of Belgium for trouble, and, whenever he felt upset, fixing his features into that neat, satisfied, vulnerable pout of the Fowler emperor. Tapping Agreeableness for fun (high above the left forehead), she wondered at something painted thus, as if telling the whole world there was nothing more to be known. She asked herself what could be the link between Staffordshire ceramic and the contents of the human head. How could anyone know? And where was Music? She looked and looked and then located it, above the left eyebrow, north-east of Order.

Blurring her vision by tightening her eyelids, Hilly saw the painted lines as cuts and the words as scars, and wondered if this was what happened when bullets hit the head in the war. All of a sudden you lost Agreeableness, or Youthfulness, although all the rest kept on working. Only L. N. Fowler would know, who perhaps tuned pianos as well, or created other Staffordshire ceramics such as flatbacks and Mason's Patent Ironstone China. She was cheating, she knew, helping her limited knowledge out by dipping into the faded leaflet that came with the bust in its wooden box with brass clip. Their house was full of such trophies from the last century when, as her parents said, people loved to have beautiful things around them, not for use, but for contemplative soothing.

How strange. She ached to be as familiar with the next century, the twenty-first, as her parents were with the nineteenth. There was something wrong, though, wasn't there, in leaning so far forward, spurning present life for some beguiling thread in the fringe of prophecy's magic carpet? If she snaked herself that far over the precipice of history, she would come a cropper, she just knew: sunk in a quicksand of metal shavings, dead hearts, and soggy charcoal.

When the war ended, as it soon would, she wondered if the British and the Germans would stop using so many machines, or if the world was already machine-minded for ever. Had not the war begun because someone with a pistol, a machine, had assassinated the Archduke Ferdinand? Would the war have come about if the assassin had used a sword, a rolling pin, a spade? Did you slaughter a lettuce when you picked it, or a radish, or did you kill milk when you made cheese? She wished Harry were home to join her in such confusion, though he would probably have vexed her no end with his Gregorian chant, that strictly masculine mooing in which his battle-ridden soul took refuge. She wanted news, she wanted lies, she wanted the year to be over, the dead to be dead, the survivors home to acclaim. She wanted everything to start again.

George and Douglas swept her outside into the tart sweetness of early April, up Market Street to the Cross and the Post Office to buy stamps. On the way back, her sullen thoughts deflected by the faint breeze blowing up from the dales (a nose-tickling mix of sandalwood and cinnamon such as never blew from the north), she began to sense war's dwindling: two more days like this, she thought, full of frocks, chortles, spinning tops and cracking whips and the war would end because no one would have the heart to go on. Rationing would end, and those who felt guilty about living their lives in the usual way could relax. A commotion down Market Street, by the Duke of York public house, caught her attention. Perhaps a pony and cart had gone through a shop window, perhaps The Wizard's, which sold cleaning materials, or Courtnauld's Ladies' Drapery.

Down they trotted, as if to help, but really to watch, only to hear that someone was lying on the sidewalk in distress. It was Mrs. Featherstonehaugh, the woman with the iron foot, who from time to time would overbalance, especially when mounting from one level to another. Born with one leg short, she had suffered all her adult life from the deep foot of skeletal steel the doctors finally equipped her with, like one of those bilevel runways for model cars sometimes given to children for Christmas. All you had to do was set a car at the top and it would run downward, speeding along the diagonal track from upper to lower level. There was no car or diagonal track to Mrs. Featherstonehaugh's iron foot, however; it hung beneath a stout black boot and gave her footsteps a grinding, hesitant quality, but at least her feet walked on the same level.

The local tradition, much shrunk from by locals, was to right her as soon as possible when she fell. The trouble was, she weighed an enormous amount and never managed to bathe, so she was always massive and rank; a composite of different odors coming from different parts of her. Those who assisted her held their breath for as long as they could, or they sloped away from her, managing to pass along the message to onlookers that Mrs. Featherstonehaugh was down, and would anybody please come and help? This message would traditionally be carried, as well, by an overgrown handicapped youth named Rhubarb, real name Artie Jessup, whose bright, shining red beak of a nose set in the plump maroon moon of his face could be seen for twenty or thirty yards. Eyes tearing, coat flapping free from its tier of safety pins, he would hare away on his mission of mercy, telling them all that Mrs. Featherstone was down again. Few would go help, though they took an enormous interest in seeing her upright, which unbreathing volunteers such as Hilly, George, and Douglas accomplished by bundling her into a kneeling position, from which they towed-hauled her by the hands into some sort of stand. Up she came, unpeeling her aromas like some elephantine cabbage, cursing her helpers, the street, the pavement, the stones, the mortar, the village, the doctors, the iron, her foot, the ankle, all of it, finally letting out an appalling shriek of "Fitch me ooam!" Take me home.

Altruistic, well-reared Hilly and her brothers backed away from the scene of their latest samaritan act, and Mrs. F. was left alone to wobble back to some kind of equilibrium while a streetful of folks watched, murmuring concise commentary: "She's up," "she's down," "she's going." She plunged horizontally, raving and choking on a gruesome spittle, while her foot rasped like a tireless wheel, starting with almost a tinkle, developing into a scrape, a metallic thump, then nothing. *Tinkle-zarp-chong* was how she sounded, while oranges and apples and slices of bologna bounced up and back down into her basket as she went spastic up to the Back Lane, politely known as Pinfold Street; she was shouting vaguely now for the police, and, people always declared, vile smoke wafted behind her as if, from the friction of it all, she had caught fire. Village legend had it so and had to be believed.

In the meantime, to an uncaring and unhelpful population, Rhubarb spread the word: "Missus Featherstunner's down again," like one whose mind the dreadful sight had blighted, his nose drooling long strings of mucus, his eyes more abulge than ever, his feet losing coordination as he went uphill. At some point, now and then, Rhubarb, having gained ungainly speed, would collide with Mrs. Featherstonehaugh, announcing her own fate to her as he repeated it upon her flesh, and down both would go, howling the howl of multiplied indignity, like entwined lovers from a Bosch cartoon, he unable to smell her, she unable to free herself from his half-erotic grasp as his swollen, scabbed hand foraged beneath layers of old blue skirts, hoping to find the rumored river wrapped in the moist mustache his betters had taunted him about. There they would writhe, unhelped, until Rhubarb at last rolled clear and went his way, announcing what he had just left unremedied as a fact too vast for him to tinker with, and all who had not seen it happen today knew exactly how it had been.

How blatant people had to be, she thought, to get themselves noticed or remembered; if you were not picturesque or weird, you made no mark, never mind how well you played the piano or fired the Vickers gun. Even Harry's face had become not so much distant as not quite specific. She knew that, if he did not soon return to reclaim his uniqueness, he would become vaguer and vaguer to her, however keen and intense her emotions about him stayed. She had to see him in some role other than war, the soldier to whom Kitchener addressed his straight-on, mustachioed poster: *I want you*. Generals did not look at people, they just sent them to other places with a cuff of the hand, attending only to their departing backs. Could she volunteer to be a nurse and go over to France? Of course, but her ailing mother and the shop kept her at home. No such romantic gesture was open to her, so her life remained curtained; a bodily longing sucked at her, some nagging and trenchant pain in her lower stomach, easily assigned to injury when heaving meat about, but just possibly a crisis in her womanhood, a piece of her crying out for a different destiny than this, as if she were embalmed or kept on the simmer. Something in her wanted to run riot, go and squander itself in the bushes behind the tennis courts at Stead's Field, where no brother—civilian or military—could give her relief. She wanted to be prey to the most awful mishaps in the world, but at least moving, warming, being vibrantly rash.

As spring waxed into summer, she began to instruct herself in stoicism, convinced that the war would soon end, but not release her from the bondage of brothers, mother, and shop. She played more music than ever, forcing her fingers when they wavered, determined to assert herself as an untypical presence among people to whom music was a hobby, a rigmarole, an accompaniment to a special cup of tea. And she became magnificent, packing all her emotion into Chopin and Brahms especially, whereas Bach and Handel resisted rather more her resolve to turn them into vessels of feeling. Market Street became her unofficial stage as passers-by became standers and listeners, marveling at the headlong, far-flung sound flowing from the open window of the music room. The more or less soulless village had come into its own on the spiritual plane. She seemed to play more often, louder and with increased trajectory; within the music room itself, they said, the sound must be like thunder. She grew reckless and undaunted, turning her piano into a transmitter to all ships at sea, rebuking a world that had gone to war instead of trying to follow Beethoven across Lake Constance. Even her brothers desisted from incipiently masculine games with dogs and fishing rods to curl up on the rug in the music room and hear her out, nodding at emotions they recognized, wishing that Thurrie and Harry could be present too, savoring the fruits of home. Hilly became more and more expressive, moving now into an emphatic way of playing she had once despised, at last converted to the use of music for purposes whose label-words reminded her of the phrenology bust that sat behind her, the unseen god of performance, the satrap of brain neighborhoods. She played to France and Belgium, in her mind's ear on tour already, mucking in with the exhausted, war-grimed Tommies, bringing them thick sweet tea and incontinent music they might, in another existence, have found hoity-toity, but now took to with unspecific hunger, making her the angel in their midst.

Hilly and Harry got through their war by closing up and drying up, conditions Clive found easier to deal with mentally than what might happen once they laid private hands on each other: tongues, forefingers, suckling, straddling, all of that. Never could he see them lascivious, although ever affectionate: always *agapē,* but never *erōs,* as if war and harmony had forbidden them what others delighted in. They would have to make children, then, in some other way, through the ear or the nostril, using saliva for seed, the navel as the little stud that would soar forward and push the other little stud inward. Something like that. Clive forced himself to see them pawing each other, but it always ended in the chaste accommodation of head on shoulder, or sitting arm in arm to demonstrate good behavior. He must have developed, he decided, from a nocturnal emission of his father's somehow taking root upon his mother, or at least finding station on her and creeping in. Could you, he wondered—could a girl—catch a seedling from the top of a piano stool?

The most amazing thing his father ever saw, Clive recalled, was the Virgin of Albert: image of the frosted sex that would be his postwar. By this time, Harry had survived by juggling with time, telling himself that there were seven weeks in a day and four months in a week—anything to make the time go by. The red-brick cathedral looked disheveled, capable of being rebuilt as something wholly different, say a fairground attraction or a baroquely consummate public lavatory reminiscent of Keble College, Oxford. On top of its battered tower stood the figure of the Virgin, still imposingly gold but cranked over from a hundred and eighty degrees to ninety-five or so, as if she were leaning toward some bodily function. Harry had felt indignant when he first saw her; after all, she belonged to the monks who sang his Latin with such purged eloquence. Then he heard the truth, that French engineers had bent the Virgin thus, much like a lead soldier from a child's fort, to keep the German artillery from sighting on it. Thereafter the hunched Virgin stayed in his thoughts as one of those utterly contrary images, both illustrious and humdrum, both holy and vulgar, a long way from the idolizing "Ave Maria" of Schubert that sometimes on a Sunday unwound itself from the window of an estaminet. He found the Virgin of Albert exotic, like a memory of an earlier lifetime tugging at him and not letting go.

When the worst thing of all happened, he was out of the line, in a field, resting with his machine-gun crew, his mind on the decoration he had never won, thanks to the antics of certain officers. By now, surely, he should have been a second lieutenant himself, although he suspected that some old-school-tie prejudice kept an expert machine gunner—a thumbs-on killer of thousands—from promotion that far; they wanted chaps who might have banged about a bit with a revolver, but not those who had fought with the bayonet. In other words, he decided, he wasn't pure enough. Officers never had their hands steeped in blood, oh no: the correct way was to fight the war with ill-concealed distaste, as if, rather than a chronic atrocity, it was a social solecism. Well, if he wasn't going to be an officer with a battlefield commission, he was going to be a sergeant-major, almost the same thing. All he had to do was look increasingly wise and develop that special tone of voice: exasperated asperity toned down for public consumption. He would look daggers but use none. His mustache would widen and thin out into a hypodermic point on either side, capable of puncturing the jaws of those who marched beside him. And on his lower sleeve he would wear a crown inside laurel leaves. Clive wished with all his heart he had got this right, doing his best to recall lectures on the subject and trying to translate Air Force ranks into Army ones—rough equivalents at best; after all, this was 1990 peering through poison gas and fog into 1917. So much of his father slid away from him, evaded, started to return the son's salute but let the hand fall to his side, and then Harry sank into the mud until only his face was visible.

Random in effect, the shell landed on a group of lazing soldiers, created a long blast of awfulness, and made a dent in the gathered humanity, scattering limbs and heads to all corners of that field, onto which nobody there would have stuck the prefix "battle." As Harry recalled it, everyone was blown up into the air, twisting and reaching, and that was in the first second or two. Knocked out by the thunder of it, Harry felt his face sprayed with red-hot needles, and then his back, but that was all. The man next to him had taken the full impact of the explosion and was dead, disintegrated, but his body had protected Harry, and this man's name—as Harry so often said with marveling gratitude—was Blood. That was what it said on his brown Bakelite identity disc.

Harry and the others lay there for an hour until some semblance of order began. There was only the one shell; but, as Tommies liked to say, it had their number on it. The fantastic thing was that Harry could walk. That so much of him was intact. But when he walked he did so with his hands on the shoulders of the man in front of him, around whose head, as around Harry's, was a thick wide bandage enclosing pads over the eyes. A line of soldiers otherwise hurt in only minor ways trudged away groaning, most among them destined to be blind. Until he was forced to stand up, Harry thought he had been killed, and, yes, there was an afterlife: not too bad, but a heaven with provision for pain, and he remembered fervently wishing he'd been able to speak before being taken. I'm alive, he wanted to say, so they might pass the word along down the line, across the Channel, to Hilly in Exington, and the rest. Apart from the sting in his eyes and the lump of hot metal stuck in his lower waist, he felt not too bad, although trembling so much he seemed to massage the shoulders of the man in front of him. No more Gregorian chant, he thought. I was unconscious, and now I'm alive. God be praised. What a bang that was. Just one. Do we get a medal for being wounded? No, only Americans do that. We get something, though; we get to go home, don't we? He smelled cordite and sulfur, dung and rotting grass. His mouth was full of gritty soil. Because he was concussed, he heard nothing, and the bandage around his head was too tight—he wondered absently if his skull was broken and if its wound in any way resembled a football injury. Honor in battle had gone roaming and had surprised him at rest, plucking him away from his habitual thoughts, slumps, and stances in a trice, changing him forever, taking him at face value as one who, having faked his age, was ready for maturer things, for man-sized afflictions. It never occurred to him that he might be among those going to be blind.

RELEARNING preposterously late in life, Clive was letting his mother arrange his arm on the table, tapping it to get it easy, then showing him how to rest his wrist so as to give maximum leverage to his hand. The main thing was to sit well up to the table and have all your arm resting in front of you, not half on the table and half off as that produced a motion similar to that of the old-fashioned ducking stool. Above all, he should not hold the pen too tight because that made it quiver, and a dot became a dash, a comma became a riding spur. The thing to do was to let the pen lie gently back against the groove between finger and thumb, and hold it lightly with the other three fingers as if it were something brittle and frail. Only then could you consider matters of the inkwell and the nib, or, if you had a fountain pen, see that it was full, that the elongated rubber bleb coated in talc wasn't like a flat tire. Some pens—but never the Waterman or the Bluebird—leaked as soon as you filled them, especially if you jumped about a lot. As you unscrewed the cap in order to write, a half capful of ink poured out upon you or your paper. It was always better, Hilly told him, to empty the pen completely before trying to fill it up. He spent several minutes siphoning ink to and fro, delighted by dark-blue hydraulics, before getting to work, and even then he fidgeted with the clip and the little side lever that squeezed the rubber tube inside. If inspiration failed, then technology would enchant. He loved the ritual, most of all the moment at which he pushed down on the nib with all his might and managed to make it write two parallel lines, sometimes with miniature blots in between them like baggage fallen from an escaping train. It was to this that he was going to devote his life, little did he know it: sitting and scratching, in all its various forms, though in recent years he had been a Luddite and refused to advance beyond the electronic typewriter that, in a fit of recalcitrance, erased what he had just written, sometimes switched margins on him, and squeaked like a maimed wistiti when he hit the code button instead of the shift. If he sped up, the machine memorized what he'd typed and printed it out at its own pensive speed. Of course, there was nothing he loved more than sliding into place at midnight, pulling the machine toward him, and setting the typescript in the only other space available on his crowded desk. He sometimes had the feeling he was working in a submarine, where the spaces for everything had been precisely figured out: no room for extras. So here, with his elbows kept in, he echoed the good boy who wrote with his entire arm on the table, to make it weightless, and kept the reservoir of his pen full. Oh, that the reservoir of his life had been the same.

What it all added up to was called penmanship, akin to marksmanship and horsemanship. If you made a mistake when writing in ink, you had to scratch away at the error with the tip of a jackknife's smaller blade, careful not to make a hole, or else you smoothed it over with spit and chalk dust. To restore the shine of the wounded paper, you had to rub it hard with one of your fingernails, which made it warm and smooth. All this was penmanship as personified in the clerks (pen behind ear) depicted on bottles of ink. Penmanship was paper husbandry: use of a soft eraser that left no orange stains; restoration of smoothness to a creased sheet (you tugged it diagonally back and forth over a sharp table edge); and something from the ancient days: scraping the rust and deposit off the pen's nib with, what else?, your *pen*knife! Some people mixed their own inks, preferring viscous or transparent runny. And it was bad manners, Hilly had told him, to scrape a pen nib against the bottom of the inkwell, setting other people's nerves on edge.

He had gloried in so uncherished an art: to most folk a pragmatic rigmarole, but to him the front door to finality. In black ink might his notions shine bright, *recoverable*—that was it, as Shakespeare and countless others had said. Death hid its face in the ink.

Merging Harry his father the boy soldier with Harry his father the revered veteran, Clive saw him writing down the names of the horses he was going to gamble on, so that would be the veteran, but also penning his schoolboy essay for entrance to the grammar school, his mind on such a word as copperplate. He knew there was a decorum of writing. Neatness counted, as did legibility; and, when the invigilator said *stop,* he wanted to go on, because this was the most pleasurable thing he had ever known: You had a mind, and here was its natural conduit, the slick slope down which its toboggan could race.

It *would* have been penmanship that his father thought about, to still the pain, wouldn't it? The half-ascetic who loved monks' voices was the man who wanted to illuminate manuscripts, and live the quietest of lives in a monastery garden, inhaling the gist of a passage and ornamenting it so beautifully that God would have eaten it. Strange to think it, his father had been something of an aesthete, manqué of course; although covertly inclined to Persian, monkish, Italian, medieval things: not a child of his own time at all except for the machine gun. It was Harry the beauty-lover who had gone to hear the bells and there met Hilly the pianist, whose music was as far from Church Row as Stonehenge from the Yorkshire woollen mills. Yet this streak in Harry had become deflected, twisted, and Clive set his father brooding on loss of sight that still allowed the pleasures of music. He half wondered if this was what Hilly wanted most of all: a cripple who was a pair of ears, to be looked after like her mother, like young Douglas: a great big funnel into which the divine panoply of music roared second after second, week after week, month after month, year after year, until here was the first man who had heard all the music in the world, except for that of the composers who at this very moment were scribbling new works. This, he perhaps thought, according to Clive, was how the balance came into things: Glut one sense and the maker of all things wiped out one of the others.

Henceforth he would be led around like a prize bull by a ring through his nose, and a couple of useless medals clinking from his breast. A man that blind, Harry thought, would be as useless as the woman with the iron foot, to be fetched and dropped off like a churn of milk, no longer human, just a relic into whose eyes you dared not look for fear of being struck blind yourself.

Much more of Harry's dreadful wound came back when Clive remembered something else to do with penmanship. Invisible ink, invisible only when it had dried. There was a packet of blue crystals that made a pale-blue fluid, and what you had written reappeared only if you held the paper close to a source of heat without singeing it. Then the script came back like a wreathing of twigs. One of Harry's tenderest messages, because he hadn't pressed hard enough on the nib, had come out incomplete: *I am y ur f iend fo   a ways,* which was a long way from the message he intended, although another read as follows: *I remember you,* coming out complete. Now, each time Harry held the unsent message to the heat he saw the miracle, pale blue into nothing into brown, but could not bear to send it. Shyly, he relinquished his magnificent idea of sending Hilly a series of sheets apparently blank. Here, Clive decided, was the key to how his father felt about sight: It had vanished into his head and could be reactivated only by some magic done with huge magnets and soft soothing pipettes full of milk.

Sight that was like a burn had sunk beneath the surface in Harry, not that his memories had failed him; on the contrary, they huddled in his outer rind, panicked and stunted, but still capable of being harvested. His father had felt some tracery leaping away from him, a tree of veins made to splash away like some shadow of blood. Or it was a fern, the sort you could press between the leaves of some heavy, leatherbound book, so that it remained for ever, etched in cochineal, what the brain could remember but no longer see: a ghost of doting vision? After that, Harry felt something move into the place once occupied by the red-hot fern that was vision's version of the finical lines in a bloodshot eye. This was more like water culled from a sensitive lagoon in the brilliant interior, but demoted now to filler—a substitute, Clive thought, for lymph, taking over. Or plasma. The pain was indescribable, but Clive tried for Harry: a fluid abeyance— not bad, but do better. A choking, then, as if iron filings had been pumped into tiny tributaries where eye honey and nerve glycerine belonged. There was that faint edgedness to all that flowed or halted. A tinge of lime came with it too, and a wrong rhythm, making whatever was within his father's eyes and blood vessels scrape against the walls of the lumen, making him want to rend the bandage from his head and rub his eyes, as we rub them to rid them of tiredness but then provoke something new, a different itch that no amount of rubbing will heal.

Was that it? Yes, but not all. Harry could not feel his eyes through the bandages, nor could he sense them internally as things in place. For all he knew, his eyes were a mile behind him, jellies on a patch of rough ground, never again to be related to him. He could be trudging along with nothing except a set of sockets. The worst thing was that the remainder of his face had begun to move toward his eyes, tugged by jerks in the shattered muscles; and this gave Harry the idea that his entire face was moving toward a certain point, would soon be nothing more than a mouth, a nose, two brows all twisted together into a miniature rosette such as some men wore in their lapels. Harry felt his head floating, going away from him, then sinking back so hard and heavily between his shoulders that he could barely walk as it plumbed down into his upper chest. He stumbled at a reeling slither, and would have tripped sideways had not his hands been on the shoulders of the man in front of him, whose hands were on the shoulders in front of him, just as Harry's shoulders held up the hands of the man behind him. Had none of them been able to depend on a dependent man, the entire column would have fallen apart into individual blind men wandering across the battle-pocked landscape, never to be found again, each hopelessly trying to unwind the bandages and use them as threads out of some labyrinth where pain bloomed bright, corrosive, and neutral. Clive knew all this, but remained infatuated with the vanishing ink, the unstating eye, knowing that how his father felt had gone forever, because his father had never told, beyond a few monosyllables.

In the holes of his head, Harry had at best a couple of rolled-up anchovies, bled brown, and would one day soon sport two high-quality glass alleys to give him a human look. This was how Clive felt, and prophesied, when he limited himself to the period of time immediately after his father was blown up, canceling what he knew of the aftermath. It was good sometimes to learn to forget, so as to reenter the instant of agony through the veil of pain, as if there had never been any future for Harry, who still was only seventeen. When he succeeded at this, Clive felt his own eyes sting and water, beads of soggy conjunctivitis cruise and finally come to rest in one corner or the other, and appalling clumps of syrup sail across his sight, reminding him that his father nearly paid the most awful price of all for being a man before his time. Indeed, as he grew older, he began to harp on his father's war adventures in an order far from chronological; to rehearse events in the usual fashion sapped their intensity. He could feel them bark in his heart only when he garbled the sequence, as if cause and effect were some kind of anesthesia and chronology was a series of cushions laid out for his wincing soul to take its ease upon merely because, like all fools, he knew what came next.

As Harry semimarched along, soldiers came and pressed cheese or bread against his unyielding lips, or hot bread smooth with bacon grease, or tilted bottles of cognac against his teeth, chipping the enamel, or tapped cigarettes between his lips, from which he took no more than a puff before opening his mouth wide to let them fall into the gulf framed by his chest, the insides of his arms, and the back of the soldier in front of him. Women came up and planted bouquets in the folds of the bandages, crying *pauvres gosses!* The flowers endured mile after mile and gave the wounded men the indecent air of marionettes, a vegetable aspect verging on the fatuous. There was no transportation, but the propaganda value of mutilated men coming home from the front like miners from a shift underground was immense; so Harry and his fellow victims walked as best they could, now and then resting one arm at a time. Walking they slept, part hauled, part pushed, which is to say that, once again, in a different format, the half-asleep soldier tugged another one behind him who in turn pushed him onward only because himself shoved from behind. The whole war, Clive decided, could have been run on just such a slow, imperfect, cooperative basis, and the only casualties would have been those caused by collisions or lemminglike falls into the rancid water of craters. These lines of the blind walked for days, always being turned and aimed, walking in ellipses or circles until somebody noticed and observed that the blind men were walking in circles again. Why would they insist on doing that? It soothed them, came the answer, until the field hospitals were ready to receive them. Led by the least useful of available soldiers—those whom everyone longed to be rid of—these men walked them rearward with a map and a rifle, letting those who fell out sit by the roadside in cold, undernourished hope. Some got picked up by motor vehicles or horses, but mostly not. Blind they sat and blind they died, their mouths crammed with cachous by well-meaning civilians, or announced with placards made from wrapping paper: AVEUGLE, S.V.P. Blind, if you please. Where had their beautiful golden boyish laughter gone; their endearing gestures as they patted their brilliantined hair; their amateurish ogling as they polished the toes of shoes against the backs of their trousers, ungainly as scarecrows? Had there always been about these men a touch of death, ennobling them at an early age, like a spray of black flowers tucked between the ribs of a skeleton? Braised by pain, they walked or sat, dreaming if they could of brand-new bicycle pumps, superb new lettuces crisp and swollen, foals in crofts gamboling on elongated legs: anything mundane, unwounded, with feet on the fender at Christmas.

Harry dreamed of goldfinches in cages of icicles, or monks walking blind with their hoods low over their eyes until they bumped into the altar, piling up in aweful succession. Harry tried to think of chewing licorice root until the fibers jammed between his teeth, or sucking on a black licorice tube dipped into a bag of pungent sugar. It wasn't much. He wasn't asking for love or credit, honor or esteem, only a little timely tenderness, and then the coup de grace by the medical profession: Oh, we have seen thousands like him, we'll put him to rights in a jiffy. It would never be. Before they attended to him, they would slip a fig leaf in front of each eye as if doctoring the private parts of a statue. As if, Harry mused, overheard by Clive, my eyes were women bleeding their monthlies out. All bandaged up. No one was listening, but he managed to formulate something to the man in front or the man behind:

"Is there another blind man in front, or what?" Hard as he tried, and much as he wanted to, Clive could not find the right image for the capillaries that in his father's eyes had given up the ghost. He thought, in anguished resolve, of threads, cottons, fuse wire, spider's webs, the faintest hairs on his hands or face, even the antennae of garden creatures almost too small to have organs, but ended up with old-fashioned red sealing wax, which, melted and pulled apart, produced strands tapering into next to nothing, a prey to inhalation, and these became his father's veinettes, through which the blood no longer shot. He could not bear to envision the remainder of the eye:

the globe, the rainbow, the lens, the matchstick dot of the pupil. He flinched almost beyond control when he thought of the eye as vulnerable. Harry had given his eyes to his country. Harry had leaned over, and his eyes had poured out. Harry had looked into the explosion, reluctant to blink, and had seen red-hot motes flinging themselves toward him, faster than the lid could shield them.

ALL THIS time, Hilly had gone on assuming Harry was missing believed killed, unable to weep because she did not credit it. The world was stupid, but not as wasteful as that. Nonetheless she often wore a veil of bluish mauve, hoping in the process to age herself; and she wondered if, clad as a nurse with big red crosses plastered on her back and front like someone galloping off to the Crusades centuries ago, she could get away with it and begin her firsthand search of the hospitals, the receiving stations, the makeshift surgeries in tents. She knew nothing of von Kaiserstein, Hastilow, or Urquhart, the human detritus of Harry's passage through the war, nor did she know anything of his private life therein. Whenever he had written her anything of interest, the censor at company headquarters had blacked it out with a tar pencil that made a line so thick and penetrant it stopped you reading the message from the other side with a flashlight and mirror. She had seen enough of the cards that said I AM QUITE WELL or I HAVE BEEN ADMITTED INTO HOSPITAL and then bifurcated as follows:

$$\left\{ \begin{array}{c} \text{SICK} \\ \text{WOUNDED} \end{array} \right\} \quad \begin{array}{l} \text{AND AM GOING ON WELL.} \\ \text{AND HOPE TO BE DISCHARGED SOON.} \end{array}$$

The rest of the card offered other such brief reviews of the situation, enabling the soldier to say he was being sent down to the base, had either received a letter, a telegram, or a parcel or had received no letter lately or for a long time. Two of Harry's cards, before he gave up altogether after seeing the censor at work through a tent flap, had bothered her exceedingly. In the first, with commendable initiative, he had gone through several lines of the card and deleted all letters except, to begin with, the B and the second E in BEEN, following up with one of the T's in ADMITTED and the H in HOSPITAL, and so on until he had Béthune; but the censor blacked out his seven chosen letters as well. The second card said H, E, L, L and the censor disliked it so much he tore it up. In other words, Hilly received from Harry routine insipidities until even they dried up and she had to depend on the newspapers for news, which was mainly about officers.

She looked over to France and saw him, better delineated from the horde than anyone else: rosy-cheeked, hair matted with mud and sweat, his eyes squinted against wind and sun, and several inches taller from having to stand up straight for so long, except when he had to hug the mud in prudence or terror. He was handsomer, more commanding, with a slight truculence in his demeanor and a new way of patting the back of his head like someone checking to see if it was still there. He looked more Latin, less dependent, more than a sergeant, almost as if he were enjoying the war, and she thought of all the male-only clubs, for hunting and cards and drinking, and decided he must never be allowed to join any such thing, even if, after the war, he were a shooting star, a Lothario, or a dashing young captain with a monocle and a sheaf of poetry books to read to her. Men liked smashing things up, but never knew how to put them together again. Not that she wanted to be a bossy-boots. She wanted him out of all future wars, out of the destructive callings, such as mining, drilling, tree-felling, iron and steel, and well ensconced in teaching, accountancy, painting, and estate management. It was said that returning veterans would have the pick of jobs, if jobs there were, and she had already, going far afield, drafted for him occupations no one knew anything about, from compiling a catalogue of owls to interviewing ex-servicemen for an album of memories, from bookcase builder to piano tuner.

"He won't want to do anything for a year or two," George the civilian told her. "He'll be done for."

"He'll never," she said. "He'll want to be back to normal in a jiffy. Wouldn't you?" George hung his head and went off to warn Douglas that she was serious and seemed intent on reforming Harry before tent-pegging him down. She wanted the estaminet out of him first, but she never gave a thought to the bordello, and certainly not to the Gregorian monks, her most doughty competition. And as she began to think of molding her black-haired hero she realized that, for the first time, she was thinking of him sensually—his brawny forearms, his large flushed Irish ears with the gristle coiled up near the surface of the skin, his hands upon her hands, cooler than hers, like two goldfish or two baby rabbits. She had gleaned the idea that war prepared men for life, made them grow up at fantastic speed, and gave them a stark sense of urgency about what mattered: family, wife, babies, the Christmas hearth, the midsummer lawn with deckchairs and scampering terrier. That war might wholly dispossess him of himself, transmuting eager volunteer into young apathetic, had never occurred to her. They would all have to come back, to a slack paradise of smokes and snooker and horse races and pint-swilling, and waste month after month merely reminiscing, before she realized that post-war meant lazy. They would no more want to be guided than leeches, no more want to lead than sloths. "You'll see," George told her.

"No," she said, *"they'll see you."*

"Well, if they do, they'll never take me seriously again. You watch out. When they look at us they'll be thinking of the dead, and how lucky we are, Hilly."

This was why she began to pray to music, or to God-in-music, with whom she was on less than confident terms. Her prayer invoked grand words such as harmony and heaven. She invoked the plumage of the dove, the agile scolding of the wren, the terrible moo of cows confined in the slaughterhouse up the yard waiting for the humane killer to thud into their skulls. She prayed hard about light people, whose word you could never count on, and serious people, who kept their word long after others expected them to. She cited Bach and Handel, Tennyson and John Masefield, in a style of prayer increasingly conversational, mixing earnestness, originality, and talent in equal measure, arriving finally at the day on which she merely willed them while she played, marking what she most deeply cared about by depressing the sustaining pedal, and hang the composer's instructions. Harry was to be brought back uncorrupted, a prize pineapple washing ashore, otherwise they would both waste even more time while she spruced him up for the fray of life. Hilly must have sounded to God like an odd mixture of prude, tyrant, and naïf, but she was truly none of these, only an economist of the emotions, knowing vaguely that music was not a waste, or children, or love.

She wondered if, after all that soldiering of his, the weird and uncouth local names left over from the Norman Conquest—Ashby de la Zouch, Chapel en le Frith, Adwick le Street, and Frecheville, not many, to be sure—might stir an unguarded nerve and set him craving a familiar pain, a French titillation, a Belgian bar, a German guffaw, a Sherwood Forester's night out under the trees. Foo, she said without injuring the propriety of her prayer, he's not that vulnerable, not after a war. He won't be, Lord, I guarantee it. I'll steady him, I'll not let him wobble. We are going to be as steady as a metronome together, hugging, kissing, playing ticklish.

The Lord must have heard her because, soon after Harry's being wounded, she stopped praying, or even willing her prayers during pianoforte stints, and began to do something new. She played as if the notes were words, perhaps transmissible by Morse, stressing them with the rhythms of conversation, yet without knowing what the words were, except that some were grave, some jesting, some funny. As an old idiom used to have it, she made the piano talk, driving up past the raised lid to the horizon black cockatoos, pared-claw tigers, lumbering hippos, vaulting frogs, squabbling sparrows, and many other manners of creatures, countercreating God's own handiwork and actually feeling that, although what she played did not in any way depict Creation, it mimicked the ways of the Creator. She felt herself bulging and splashing. Icebergs ran from her eyes, formed themselves, and crashed past her midriff. The ivory in the piano keys reverted to tusk and she played something akin to a comb with pointed wavy teeth. It was heavenly because, once upon a time, God's mind was empty too.

And on that other level of her life, she served chops, steaks, brisket, lift, and liver, handing over parcels that bled when she hoisted them, and the stabbing ache in her stomach continued, yielding only when she punished it with her fist, telling herself never to hoist anything again, never mind how much George and Douglas giggled. Her mother was fading, but with impeccable Victorian hauteur, a woman summoned from far away but not heeding the summons lest she upset her children in time of war. A Fitzalan always put up a fight, even if in the wrong. Then the word finally arrived that Harry was dead, and Fitzalan life went on as usual, Hilly, although frozen, repeating to herself "They're wrong, they're wrong." Nonetheless, well brought up, she wore black and, around her neck, an inch-wide band of black crepe which in certain lights resembled a gash. She walked, played, and served with a severed head, mentally adrift in the domain of music, where harmony prevailed; you simply had to find the key.

Recovering, or inventively corroborating, all of this, Clive felt his head flush and swell with shame, chagrin, and the overall sadness of things. Diving into his father now dead, his mother the creaking gate now beginning to grind, moved him and appalled him; he thought of all the life that had rushed through them, chaotic and unbidden, using them (he supposed), but also inciting them to grandeur and stoicism, love and panic. Would it not be better to leave it all be and content himself with having loved them incurably well? What if he had misremembered his father, misheard his mother, mistaken them both? No, he wanted to rest in the ample forecourt of their conjoined lives, reliving them until he had become a raving pariah alone on a mountain with metronome and revolver, a plastic bag around his head to keep the bullet from making a mess against the—he was going to say *wall,* but realized where he had imagined himself as being. It had to be gone through, this final or next-to-last auscultation of the mighty, manipulative lovey-dovey their lives had been, and his mother the midwife of the whole operation, august figure against a background with Bach and Tennyson in it, they themselves escape artists locked in by memory. He had to do it, entrusted to take his parents' lives into the future, in something he had not yet written.

A PRACTICAL, down-to-earth person, Hilly nonetheless began to feel uneasy about her own body, the echo and counterpart of Harry's. What bothered her most was the skeleton, feeling it undulate and sway as she moved about, keeping her rigid and together but surely warning her of horrors to come, far worse than what happened in the slaughterhouse. Her mother, before she took to her bed, had begun to stoop and shorten, and that was the skeleton beginning to lose its trim, its command. Why the flesh and muscle outlived the bone she could not fathom, but she hated the disparity and called the designer into question during long sessions of Bach played with almost vocal smash. Hilly wanted Bach to be more defiant and hostile, and played him thus, with scowls, tight teeth, and sometimes a tapping foot. Belligerent she called him, seeing the curly, robust lips and the dimpled heavy chin above a tunic; actually, he looked like a general, at least in all the pictures of him she had seen, but she demoted him to sergeant, making him useful and agile, letting him remain tubby but depriving him of his wig, and getting that right hand out from behind him to shake Harry's on the inevitable return. Bach was the keeper of the flame, the custodian of the gate, the guardian of harmony, but she wanted him less even-tempered, open to the tumult of war.

How ingenious this maneuver was, and how dangerous, Hilly never realized. She was using what she adored to save her the pain of one she loved. She knew, without quite formulating it thus, that those who collect enough chamber pots will probably find the Holy Grail; but she never dreamed that making chalices of chamber pots by relating them to the Grail would undo her devotion to Harry: outdate him, formalize him, make him vague and representational. She was not making Harry into a saint, but into a cast-off relative of the impecunious Bach, whose music was that of accommodation, reconcilement, whereas the feelings she had most of all were indignation and frenzy. Had Harry written to her daily, and not been censored, she might have felt different; as it was, she had to fight a vacancy while she sensed the clustered disasters of war going on, run by bloodthirsty old men to whom the lives of those they sacrificed were as so many bus tickets. She wondered if men who, as boys, had played with toy soldiers became less careful with real men's lives, or the other way round. Familiarity bred, not contempt, but familiarity. Of course. She wanted the generals to fight it out on their own in a space the size of a boxing ring, with the troops as audience, booing and cheering. When in severe distress, after wonder turned into gruesome imagining in spite of her efforts to keep the war at bay, she played counter-music, defying the composer's instructions, just to see if the roof of heaven would fall in. Now, when she laughed, the laugh was followed at once by a sharp, birdlike clearing of her throat. When she could not sleep, she stroked her breasts with automatic languor, sensing she was going to waste.

Clive withdrew the thought, the contrived observation, wondering how the devil he was going to stick to fact or even find it; no use embellishing her, he scolded himself. He wanted to know, but he dared not ask, and he instructed himself never to guess, never mind how plausible the result. If only someone would come along behind him and take over, less intimate with Hilly and less inhibited about asking her, under the circumstances, what she might have done. He was wholly daunted by the image of ninety-four while trying to tune in to her teens, the war-widow before marriage. She would watch him with those gray-green eyes and comment gently: "Thinking hard today."

"As usual," he'd say, trembling.

"They say if you don't use it, it withers up."

Oh, he thought; if only it *would* wither up, but it—the mind, the memory, the love, the mind fed by the memory flayed by the love— shone remorselessly, like the golden word hoards of all the caliphs of Asia, a shower of forbidden miracles, the most of which was how to pretend you can read your mother's intimate mind of seventy-odd years ago, she never having told a soul unless perhaps Edith, who never in all of her brightly enameled arias sang family secrets. What did Hilly do when she couldn't sleep? All he could say was: She waited for sleep.

Trying to muster his materials, Clive lined up Harry, Hilly, George, Thurrie, Douglas, Kotch his sister and Bruno her dog in his mind, and wished hard to have them all in a thimble, interacting, not separated by long relay races, international boundaries, and final cate- gories such as life and death. He wanted them all in his arms, say, or at the same table. Then he realized, with a cerebral jolt, that only his father was missing, and that he should be doing better, getting his father nearer the scene of diagnosis, Hilly to accepting a life without him (devoted to Douglas and her mother, the two weakest); but all he could see was the leaning Virgin of Albert, whose fall would portend war's end, although, to him, she was executing a flawless dive into nonexistent water, arms outstretched, the rest of her taut in streamlined sequence. Beneath her the church stood like a broken biscuit, passed by thousands on their way to the battleground of the Somme, and hundreds of the so-called walking wounded, among whom came Harry, his bandaged eyes impervious to the tear gas they had marched through, led by a soldier with a gas mask, walking them toward peace and quiet. Harry knew his bandages would have to be soaked or they would never come off, and then he would know.

In this he was wrong. Harry, they told him, you are blind, you may always be blind, you may regain all of your sight or some of it. Who are you? he asked, and they told him, but he wondered how they knew; he felt his eyes were on the verge of seeing, he could tell they were moving according to his will and getting ready to focus. All those talking to him had to be patient.

Rid of the worst shrapnel, set in a wheelchair, he found himself being lectured on the virtues of being blind, or, rather, on all the wonderful things remaining: the other senses, given him like four toys. Give me something bright to look at, he told them. Shine lights. They told him they kept doing just that, and he must try to adjust; a counsellor was coming to see him (he winced) and explain to him what sensations to expect as the tiniest shrapnel began to walk out. Don't rub, don't scratch, he heard, you will make things worse. Off went the telegram to Hilly: *Wounded, all right, tell Church Row. Love, Harry.* Stiff upper lip. Stiff upper lid. They dressed Harry in a blue tunic and rolled his wheelchair to the terrace, where he began to live again and put on weight, receive letters from Hilly and try to imagine how his monks had sounded. It was, he told himself, as if all of them had had their throats cut.

Very dear Hereward,

Your first letter, perfunctory as it was, was not in your own handwriting, which suggests to me that your upper right limb is hurt, your writing hand, silly, or something even worse. Please explain this fact. You sound generally fed up, as we all are here. Mother has become crotchety, and Douglas, though tall, seems anemic, so we are forcing him to drink beef broth and eat minced steak. It makes him sick, the mince does, and I wish we could send it out to you, not what he has vomited, but the meat pristine as it is at first. So much for that paragraph.

How do you like Belgium? What are you reading? Is there any music in or around that church you mentioned with the leaning angel? Bach keeps me busy, but I don't give in to him, and I sometimes play his music my own way, which makes him cross in a very German way. Perhaps I should not be playing German music. They may drag me out and tie me to a cannon wheel. We have been playing tennis, but it's too much pit-a-pat. I would prefer something more irregular. George and Papa are well. Thurrie is somewhere in France, I think, from last account. We are all tired of war, but relieved that you are alive. The report said that you were missing, then dead. You are like a resurrection, although not religious. A parcel of surprises is on its way to you. Be good. Get lots of sleep. Tell us about your injury, please. We miss you, I especially.

Love, Hildred

Basing this on Hilly's reluctantly offered paraphrases, Clive wondered at his effrontery, mouthing the words as if she had written them. What was this pedantic need in him, to know how they managed it without any of the conveniences called modern? First Nurse Mallow wrote for Harry, and then a bilingual sister called Binche, who told Hilly the truth and then mortified Harry by informing him what she had added to the letter he dictated. Now he was a publically blind man, unable to keep his secrets any more.

Nurse Binche began her duties in a serious manner, taking extra time to unbandage his eyes, which operation felt to him nothing like unwrapping a turban but more like someone slowly twirling his head, tapping little messages through the decreasing layer of muslin and tugging him gently this way and that in a horizontal St. Vitus's dance that did not end when she had finished; his head went on wobbling in the medium called air that you could never see, blind or not. What are you doing now? he would say, and she would always give him the same answer: All that is good for you, in her glaciated, slow English. He did not see the little raised bed she made from lint soaked in antiseptic, setting first one eye and then the other in a little rectangle that allowed for the curvature of his upper cheek. From a tiny watering can she poured boracic solution against the puckered, bloody whites, almost cooing to him; and it all felt polar cool, the lint, the liquid, her hands, just the thing he had dreamed about in the heat and sludge of the craters and trenches. Each eye took five minutes and she called it irrigation, carefully directing the spout to all areas of the eye, sometimes pouring for a long time and making a flood, sometimes doing just a quick tip to soothe an area neglected. For the moment at peace, Harry felt he was being christened in an unusual way, though the lotion felt astringent, especially in his left eye, the worse hurt. Other days she encouraged him to use an eyecup, handing it to him full and then helping him to bring it into place with a sudden plunge, always careful not to jam it hard against whatever was beneath it. Then he held the cup in place and tried to blink, finally removing it with a tip followed by a groping thrust toward her voice. Sometimes he messed up, spilling boracic on his chest, but mostly he got his eye, grateful that the water used in the solution was tepid. At the moment, this sluicing was the thing he wanted most in life, and he got it every three hours. The hospital staff filled him with eggs and crusty bread, made him strong sweet tea that reminded him of the army, from which he considered himself well and truly severed, stroked his head, combed his hair, cleaned his ears and nostrils, and waited for changes. Strong lights came and went unnoticed as he tried to accustom himself to being a baby, much of the time in bed.

But he also ventured out in his wheelchair, escorted on short promenades by Sister Binche, whose protégé he had fast become: partly because he reminded her of her brother, captured in the Somme, partly because she felt for the blind, the deaf, the dumb, possessing a special vicarious gift, a tremendous capacity to discover how it felt to be another. In Harry she discerned something copiously ascetic, perhaps mistaking the bareness of his early life for girding of the loins, self-denial, the beginning of the via dolorosa. She treasured him and taught him some words of French, and after a few weeks they were able to hold private rudimentary conversations about the weather, food, and the Vickers machine gun. Harry told her about bread dipped in bacon fat, von Kaiserstein, the book lovers in his home in Exington, the Gregorian chant, the record, the mess book, Hastilow and the major in no-man's-land, and the man named Blood found on top of him, shattered and dry. For pain, of which he had a great deal, she gripped his fists and almost wrestled him, sometimes also letting him bite the heel of her roughened hand. Older than he, she saw him at the beginning of a career as one of life's victims: a *mutilé de guerre,* a phrase she had candidly taught him (which he said as *matelot de gair*). She did not give him much chance of seeing again, and she would soon have to inform him of the need to learn Braille. But not yet. It was a month since he had been wounded, and not all the right surgeons had been to prod him yet, although he himself described himself to her as a goner, a useless blighter. There is still Woodbine, the American, she said, who will be here soon. Let him see.

Harry wanted the issue final, so that he might evolve an absolute attitude and become one thing or another. Having already told Hilly to forget him, to find a stockbroker or an officer, he regarded that piece of business as transacted, and stopped writing, at least until Sister Binche rebuked him and told him not to be so sadistic (a word he did not have). He still did not know her first name, and had not asked it, resolved in some reciprocal maneuver to deny himself things in much the same way as blindness denied him her face, though he had felt at its high cheekbones, the deep compassionate chin, the gritty-lidded eyes.

She was black-haired, she told him, and therefore must be rather Irish-looking, he thought, with that combination of light and dark, and fair-complected too, with freckles along her arms but none on her chest. Ari, she called him, or Sergeant Ari, making him feel important and imposing. The double eyepatch made him look like a man going to meet a firing squad. She tried to bandage his head down low, screening the eyes just enough, but giving them air, a touch of breeze or her own mouth gently blowing at him to get his attention. She had removed much of the crust from the roots of his lashes and increased with minor coaxing their natural flexure away from the surface of the eye. If this attention soothed him, he never said, accepting it as the due of a blinded man who wondered how terrible he looked.

"Am I a monster?" he asked, hoping never to hear the answer, the white lie.

"Only in your mind, Ari," he heard. "Before you label someone a monster, you must consult his soul, and, if that is in good working order like a chiming clock, then you say the clock is wonderful, like a polar bear in bedroom slippers." Sometimes she went off like that, clinching all with an image that crackled like a firework even while seeming to go off the point. She stroked his arms, his shoulders, tugged on his ears and his toes, and, one night when everyone else was asleep and he was groaning with tiny penetrant pain, she slid her hands beneath the sheets and opened his hospital pajama trousers, exposing himself to himself, hand-galloping the virgin he hardly knew he was, and the headache went away, as well as his memory of what he had considered the happiness of his previous life. "There," she said, "now we've been introduced. You have a beautiful build. I am going to visit you again, Ari, and show you what to do." He knew, but he had hardly had time. His seductions had been toward death, and only young men at that. His orgasms had been those of panic and terror, when the rear end puckered and retched. His only sadness afterward had been his distance from the animating premise of the war: Why was it being fought? Fabienne, he said; it doesn't sound like a woman's name at all. At least (he told her), it won't matter if I get any of it in my eye, will it? Where it's going, she reassured him in her slowest French, it won't have any chance to get into an eye, *mon trésor.*

He was not, he knew, being unfaithful to Hilly because none of this figured in his relationship with her, and probably never would. One day he would tell her about it, much as if confessing a trip to the dentist. Well, perhaps not quite that, but like gambling, shooting pigeons, letting a greased pig loose in a sedate club for footsoldiers. This experience in the loins had come too late, now that he was a dead man; wouldn't it have been better to have something to compare it with, such as making love with his eyes on the beloved instead of trying to make a difference between dark and dark, between bandage dark and sunshine dark, aghast that, there in the bed as he shoved and stabbed against her, his eyes had only the pawnbroked glory of two bullet holes or, as he invoked one of the oldest soldierly curses, two pissholes in the snow? Better they should bandage his penis to his leg and wait for it to wither, fall off, like the feet of Chinese children. It was no use going home a sexual success but a flop at seeing. I, he told himself, am only an invitation to blindness; living with me, or even bedding down in the ward in the small hours, is only like asking someone else to be blind too. What he had entered was a newly opened wound that she thought was only her normal organ, whereas he knew he had maimed it, set it in a different category altogether, among the sponges, the roots, the funguses, the cuckoo spits. No: She was still herself, refusing to tell him how many men she had handled, how many had entered her, little knowing that death had lain with her and irrevocably joined her to the league of the helpless. He could not understand that she worked by means of sentimental convection, which meant moving huge areas of feeling around within her, never losing them but frequently combining them in new ways, linking a newly discovered Patagonia (Harry, Ari) to a Latin America already within her possession. She lived by comparison, by agglutinating man to man without ever thinking herself a nymphomaniac or even promiscuous; she was creating a piebald lover, a Joseph's coat of satisfactions. Her memory belonged to her much as, sometimes, she belonged to several men in the same phase, or even in the same evening if she could manage it. She was open, she decided, and she should be filled. One day Ari would be sent to a hospital in London to be put through further ordeals, and that would be that. If she had unhinged him somewhat, she had no idea of it, choosing rather to think of herself as the angel of satiety, as capable of kissing and licking blind men's eye sockets as their genitals, once you became accustomed, she mused, to the local texture, the topography, the patchwork aromas and the rest. Having risen high in her profession, not least on account of an imperious contralto voice and a way of cowing doctors by raising herself to her full six feet, she had become accustomed to the often-vaunted embarrassments of having a body. The soul was a greater obstacle by far, so she wanted to at least settle herself in the flesh, as it were, and come to terms with all the organness there was. She presumed that, when the Almighty first formed flesh, He did it out of boredom with abstract ideas. He made the dirty bits to drive his masterpieces crazy.

WHAT, Clive wondered, was he doing to Harry now? Had son ever probed or been so fanciful before? Based on Harry's hints, how had all this come to be, granted the outlines of what happened? Clive half-expected his father's ghost to come treading down the hallway outside Hilly's door. This was Hilly's apartment: Hilly the betrayed, if those old stories his father suggested and Hilly dismissed in a rage were to be believed. The question was not Had Harry ever done this? but Would he have liked to? Was his son belatedly giving him things that Harry would have wanted? Well, perhaps not exactly like this. Harry had had desires, though, and untapped ones at that. He was a blast furnace on hold, born, Clive believed, before his generation knew anything about oral sex. Oh, he wanted everything for Harry, he wanted him to have been an Ari; and, in a very distant way, he wanted him to have had it for his son's sake too, and the son's mother's, so that Ari his father should, although blind, have become a man of the world. Like Bach. Always-Bach, as Hilly said, always smarting about the games Harry-Ari was supposed to have played in France—or was it Belgium?—when he was recovering. The son was imposing a rite of passage from within on his own father, and the mother was still here, getting on for a century later, never to be appeased.

Imprisoned by the bliss of genuine recall, amounting here to Hilly's eyewitness, Clive let Bernard Ditcher, the suitor of the moment, make his lethargic approach, burdened as he was by three Great Danes, a tennis racket, and a wet sheaf of flowers. Presumably his golf togs were within easy reach, like his father's fortune. Shortsighted (a weakness Hilly was merciless about), he pottered toward her, spouting in a wry squeak his constant line: "Turned out nice again."

"We could all—" Ditcher got no further.

"Could we, then?"

"I was thinking."

"I could tell," Hilly snapped, faintly aware that, if she was going to have to go to the ocean bottom for the sake of money, all hands lost, then she was going to go under protest.

He tried again. "Hilly—"

"Hilly, is it?"

"Hildred, I thought—"

"Formal today, are we? That's nice."

"How do I start?"

"Have you," she inquired icily, "met Mother?"

"I'd be most happy."

"Well, you won't, she's not well."

He tried again, but she eradicated him, asking "Have you heard about Harry Moxon?"

Yes, he had, and his heart bled, but he hadn't come to talk about Harry.

"It was your eyes that kept you out of the war, wasn't it, Bernard? No wonder we're losing. I do declare, if I'm going to have to settle for somebody with bad eyes, I'd prefer a blind man to one who can only squint. Wouldn't you? It's not a matter of eyes, though, it's a matter of principle. I can't really see what you're doing here. The flowers are lovely, thank you. Now, wouldn't you say there's something frivolous about Mozart, compared with Beethoven? Don't you think Haydn's a bit, well, *powdery,* like one of those wigs? Are you good at talk? At music? Wouldn't you like to begin? I'll soon be in my Red Cross nurse's uniform. They're waiting for me over in France, you know. Are they waiting for you too, or have you put your shoulder out of joint carrying all that money?"

The lower bourgeoisie, Clive thought, was attacking the upper middle, and with dazzling success. Poor Bernard Ditcher needed a scriptwriter even to come within Hilly's scalding orbit. So many emotions harrowed and propelled her: hate and grief and fury and pique and pride. She was suddenly the custodian-to-be of a blind and lonely man who could no longer even write to her without the intervention of some foreign slut of a nurse, whose spelling—well, her spelling was all right, which only went to show how boring she must be. The Bernard Ditchers, more ghoulish than she had ever thought men could be, prowled around her like jackals, little aware how tied she was by the shop, Douglas, and her mother. Douglas was covered with hives, blinked nonstop, and needed excessive sleep; born too late, he was the obverse image of the biological tantrum that laid her mother waste. Having a child had sapped her, and seeing him made her worse.

Yet here they came, licking their chops and fawning, in plus fours and panama hats, with dogs or flowers, little scarves of silk or paintings of the Brontë country, as eager to sweep her off her feet as reluctant to help her sweep out the shop. The Ditchers, she told herself, were the rump left over from heroism, meaning the ones not fit for war, like George the ace metallurgist. Here they slithered, eyeing and noting, ready to invest in her and, no doubt, dictate to her what kind of music to play for their half-hatched friends at silly garden parties. Hilly knew now that, no matter how cruel she was to them, they would bounce back with armorplated hearts, as adroit at the war of love and courting as Harry had been at that of death. The pain in her stomach had still not gone away, even though she no longer lifted; something was out of place, she was sure, and the only vent she had for her rage—hurling a bag of salt at the wall of the washhouse until it burst—did her no good either, dragging anew at what was skewed or loose, making her feel bilious, one of the well-spoken doomed.

Bernard Ditcher took his leave with no sense of defeat, attributing all she said to women's being funny most of the time: high-strung bitches good for one thing only. You had to humor them, especially the clever ones, or they put the needle into you and twisted it. He would come again, he knew, sensing here a woman about to crack, to accept whatever life forced upon her because—well, *because,* as they liked to say when trying to come up with a reason for arbitrary finality. The British, Clive noted in his depressed way, regarded social norms as facts of nature, and nature as a convenience meant to keep them calm.

Brooding on Harry, with special attention now to words such as bloodshot and sightless, Hilly felt impelled to go to the Continent, to get him, to get at him, to see him through, but there was no going. She was mothering everybody save the one who really needed it, and she imagined the starchy nurses being uppity and taut with him, laying down the law and commenting sarcastically on the excellent English he spoke into his letters. When she whispered to him, a huge whooping crane would come out of her mouth and fan him. When she touched his wrists, goldfish would slip out from under the skin and cool him off with their polished flanks. And when she blew gently at the bandages over his eyes, new eyes would start to form there in the muslin-swathed darkness, eventually to hatch out with a potent, exact slither. Oh, she would know what to do once she got there, and she would bring him home, to Market Street, and play the piano to him, all *largo* and *lento.*

The thing to do was lure him into a curative trance, sitting and nourishing him until he began coming back to life, with all the right flavors wafting through him, the juices, the syrups that impersonally seeped. Cure from within, she said. Whoever wishes to be cured must first expose his wound. *Boethius,* Clive murmured, I knew she knew Boethius. I got Boethius at my mother's knee; I still do. In the old days she had a quote for everything, as if literature had anticipated all of life and always had a phrase. Now, is that like all those plants in the Amazon? Is there, somewhere, a natural cure for everything? Are we living in a planned universe after all?

Gradually Hilly lost her free-ranging bluster as her letters from Harry became more and more stilted, reporting a nullity she found easy to explain, but not to accept. He was in good hands. It was amazing how long he had survived when, daily, she heard of young men, local and distant, who had died during their first day of battle, cowed by what was going to happen to them, cut off from music, tenderness, grass, books, and clean linen.

Who, she wrote to Harry, is writing your letters for you? Left-handed? Does she have a name? Would she care to write directly to Hilly, adding a little postscript or even tucking an extra sheet of stationery into the envelope? No censor spied on them now. Could this same lady some day actually guide Harry's hand and thus, never mind how untidily, get Harry to write a letter of his own? Fabienne Binche did guide his hand, but away from letter-writing to zones of intemperate, lubricious warmth, even telling him during the prelude of things a blind man might attempt with two, even three women once the geometry had been worked out and the pillows arranged. Did God, Harry wondered, no longer strike anyone dead for disgraceful behavior? Was he entitled to everything because he was blind?

Amazed he had survived the war while knowing so little of life, Harry caught himself in the middle of the thought and wondered if indeed he had survived. Being alive was one thing, but being alive blind was like being made of gun cotton: One touch and you went sky-high. That just about summed up his days and nights with Fabienne Binche. Diligently she piped chemicals into his eyes while he wished them ever cooler, but she taught him hygiene in other ways too, coming to him, after the lights were dimmed, with a basin of hot water and a rather coarse-feeling washcloth with which she laved his glans after gently peeling the foreskin back. Until only days ago, Harry had not realized the skin retracted, and he now, perhaps alas, linked erection with the act of washing; you never did it when you were soft. Back he lay, humming something Latin from the Gregorians, while Fabienne Binche worked upon his privates the office of the portable bidet, astounding him with a flick or a finger snap as if she were supervising a frisky kitten and delighting him later in the performance with cold cream and eau de cologne until he felt wholly spruced up, for either the fray or a good night's sleep, depending on her mood and her hours. It might have been paradise save for his eyes; he certainly felt ministered to, delighted to have the bulb of his organ aired in a foreign place, sometimes trying to figure out how far his new life, in which ecstasy and pain combined equally, was from the old one, in which he had neither. If this was France, or Belgium, he wanted to stay here for ever, blind or not, and he seriously tried to keep his mind from next month or next year.

His conversations with Fabienne were much the same, day in, day out.

"Who is he?" she murmured. "He's an ugly young soldier full of love." Then she sang, with buoyant nasality: "Will he always be blind? Will he never see if the beauties who attend him—have warts?"

To which Harry said nothing, but hummed voluptuous contentment, little realizing how much a novelty—and little else—he was in her complex and erotic life. Because he could not see, she read aloud to him the sexual properties of his body, from the little steamy fizz she milked from him in the beginning to the splatter of hot gruel she fostered in him after a week or so, exclaiming in delight as it popped upward in the half-light of the ward. She taught him names. She said his body was an aviary of flightless parakeets, each wrapped in fragrant Armenian paper. She taught him how his tongue and hands might do duty for his benighted eyes, and how his sharp military nose had lain in abeyance for too long.

And so as Clive, master of these ceremonies—heaped up against the thought of his father's never getting well—envied him and smiled at the benign hoax of the whole memoir, Harry began to think of himself as lucky, master navigator and master cocksman in one, at last come into his own, severed from the prosaic saunter of engagement and marriage; become instead the roué of the ward, a man who almost missed his disgraceful vocation, now fit to be greeted by the male nurse on his morning rounds with hot chocolate: "Good morning, English bums, good morning, American bums, *shokeaulah, shokeaulah.*" Harry wondered about the other patients and tried to estimate how many of them Fabienne had likewise sacrificed to her own imperious mucous membranes. He didn't care if he was the only one or one in twelve; he just knew that he never again wanted to be without this oozing extreme of life that gave the lie to war, blindness, disappointment, lack of hope, loneliness—everything. In a way she was too old for all of them in there, but in another she was the perfect tutor in lustful friendliness. She loved what she smelled while tasting. She loved what she tasted while smelling. She loved what she smelled and tasted while touching and listening. She was a waning phantom, already beginning to suffer from varicosity behind her knees, little bouts in which her ankles went sideways, and, she was sure, prey to sudden extra heartbeats that winded her. Well, she was going down in flames, willing to waste nothing so long as she had it.

Here she came, breathless from being big and having to move neatly through the hushed-down ward. Harry felt a little bird heave upward from his chest, and all things begin to twitch and stiffen. Her very approach, in rubber-soled slippers, was aphrodisiac; Harry, a poor sleeper, was the only one regularly awake, with his organ in his hand, his other hand behind his head, smoothing him to an hypnotic and callow rhythm. Here she came, the vestal of the hot-water bottle and lavender soap, willing to tease him by threatening his penis with a scrubbing brush ("Feel at this, *mon grand*"), but ever disposed to baby him and bring him to climax in the same breath. She would coo and urge to ready him for a public appearance, with his prowess in his pants to begin with and then lofted high in front of the other blind men who to a man cupped their ears for sounds of friction, imminence, bliss, and decrescendo. Noncommissioned officers, she found, were reluctant to lie back and be serviced, whereas everyone from lieutenant upward seemed only too happy not to exert himself, not while the night-prowler toiled. It was the strongest orgy she had ever known: muted and impeded. Now she knew what the thought of death, hemorrhage, or amputation, did to the standing penis, making it into a fugitive conical piece of candy busily scurrying for cover in its root. She was as accustomed to last rites as to first spendings, preferring, with the one, to weep later in her little garret atop the hospital; with the other, to let the seepages dry and flake away, having had a brief tumultuous dignity in the arena of the wounded man's groin. Life was like that, she thought, as Clive nodded yes. Life spilled, out or over. To die was to go. To come was to die. Those who had never come much were never at ease with death.

All of a sudden, Clive came tumbling out of his father's gold-and-ivory Venusberg, astounded by the prelude to his own conceiving, aware that a conceiving was merely one "take" amid a thousand pops. It should be more dignified, he decided. My father had the life over there he talked about; all I am doing is consummating it for him, giving to his ghost what he never fully told me, when delicacy or rudely remembered satisfaction made it too private for anyone to hear. That he had something of keen, humming high flavor is enough for me; I want him to have had an ecstasy other than that of the mind, and a pain other than that behind his eyes. This has nothing to do with

Hilly. I want him to have felt the edge of a desire so keen he must have thought the universe had designed it to be that way. I wonder. I doubt it. Let's not over-dignify the old breeder's bribe, the sperm-bearer's *Kyrie*.

Released from his stage-managing chore, he began to think of actresses he would have liked his father to have had, pandering backward for him from Barbara Carrera to Daphne Zuniga, from Persis Kambatta to Mimi Rogers, no doubt evincing his own tastes, but impulsively wanting the war hero to have his traditional reward: home to beauty and the standard tribute.

ONE WARM sunny Sunday, Fabienne Binche and several other nurses took the ambulant blind on a little outing, the first of many planned, although some of the doctors in the Red Cross hospital had argued that those who could not walk would feel resentful. In the end, however, it was decided to send the first group and see what happened. Off they went in two ambulances and within the hour were lining up at the entrance to a museum, marching a few steps forward (some, still military, got it right; Harry shuffled, to show his exclusion from the war).

He reached, he found something bulbous and concrete: the arm of a mighty statue that blocked his path while, elsewhere in the echoing gallery, other blindfolded men in blue tunics hesitantly made contact with pieces of marble and stone, wondering what they were feeling at. The public were never allowed to touch, but this was a special occasion: not a guessing game, though it degenerated into one as the men slowly came to life and a long-lost ribaldry lifted its tactless head. Those listening pretended not to hear what the men whispered and shouted: "Goliath's balls, to be sure!" "Jack the Beanstalk's stalk, lads!" "My old woman's backside, frozen stiff." It was perhaps the first serious laugh they'd had since entering the hospital. Harry enjoyed the coolness of the various statues, responding to the muggy weather without the gusto of the others, and wondering if this laying-on of hands would extend to human bodies as well. Or were they all, the blind ones, already so sated with Sister Binche as not to care? He asked, was told that only she, of all the nurses, made the midnight rounds, and not with everybody either. She played favorites, and had been known to overpower a given soldier for a week, then leave him alone altogether to wonder what he had done wrong. Nobody else, it seemed, had come in for as many attentions as Harry, for whom she had developed a soft spot, banned in the daytime but allowed to pulse and bulge as soon as the sun had set.

Alas for art and therapeutic visit, several of the livelier young soldiers had opened their flies and were attempting lewd overtures to what they presumed were appropriate places of the statues in front of them; only a Turkish bath was missing as they pushed and clasped, yelling obscenities about the white cliffs of Dover, blindness from self-abuse, hollow spines from tossing-off, and the big shots of their schooldays who kept enormous stone jars of sperm under their beds, the tribal law being that you must never let any of it get away from you. It had not taken long for the blinded men to revert to adolescent atavism, to fast, impromptu exchanges about swishers and danglers, knackers and bollocks, jam rags and horse collars, all of it diffident and amateurish, just the sort of thing they said in the trenches, not to hymn desire but to vent their nerves. For a while Harry, more conversant with the peculiar turns of Fabienne Binche's mind, thought there would be naked human beings, women certainly, in between the statues, awaiting only a soldier's touch to erupt into lascivious life. Then he thought that he and his mates were supposed to strip naked except for their head bandages and go through the motions that several had attempted while more-or-less clad.

In the end he decided this was one of those cultural expeditions he had heard about. Music would be next, followed by a visit to the herb gardens. It was all a way of killing time until the doctors could think of something to do, until each man's future was a certainty. This was a brothel of stone, he decided: though, if a man's desire was hot enough, the statues would melt. He suddenly longed for a Vickers machine gun to lay waste the humanity surrounding him: nurses and soldiers and all. He did not want to see, hear, or any of the rest of it. They had been brought out of the hospital like lunatics from a mental institution, made to look silly and conspicuous, aired like dogs on an aristocratic whim by people who should know better.

Clive agreed. His father's ruddy skin was pale for all the summer's heat. His hair rose high from the inner perimeter of the bandages and had that slept-on look. His gait had become unsteady; he walked with an invisible tureen of hot liquid balanced on his crown. For all their vulgarities, the blind soldiers conducted themselves with hesitant delicacy; every now and then, among the solid stances of the statues, they groomed themselves with one finger raised to the cheek, testing that area for scars or scabs, then another finger tapping the concavity between chin and bottom lip. They believed that the eyes, once mauled, led the rest of the face downward to extinction too, and they were not going to be thus consecutively wounded without knowing about it. An arc of whirling knives surrounded them. They breathed shrapnel as tiny as grains of sand. Their lips dried so much they made a glow and sometimes caught fire. Blocked with drainage, their nostrils soon clogged up on any outing, and the return journey became mainly a matter of blowing into khaki handkerchiefs, which they then folded back up into the rectangular creases left by the smoothing iron, in effect sticking the little panels together with thumb-flattened blots of blood, which stuck better than anything: one of its main duties, Harry thought. Blood is God's glue. God's in his heaven. All's right with the world. Human skin is blood's best blotter. All nice outings come to an end. I have to keep up my strength for tonight. Odd, you'd think people would find us disgusting, but for some it just sharpens the edge of novelty. People could pull all kinds of faces and we'd never see a thing. They could rent us out to the most twisted sinners in Creation, so many francs a go, and extra to lift up the corner of the bandage and have a peek into the twin gloryholes, nothing of the eyes left but two cooked raisins.

On their return, all the men had their eyes bathed. In case we saw anything, Harry thought, they are washing it away. Off. They don't want us to go getting fancy ideas about having a look at things. A good *shufti,* as the Arabs put it. I don't deal with hearsay. Nobody could tell him what Sister Binche looked like. No nurse would. Could she, just perhaps, be blind herself, not a nurse or a sister, but an overeager blind volunteer for whom night rounds were as natural as graveyards for the dead. Unless she was Hilly in disguise! A poor thought, this, but it led him into Hilly's hinterland again, making him tell himself he was comfortable with his decision to give her her freedom. He knew about the Bernard Ditchers, and wondered if any kind of civilian cowardice could get them sentenced posthaste to the front trenches, and, with any luck, blow their heads clean off the first day. So it was now to Hilly, severed into inveterate loneliness, that his flinching mind began to turn, for once facing the facts: the full, embarrassing crowd of them all pointing a finger at his head and blaming him for faking his age in the first place.

"Harry showing off!"

"Harry," he bugle-called back, "in a poor way now. Don't you tell."

"Oh, we will, Harry, count on us."

They were nobodies, people who always stood when the National Anthem was played, but in their souls sat down, asking only to be overlooked. Hilly dwindled as she floated away from him into immaculate vacancy, his name no longer on her lips, the wound in her heart healing fast, her whole being gladly and unlovingly shut of him, and relieved to be so. He saw a blind Harry helping in the shop and chopping off his hand with the meat cleaver. Reaching out to take her hand and butting her in the groin. Playing tennis at Stead's Field and swatting a bird with his racket. Harry the unhandy.

Whether Hilly eventually married Harry or not was beside the point, since she had received him into her tropic of adoration. What had happened to him qualified him enormously for special reverence, like a madman among Red Indians, she thought. Negating herself for her mother or Douglas or the business was one thing, but becoming Harry's guide and custodian, whispering *Come this way* or propelling him another, was akin to learning to play Liszt without a flaw. All she would do henceforth was practice, after a while setting the spiky text aside and doing her oblations from memory.

Clive shuddered at the contrasts between Hilly and Harry: depravity versus virginity, worldliness versus innocence. He could understand them both, his parents; his emotions were so much theirs. He almost persuaded himself that Hilly's rapturous lustlessness was really an acute form of desire, that Harry's newly awakened libido was the only form of prayer to evolve in blindness. He knew neither of these conclusions would have been true, but the drift of his mind, tampering with their lives almost a hundred years ago, went that way. He knew that he was going to put the two of them together again and, out of that protracted encounter, produce himself, like a conjurer his rabbit.

Hilly, conscious of at least two types of pain, began to find in her head music between the lines: not notes she played, but notes she heard from out of nowhere. She realized she was composing, nothing grand, but obstinately intrusive—not like Bach or the others, but clamorous, melodramatic, making everything a little hostile, a bit more crowded. Her ear accepted it all as if bribed, but she never thought of writing the melodies down, not until later, and they were not melodies anyway so much as battering chords to crack windows with. She knew only that, under so much pressure, she was more into her music than usual, letting it regale her while she wrung its heart. She thought of herself as being more musical nowadays, more like the people whose writings she played; and those who passed by the Market Street music room thought of her as the muse of war, without exactly using that phrase; she paraded naked emotion to the daily shoppers, to the boozers from the pub and the potted-meat buyers from Mrs. Anthony's shop opposite. Even the kids, spending a half-penny on mint imperials or a stick of shiny black licorice, took her for granted, not whistling to her tunes (which they couldn't detect) but making a compatible noise between a hum and a drone. Hilly Fitzalan's not half pounding it out these days, ever since Harry Moxon copped it: Blinded he is, in a French hospital somewhere over there.

Like that: not red-letter news for Rhubarb to rush all over the village with, inevitably felling the woman with the iron foot. But, sturdy enough for comradely diffusion, it even reached Reggie, Rhubarb's brother, the village shoe repairer, alas so spastic that most of his hammer blows missed nail, sole, and last altogether. He had to aim at the wrong place in order to strike home, to dupe, as it were, his galvanic nervous system.

After a while, since there was never much to do in Exington apart from billiards, snooker, and the pubs, people began to make a point of walking past the butcher's shop to hear the music, and Rhubarb actually got to make his rounds, incomprehensibly saying to all he passed his own version of events: "She's playing hard today," said as *Zhblayin,* which was enough, since all knew the signal and had been translating Rhubarbese for years. They brought their dogs for the walk, and some yapped over the sound of the piano. Other people unearthed bugles and trumpets, kettledrums and concertinas, and there would be an informal, straggly concert, with Hilly playing oblivious to them all, although hearing them with the fringe of her mind's ear. Their traditional gathering place was the covered entry to the slaughterhouse yard, with room for some dozen players who found the acoustics tremendous, deafening themselves while half following the piano from above. Such was the village's impromptu response to the kaiser and all things German, which most of the music played happened to be.

EVERY SO often, to while away the days, Harry talked with the other blind men in the ward, asking them if they had done the noble thing and severed their connections with sweethearts back home. Most of them had not needed to. Only their families wrote to them now, and perhaps even those letters were fake, concocted by nurses; Harry wondered about this, unable to decide how stock a letter would have to be before someone else, a stranger, could write something just like it. Surely not, he thought: There are always family secrets to snigger about, little undusted corners that an outsider would never know, like my mother's habit of combing the soap to get all the stray hairs off it.

He had broken with Hilly because of Fabienne Binche. To him, his infidelity was abstract, happening not between Hilly and himself, but alongside them; he was not expert in callousness or craftiness, in deceit or shame. He just knew he had passed a certain point beyond which he and Hilly would be profound hindrances to each other. When the soldiers asked him, he dodged behind formulas of romance and announced that he had withdrawn his suit, a fact of which she had been informed. He wondered where he had picked up such a fancy phrase, which sounded like an insult to a tailor or a laundry, and if there were actually people who talked like that. Prim or stiff, it served his purpose, stifling further questions and setting him up in the ward as a bit of a gent, at least a man with airs. He was a sergeant after all, almost an officer, and would have been a medal winner several times but for the accidental deaths of certain sponsors.

Hilly at that moment was doing research into the life of Bach, whose reading tastes were undeveloped, and whose handwriting was an uncouth meander of the pen, not to mention his awkward German and the confusion of his ideas. All this she learned with awe; but her mind fixed on his blindness. Bach henceforth was the man who had undergone an eye operation at the hands of a certain John Taylor. Before Taylor operated, Bach had failing sight; after it he was blind, although shortly before he died his sight came back for a while. In that brief reprieve he worked night and day to revise and copy *The Art of the Fugue,* one of his final works. Glad to have found something related to blindness in the zone of music, Hilly bought a cheap copybook and began making entries on Bach's blindness, hoping to have a mass of information by the time Harry returned home; she was eager to imagine certain moments not documented in her books, much as Clive filled in the gaps in his reconstruction of his parents. Bach became three-dimensional for Hilly now—not just a composer, but a man who sprayed the world with children, whose salary had once been paid in measures of corn, trusses of wood, and whose living conditions were gloomy and unsanitary. One day she transcribed all her findings on Bach into a music-manuscript book, writing them along the staves like music to be played. Given enough libraries, she would soon have a Bach exhausted and laid bare; she could play to Harry and, in between pieces, read to him from the life of the master. It would be one way of reaching Harry, especially with stories of the young Bach copying by the light of the moon an entire collection of instrumental music, and almost ruining his eyes. It would be a way for Bach to go to war, and there might be conversations between Sergeant Harry and Sergeant Bach:

SERGEANT HARRY: Does the blood sometimes run down onto your cheeks? Perhaps it isn't even blood.

SERGEANT BACH: I always thought that was music.

SERGEANT HARRY: How much pain, mate?

SERGEANT BACH: More than you could stand, Moxon.

SERGEANT HARRY: How do you know that, organist?

SERGEANT BACH: Because I'm a believer and I stand with one
foot in the grave.

Hilly intended to develop these conversations, so Bach wouldn't be
quite so arrogant and Harry wouldn't cave in so easily. As she already
knew, the composer had written music for one patron who suffered
from insomnia—had composed his *Goldberg Variations* for Johann
Gottlieb Goldberg to play for Count Karl von Keyserlingk, and put
him to sleep at public concerts. This Hilly would do for Harry,
making those maimed eyes close in yet another way, sealing off his
mind but not the sleek tympani of his soul. What kind of a world
would it be in which a Bach-proffering Hilly did not await, for a
lifetime of musical buff, the blind man Harry, whose life, in a sense,
and certainly his future had gone into thin air all because the crown
prince had been shot—of whom the writer Stefan Zweig said "He
lacked all the qualities that Vienna required in a man: charm and
amiability"? Hilly's grasp of history was not quite firm.

"You've done me some damage," Harry told Fabienne Binche.

"Look what the Germans did to you, Ari Vederci."

"That's different, woman."

"Well," she said, with haughty tenderness, "before, you were blind
down below. At least that part of you can see now."

"I suppose," he said hesitantly, "women exist to do damage to a
man. Which would mean that philanderers fall apart soonest. I wonder, though. Perhaps the ones that crack up first are the ones who fix
on just one woman, and so give her unnatural power over them."

She scoffed. "Unnatural, Ari? It's the other way around. It's men
who deal in the unnatural. Wars, politics, money."

Harry gaped, vowing, ill-equipped as he was, never again to launch into theory. "Right," he said. "Maybe."

"One day, Ari," she said, "you'll know."

"I damned well will," he blustered, "and then *I'll* be the kaiser."

"And then, *mon grand,* rapture will be like a buttered muffin. By then, everything will be too easy, and the challenge will have gone out of life."

Inclined to complain today, he said "I'm not sure you haven't blinded me down there as well," and set his hands finger-touching on his chest. Away she marched in a crackle of starched linen, unwilling to argue with a recent convert.

He was slowly learning to reassemble his body, since his eye wound had unsettled everything else, creating new relationships: new tensions, new alliances. He would never have believed it, but after an hour or two of being put on anew his bandage felt heavy, sagging and cumbersome, pulling his eyebrows down toward his cheeks. As a result, he was constantly shoving it upward from an imagined droop; up and up it went until the eye sockets came into view and the clandestine light that he no longer reveled in slid over the hurt part of his face, and the eyes in their nacelles did nothing for him at all. Harry sensed he was lighter, less bulky, and decided that food you could not see did not nourish you. Nowadays, when he had speared the morsel, he brought his fork close to his nose and inhaled; the aroma was always better than the taste, but that was no doubt because he was accustomed to army fare and this was French food, the best cuisine in the world, at least for those brought up on it. He missed his bread and bacon dip, the bully beef, the metallic-tasting tea. Here he got coffee, eggs and ham, soufflés and baguettes: delicious, but in a profound sense alienating—food for a toff, he thought. There was something else wrong with it: It was peacetime food, and, unless the war had suddenly ended (he envisioned a separate peace signed by France and Belgium while the British went on fighting), inappropriate, as if life was going on as usual while the cream of manhood was mashing itself into fertilizer not twenty miles away. He had thought of refusing such food, and of encouraging his fellow-wounded to do likewise; but what the hell, he thought, we might as well tuck in while we can. No telling when, in the dead of night, with our nightshirts flapping around our rear ends, we'll have to get out of here on the run, and only the blind ones know the way.

There had been a blinded nurse behind some screens: a critical demonstration of war's futility. Harry had asked to be led to her, had spoken and touched her hand, then placed a kiss on her arm, all without so much as a sigh from the Belgian nurse, who had other head wounds too. Today she was not there, Fabienne told him: died during the night. A soldier was already in the bed.

Harry was still waiting for the American doctor to brave the Atlantic and see him; but Harry was impatient for everything.

"Take it," a young corporal told him, "take it in twat."

Harry was puzzled and said so.

"Like you was a twat, wide open, see, sarge."

No, he couldn't see it, but he enjoyed the expression's bluntness. They all envied him, most of all the hairpin he found under his pillow one morning and returned to her with courtly elaborateness. "Or I could pick my teeth with it."

"No fear," she told him. "In this country teeth're rarer than cognac." Eventually Hilly would see him, no doubt escorted by Kath Kent or that woman who took Hilly to the music exams—the chaperone—and she would be polite, but it would be clear from her tone that years together had been canceled, the years to come had been shifted to the Bernard Ditchers, men with a bankbook over each eye, a dustbin lid in front of their private parts. Perverse as he could often be, even to the extent of openly saying he'd rather fight alongside the Germans than the French or the Belgians, Harry held on to something sensible, counseling himself: Steady, lad, steady. The Bernard Ditchers will be feeling so guilty once the war's done they'll have jobs galore for the likes of me. Eminently qualified for a job in civilian life: dead shot with Vickers machine gun; much experience of escorting officers on reconnaissance in no-man's-land; capable of living on mud, soil, or whatever's trapped in the seams of a sandbag. And blind too. Excellent references. Young, obliging, ready to salute. Why, he said, I could run a first-class brothel in the city after what I've learned in here. It's called the laying on of hands preparatory to the shoving home of you know what. I could handle and guide stallions on the farms, a bicycle lamp in one hand, the enormous cod of the horse in the other. I can hardly wait: My mother *will* be proud.

The blind man, Clive was thinking, feels life from the wrong side, if indeed life's a tapestry. In a way he was fretting to be off and about, getting the disaster on the road as we say in the States; but he would have been just as happy to stay in the Red Cross hospital, learning to adjust himself to a more and more refined sense of doom. He would taper off into nothingness, cherishing such words as "dim" and "gloom" and gradually forgetting what a plate of eggs and ham looked like. At that moment, overcome by both memory and memory augmented, Clive would have given his own eyes to Harry to save him the gradual dismantling that came with such a wound, its absoluteness becoming central and his entire biological life grouping itself around it. It was an idle gesture, as Clive knew, knowing the outcome, being the boy, the son, the seed, the heir—a laugh, as Harry was always an Elizabethan, spending all, with not a shred of the Victorian hoarder in sight, whereas Hilly had been brought up to respect everything: the piano tuner's ear; the ball of hair, shiny and hollow, plucked from the stomach of a dead cow; the trousers press that made knife edges girls kept away from; the sustaining pedal that seemed to let sound stretch out and walk. If Harry would only sit in a chair by the fire, Hilly would remind him of all the world, from the forget-me-not to rosemary for remembrance, from the names of the local rivers, to the names of the local railway stations from Exington (LNER: London and North-Eastern Railway) to Reresby (LMS: London, Midland and Scottish), locomotives apple green and maroonish red.

WHATEVER signal the village had awaited, it heeded Hilly's with hooters and drums, bells and whistles. It was like prewar days, when so-called jazz bands, dressed in black-and-white tunics vaguely nautical, marched from the rectory to the Top End, blowing kazoos and followed by small boys who blew on combs wrapped in tissue paper. Hilly and her street band played burlier stuff, and thus tapped a font of smothered feeling, from bereavement to the jubilation of the soft-job brigade, as yet another day passed and the village went unscathed. Now the band spilled out into the roadway, blocking what little horse-drawn traffic there was, and the effect was that of an ovation in front of a palace window from which a dictator, a king, almost any bedecked portentous worthy, would soon emerge to flatter and harangue. But it was a serious-faced young woman who popped her head out, calling something quite lost, the cessation of her piano unnoticed amid the din. Seeing her, they blew and drummed all the harder, perhaps inciting her to leap toward them, perhaps inviting her to go back and play that much louder. The woman with the iron foot soared up to meet her, lashed to a ladder manhandled by half a dozen middle-aged men with stuttering feet: Mrs. Featherstonehaugh rising from a nonexistent witch's fire, her metal boot gleaming in the sunlight, not something to play unless she banged it against a thundersheet or a piece of corrugated roof.

Hilly bawled at her, at them, something impolite and unworthy of a Fitzalan. She wanted to play in peace, mustering new conundrums from the depths created by the sustaining pedal. Mrs. Featherstonehaugh swayed and reeled atop her ladder, midpoint between being a victim and graduating into leadership, wetting herself in huge releases that ran down her legs and the ladder, her mouth by now working incessantly to produce a costive froth. She was yammering something, but so were all the players, and then, thanks to drunken shoves from below, she was at the window, face to face with Hilly, whom she failed to recognize.

"I'm coming in," she cried, but Hilly at once withdrew and began to haul the window down, trapping Mrs. F.'s arms, which made her scream above the general racket. Hilly opened the window again as the top of the ladder barged in at a sharp angle that jammed it and stranded Mrs. Featherstonehaugh and her black greasy coat. Down below, unwatched, Reggie Jessup had begun to hammer the foot of the ladder as best he could. But he managed to hit wood by aiming at gaps, and roared his delight until trampled underfoot by those who hauled the ladder down before it smashed the glass. At the window appeared Hilly's mother, gaunt and ghostly, a poker in one hand, hot but not red-hot, her beaker of stout in the other, toothlessly threatening them with Ben the Great Dane, scalding water, hot lead, fresh offal, and rotting blood. She sipped her stout, beat the poker against the ladder, shoved it into Mrs. Featherstonehaugh's streaming face and effectively branded her there and then right in the chops, which produced a scream heard well above the crescendo of the mob. The ladder slipped down, Mrs. Featherstonehaugh tottered backward, then went down with it, howling, and Hilly's mother slammed the window shut on the scene of yet another disgrace.

Hilly saw her mother's haggard, harassed face assume its most appalling hue, as if the stroke were on its way at last, snow and soot gathering in a vast aerial bunker of cumulus cloud; but it was only an old woman in a barely contained frenzy, violet with fuss, the rings under her eyes bulging forward, a French-polisher's brown.

"Music!" said Hilly, making light of it.

"Uproar, child," her mother said. "Don't you know the difference?" Hilly at once withdrew her attempt to dismiss the goings-on outside and drew her mother's attention to it all, bit by bit, to vex her and drive her away.

"All because you play, madam," her mother added, "with the window open. Which you began to do for your romantic soldier, the blind Moxon boy. If you played in privacy, none of this would happen. You have made an exhibition of yourself. Pleasures denied, hussy."

"*What* pleasures, Mother?" Hilly asked. The hand was across her face and traveling through distance when Hilly realized she'd been slapped, there in the music room. Never a room given over to punishment, but, at best, since it faced west, it was a room for spanieling—lying on the rugs in the full spill of the evening sun—at worst a room in which a careless hand received the rebuke of the piano teacher, most recently Mrs. Barnaby Wainfan, who used a frail tap with a pipe cleaner, no one knew why.

"Recite the pleasures," Hilly's mother snapped, her mind as far from spanieling as could be, when Hilly and her brothers just lay there and gurgle-giggled, tickling one another and shooting their legs high in the air to ride an invisible upside-down bicycle.

"Little Douglas," Hilly began. "Big George and big Thurrie. Serving in the shop. Lifting beef in the back yard. Cooking for everyone. Filling Papa's pipe—"

"Said without relish."

"Done without thanks, ever," Hilly said with tense defiance. "Slap me again, Mother."

No slap, but the screwed-up face fluttered, the old lady sank sideways at carefully planned catching speed, and Hilly had another carcass to lift, although her innards told her not to try it, to let the old hag drop with a thud.

"Caught you that time," Hilly said, wincing at the pain in her stomach.

No answer. The poker had rolled away, the etched glass had ended up under the piano, the moment had subsided, though Hilly wondered if she could ever do anything bad enough to make her mother strike her with the poker. Had she really rammed it into the face of the woman with the iron foot? Burning her? Here came Papa, ever affable, voluminously attuned to the angry postures of his beset wife. "Right bloody row I'd humane-kill them all wouldn't I if I was a nastier chap than I am." He said this in his habitual unpunctuated huff, never meaning any harm, never doing any, but keeping up the bluff hectoring front in case somebody suspected what a softie he was behind it. "Than I am," he said again, as ever completing himself with an echo.

"Is she well or is she poorly? She's no good standing up and she's hardly the Expeditionary Force sitting down. She is a woman who like the nineteenth century has done its best."

Hilly waited, as they all had learned to do, though they might just as easily have learned not to. "Done its best," he said, and it was over. He picked his wife up like a paper tassel and carried her across the landing to her private room and the canopied bed with its satin-wrapped bucket to spit into, in its bottom a half inch of Izal, a kind of limewater.

Some day, Hilly told herself, he's going to saw her up, chop off her arms and legs, treat her as a beef. Her father was too powerful merely to be cutting up cows; he needed buffalo and bison, musk-ox and Clydesdales. They needed him in Belgium and France, heaving those ramparts down, demolishing the hills of sandbags behind which the enemy hid. Yet, and this amazed her, he had a tenderer soul than she, not that he was much given to tears, which he always construed as an apology for not feeling more sympathy. He knew how everybody felt, even if he gave no sign. He just knew that most folk were not up to the catastrophic job of daily living. He had seen so many dumb animals hit the concrete floor of his slaughterhouse that he knew about being doomed, about the murderer's eye on yours, and he allowed himself an enormous range of gentleness. He always assumed that people were hurting, never mind who, and Hilly had sometimes thought of calling him Papa Appassionata: a fancy name, true, but something to honor him by. What did he say? "You all hurt, I know, I know. Now, which one of you wants mothering first?" They all waited.

"Mothering first." That cleared the ground, and the first child to be comforted lay across his giant paunch, face buried in the charcoal-gray waistcoat, hearing the low cluck of his watch as if it were his heart.

Whenever her mother came after her, slapping and chiding, Hilly got that old skeleton feeling; she was a see-through, a structure as open as an umbrella stand, fretted and slotted. That was when the flesh lofted away from her body toward the war, the shop, and the slaughterhouse. When her father quizzed her in his usual bumbling way she felt more intact, less exposed, knowing she could get away with a fib if she had to; he did not care that much, so long as they thought him the kindest Papa in the world, the only one to smooth them down with honey and cream.

When she played, though, everything changed; she flourished un-parented: music's daughter, warmed by an arc-light powered by self-esteem as much as by electricity. Her head sank forward and sideways like the Virgin of Albert cathedral, festooned in a web of combed waves, golden and taupe. Her chest split open to receive an ornate intrusion of the supplest ivory decorated with Balkan fronds. Lower down, she felt a solid mermaid tail, slithering up warm and spiced until she had the creature's head behind her mouth and the fin between her legs, peeping out like the famous winged orchid of Lichtenstein, more than once mistaken for an elliptical-winged butterfly sitting on itself. Hilly was capable of the most amazing special states, of metamorphoses all the rarer for being wholly unobservable—though she had recounted them at school and actually coached other girls in the preparations for change: deep, intoxicated breathing; the tensing of all body muscles to the breaking point; pressure of top of left foot on rear of right heel. The body, she taught, was there to be exploited, made to serve the soul, and she initiated dozens of them into feeling like a fish, seeing like a bird, touching as a slug or a snail, going to sleep as a deer, a stoat, a newt. It was during piano playing, however, that she taught herself the most advanced maneuvers, as she winced and flinched with the music; not simply compensating with the rest of her body for an arm thumped down or lifted high in a bar's rest, but elaborating the tension felt into rigid twists of her frame. It was as if her hands dealt with one language, her body with quite another. Was the one connected to the other? She was never sure, but she hoped so; she would not have enjoyed writhing and fidgeting to some tempo, some lilt, not within the music at all but merely the physical by-product of its being played, akin to the mess on the palette after the painting is done. She wanted all parts of her to be in accord when she played: the music dominant, the body the inspired executant, all in tune.

She adored change, keeping in reserve for her broodings on it a slew of special words, to be said in a special way, from *crescendo* to *fe-cun-dit-y* (which word she used most of all), from *growth* (said as *grow-eth*) to *swell*. Change safeguarded her, but so did magic, which was change at its most inspired. Soon, she hoped, a shimmering beast, a griffin or a vampire, would come and gather her up. If not a griffin with gold-leaf eyelids, then a guzzling vampire, harmless but staunch. In her desk in the music room she kept an eraser cut in the shape of a vampire's head; she had had it two years, nicknaming it Old Toothy, and liking to set him on top of her papers as the guardian of her ideas; as she used him to rub out words, horses, dogs, and clouds, his chin became smaller and smaller, so that now she was rubbing with the bottom of his lower lip, and the sharp points of those canines had long since vanished. Sometimes Old Toothy had the face of war: scarlet, bulge-eyed, mouth thickly and asymmetrically contorted. He too changed. He was only rubber, after all. From time to time she had equipped his bulbous eyes with pupils, to humanize him a bit, but she had never liked the result, so her little red rubberhead had eyes of an opaque blue glaze, eyes that were all pupil, as with the dreaded *shf* disease that came to the purpure-dyers of lower Mesopotamia, who had fecklessly rubbed dye into their eyes, blotting out the whites. If Hilly found the world malleable, amazed as a small child at what the body could turn a three-course dinner into, she found herself similar, knowing, though, that the mind could change the mind and was the most fertile crescent of all.

DOWNSTAIRS that evening, with the shop closed, the piano's lid down, her mother fast asleep like someone poleaxed by lightning, and Ben by the fire across her father's feet, she heard a knock on the door and found Mrs. Featherstonehaugh standing there, mouth wide, her index finger aimed at it. Had her mother truly pokered her in the mouth? What the woman said was uncouth and labored, but it was clear she was demanding some kind of restitution for the damage done her that day. Had it been the era of ice, there would have been an obvious remedy; instead, Hilly, after a moment's thought, went into the pantry and came out with a long pork sausage that she popped into the proffered mouth. She saw the fit was good and closed the door. When the knock came again, Ben charged it with all his force, winding himself a little, but putting the woman with the iron foot to flight. Hilly and her recumbent brothers heard her chink-scrape away, wondering if she had begun to chew the raw sausage, and began to gossip about the new rowdiness in Exington, all brought on by Hilly's piano. "We'll get Edith to sing," George said. "All we need is a choir." All they needed, Hilly told them, was peace and quiet in which to play the piano as it should be played. From now on she would close the window, she told them, anyway until Harry came back. She knew the month and had it written on a piece of waxed paper from the shop, on whose matt surface the pencil's lead deposit gleamed a humbled silver. He was coming home, and that meant two things: More of him was coming, and so was less. At this point in an old-fashioned nineteenth-century novel she would have been unable to take a breath; but Hilly was a twentieth-century woman, even if only by a decade and a half, so she kept calm and told herself the time to get worked up would be when the week, the day, were fixed, and she might be able to count the number of breaths or heartbeats she would have before Harry came back in triumph.

RECOVERING these halcyon days of Hildred his mother, Clive shivered with delight, having got most of it correct. That was exactly how the old Fitzalan family lived: kindly toward others, but only to a point, after which came magnificent tribal things such as homework at the big teak table, each child with a pile of books that grew taller over the years, and the huddle on the rug with Ben, the real center of it being Douglas, however, whom they hugged to death to make up for what an older mother had not been able to leak into him. Without Thurrie, however, the huddle wasn't quite right; and Hilly thought it would have to oust Douglas for Harry when Harry came marching home in front of the black-and-white jazz band or even the raucous motley of today. Why did piano music rouse them all so much? They could hardly be that sensitive to it. Any kind of music would have set them off, she decided. No, Clive thought, Rhubarb running around, some chronic frustration in the village (mud- or manure-slinging), would have been just as appropriate. It was summer. The schools had just closed. There was a heady yellowness in the air. People were fed up, he thought, with being fed up. And Hilly, the haughty princess of this revel, was a woman poised to attempt something—embracing Harry's return to village life—she might not be able to manage. In characteristic Fitzalan fashion, the next day George and Douglas and Hilly blindfolded themselves for an hour to see how Harry would feel. Hating it, they shouted loud warnings and semihysterical cries of reassurance, even sliding a garter over Ben's eyes, which he soon pawed off. Mutiny was in the atmosphere. A blinded pal was coming home, to be made much of, to be led to and through familiar haunts, and they felt themselves trembling for him, trying to list mentally things they must no longer do. There would be no more fancy dress, would there? No more parties of that kind? A brand-new orange strap would link him to Ben, and Ben would scout for him. No more bats and balls. No more photographs. No more hilarious handwritten messages passed from one to another.

Clive could feel his mother heaving with sobs, then taking a deep breath to give her strength to do it. He heard her practicing lines of questionable tact: "Can you feel the weather on your face?" "What's for dinner?" Only a huddle on the rug in the dark would help, and then Harry's much deeper voice, his postwar voice, telling them all about it for ever and ever, while God worked out how many times he could tell his tale before everyone got bored, and then he would be reduced to telling the village, at long last Rhubarb and Reggie Jessup, Mrs. Gloistius Featherstonehaugh, Kath Kent, and the rest of the rank and file. One day, perhaps, he would throw his head back, roar with pain, and tear off his bandages, letting them see how he felt about the twin scabs in his face. And he would tell them about the raiders who, with blackened faces and small bottles of rum, dashed through the enemy wire and took a few prisoners for interrogation. He had lived his life as part of a different race, blown up for love, for gall, for pride, for wanting honor too soon, like a boy of ten composing his autobiography. My dad, Clive thought, wondering if he should whimper for him: Can my father see me now? Will he approve? What sign, such as a reverse salute, might he make? Which was the less respectful: imaging his dead father coming back from the dead or his live mother falter toward them?

The rowdyism in the passageway between Fitzalans' butchers and Nettleship's confectioners continued. Musical instruments that never had been musical instruments now caught the light of day. Folk drummed on lettuce boxes, old coconut shells, sheet-iron fireguards, and lengths of defective piping (whose assorted holes gave each length an individual pitch and tone). Hilly played on behind the closed window. Dogs joined in, brought to bark and yelled at until they did. The village was having an harmonic nervous breakdown, and only just in time.

ONE MORNING, Fabienne Binche seemed in a hurry and her habitually seductive voice, in which languor competed with bustle, had an edge of pure officiousness. Dr. Woodbine was coming to see Harry and give an opinion, so first they wanted Harry awake and then Harry anesthetized. It would take all day, or so Harry surmised, sniffing, as he had learned to, the noble American at loin level, and discovering from the whiff of smegma that Woodbine went uncircumcised in the world and was none too punctilious about washing himself. I'm like a bloody dog, Harry thought. They always come and sniff at you right there. Then he was all shudders and tremors, with the pain slicing clean through his head. The area around his eyes felt like hot soot. His nose oozed blood all the time. His face was being tugged by a puppeteer far away, the lines connected by fishhooks. When it eased, Harry began to recollect the velvet seat of Hilly's music stool, with its lovely fume of lemon furniture polish and combusted groin sweat: not Hilly's only, but of players and Chooners and examiners since 1800, all those innocent unfragrant bottoms sitting it out. Ten minutes later Harry passed out and Dr. Woodbine began in earnest, removing more and more tiny bits of shrapnel. A dapper colonel entered the ward and, with permission from Fabienne Binche, left a decoration in a packet on each man's bed, bestowing on each bandage a kiss. There was no speech, no music, no fuss. Had Harry through some miracle been able to see him, he would have recognized von Kaiserstein, the vanished enemy, now refurbished as de Yturri, but whom Harry in his right mind would have recast as Pierre de César. What was this decoration? Awarded to officers for gallantry and to noncommissioned officers for professional services, it was the Belgian Order of Leopold I: plum ribbon, brown metal swords and crown, green leaves upon which sat a white enamel cross and the legend *"L'Union Fait La Force."* Rather than depending from the ribbon, the award was pinned to it. Harry missed his kiss, and a second glimpse of Kaiser-stein-Yturri's white shirt. Harry's eyes, like those of the other seven NCO's in the ward, had been decorated, and in fine fashion. No one ever queried the Belgian colonel's bona fides, or the fact that he was wearing this same decoration himself. A true Proteus of war, he slipped in and out of uniforms, from one front line to the other, from headquarters to headquarters, taking note with fastidious aversion and, periodically, collecting notes from such of his agents as Sister Fabienne Binche, to whom wounded soldiers talked impetuously. Clive smiled at this index to his father's busy war.

NO VILLAGE could keep up the pace Exington and its revelers had set, if revel rather than riot is what its impromptu musicians had in mind. The rowdy gatherings went on, but only once or twice a week, got going by Rhubarb in the street as summer blew hot and the ice-cream cart creaked to and fro, its yellow custard never cold enough. The best technique was to wait for the jingle of the cart's bells, then dash out into the street with a glass. What Hilly liked to do was cool a jug and take that, get it half-filled, then pour milk into it and make a paste, which she then set on the piano on a thick doily and ate with a tablespoon. Later in life she would advance to one-pound slabs of white ice cream situated on a dinner plate and eaten with knife and fork as if it were something hearty made from a dead animal. On she played, in the summer of 1917, no longer connected with the buffoons in the street, although now and then she caught a bar of tambourine or tuba, wondering if Kath Kent still took the children of the well-to-do down to bell-ringing at the church. Un-married, Kath would always remain so, never having had time to meet young men, always ferrying, fetching, and carrying, her role with children pretty much that of Rhubarb with rumors.

Hilly was always planning her declaration of independence, never quite knowing how to manage it—the piano would have to go with her, all her clothes and books and toys, as well as Douglas, who, although four years younger, was now surpassing George in metallurgy at the local technical college. But how would she do it? By enlisting the aid of Mrs. Barnaby Wainfan, whom folk credited with a raffish past in Liverpool music halls; Kath Kent, the ever-ready; and anyone else able-bodied enough to lift and unload? Would it be London? She saw herself trekking off south to set up shop or house with Harry, but Harry was only going to be another burden, she could see that. It was like a game: lose George, win Harry. Go back to square one. It was serious and appalling: She had to work out if she really had the courage to adopt a blinded man, never mind how fond she might be of him, and virtually become his Saint Bernard, always pointed out as an icon of female self-sacrifice: a wonderful pianist, but . . . Did she wish to sink without trace in the second decade of the twentieth century? Did she want to be as obscure yet as well-known as the little heroine of Gene Stratton Porter's novel about coming of age in Indiana? No, the book was real: that *Girl of the Limberlost* was a legend in America, a cipher in England. What was Indiana, to whom? You couldn't be much farther away from home than that, unless locked into some long-suffering role in one of Mr. Kipling's stories. She knew she wanted to devour certain of the usual formulas; she wanted love declared to her with pounding rhetoric, her swain on one knee, perspiring, her father ready in the offing to huff and puff until all seemed lost, when he would relent with bombastic self-denial, like a tree ripping its own bark away. All that. Yet she also wanted things not abstract at all, such as applause, fame, and the friendship of the gifted. She was still pondering the impossibility of both when the second erupted upon her.

Requests had come for her to play concerts in the surrounding villages, as well as in Sheffield and Chesterfield: nothing too stuck-up, mind you, but, as some of the letters said, any Chopiny sort of thing, with a tune. She agreed, brushed up what she regarded as her FFFF repertoire (a Fair Field Full of Folk), as distinct from her Royal Academy of Music one, and took it to the outskirts, playing in a manner more exaggerated and sentimental than usual, laying it on a bit thick, but infiltrating a little stern Bach into the program, just to show them music wasn't finished. Some evenings Edith went and sang with her, seriously quizzing her after Mrs. Barnaby Wainfan had fallen asleep in the coach.

"What will you do when he's here?" Edith suspected she herself, loyal only to a point, would flee.

"Take him in charge" came the heroic answer. "See to him. His mother won't. She *would,* but she doesn't know how."

"But—marriage?"

"He's not asked me," Hilly told her. "How could he? He was only a child when he volunteered, and now he's a—he's a sergeant. It's all going to take time. I'll ply him with elder flowers, wild thyme, lemon balm, hyssop, sage, dandelion and burdock, all the *natural* things, until he's ready. I'll give him back to nature, and perhaps nature will show him the way. Girls are much more advanced than boys, anyway."

"Yes, that's what George tells me when he takes me out to collect birds' eggs—thrush, sparrow, skylark, mainly—and instead of bird's-nesting he forces me up against the crumbly north wall of Brunts' apple orchard. It doesn't do me much good. It would if George had never heard about it."

"You leave my brother alone," Hilly said, "It'll be your fault, not his, if something happens."

Edith sang something Italian and seditious under her breath, and woke Mrs. Wainfan, whom only music could stir.

By September, Hilly had played two dozen concerts. Popular in the vicinity but unpopular at home for deserting her chores, she had become the official personification of girls who yearned for their gentlemen to return. The money from her concerts went to a soldiers' benefit, and her fame went not to her head but to her mouth. She began to speak, genteel impetuousness. Women left behind and committed to scorn the soft-job brigade showed up at her concerts, having

little else to do. "Drink to me only with thine eyes" she openly
dedicated in her mellow, stern voice to "the Bernard Ditchers," on
one occasion, after a tiny toot of stout, ending her preamble more
forcefully than she'd planned: "So it is for those who still have their
eyes and are not bleeding second after second into a sloppy pad, and
still have their arms and legs." Then she thought of George, who
wouldn't have minded soldiering, stopped talking, and began to play,
nonetheless having made her point.

"That was your Ditcher speech," Edith told her.

"Hang Ditcher," she scoffed. "I'll do a Hereward instead." Her
tenderest piano essays brought them to tears, more than all the Sunday
morning sermons, pious editorials, or leaflets passed out at the post
office. It was she, who in her deliberately lento moments, told them
in full about the carnage, the waste, the horror, the indefensible
brutality of the war, drawing a clear line between music and butchery,
between a butcher's shop in Exington and a butcher's shop occupying
the whole of Belgium and France. When she and Edith, two virtuoso
young women fast gaining in public poise, performed Frank Bridge's
Two Songs for Soprano and Piano, written in this very 1917, the audience wasn't quite sure what it was hearing, but it was enough to make
them dismal, and some wondered where and how the two young
women managed to find such songs. Mrs. Barnaby Wainfan was the
answer. Thanks to her well-connectedness, she eventually got her
hands on the next three Bridge songs, making a total of five, and
thanks to her Autolycus-like talent for nosing out scores in the Sheffield music shops Hilly began to assemble an unusual, if somewhat
pirated repertoire. Speaking began to frighten her less, and her hands
kept wanting to improvise; all the time she wanted to play with an
orchestra, becoming submerged no doubt, but making such mighty
music as to daunt the birds.

Looking back on his mother's efflorescence as pianist and performer, Clive at last decided she had done a Mrs. Miniver for World

War I, at least in her own area, mustering the hearts of grieving women, stirring men with something less than a battle call, but stirring them all the same. Between Mrs. Miniver's champion rose and Hilly Fitzalan's bravura piano, there was little difference. Both were epically English, incorrigibly wholesome, and a mite snooty. He marveled at Hilly's grasp of the arena, her knowing whom to insult and whom to make weep. It must have been the ghost of Bach behind her, Bach the blind, at last recalled to duty. For a while, he thought, she had decided to give up everything for music, even Harry, at last making the break; but young Douglas must have swayed her without saying a word. She saw his face and knew she was doomed to remain an Exingtonian, at least until he was able to scoot off on his own, into his own Xanadu. Something in her reached farther and farther away, her arm elastic, but it always came snapping back to home and beauty, as if the outside world, which she had seen and excelled in, were not real after all. Could the chief nourisher at life's feast, he thought, be also its Scheherazade? She played fluently, heartfully, and with nimble brio while Edith sang from operas without ever being in one. Art was ablaze and uncontrollable in his mother in those days, and Clive lingered in them, a fan, a reverent peeping son.

Beckoned on by Harry, Clive allowed his mind to move toward the target of seeing, a literal target with bull, inner, and outer, except that it was no longer one of seeing but of exorbitant pain. It was almost peaceful in the center but agonizing at the outskirts, with a spectrum of sensation ranging from tingling and prickling to hot needle and acid drop by drop. Dr. Woodbine had finished, but the legacy of his ministrations went on, converting Harry from casual hedonist to convulsing victim as the anesthetic wore off and he began clutching, rubbing, trying to thumb both eyes into submission. Woodbine had removed as much shrapnel as he could, and he had also scraped the insides of the lids. Harry wanted to be unconscious again as soon as possible, but no oblivion came to put out the caustic star shells that dominated his vision. Fabienne Binche came and went, almost inured, but feeling dried and pointless, giving him what relief she could while Harry prayed for green water, cold; for warm vinegar; for ice; for raw steak; for a ball striking his eye hard enough to knock it out: a hundred-mile-an-hour ball with sharp stitching to slice the eyelids. After the routine euphemism, Harry had relaxed and lain back, believing in the words offered him: discomfort, some pressure, a bit of a push. If this was the price of cure, he wanted to go back blind to the front as soon as possible, complete with eyebath and bottle of boracic. Exhorted not to rub, he waved both hands madly in the air in front of him, manufacturing a draft, spending energy that might have gone into pain. Clive thought of all the bothersome lotions ever squirted into his own eyes, such as sulfacetamide sodium, but they were as nothing compared to what burned his father. All through the night, held down by Sister Binche, Harry tried not to weep, heaved his head about and clenched his teeth, sank his nails into her hands and held his breath. By dawn he had fallen into an exhausted sleep, unable to attend to his suffering any more, little knowing that the optic nerve in his right eye had been freed of metal and might even begin to function again.

Clive, who knew the outcome, held the ghost of his father tight, resubjecting him to the experience but, in some shared and fortunate interim, healing him at speed, wanting to get him home, back into the right clutches, away from his Red Cross Venusberg. Was it osmosis that made his eyes tear whenever he thought of his father? Grief? Shame? Taught as a youth how to do it—by his father, of course—he applied fingertips to his eyeballs in their pouches of skin and gently maneuvered, going north, south, west, east, with each tip, pushing gently against the curvature of either eyeball, then described slow circles until the rhythm and the slow rotary motion had lulled him into a trance that could never have been his father's until years after. No one was better than Dr. Woodbine, that huge man with snowdrift hair growing in and from his ears, breath that smelled like scallions, loins that—or so Harry thought—needed a scald in a bidet. Never mind, the man, from Baltimore, had come 3,456 miles, as Clive put it: no, farther, because he had come to Belgium, beyond Southampton, scheduled for an operation each day. The ward soon filled with writhing, gasping, hissing surgical successes who created, new every morning, an indecorous moan as background for everything else, such as food spilled or thrown, glasses smashed, sheets torn off the bed and thrown vainly across the new head bandages as if to smother what was blazing underneath. Dr. Woodbine sapped these blinded soldiers of lechery all right. He himself ate enormous meals both before and after he operated, devouring fried potatoes and thick grilled ham. He must have had problems of his own, gastric and cardiac, but he never mentioned them and continued to operate, moving like a dancer, sucking in his paunch the instant he approached the patient's head.

Fabienne made much of the Belgian decorations that hung from the foot of the beds, explaining this or that facet; but no one paid her much heed, certainly not those in recovery, not even those awaiting Woodbine, who took the trouble to come in and view the decorated beds himself, saying it was swell, all swell. But she gathered that the blinded men weren't Belgians, did not think of themselves as Belgians, were unhappy to be taken for Belgium's allies, did not wish to be in Belgium, and couldn't find it on the map. When von Kaiserstein returned, complete with ambulance, Sister Fabienne Binche of the erotically adroit hands and the ever-wet zone took her leave and went eastward, her job well done, a Florence Nightingale in wolf's clothing, all hearts broken behind her, and many male virgins converted to what some of them called the old knee-trembler. She considered going off with a souvenir of each man, a hair here, a splash there, but dismissed the idea as coy; she contented herself with a kiss, and collected up the medals before departing—von Kaiserstein liked to economize, and his job was far from done.

Except for this. As a nurse genuinely impressed by Woodbine and his Baltimore ways, Binche handed him a Belgian medal out of something approaching reverence; he took it, but promptly put it back on Harry's bed after she had gone, the purpose of her departure being ostensibly to pick up medical supplies. The other medals went away with her, fireflies of valor, to be temporarily bestowed elsewhere, say a hundred miles farther on. As Woodbine told it, Harry became confused:

"Gave me ya medal, son, she did. These nurses. You got it back. Here, feel."

"What medal?" Harry asked. "Did you say the Binch has gone?"

"She'll be back. You got your medal right here now at the foot of the bed. Funny dame: She took all the others, maybe to get them polished. You got the first one back, I guess. These Belgians, they sure ain't French."

Harry was dreaming of Hilly playing tennis in a wide-brimmed gray hat, from which a mauve bird lifted off, aghast, each time she struck the ball. Harry and Hilly would go for walks again together, newly taken with each other. The ball in the dream was a disk of light sent from America by sea, a gift from the westering sun of San Francisco, a flash from the heart of things, from the place where all medals melted, all bandages came off.

ASTOUNDED by the needle's point that fast became a hole made by a knitting needle, then by an awl, Harry felt generous toward the source of light for not having gone away. Painful as it was to do it, he squinted and squinted, half expecting darkness to win out, but nothing went wrong, although the creatures he saw undulated and sagged, billowing and feebly signaling. These were the people who had been alongside him all the time, watching him watch nothing. Where was Fabienne Binche, then? A total apparition? They told him she had been seconded, which sounded vaguely obscene, but it meant she had been sent elsewhere, nobody was quite sure where. So he had never seen her, and was unlikely to do so, to remain forever haunted by a lubricious phantom of the everlasting night. But seeing again, never mind how mottled and unsteady a world, dulled the ache; it was as if the world had been given back to him. He knew that craven and craving depravities took place in the dark when heart lost hope and body shed its pride. He saw a world little changed, except for Dr. Woodbine's pink cheeks and his huge hands, which had been as intimate with Harry's eyes and their tender sockets as Binche had been with his genitals. Had he grown up? Who was he to formulate such a question? Looking at his face in the steel shaving mirror, he saw the same young, questing Turk, serious but even-tempered, more Scottish than Irish, he thought, having a darker tinge, a steadier gaze, a promise of something stern. It was his father's face minus the waxed mustache and its sharp, tapering points. Harry's mustache, shaved away by the nurses, had been a sergeant's, allowed luxuriance to age a boy; and he was glad to see it gone as he no longer had men to command, no Vickers, no revolver, no maps, no bully beef. He was a convalescent, that was all, but he had had an extraordinary blindness, led into riot by an invisible siren whom he might just have invented.

When he opened the package, however, he knew she had been real, for there, stitched elegantly above the right-angled Virgin of Albert, sat his name: Sergeant Ari Moxon, in red on pale blue, with the dates of his hospitalization: no message, no endearment, but the Virgin and her tower in full glorious thread. It was something to treasure, and perhaps something to hate. Each corner formed a half-cross as the two edges of the stitched frame continued about three inches outward, having intersected. Had it been rolled up, as for a cardboard tube, certificate-style, Harry might have squirreled it away under his pillow, or into his kit bag. Done up in a frame, however, it was a public object clamoring for a nail to hang on so as to announce itself and the feelings it embodied. A nurse had already hung it, and now, after showing him, she set it back for him to admire with his newfound eye, which of course meant he had little idea of how far away it was; and that matched his sense of Fabienne Binche, whom he now loathed for being gone, for not being there to watch him take the sampler's measure and delight in its contrasted threads. Couldn't she have waited? Just a day or two? There was something sneaky about her disappearance, as about the Belgian decoration presented him by the man who spirited his bedmate away. Who had told him it was a man with a monocle? A man obsessed with handing out medals? He could hardly believe it, having long ago consigned von Kaiserstein to the gallery of dead imposters. More than he needed to go on making love with Fabienne Binche, he needed to know all about her life. She had suddenly become worth knowing—ogling, following, eavesdropping upon. Could he but aim his blows, he would wallop her one in the face, breasts, and belly. Because she had had relations with other men in the ward, he desired her all the more, but his desire for knowledge was greater than that for her buxom, fluent parts. With his hesitant new eye he wanted to interrogate her, watch her doing all the abominable things she did without him, tasting and fondling other men as if she had no primary sweetheart stuck there in the nest of his blindness.

They were all blind, he told himself, except for Bicester pro-nounced Bister, who also had come back from the ravine of blindfold misery. When had she blown out the candle? When removed her underwear? When untrussed her six-footer's breasts? Had she come to him without makeup? How had her face been at moments of acutest pleasure, taking or receiving? What had she been? They showed him her photo, culled from the files, and she was hardly as he had imagined: drab as a clock, heavily mustached. Still, why no letter? Why just a sampler, mute as a blind man?

That afternoon he took the first of several sedatives for excitement brought on, most supposed, by seeing again. His semijubilant pres-ence upset the others so they moved him to a smaller ward of seeing men who had lost limbs and had a whole series of quite different complaints, none of which he heard. He wanted to see the past, the gone, the irrecoverable, almost wanted to sink back into the prickly oblivion he had assumed would be his for ever: Two black eyes and I make three—what rotten company they be, as the song said.

The talk was of London, the famous eye hospital, the resonant blue tunic he would have to wear and the red tie to flaunt the blood shed. And a white shirt. He grinned. Next thing, von Kaiserstein would be his new surgeon, and Sister Binche, restored to him, his nurse again. His sight seemed to be improving daily; the world was regaining its colors, its corrugations, its taper to the distance. Off went the telegram to Hilly and his mother, giving no details but telling them he could see and would soon be transferred to London, one of Dr. Woodbine's successes. From those days onward, Harry loved America, from which someone braving torpedoes and submarines had come as a midwife, delivering him all over again as a blue baby, able to go back to his competition essay and choose his topic: Write about being blinded or being in love. Either would take him a lifetime. Well, enormous thing, he told the sun, I'm not afraid of you any more; I shall never turn you down, and I wish you blazed all night. I can't get enough of you, sir, I am your batman and servant, your swain and your retainer. Take you for granted? Not I. I am more complete now. There is more of me worth having. Most folk only achieve 50 percent of what they could be; some, who go through the valley of the shadow (which includes joy past desiring too) get up to 75, don't they? And others, a very few, almost reach maximum for having guessed at something massive and unknown. They grow up just from the enormous effort of wondering what it is like to be complete. These are the big imaginers who never lie to themselves, who know that life feels incomplete without ever telling others what it is that's missing. They keep their ogres, their mermaids, to themselves, letting the presence of delusion fuel them. They never go into details; they accept it as the unknown familiar challenging them, making them abstemiously hope.

Where had that word come from? The officers' mess? He had said it all through his army years, telling the teetotalers and the drunkards, when they asked what he was, that he was abstemious, not an abstainer, one who never overdid it: until Nurse Binche. The image of her went with him everywhere, making him a craven dependent, preparing him for no other relationship because he had been uniquely savaged in the tender corms of his being. Henceforth Harry (or Ari) viewed the world as an accomplice with whom to commit an abominable act; he thought he had, deep within him, an untapped, untouched other self available on call like a trained spaniel, who would do his good behaving for him while the roué, or the desperado of the flesh, went his gruesome way, itching for vice, his heart full of shrapnel, his head full of rage. He had never known he needed that side of life, and here he was already deprived of it. For lack of sensuality, he would now have to push even harder into grave stateliness, or he would not have a life at all, and his fellow survivors would chide him for not showing the right degree of wholesome gratitude that all survivors came up with, as if bowing to the Almighty for choosing well. But he wanted to be Ari; he wanted to be Harry no more.

He should have stayed, Clive thought, in France or Belgium, but the army told him what to do; he couldn't volunteer his way out of this as he had volunteered his way in. He would no doubt have become a bum, at worst, or a diner-out *mutilé de guerre,* at best. But he would have had a chance to choose his life each day, going to the dogs, drinking the dregs, in a country where the stiff upper lip never existed. He should have gone to France so as to have no home to go to: a place to revel in, far from domesticity. He never wanted a son. He wanted Fabienne Binche, his nymph.

NOT ALLOWED on deck during the Channel crossing, Harry practiced looking at people and getting used to having a single eye patch; he learned to resist the temptation to tug the patch away, then let his hand ride it back at the limit of the elastic's tension. What anyone saw while the patch was off he never knew, but he fancied they concluded it was raw flesh and lacerated white. He felt a bit wild nowadays, blooded by Fabienne Binche and reprieved by Dr. Clement Woodbine. The war was behind him, along with the worst of civilization; and what he did from now on would be his own business.

"What happened to *you,* son?" It was a familiar question already, to which he answered, mostly: "Lost two eyes, got one back."

"Well, you are a lucky bugger, aren't you. Lopsided for the rest of your life!" Harry sniffed and looked away, far out to sea. Life from now on was going to be the always promised wonder: no more deprivation, waiting, slump. He had done his share and could now count on living off the fat of the land—not that he thought there was any such thing as justice; he simply believed in some arithmetical balance to things. After all, he wouldn't be of much use in a war, but the war didn't have to end for him to be of use on the home front. Yes, Clive thought, he believed in a world that made sense. No Buddhist, certain that the world is mainly disappointment, Harry actually got his medal, never mind how deviously, by whatever fluke. Now *that* was a decoration, the real thing, like a piece of the sun chariot falling from heaven.

Harry had been gone three years, but had aged ten without looking it, and now he had to confront Hilly, who simply had become better and better at the piano: a virtuoso celebrity operating out on the fringe of the family, almost energized enough to break free. Clive wondered if they could not have set up house together in London, then remembered he was thinking of 1917; besides, Harry had to live in the Eye Hospital. Nonetheless, Clive wanted them together— wanted them to have been together on alien turf, fleeing, loving, and he backed into them through history until he found a happy pair to come from. It was these days his mother never spoke about, though she had a perfect memory for sitting by the Thames, having a lager together in a riverside pub, eating fish and chips from newspaper in the street. The tourist part she told with grateful finality, but the emotional one she left alone: It never happened, it never needed to be talked about, it had been a dream different for each of them. After three years, she said, you just don't jump in and cross-question a blind man. You assume it has all been for the best, and, while you get to know each other again, Bach is pleading on your behalf—"You can't say behalves, can you!"—with God, or whatever brings sweethearts back together again, with all their quirks intact.

"Yes, Momoi," he said, calling her by a name he'd invented years ago just to make *Mommy* a longer sound. "There was some nurse."

"Oh, there were several nurses, Belgian and French."

"I mean one he was sweet on, if you don't mind the expression."

"Talk as you like. There was a *lot* of wild talk at first." She was playing piano on her knees, her gaze aimed high into the corner of the room. "Confusing," she said. "First missing, then dead, then found, then blind, then not blind, then half blind, then coming home. Six months for each, if you see what I mean. He had complete freedom from the hospital, but we had hardly any money. Anything I made from concerts was paid to Mother."

"Via Mrs. Barnaby Wainfan!" He saw the woman again, never having seen her: a wide flat hat like a cymbal, pince-nez giving her the face of a European governness, and the black silk ribbon around her throat as if to hide or restrain a goiter. He wondered if Mrs. Wainfan took 10 percent, or kept books, if the Barnaby was a husband's name or that of her mother. Hilly could not remember. Her mind was on Clive's departure, the way he had been gathering up his things, never mind how surreptitiously. Whenever he came over, he left certain things at her house, to give her the sense that she was still looking after him, after anybody: his Polaroid camera; a couple of pens; a yellow pad; some suntan cream. These were the tokens of intimate endurance, a homage to a full childhood, to the years when he came and stayed with her, sleeping on a hideaway bed in the living room. Now she stood guard alone over the future, almost wishing she had never had children, because they made you not want to die, made you outstay your welcome.

On and on Clive went, quizzing her about London with Harry, as if it were a son's business: Harry's confession, his slapped face, his apology, the dreadful words (you don't slap the face of a blind man; you don't betray a sweetheart with a foreign nurse, or an English one, either). It had been misery: no celebration or making-up. By the

Thames, they had sat four feet apart, and on one occasion somebody had come and sat between them, unaware that he was separating a pair. But, she eventually thought, soldiers will be soldiers. I have been on farms. I know what life is about. He's mine still, I hope, I think, I pray, worth a dozen Ditchers from the soft-job brigade. Some things were going to the grave with her, part of family honor, and Clive could guess and guess, he'd never get it from her.

So, Clive decided, Harry never told, explaining the sampler away as a gift from the nurses as a group; each had done a portion of the work, he said, usually during the nights. Each man got one. It sounded implausible, but it would have to do. Would she have made any more sense of the officers' mess book and the record of Gregorian chant? She liked the Belgian decoration. But she never saw Harry's shrapnel, which he tossed over the side of the cross-Channel steamer, honoring the tunny and the sharks.

By the time he got to London he was de-Fabienned, squinting and blinking, but alive in Hilly's presence and able to kiss her with accuracy. She marveled at his well-kept hands, not those of a returned warrior at all, until she recalled that mud was good for the skin. Clive backed away, unable to sustain his incursion, happier to envision her looking at him and marveling that a man could be blinded, so profound a change, with so few facial alterations. It was uncanny how intact he looked, apart from the eye patch. Had he remained blind, would he ever have come home? Probably, she thought. But not to her and Exington; he would have become a Chelsea pensioner, with bed and board for life and a fancy uniform to disguise himself in. At the drop of a hand he would go away too, if he offended, determined not to be steered around the village by the likes of Kath Kent, all grown up and still the omnipresent escort.

As Hilly walked Harry from the hospital to the bank of the Thames, she noticed how both men and women gave him a half bow, some of the men actually raising their bowlers or trilbies to the wounded man above a look in which pity, pride, and even envy mingled. Here was one who had come back the worse for wear, planted deep among them to remind those who got off easily. Walking with a ghost, she began, but changed mental direction, correcting herself: Walking with a legend. Yes, that was better. Nobody knew who he was, this sergeant with not many battle ribbons, but they saw the eye patch and that was enough. He was none of your shell-shock cases; this man had been genuinely wounded and, oddly enough for he could walk quite well, equipped with a cane as part of the generalized insignia. It was a white cane, of course, ideal for brandishing at the seagulls who cruised low upriver in search of crusts and offal. As she negotiated Harry through the throngs, in a way Hilly felt ill at ease: He didn't look wounded enough compared with the others in blue tunics being wheeled along the embankment. There was just this little flaw in his eye, which almost nobody could see, and the rest of him was right as rain. But she thought, there were thousands with wounds nobody could see at all, or heal, and these never saw the light of day. Harry was quiet, as he always had been, but every now and then he would avert his head to track some bird or a barrel organ, like some open-air public speaker in the act of routine obeisance.

For hours, in dutiful taciturnity, she watched over Harry as he exercised his face, sometimes turning to confront her with a whole series of impressions, choosing from a bazaar of faces but finding they all felt the same from within. "I love shelves," Harry told her, "I don't like stuff all over my feet, or where I want to sit down." In no time he would go from a face of youthful craving to one of older disdain, followed by middle-aged bittersweet and even older diffidence, both high-strung and stoical. Now and then the joy of being in his teens shone through, but mostly overlaid with pique, hurt, insult, bewilderment, self-pity and pride. No emotion lasted on his face longer than fifteen seconds. It might have been someone speaking to him internally, haranguing or cajoling, and his response showed right away, only to be swallowed up in his next expression. In this way he was nobody special, just somebody inscrutably tender, trying to tell humanity not to go over there, not to look, not ever to do anything like this again. See what war had done to a young lad barely into his teens, barely accustomed to kissing, even under the mistletoe.

Hilly tried to entertain him, but he seemed unable to respond, mellowly assenting to whatever she said, fighting back with nothing at all. He had formed a crush on a nurse: that was all. Wounded men did, or so she had heard, although how people knew such things eluded her. Surely the wounded were the last to talk. Maybe the whole thing was a myth, a piece of sentimental chicanery put out to persuade the public that nothing was serious. Hilly had never been in hospital to stay, as she put it, but she could imagine how lonely it was in the wards, and she was enough of a mystic, a forthright transcendentalist, to know how easily the mind invented what it needed. She would wait for Harry to come back to normal and then spirit him home. The army, she decided, would hardly need him any more unless it was truly desperate. Closing one eye to get an idea of how his world looked, she marveled at how things flicked sideways, at how unreliable eyes could be. He would try to recover it, but it would never come back. Some day, perhaps, Harry would graduate to one of those eye patches with slats that let the light in, or to a pair of spectacles with smoked lenses; even so, nothing would change. He would still be tremendous at aiming a gun, using telescopes or microscopes.

She took him to Catholic churches to hear the music, but it was not Gregorian chant, and he fussed, telling her he preferred opera, of which in London at that time there was almost none. No, he said, that wasn't it either: What he wanted was a boy soprano whose almost machinemade high pitch came from a mouth too innocent to curse, though he knew better. He wanted something impossibly fine, he said, such as bore no taint of war, not even the benign contamination that came from peace. So they went to recitals, and he began to settle down even as her fingers itched in emulation. The music tamed him, made him easier to talk to, especially the "Moonlight Sonata," so-called, and some Bach played in a church—murky, bridling, miserable music as he found it, full of browns and grays, aimed into the holes in the firmament. Again and again Hilly reminded him about Bach's blindness, and its cause, and Harry shook his head. "He was worse off than I am. Just imagine. Operation got me some sight back."

He liked the truculence in Bach, claiming the composer as one of his own to make up for all those who had been killed and whose names he recited under his breath as if they were Latin and he was a priest intoning: Hick, Butcher, Boon, Dodemaide, Parsons, Tedstone, Bunting, Spooner, Hookey, Needham, Slack, Gard, Tungate, Leather, and on, and on, lest he forget them, lest the one chance they had of coming back to life be lost because one old comrade remembered the face but forgot the name. The war had flushed them away like so much refuse, and this was a pain far worse than the one in his eyes. Indeed, Hilly wondered, his expression keeps on changing so fast because he is trying to recall all those men, perhaps even trying to *be* them in some way: one who stammered, another who had a nervous cough, another whose trousers kept slipping down, another who hummed the national anthem, another whose cigarette always dangled from his bottom lip. Like that. She asked, and he said he was trying to keep them all in mind, but they became foggy, their names no longer fitted them as they always had, or so he thought, which meant that Hick should have been Butcher, say, and Butcher Boon, meaning that all of their lives had been a waste. They amounted to nothing more now than a box of unattached characteristics, shaven, cropped, and blanched, better off with numbers to be called up by, which only went to show how clever the army had been in the first place to assign everyone a number to be forgotten with. No doubt these dead no longer spoke English; just some lingo like Esperanto, heavenly version only, with all the soldierly curse words left out.

"Don't be blasphemous," Hilly said, chiding without meaning to. "There's no need."

"War's the blasphemy," he said. "At least I got my money's worth, didn't I? Most of those who volunteered never came back. Or never will. At least I have something to show for my stupidity, don't I? I'm really grown-up now, in all sorts of ways."

Nothing to boast about, she told him. "Hungry?"

"I'd like a fresh start," he said with a wrenching sneer. "These two eyes poached on toast, and a couple of new ones wrapped up warm for afterward. I'm sorry, but it sometimes gets the best of me. See: I'm not that grown-up after all."

"Who's to say the Almighty ever grew up?" Hilly knew that only extortionate comparisons would crack his mood and get the old Harry grin going again. Away they strolled, walking to kill time, as Clive decided he was really getting them now, tuning in with congruous intuitiveness, faking nothing, pleading nothing, neither imposing nor distorting. It was almost as if he were already born.

Now she carried Harry's cane for him with a touch of blasé bonhomie, as if to exclaim how wonderful he was for walking blind along the rim of the Thames Embankment without falling in. Did a warmer current flow from her hand to his, as if some preposterous self-sacrifice had been gone through with? Was his heart opening up to a new, almost unphysical emotion? What Harry had felt as a young boy had been almost perfect: Hilly was music, and he adored both, without ever having heard the concerts she played in Market Street and then in various halls in the county. Perhaps, Harry told himself, this feeling was only a gladness at being alive, at being out of the war. It was new, but not what the authorities would call love. Simply, Hilly was back, and Fabienne Binche, Gallic phantom with rubber hands, was gone, no doubt bedding down somewhere with von Kaiserstein. Harry was not sure, but he felt some purged, inviolate, cool thing sweep through him, making him babble the Bible, getting it wrong, but confident enough to think he was no longer in the valley of the shadow; instead, soft- and barefooted in green pastures, squashing buttercups and daisies.

Hilly away from home was calmer, more attentive, and, minus her piano, less of a muse. She was affable, after the first slap after the first slip, and tolerably poised, assigned as she was to be the escort of honor. And Harry felt just a bit the hero and wanted it never to end, knowing that when she took him home he would not be wearing his wounded warrior's blue, red, and white.

Hilly never got used to the things passersby thrust upon them in the streets: boxes of chocolates, slimmer ones of cigarettes, and flowers, flowers. Here people came, nothing farther from their minds than running into Harry and Hilly, and suddenly they had in their hands the very thing to give them, with the thanks of a grateful nation, and so forth. Thousands, she thought, must promenade daily with the carefully chosen reward impeding them; but there were so many wounded men in London it wasn't hard to find a willing recipient. At concerts or the theater, she sat beside Harry in the best seats, alongside men with no arms, no legs, no faces, their canes and crutches carefully stowed in front of them by army nurses with miniature rustling capes behind their heads to hide their hair. Or were these women nuns? Always installed an hour before the show began, these destroyed men had to sit it out, wetting themselves or turning frozen to stone, as little occupied by the music or the play as by life itself. Some of them would even arrive with the day's booty, a fruitcake or some fancy small cheeses arranged in a tin, held by the nurses. They were not fed during performances, of course; but surely, she thought, as soon as the curtain fell, the nurses would move along in front of them pushing kneaded-up balls of fruitcake into their mouths, observed only by the stage crew. Nothing was eerier than those theaters in which, with everyone else gone, the maimed got their toys back, their little snacks, and then were hoisted onto whatever contraption enabled them to get about. Lord Kitchener had sent for them and had returned them soiled. Harry took little notice of those worse wounded than he. Having seen everything at the front, he had no need of civilian sideshows. He wanted the commonplace, not the outrageous.

"Terrible," she whispered to him as they walked up the slight ramp to the outside world.

"War," Harry informed her, "isn't a Sunday school picnic. Somebody has to get bashed about."

"I'm glad I'm in London, then."

He asked her why, wondering if she might not be homesick, which he himself would never be again.

"Because London's more general, Harry. You don't know these people, so you don't care as much. You see the wounded men against a background of strangers, who sort of tone things down a bit. The wounded at home, like you, are your own, and each one makes you writhe."

"You're a devil for sharing pain," he said, and inhaled the night air, still alert for poison gas: mustard gas mainly, from the Germans; the Allies used chlorine and phosgene. Harry knew these things and had worn on his lower left sleeve the proficiency badge of the machine gunner, telling the world he was an expert with the weapon and knew almost too much about the way the war worked: how it killed, how it failed, how it would be the last war of all. He understood what she said about London, toward which she had always yearned as a performer, an artiste, a Licentiate of its Royal Academy of Music, to which they had had several walks already, treading the hallowed ground of bourgeois pastoralism as if it were Gabriel's own.

"You're getting better," she told him. "It's in your walk."

"It's in my trousers, you mean." He loved to shock her, and this was new.

Hilly said nothing, thinking: You took the rough with the smooth. You got your sweetheart back, but he came home as a man, not a sugar doll. Skivvying for her mother and her brothers, she had often noticed, when sewing, how she always got the wispy end of the thread into the needle's eye at the first attempt, but how the roughness of her skin pulled it out and away again the instant she tried to let go of it. A pianist's hands should not be cracked, should they? but soaked in neat's-foot oil.

Next day by the river, pursuing the unvarying routine of their days, she took out from her purse a small mirror and held it in front of them, adjusting it like a photographer until they fitted exactly into the little shiny frame. She was strong-featured, her face an elegant polygon of straight lines and unflabby planes, almost Greek, whereas he was ruddy cheeked, a little plump around the mouth and below the eyes, and afflicted with a look of utter oblivion, as if he were nowhere, had been nowhere, were going nowhere. She looked at him looking at them both, inquiring of herself if they made a handsome couple, bound to click sooner or later. He thought of the phrase *the issue of my loins,* while she tried to attend to their eyes, especially to the little leaden dot of shrapnel in his left. It killed his expression, ruined the focus, made him a bystander even when examining himself in a mirror. This was the pupil that looked backward, into the man who had suffered and almost died. Harry would never wink again, she thought. Nobody would ever dare to kiss him on that eye. Only Doctor Woodbine might touch it, and he was already a man in the past, sailing home, having taught his skills.

"There," she said, "look at yourself: the most handsome wounded man in the world."

She had wanted to get it all into one sentence and have done with it for ever. And now she had.

Their lives would open out or close up; Clive, the passionate spy, already knew the outcome. But was their being together, their coming together, the one or the other? The leaves of the poinsettia, he had noticed, did not fall the shortest way to the ground, but because of some aerodynamic quirk forced on them by their shape made their first and last flight in two stages: downward and outward at perhaps forty-five degrees, and then more or less straight down. But that penultimate cruise told him something about the poinsettia's addiction to life. What was the word? Marcescent: defunct without falling off, like the hands of certain paralytics. The poinsettia's leaves wanted to be marcescent, but they had to go, so they fell flying, even in extremis. His parents would fly too, once they had had some practice at being together again. He sleepwalked into the dubieties of their extended preliminary, itching to have them move ahead into glory and jubilee instead of hovering, pausing, talking it over and over. If they had only seen him then, at that time, would they have dawdled so much? Each respected the dawdler in the other. Harry had been seduced and traumatized. Hilly had begun her career. They confronted the world with a new desire, for which Clive knew no word: They wanted to fall off each other while remaining alive. Was that what happened when a woman had her heart broken by a man she hero-worshipped? If she was going to tend to him, though, her only option was to recover.

Then, as it were, came Hilly's turn, her own war. After walking in the rain with Harry from the Woody Nook to Never Fear Dam to Ridgeway and then back by White Moss Bridge and the Old Mill, she had gone down with pneumonia, aware in the midst of her babbling delirium only of soggy clouds, metallic and fumy, trying to choke the breath out of her. For two weeks she lay, as her mother told Harry, at death's door, neither shelled nor machine-gunned, yet silently invaded, taken over, with nothing more to help her through than systematic prayer by all who loved her. When the fever broke she began to spit up mucus into a white enamel pail, and then, smudge by smudge, her hair began to fall out, fluffing onto her brush until she was almost bald, and all she could think of to cheer herself was Elizabeth the First, then Elizabeth the Only. A year later, after enduring witticisms galore, she found something between her palm and her skull, and it was hair beginning to grow back, soft as smoke, curly, like a tender crop from paradise.

II

EXINGTON

A Porphyry Made with Strawberries

SO, AFTER MUCH debate and feint, their conjugal life began with
a marriage that had the dry fragrance of a bouquet thrown to them
decades ago, caught, then made permanent by talcum powder, kept
in a high cupboard with cracked basins, dead clocks, wobbly candlesticks, and defunct letter racks. At the Fitzalans', of course. Harry,
graduate in erotic preliminaries, yearned to initiate lovemaking, yet
noticed in himself a reluctance, sensing that Hilly was too ethereal.
Urgency fanned him on, though, and he was soon prompting her to
read discreet, plainly bound manuals of love and technique, knowing
full well that the only useful manual in such matters was impetuous
experience. He needed not to read about it all, but she, he supposed,
needed the full course to make her earthier, that was it. She laughed,
and told him anything a goat or a pig might grasp without a single
word of English would occur to her too: natural, unfussy, improvised.
Harry the rake was making a lot of to-do, whereas Hilly the innocent
was lying back like an odalisque.

Well, thought Harry, perhaps she's been more places than I know
about. She's had *experience*. She'll be critical. These bints often are.

Lord love us, Hilly thought on her wedding night, each is a pig in
a poke to the other. He knows all about killing from the war, of
course, but so do I, being a butcher's daughter. All we lack is knowledge of the positive thing between men and women. We'll have to

202 · Paul West

try, it's too late to turn back now. We could get away with not doing it for years, almost as big a secret as having a child.

Their wedding night at the Fitzalans', in a large, echoing, damp chamber near the music room, was the prelude to a different life in a terrace house only yards away, not yet ready for occupancy; but it had four bedrooms, a best room, and a living room, lit by gas, sealed by slate, backed by a puny garden, fronted by a little lawn the size of a grave plot. A couple of steps rose from the iron plate that covered the coalhole, down which deliveries would pour to the cellar.

"Here we are," Harry said, smoothing the edge of the sheet down over the comforter, "almost in our own place."

"Here we are," Hilly said agreeably. "I suppose we ought to start."

"We can always wait," he said, "until it's a place of our own."

"Just like two corpses," she told him. "Just look at us."

"Waiting," he said, wishing with all his heart for Fabienne Binche, the medal-touting slut to whom blinded men were easy game.

There was only a candle, so Harry blew it out.

"I'm frightened now," she said calmly.

He would light it again, he said. Think of the bed as a tent; he raised his knees and made a tentlike shape. Tents, he said, were quite soothing, once you shut the breeze out.

"This," Hilly told him in a stern and nimble voice, "was the house I was born in, so I don't feel *that* scared."

"No, you wouldn't. I was thinking of myself: the guest, the visitor, the chap from outside. It's different for a man anyway. He has to be, well, primed."

"He has to be well primed?"

"He has to be ready for it."

"Or he can take his time."

Harry agreed, trembling with Belgian memories, sickened by sudden and inappropriate nostalgia. He adored her, but sexually she was bland, neither exciting him nor exactly disappointing him either. He had no idea what he wanted, or if lust had any place in marriage, even for one-eyed men with bits of shrapnel in their backs. He didn't want the bed to squeak or Hilly to cry out; all his years in this house he had been enjoined to behave politely according to the excessive etiquette of one who comes into the household as a changeling, a transplant, blundering with wanderlust and seething with self-promotion. They would all be listening, he knew, the brothers lying there in the darkness holding their tools and waiting for the first spurt of union. He and Hilly had gone to bed last out of pure embarrassment, not having dared to make the first move, almost as if they were going to savor each other by the dying fire as hearth beetles came out for their first patrol of the night and George's leather harness creaked while it cooled near the ceiling, ready for his next ride in it, harnessed tight so as to dangle by his armpits and straighten out his back. People seeing George for the first time as he rode the upper currents of living-room air like a dead parachutist laughed and then caught themselves, bowing their heads in reverence. Then George would say his ghostly hello.

"Dreaming already," she pronounced. "You."

"I've plenty to dream about."

"Perhaps we should get up now and I'll play for you. They will wonder how we managed to be so quiet."

"And they'll be looking for blood on the bottom sheet in the morning, woman. I'm on my mettle tonight."

"You daft specimen," Hilly said. "This happens to be a butcher's shop. Do you think I'm above squeezing a bit of rump steak to put a few household spies off the scent? I've been here donkey's years. I know how most things are done."

"Well, I'm not very stiff," he confessed.

"Then we'd better feed you up," Hilly told him. "You need proper rations, young man."

"You don't mind me talking about it like that?"

"It's not important. Eventually things will happen," she said. "In time. Don't badger yourself."

There they lay, becalmed, astounded to be lying thus for the first time in their lives, he thinking he had to go to hell to qualify for this, she believing her life had to slow down now, a Harry beside her. They held hands with tender quasi-obscenity, trying to remember the right words. They kissed, then laughed. Hymen, she thought: When you can't see it, how can you tell what it is? He'll never get near it tonight, not with a gladiator's sword. Harry began wondering if he should play with himself to start the excitement, but he lay unmoving like someone born at horizontal attention, awaiting the officer on duty. War was easier, he decided. No, *she* told herself, the most awful music examination in the world with the spikiest examiner. They touched toes, murmuring; they had done this before, in the River Moss and down Pipworth Lane in the marshes, where peewits fed. They kissed, but this was familiar canoodling, even allowed in full view of Hilly's mother, who advised them on the right degree of lip pucker, the delicacy of angle, the art of holding breath. Kisses, she had told them, were not wet, or sloppy, or long. A kiss, she meant, was dry minimal recognition of the one by the other, like a lip curtsey, a face blessing. So now they kissed a little bit hard, barely pressing, wishing they could talk while doing it. Well, they could, they did, mumbling into their teeth, actually seeming to use the other's lips to murmur with. This was it, then, the courtly or demure version of the marriage bed: the warrior and the musician, cuddling like two re-united refugees, more aware of the pianoforte in the room across the landing than of private places unsummoned, as yet, to this ritual of the night.

All everyone wanted them to do was make a mistake. Let out a whoop. Or a shriek. Any sound would do. So they tensed up together in umbilical proximity, murmuring about war and Chopin, the new house ready for them next week, the need to have pictures on their walls, "but, please," Hilly said, removing her lips from his a little to make her point, "no dying Highland steer!" Unimpelled by their buried natures, they felt uniquely befriended there in the cool bed of a May night, having spent years dithering and pausing, imagining what it would be like to be uninvigilated, being illicit by permission of the Crown. It was 1928, ten years after the war had ended, and their lives postwar had been almost the same as their lives before it. In a sense, they had put passion behind them before getting married, each tutoring the other about how to live, as if their troth, so-called, were mainly defiance of time: How long can we manage before we give in? They were a famous duo by now, practised hoverers at the gates of bondage, and monumentally faithful. So dear and close they were, so tenderly mutual, they had shared and lost dogs, seen all their friends married and breeding, and yet had gone on and on in their interruptible sublime conversation, less a marriage of minds than an alliance of whispers. They seemed oblivious of all others. They had walked on burning coals and not noticed, each pondering the other's question, not about profound matters but certainly about pain, rivers, stars, blindness, the sustaining pedal, bison and Bizet, cows and Couperin. Each had advanced so far in a discipline as to seem authoritative to the other, so there was awe in their affection now. He confided to her again his love of Gregorian chant, which she took gravely, while she re-explained to him the rigors of being a wartime pianist hired to entertain the troops, who of course didn't fancy her kind of music at all.

Of the flesh they said almost nothing, postponing what they knew the words for—defloration, climax, withdrawal, and the rest—as if awaiting a letter authorizing them to go ahead and do what the world lived only to do. They ambled and strolled, traipsed and sauntered, aristocrats of belatedness, not in the least worried, just cruising about as if they intended to live for ever: two alert dotards who felt that life owed them some time off, some rehearsal, before they knuckled

206 · Paul West

down and behaved like everyone else. They were radicals, having
suffered a steep or sharp fate while warming up, as it were. Each was
the other's child, indelibly, for ever and ever.

Harry did, however, pat Hilly's stomach in a good-night gesture,
vowing to be a good Belgian to her before the week was over, and
for lullaby summoning up ribald images of Sister Binche at her most
lascivious; he had not expected to be drawing fleshly sustenance from
so far away, from a woman almost a myth. Certainly, during the long
interim between 1918 and now, he had pawed several young women
in the dark of country lanes, sometimes even walking home with a
souvenir stuffed into his pocket—underwear, although a handkerchief was enough—to be stashed safely in his army kit bag next to his
button stick, discarded eye patches, his revolver, the Uhlan sword, the
bayonet, the khaki-bound army bible, his copy of *Field Service Regula-
tions: 1909,* reprinted in 1914. To him sex was an enormous hinterland
into which he had not penetrated, though he had as they say "entered" the women in the lanes. He wanted satisfaction and was
beginning to think it lay in the right blend of lust and hatred: not the
natural, spontaneous efflorescence of love, as he would have preferred, but some bitter paradox made of loathing, desire, resentment,
and, yes, love and liking. The sensations and emotions that sharpened
lust bewildered him, and he wondered why sex seemed an act of
violence after all. It was a pagan, Hunlike thing, he thought, not
something to be proud of, yet not something to be deprived of: an
agonizing rainbow thrust through him, sending his nerves into an
explosive twitch. As soon as it was over, it was over; there was
nothing left, not even of the savage pique in which it had begun.

Hilly, better informed than he, had lived without it for so long that
she was almost invulnerable. When it happened between them, she
would be able to tolerate it without achieving much pleasure; she
would look the other way and abide. She had noted, of course, times
when her loins felt choked, bulging and rubbery, apt for stirring up,

yet easily looked away from. She set a hand upon herself in a grip that
nearly punished her flesh for discomfiting her so, squeezed chidingly,
and let go, sensing the blood change direction and, defeated, lay siege
to her liver or her appendix. She would stare it down, she told herself,
until the crack of doom. She had saved herself for Harry, such a long
saving too, and it was no use rushing into it when he was not ready
or ripe. A hurt eye, she told herself, made for disasters below; after all,
she had grown up with three brothers. What remained to be done was
to arrange their wedding presents in the new house: the silver-backed
hairbrushes on the dressing table, the huge bottle of eau de cologne
beside it like a chubby minaret, the cutlery in the drawers, the biscuit
barrel next to the seven-day chiming clock, the heirloom barometer
on a safe hook, the coal scuttle on the black-leaded hearth. First the
household gods, in all their pomp and panoply, and *then,* perhaps, the
act long deferred, put in second place after blood and war, decorum
and dawdle.

She was not a theologian, but nonetheless wondered about Catholic thinking, which installed in something called ante-Purgatory the
souls of those who had postponed their reconciliation with God.
They waited in ante-Purgatory for the same period as they had held
off, then went ahead into Purgatory proper. Had she herself not done
much the same, postponing her union with Harry almost to the point
at which they might never need it? Why Purgatory, then? Why had
she thought of that, as if a wedding led to punishment? Bridegrooms,
she knew, leapt into their marriage chambers, and chambermaids, the
morning after the wedding night, flaunted the bedsheet at the open
window. It was more paradisiacal, wasn't it, than purgatorial? It was
the elongated waiting that had seized her mind. Harry had no desire
for children, having seen too many massacred, but she wanted nothing else, after music. She had conquered music, and now she had to
conquer the brute deed that brought forth babies. A snap, she knew;
nothing could be more difficult to learn than music. The better a

musician you were, the more you knew how difficult it was to excel, and you taxed and winnowed your gray matter until the perfect tune appeared, like a baby being born.

They slept the sleep of overritualed uneasy guests in a crowded house full of their own childhood.

Only a week later, after some carefully undertaken sexual incitement based on Sister Fabienne Binche, Harry laid siege to his Hilly with much puffing, heaving, and cursing, while she undertook him with a half-smile of ruptured indignation, not quite able to establish how it felt: a blunt battering; a gentler heaving; a sharp stick-'em-up out of Dick Turpin's stand-and-deliver; something like celery and bologna fused, not so much painful as headachy, but in the wrong place. What a barren act, she thought. Even he does not enjoy it much; someone has told him to, so he does. But it bothers him, I can tell, and makes him sweat, a virgin upon a virgin. What incompetence we share. She hardly even felt him find the way, enter, and, waxing and waning, perform. If this, she thought, is the best carrot that God could come up with to tempt us to breed, He cannot have been all there that day. It is not even delicious, or delectable. We could live a happy life without it. Chimney sweeps have more fun. I have seen animals mount animals and all the time presumed they felt some pleasure, but this is hardly as pleasurable as moving the bowels. Its reverse, I suppose; it lacks loveliness. Just think, I might have married many years earlier than this just to find out what it was all about. Poor me. Poor me is what I would have been.

"Well," Harry was saying, "we're done."

"It isn't much, love."

"It'll be better, I swear."

"Not if you swear at it, King Arthur."

"I think we were designed wrong—some women anyway."

"What can you mean?"

"No," he said, shuddering with humiliation. "You spend half your life trying to get it ready, and the other half trying to make it work, get it in, and then there's the pushing part. I'd rather be a bullock."

"I would call it," she said with purring hauteur, "one of life's optional pleasures."

"Oh, there are those who enjoy it," he said, "they like nothing else. I know men who go home every midday, not for a meal, but for this. Imagine."

"Do they walk far?"

"Some would walk on water for it if they could." Harry was wondering if his triumphs with Fabienne Binche had ever happened. Had his foreign prowess been a daydream, like his Belgian medal? Had something tinkered with his memory? Or had they waited too long, idolizing each other but gradually shriveling up inside, so that in the end he lacked the stiffener and she the feel? Jack in the box had met Jill in a pail of water, and nothing had come of it. Should he bathe his tool in vinegar and try again? Or was it rock salt? What fed the urge? Eggs, meat, oysters: He had not been in the army for nothing. Yet what could *she* take? Some women's pills, as the world called them, likely to liven her up and strengthen her holster. He wanted to be quit of the whole wretched business, convinced now that Sister Binche was right: Sex was better in the open air, not buried within a woman. For men anyway. Hilly, however, had already convinced herself that, while it did not please, it was amusing, and led to mighty changes in a woman's condition. It was worth a thousand heaves.

The instant she moved, she felt some kind of change anyway: a flooded, queasy sensation, as if a sudden untimely period had begun, but this was merely Harry beginning to leak out of her, as if rejected, though she had no way of knowing. She was not bleeding. She was drooling and pooling. The preposterous thought struck her that her very own mother had been in exactly this fix some time ago. How,

she asked herself, could this business so dominate women it an-
nihilated whoever they used to be beforehand? Why did they all think
it worth it?

She had become a genital spittoon, that was all, and that was all she
would ever be now, since Harry had a licence to pump her up every
Saturday night, lightening his load of gruel at her expense, making her
what she hated to be: slithery, slimy, waterlogged. If sex had been dry,
she would have loved it. Push and pedal, she heard from somewhere.
Would her brothers want to do this to her if she asked them to? Why
had her unaccommodating, far from saturated mother settled for this
farce? Had all men the power to drag women into it? She asked and
Harry stammered, unaware that there could be a female's attitude at
the other end of his penis. To him it was enough to bleed white, as
a saying of the time had it; fetch his spunk, as another saying put it,
and withdraw into ceremonious glumness. A nose blown.

He vowed to get her using cocoa-butter pessaries and reading the
manuals before a next attempt. Although he loved the notion of
children, he loved them for other people, not for him. He saw a
future of light work, thanks to his injury (mainly supervising others),
gambling, monk music, and, now and then, a pressure-killing squirt.
In mock humor he recited to himself his favorite line: I bear the seed
of my own destruction within me. He longed for the perverse Binche
and her rubber gloves, even the twirl of her mustache across his glans.
In a way she had unfitted him for procreation. He now saw what his
Belgian decoration had been for: service in front, not in the marriage
bed. *Jaille, mon choux,* she would say to him, and he squirted, as unable
to resist as to see. He had been honored for being copious, that was
all. When he got older—no, he would always be this age: He had
grown up all he was going to, and he would die as he had been
prepared to die, a mere youth in the trenches. He was not going to
develop. He was like a cross on a grave, a fixture, a man whose life

was all in the present, fumbling from day to day, his future already squandered.

And he never recovered from this premature decline, this pawn-broking; it was as if he had lived his life already and his remaining years were a pseudoblissful charade, himself a caricature somewhere between war hero and water pistol. He no longer felt the need to bestir himself, to try, to aim, to achieve; he was a postscript man, that was all, handsome and almost finically gracious, a magnet to women, until they came near him and he felt the dry fluttering ash rise into his mouth from his core. He had been had already, he said, granted a measly pension for his eye, but naught for his mind. He could go to another war with consummate confidence, for war was all he knew, and the compromise etiquettes that attended it. Hilly knew there was something broken in him somewhere, but not exactly what; she knew only that he had flamed and died in the same moment and had to be dealt with gently.

Pondering some of this, Clive writhed, loving his father as a young man, wanting to kill those who had killed him without killing him. All his contorted rage poured into the word *subaltern,* standard term for any officer below the rank of captain, but also meaning *of inferior quality.* They had taken his father's original quality and thrown it away, or left it to twist and rot in the rain. That had been the end of Harry the historian, Harry the accountant. And now, for a while, Clive realized, would come the end of Clive the viewer, doomed by powers beyond his control to take a back seat, so as to have a preamble to his own birth, lest he interrupt it in a bout of irascible fellow-feeling predicated upon the trashing of his young-man father. He would reappear, he more or less knew, but merely as an usher, a bouncing baby voyeur, no longer allowed to watch his youth in an adult fashion. Perhaps the powers would be generous to him. He prayed for this, knowing the limits of collusion. Doomed to remain a twinkle in Harry's eye, he addressed himself to his mother-to-be, and left well alone.

IN ORDER to reach his job, Harry had to rise at six and walk to the
railroad station: slightly more than a mile. He bought a little square
of green cardboard that was a day return and took the train to Staveley
Iron and Steel, where he supervised the repair of red-hot ladles full
of molten iron. A man with a war record such as his was peculiarly
suited to so dangerous an enterprise; he enjoyed the open-air quality
of it, the faint echo of wartime in the peril, and the sense of being a
sergeant all over again. What no one knew was that, walking to his
train up Market Street, down Station Road, mainly past flowering
hawthorns, he kept his left hand behind him, working the right as a
piston for full military effect. He strode forth as if on a parade ground,
going to war again, proud that, in the end, the Allies had won. This
was the delicate, functional postscript. He was a veteran, a husband,
a man with a destiny. On his return journey, he bore the daily paper
rolled up like a baton but with his right hand behind him, to the same
cadence: a slowed rat-tat, "Lilliburlero" or another march whose
name he couldn't recall.

A sprig of hawthorn in his mouth, twizzled as he walked, brought
him no bad luck as far as he could tell; superstitions affected him little.
He was walking toward wife and home, enjoying the secure, sturdy
feeling this gave him, not toward some hellish destiny devised by a
brass hat with red tabs on his collar. Best of all was the radio set that

sat on the sideboard: enormous, with a short-wave tuner that, late at night, would bring him the sonorous drone of monks from Rome. He relived his war years while Hilly slept, her mind on her parents' home only a few yards away, where the piano sat unused. Soon, Harry knew, he would be able to sit up all night reading while the far European stations bloomed like narcissi of the night, urging him toward them and making his mind glow with secrecy, love, health. That he was half blind deterred him little; he had seen all manner of mutilations in hospital, and he ranked himself among the lucky ones. His progress amused him, from Church Row to Market Street: three hundred yards. Number 7 Market Street to Number 17: hardly a distance at all. The other journey, an expanded irrelevance, had taken him from Church Row to Belgium and back, during which he seemed to have lived much of his life and, surely, a good portion of his death. When you had paid so generously with blood and pain, your death would be trivial at most. He mused on these matters while walking to the London, Midland and Scottish station, then cruising in his third-class compartment to Staveley Works, not in the least put out by the humble nature of his employ (a phrase he had heard somewhere, perhaps read in the Bible). People looked at his dead eye (he wore no patch) and knew, according to the high sentiment of those times, that they were here because he had gone "over there." He had given that eye for them, though how they knew he had not lost it in some Saturday-night beer brawl he had no idea. It must be that the saved could spot a savior at once.

Indeed, posttraumatic ecstasy almost overshadowed his comparative happiness in marriage; he was happier to be alive than to be in love, as he surely was, wasn't he? without lusting in the least. Oh, he went through the motions with Hilly, as a man should, but he found the whole union stagnant. He had already written away for the marriage manual and a three-month supply of cocoa-butter pessaries, enclosing the requisite postal order, and checking with an X the box for plain wrapper. It was all routine, though; there was no obsession, no hunger in it, as there had been in Belgium, where he had been a blind white fish with a live wire in his pants.

So this was marriage, a scene of comeliest calm; it could almost have been one devised by Hilly's mother, an expert in unrewarding doldrum. He had already begun to gamble, dividing his wages into left-hand pocket and right, with the gambling money and his winnings on the left in a little Bisto tin that made them rattle until he slipped into it a length of cotton wool plucked from a cloud in a blue, medical-looking wrapper. He walked with his winnings cushioned, the better, he sometimes fancied, to hear the birds; and he became very good, a dab hand at picking winners. In only two weeks he had to find a bigger tin, which Hilly obligingly produced. This one had held Finnon Salts, which you sprinkled into bathwater to ease your rheumatism. A larger wad of cotton kept the money quiet, at least such of it as jingled, and Harry became adept at folding the huge black-and-white five-pound notes as they began to come his way. At this rate, he thought, a hiding place was what he needed—for the money, not for him—and this time it was a biscuit tin cached in a locker allocated to him at work. His attention was on the red-hot ladles that sometimes spilled as volunteers repaired them for double wages, but his vaulting Promethean self rode with the jockeys in their flamboyant silks and flaunted itself inside the winner's circle after each race. His only vice, he knew, was not knowing when to stop: he gambled enormous sums of money, at least in comparison with his wages, and sometimes came home with only his punched rail ticket to his name, all the rest sent swooning into the never-never.

Hilly was speechless, though not for long. He had never known nagging, except from sergeants major when he was a private, but now he did, and he felt Hilly was a killjoy intent on blighting the one compensation he had for being blinded. Surely she, the archdruid of romantic beauty, should understand his need for glamour and thrill;

she did not, invoking such prosaic words as food and bill and rent, emblems of a world he hardly knew existed. He had staggered out of hell feckless and somewhat otherworldly, content to work for a living, as folk said, but also a superman emeritus. The war was over. Nothing else mattered. Ortega y Gasset had already said that men invented love while women invented work. Harry knew nothing of that, but droned away at his job, getting an occasional burn from spattered metal, and for the sake of peace giving Hilly a specified portion of his wages each Friday. He wanted to live recklessly, with spry abandon, but Hilly tamed him, in short time making him into a well-spoken, modest gentleman who seethed when George said he had just bought half a racehorse with money made during the war. Harry never put money on George's horse, name of Araby, although it often won or placed. If Harry had not been his old pal and brother-in-law, George would have cut him dead; but Harry would have severed George's throat for being a coward and a profiteer.

All Hilly wanted from marriage was children, but all she got was the obligation to teach music pupils at her parents' house, two each afternoon. Harry had this frisky gristle appended to him, the wrinkled pod that went with it, and he spent his seed on a weekly basis; but nothing came of all his puffing and expending. Hilly wanted to be pregnant and, after reading the sex manual, dropped the pessaries in among the nasturtiums and tulips, wishing them no ill, but determined to let life's juices have their flow. She told him, but got only one of his roars; he refused to discuss it. He hid his winnings, much as he thought she capped his sperm; she planted his pessaries and helped herself to his minor wins while he twiddled the knobs of the radio in search of a Gregorian monk with umber throat and boyish chirp. A pattern of living had begun to exert itself, and it was not one of communication. They had begun to veer apart, politely but defiantly; and so, feeling they were breaking the rules, rather than wanting to put things right between them, they went away to the sea for their never-taken honeymoon, agreed in this although in nothing else: A week at Number 7 had been like a medical examination.

After strolls together on the cliffs, the wide asphalted promenade, and barefoot in the slop of the beach, they went their separate ways for a while, she to the pier where a dance band played. She went and crouched near the drum, beating out the rhythm with her pretty satin-shod feet. He went first to a department store, where he bought a tie with club stripes of white, silver, and pale blue. He no sooner put the tie on, in the store, than he marched off to the nearest bar, where, perched on a stool in his first Grand Hotel, he suddenly found himself accosted and embraced by a distinguished-looking gent who seemed to know him, had also been in the war and Belgium, although he had never felt the ministrations of Sister Binche. Impressed and gratified, Harry became voluble; he didn't know the man, but liked him. As they parted, after agreeing to meet again, Harry got the point: The tie he had bought was much the same as that worn by the Edinburgh Academicals, and his afternoon companion had recognized a fellow-graduate, presumably a fellow-officer. Harry had vaulted into the upper leagues without even trying, without even a miniature medal in his lapel. Surely this fellow wasn't another Hastilow, was he? He'd gone, leaving behind him a potent aroma of cigar that swirled around Harry, cloaking him. Once again, he had glimpsed the ark of the covenant, socially speaking, and had smoked a cigar with the exact same poise as the other. Harry's meticulous pronunciation, picked up from the officers he had dealt with, and his expertly manicured nails, could fool the world, as might the wad of fivers in his inside pocket. He was ready for the high jump, away from marriage, rent, father-hood, and in-laws, knowing now that he would end up in a Belgian colony, running a brothel with Sister Binche, spending his days at the local track and his nights beneath the big fat poppy of her bulbous lips, mustache or not.

An hour later, though, he was reuniting with Hilly at what they called their "private hotel," which meant without a bar. No Grand or Imperial, this, but a dank lodging house with strict times for meals and only a jug of cold water and a basin for a bathroom. The basin and bath were down the hall, behind a door of frosted glass, and the toilet was at the hall's other end, where a thunderous box poured water when they yanked the chain. Somewhat in his cups, he let slip at high tea that Hilly could play the piano more than well. The Edinburgh Academical in him was talking. Hilly gave him the look that turns statues to salt to make them useful and explained that she had a headache; but the throng persisted, pleaded, groveled, and finally got her to run through some popular favorites with a regnant scowl, rushing through the whole performance to keep an appointment with the bathroom. When they locked the door of their little bedroom, she turned on him and launched salvo upon salvo.

"My music, Mister Man, is a private matter between you and me, if indeed it is between us at all. I am not an entertainer. I am not a barrel organ with a monkey. I am not an organ-grinder. If I choose to play, I play; but I do not play in boarding houses that smell of cabbage and vomit. I play when I choose to, and I play to people who can understand music. I am not a skivvy. I do not play on holiday. I do not want to be popular. Let them go to the pier, where there's music galore."

Dumbfounded, Harry knew he had done something wrong and crass, but he had no idea what to say or do. After some moments of brittle confusion, he reached in his pocket and withdrew a couple of five-pound notes, handing them over without a word. "Get yourself some chocolates," he then said, knowing he had just made a worse mistake as Hilly glared, gaped, and at top speed began to wonder where the money came from.

"I found it," Harry said lamely.

"You found it. At the Mint, I suppose."

"People drop things."

"How many more, then?"

No, he told her, guiding her hand away from his pocket. They could add some furniture, she told him. She had seen a lovely mahogany table in Morgan's, with a spare leaf. It would just fit. He was not hearing her because handing over the money had reminded him of Binche and Belgium, even though he had never paid. Something mercantile and unsentimental had quickened him at the core; his mind's eye grew lascivious and frenetic. Not horses, he thought, but Puss in Boots, giving him the requisite flick of pain. It would have to be pain or contempt, something like that: the struck flint in the flintlock, the tang of vice that Edinburgh Academicals preferred and paid for. Harry suddenly felt he was being assembled piecemeal toward a final product he could not envision, but for sure it was a half-blind man with European tastes. Once you have eaten French bread, he thought, the rest of bread is only slices. Belgian, then.

All he had felt about Hilly was pride, but she felt she had been exposed, as if her kind of music and attitude toward it had been ridiculed. She had a point, but it had nothing to do with music; it had to do with not wishing to be in any lodging house or private hotel. She had married down, the very thing her mother had warned her against, and here she was among the common folk, humbled and traduced, with a blind man like a barker yelping her wares. She did not want to be consumed, or to oblige; she wanted to be utterly private, confronted by no one. If she could not be pregnant, she could at least be fertile in another way, hearing music she never played. If Hilly was a mystic, then Harry only treated her like a public oratrix. He needed someone who lived outside herself, who had not already been where he wanted to go, who was another innocent aspirant. He had married a muse, but he needed a nurse.

THE HOLIDAY done, and all its demands met with compliant exasperation, Hilly and Harry carried their small suitcases to the railway station and boarded, wishing holidays (or honeymoons) were longer or, even if they were short, there was no obligatory return after them, so you just stayed put awaiting the next war, living on fish, sleeping between discarded Sunday newspapers. This being Saturday, they could rest up all day Sunday and then set to with a will, ready for the Calvinistic thou-shalts of Monday. Life could be bleak so long as it made money for you. Picked up at the Renishaw station (not the one that ushered Harry's train off to work), they thanked the Lord for pony and trap, for Thurrie who drove it, and were soon at the brink of their new life again: Enter the passageway, turn right, go past two doors, curse the intended garden, the uncut grass, and unlock. Recoil from the smell of locomotive, like children perched on the bridge as the train belched through below, covering all in a graphite cloud.

There had been a greater than average fall of soot, filming everything including the carefully set table for their return; they had laid it out before they left, so they could boil water and sit down to a quiet meal on tongue and ham brought from Scarborough and by now sliding about in greasy packages in their suitcases. At once Hilly found dishcloths and set the kettle going. There was no other hot water as there was no fire to heat the boiler. Off with her finery, including the

wide-brimmed cream hat that kept the sun away from her fair com-
plexion. On with her apron and kneeguards. She scrubbed for several
hours while Harry tuned the radio, finding good polishing music, as
he called it, at least until she screamed at him to go and unpack in the
front room where the aspidistra sat in the window. Off he went,
wondering if he went high enough in the house the smell of soot
would disappear. When they at last ate, they had no appetite; Hilly
already had a migraine from stress and upset, and the plates they used
had a smeary veneer, a tincture of engine smoke. "From now on,"
she whispered, "if we have any more holidays, we are going to jam
up that fireplace. I knew something bad would happen the moment
I turned the corner on to Southgate. You can't move without catas-
trophe. We live between two sets of soot. One comes in with the coal
and floats up from the cellar. The other comes down the blessed
chimney. This room is where they meet, and we live in it. It's time
to get out now, if you ask me, back to Scarborough."

It had been against such a mishap that they had brought with them
from the sea a little store-bought magical envelope full of sand and
tiny shells: Poseidon to banish smut. It had not worked, so Hilly
threw the packet into the poorly catching fire of sticks and twisted-up
newspapers from foreign parts. Harry had assigned his mind to something cheerier, namely the number of rooms they had between them.
"Six," he announced. "Where I came from, there were only four and
twelve people to share them. Next door, at Fitzalan Palace, they have
six, counting Jim the live-in, to spread out over six. We're better off
than any of them. Three rooms apiece. Isn't that a wonderful thing?"

Hilly could hardly see him for the shimmer and sawtooth dazzle
that came with her headaches. "I suppose that's because you want to
get as far from me as you can. Sleep on the top floor if you want. I
saw you watching that waitress when she bent over the tables." Harry,
who watched everything female, and twice as hard as other men, had
no idea what she was talking about, having decided long ago that one

of the chief pleasures of sex consisted just in the looking. Peering and lubricating up were two of the main pleasures. If the law had not banned it, he would love to cuddle up with a good book, perhaps something by P.G. Wodehouse or Edgar Rice Burroughs (*Tarzan of the Apes* had come out in 1914, the year he went to war), and a nice depraved young girl in his lap, his hand up her skirts while she made popping noises with her mouth. Something that carnal and aloof would have pleased him much; Sister Binche had helped define him as that noninjurious species, the languid sensualist. He didn't want children, not of his own. He didn't want earnestness, loyalty, routine. He didn't want work or holidays either. He wanted a lot of slow, overpowering fun. Above all he wanted French bread and the sound of distant cannonfire. He was wholly unfitted for civilian life, at least among the Moxons and the Fitzalans; but he had no way out. Monday morning, the red-hot ladles would await him, the Renishaw to Staveley train puffing steam, the pay envelope on Friday. Only the week's horses and their courses sustained him, almost as if he were pointed backward into the pageantry of the Middle Ages. If he couldn't have that, he told himself without the least melodrama, he would shove his head into the molten metal in one of the ladles, leaning bent over so as not to scald his midriff, then pushing his head lower and lower against the fierce gust of red-hot air, making it yield as he thrust himself toward it, still without having even singed his front, though it hummed hot. He could imagine the commotion and the headlines: ONE-EYED VETERAN INCINERATES HIMSELF. Or he would unbutton his trousers, reveal himself to any who might be watching, and jerk off in the general direction of the ladle, only at spasm shoving his head into the dull humming blaze. It was one way out, he thought, no worse than some he'd seen in the war.

He wasn't having much of a life just now, and he knew that he and Hilly should have stayed apart, living with their parents until the end of their days. Married, they got too much of each other, more than they needed, though perhaps they could have handled the amount ten years earlier, before they had thought things through. It was too late for intimacy now; he wanted someone to station him on the promenade at the seaside and leave him alone, watching the sea lumber out. He wanted to hear the rest of his life drifting away unused and unappreciated. Had he been an officer, he would have been treated in hospital for battle fatigue, then known as shell shock; or if he had fought in a later war. He knew vaguely what was wrong with him, but had vowed to say nothing about it. He was no longer anyone in particular, he felt, but a sign, an emblem, a cameo. People pointed at him, and his behavior, and said that was what war did to a decent man, wasn't that a good enough reason for making it the war to end wars?

He had heard all the bromides and the rip-roaring slogans; he just wanted no more of church and state, well-educated people preaching the need for cannon fodder. His friends, the Germans opposite, understood this too, and he sometimes felt the common soldiers, the foot soldiers especially, should declare war on the politicians, the generals, and the clergy, the liberals and the besotted orators. The soldiers and the whores, he told himself, in one sublime body, putting everything to right and creating a world society without flags. That would mean years and years of shooting, in courtyards and drawing rooms, women and children too, just to snap the circle of high-mindedness that got wars off to a good start. How he loathed high-mindedness. Given a different era, he would have been a terrorist. Granted more energy, he would have become a communist. As it was, he became a chronic anarchist, reserving his finest sneer for high-minded saviors of the nation. The trouble was, most of his fellow-anarchists were dead; he was one of the few, not one among the few who would fly in the Battle of Britain some twenty years later, but one among the first few, sometimes called Old Contemptibles. They had barely enough members to sell imitation poppies in memory of the fallen.

Unstrung, racked with pain, and never quite able to pay her bills, Hilly watched him day by day become an automaton, sleepwalking to work, sleepworking while there, sleepwalking home: bemused, compliant, terminally humiliated. She had no idea what to do beyond caressing him at six o'clock when he knocked on his own door before entering. A man so deferential while seething inside was something to behold, and perhaps to lock away. While his dead eye shattered again and again, frozen in the blur of old splinters, his good one roamed the postwar playground with merciless stoicism, amused but offended, making him wonder why he had almost died for this—for the Georges and the Bernard Ditchers, for the schools and colleges that went on as before, as if the poor had been well and truly abolished in the best of possible wars. He isn't here, among us, she told herself; he has become a statue to dubiety. I am superb at English, but I can come up with no phrase that altogether sums up the sharp details of what has become of him. In bed, she began. Yes, in bed—let's be blunt about it. In bed he seems miles away, more distant than when at table, when clipping the lawn with shears, when watching me cook a late-night supper.

She knew what to do when she felt like this, alone in the styptic quiet of a house smelling keen with furniture polish and disinfectant. Out came the medals from their shallow cardboard box swathed in tissue paper, the box's eight corners all broken by the postal service, making them into flaps between which the medals tried to slither out. She sat them on her work-worn hand, covering the lines of head, heart, and life. He never wears them, she thought with attenuated gentleness, except when at the Cenotaph. There was a time when he had been home a week, a month, and now he seems to have been here wounded forever. He *was* wounded. The war went on. The war ended. All kinds of remembrances began. The peace was full of the dead war. The country was full of the maimed. Blind heroes stood at street corners, trays of matchboxes arranged in front of them. Others hawked shoelaces door to door. Groups of four or five sang patriotic songs outside post offices, Labor Exchanges, and barber's shops too. Sometimes a three-legged messenger dog accompanied them, walking with a list. It never ends, she thought. He should have had more to show for all those years in the trenches. The tissue paper smelled of almonds and soot, perhaps the aroma of tarnish. The bronze medal hung from a ring. Its ribbon was red in the center, with green and violet on either side, shaded to make two rainbows; but what held her eye now, as ever before, was the winged figure of Victory, prim in a toga, one hand uplifted to cup sky as if testing spring water. The figure's head looked detachable. The feet had begun to melt, she couldn't think why, unless the figure was standing in the mud of the trenches, or in the boiling fat that poured out of cooking bacon. The side of the face in shadow had a halo, not above but alongside.

The brass medal was all action, though, with St. George on horseback trampling the eagle shield of the enemy powers, and a skull and crossbones (for good measure), while the sun lifted above all like an extension of the ribbon's orange watered-silk center. She caressed the medals and rubbed them with her hankie, thinking he must have worn the king's head outward, certainly in London in his blue uniform of the wounded man, so Victory and St. George were what he wore against his heart, hard against that rough material. Jangling when he breathed, they were what he got for giving what he gave: simple equivalence, according to the politicians of the day. Her mind fell into the phrasings of Decoration Day formulas, usually spoken against the echo of crimped trumpet notes and a distant shuffle of traffic: the music of remembrance, of pain minified and jubilation made into a graven image.

At the Cenotaph, she thought, but lost her drift, just seeing him at the concrete breechblock inscribed with the names of the local dead. Was it concrete or metal? She did not even know. The word meant *empty tomb,* and she winced at its awful sound, the bony whisper it seemed to release. She had never heard anyone say it with any degree of confidence. Who were those men to whom he bent his head, half saluting as if ashamed? Bob Woodcock, Stephen Rais, Granville Burdett, Alec Marsden, they too bent over, like inbred ghosts: husky, distance-scanning men with emptied smiles and fresh-rinsed eyes. The few, as Harry called them. The platoon of the remainder. They went down in hundreds, she reminded herself: both sides. He did not have to aim, he said. He just looked forward and fired. He just pressed down with his thumbs. One of the officers, Ferrers of B Company, honor-mad, had charged the German machine guns, sword in hand, monocle in eye. Monocle and sword had reached his family a year later by registered post. "A big difference," Harry had told her, "between medals and decorations. One means you were there, and being there was apt to be the biggest occasion of your life. But you didn't have to have done much. It depended. The decoration, though, is for being brave in action, really sticking your neck out. Or for impressing the right officer." He gave a fleeting sneer. So these, she told herself for not the last time, and with a disappointment that made *her* ashamed, were medals only. His bravery had been in being blown almost to pieces.

Then she unwrapped the Belgian medal for the first time, wondering what it stood for. What had he said about it? Had he even worn it when he wore the others? The language on it was French. The whole thing looked fancier, more expensive. She wondered if she would dare to ask him why he had it, perhaps for some brilliant exploit in Belgium. It must have been for something outstanding, on which to predicate the rest of his life.

"Oh, that," he said wearily on entering. "It came to me in hospital. These foreign brass hats, you know, kept traveling around and leaving medals on blind blokes' beds. Haven't I told you this already? And little bits of carpentry too, made by the locals. Souvenirs, see."

No, she persisted. "Is *this* a decoration?"

"Let's put them away," he said. "That war's over and done with. Once upon a time I thought I'd need them, to make me feel better. Not any more. I'm one of the toiling poor now, as honorable a vocation as a man can get."

"What *is* it?" she demanded, at last out of patience.

"A decoration," he snapped. "Now be *said*. There are other men with far better, who did much more than I did. It's a bloody consolation prize from the damned Belgians, that's all."

HAVING MARRIED late, to fulfill a troth plighted ages ago, they seemed now to glide past each other, murmuring gently but out of touch. In theory, the more people suffered, the more the good Lord provided them with, to make up; but Harry and Hilly, awash in sympathy, could no longer express love. Perhaps they needed an enemy thrust down their throats—her mother or his war—in order to mobilize their affections. They hugged and patted, kissed and smiled, but without the promised amatory impetus. Hilly contented herself with thinking that it was like an arranged marriage, in which, over time, love grew into a mighty thing superior to infatuations of a week or two. Harry blamed himself for having been, as he put it, spavined. It was almost a middle-aged debut between two people of extraordinary fortitude who, almost too good at soldiering through, could not quite become one flesh even when their defenses were down and their enemies had fled.

Still determined to begin a family, Hilly went to see Dr. Sinclair on Southgate, opposite the ample manse that housed Ruthin College, where she had taught English. It was like taking her English to the doctor, a gruff, generous man who rarely sent out bills. He told her he thought she was fertile, but that her womb was pointed in the wrong direction. So began a long series of painful manipulations done at Jessup's Hospital; Hilly felt deformed, inadequate, uncouth, but she determined to show them her capacity for bearing pain. Off she would go on the first bus of the day, and back she would come, hardly able to walk, an hour before Harry arrived home from work.

Increasingly, however, she felt the price she paid for her first baby was unbearable: After three visits she thought herself entitled to twins, but she as quickly withdrew the notion; after five visits, a genius; after seven, an angel. The trouble was that, in order to test what was being done to her, she had to let Harry have his way, which was sometimes rough because he became excited by abstract automatism when finally in the saddle, recalling Fabienne and flogging his erotic imagination with teleported vignettes. Hilly soon began to associate pain with coitus, and made Harry desist, for which he compensated by gambling undue amounts on wrong horses, as if to annihilate himself in the saddle in a different way. He succeeded, and took his wages to the bookie too. Hilly was rather glad to have something to explode at him about, having long chewed her lips in purposeful silence while he heaved away.

Marriage had come to feel like an enormous barrier to what used to be their affection. An elephant hide got in the way, thwarting and parting them. Not being religious people, though willing to go through an occasional ritual, they found refuge in politeness; their old, altruistic sarcasm died; their playfulness became slow motion. With marriage, everything had turned deliberate. There were things that had to be had, never mind the pain and tedium. Everyone said so, and both Hilly and Harry felt their lives being designed by conspicuous failures in the shops, the pubs, and at the bus stops. Had they at this point decided against children, they might have thrived, but Mrs. Ford, Mrs. Levick, Mrs. Anthony, Mrs. Lewis, Mrs. Wallace, Mrs. Sharman, Mrs. Courtnauld, Mrs. Morgan, and Mrs. Mallender soon put paid to any such idea. It was late already, they said. Hilly felt obliged to oblige, so her visits to Jessup's continued, her only other problem being the old one of how to test the rearrangements of her womb. She felt she was paying for some crime committed in her sleep or while playing the piano with exceptional abandon. Whom in the widespread universe had she offended? Slave to forceps and rubber gloves, she dreamed of being at last, blissfully, sewn up and sealed with candle wax, or even the bright-red sealing wax that closed letters. Had she walked out and never come back she might have fared better, although condemned and ostracized by the ladies.

In a way she was choosing between maternity and music, between music as a concert pianist and music as a teacher. Women of her station and situation just did not take a hike, however, and, besides, Hilly had not the means. If she had, she would probably have gone and found another man, one less fraught with complexes and wounds, or indeed more fertile—she was beginning to wonder if Harry's intermittent salvos were dead to begin with. She continued to try to grow an extraordinary secret fruit inside herself while Harry took only a limited interest in what she dismissed, at least in talking with him, as women's troubles.

To Harry, all women's troubles, so called, stemmed from menstruation, about which he had heard a good many vengeful and grotesque jokes while in the army. He had noticed how the high-strung Hilly became a hectoring banshee once a month, as apt to scream at him sustainedly as to point and flail right in front of his face. "For God's sake shut up, woman," he would say, "and leave me alone." A wife who had recurrent migraines (a malady he thought she had invented—*he* had never had them, after all, even during bombardment by star shells) was enough, but one who went virtually berserk a dozen times a year was too much even for a veteran. Were there books about it? No, nor were there pills to correct it. Like the weather, it came and went, came and went, and he developed a new idea of purdah as the tent where the men went to escape the hysteria of their women. She made him tense and caused him heartburn, which he eased by drinking huge quantities of sodium bicarbonate, which made him (as he put it) "rift," easing his indigestion. It was more likely, though, that he was upsetting some whim of the vagus nerve that made his heart fibrillate; the huge burp shook the vagus up and, sometimes at least, made it reset the sinus node of his heart to a normal rhythm. On she nagged, and on he gurrumphed. At times he took the fizzy drink before she had begun, and the subsequent tearing loose of air set her screaming like a Pavlov dog.

One smile at this mutual percussion would have ended it for keeps, but Hilly and Harry allowed themselves to settle in their ways. It was true that she got hysterical, but she was in chronic pain. It was true that he was feckless about what she went through, and dulled his mind with deadhead prejudice. They began to take a malicious delight in thwarting each other. Hilly asked Roman Catholic friends about the likeliest time in which to conceive, and he took to coitus interruptus, just to make sure the Dutch cap and the pessaries didn't betray him. When he laid hand on her in bed, she at once envisioned the faces of pearly babies to get her through the ordeal, always hoping this would be the last one. You should, the hospital told her, be all right now, after all this. Your womb is smack in the correct position. Hilly felt as if she had been reborn, though wondering what on earth else was wrong with her. Had she been younger, would none of this have happened? Once upon a time, had her womb been flawless, as well-aimed as those air vents on the decks of ocean liners: scoops on top of cylinders? Yet she asked her mother nothing; viscera did not exist for Victoria Jenny. Her daughter, so adept at music, asked herself if there were not some way in which to cherish the miracle of humanity apart from any human relationship. The most tender passages she managed to play, or hear her pupils mangle, got her thinking about the unique exquisiteness of an Earth repeatedly peopled, but the idea went no further; she wanted only one, she said, girl or boy, so long as the girl would not be a music teacher, so long as the boy did not go to war. Everyone counseled her, displaying gross tactlessness in appraising her innards, as if she were a cow for sale. Most of them knew something about pregnancy and birth, but they had only the vaguest idea of conception, which remained a mechanical mystery known only to a haphazard-minded deity.

Harry took to revisiting Church Row, where he saw his mother withering and declining, like a violet grounded in salt, and his father, the ex-miner whose leg had been crushed in a fall, still trying to claim compensation. He presided there, in that humble house, absently nibbling a beef sandwich with his trilby hat still on his head, wondering how he had stood it all those years, but eventually calming himself with a vindicating dream: Paolo and Francesca reading the book together in Dante's delirium, except that Harry's booklovers were his roguish, dramatic-eyed sisters and equally roguish but duller-eyed brothers, at it even now. They lived their childhood still, reading all weekend, incorrigible maintainers of a pleasurable cult. To read, they lay upstairs three to a bed, every now and then rolling off to empty an inconvenient bladder into the chamberpot beneath, but taking the book to crouch with, not shifting their juvenile eyes off the page until one of them had to undertake the trickiest feat of all and, with book in one hand, pot hugged tight against the ribcage, go empty the pot into the bucket on the landing, its top camouflaged by an old veil. The return journey was a less precarious read, of course, but nobody had ever gone toppling drenched down the steep and narrow stairs, book and all.

It was bound to happen, they always said in the dream, but only to Harry, who had blurred the sensitivity of his thumbs by having fired machine guns for so long. That eye, they said, wouldn't help him on the stairs. He agreed and smelled the same old smell coming from under the beds, thanking providence they weren't French asparagus-lovers. Grand ambitions he had nurtured in the fetid silence of that little house, whose women never screamed because they had never had the education that taught them how. He had aimed his desires outward, like sparking rockets, through a window or a series of open doors: out the bedroom door, down the stairs, through the doorless doorway at the bottom of the stairs, and through the one and only doorway to the outside. When the doors were closed, he willed them open, and, when that failed, he went and tied them open with his suspenders.

He marveled at the simultaneous decorum and indignity of his early life in this cubic hovel, where he had said perpetual vespers to himself. Then he had lit out, speeding to the flashes of orange gunfire on the horizon, knowing that in order to come back he had to throw himself away. He had come back a hero of sorts. In those days you were a hero for still being alive. It depended, he supposed, on how many were lost—how many million. Now, who did the counting?

Before then, he had been glad to march from the earth closet in Church Row to the water closet at the Fitzalans', supposing that one day he would do his business in a closet that flushed milk. Anything better seemed normal in his optimist's head. When he went back home, after time with Hilly at hers, he would fumble for what wasn't there: a foretaste of the half-blind man. You get what you reach for sooner than you anticipate. Thanks to Hilly, he now knew that to expect was vague, whereas to anticipate was mighty specific. What a joy it was, even while she was screaming with pain, nerves, or rage to have precise control over the events of the day.

Hilly began to evolve ways of justifying barrenness, or lateness. She preferred the latter, accepting the assertion heard somewhere that a child born late in the mother's life is brainier, although perhaps prey to sickness and flaws. With a penchant for exaggeration, she soon had the vision of an extraordinary child born when the mother was fifty, sixty, seventy, babbling in Greek or Sanskrit while taking suck.

She did not pray, but willed hard, trying to picture the faces of her babies, and having with Harry pretend conversations that went like this:

"Why don't we do without, for a change? More natural."

"Without what? Oh, I get your game. Trying to tie me down."

"Just thinking up a bit of future for myself."

"You've got the wrong husband then, lass. Try Bernard Ditcher. I'd sooner go blind in the other eye." On they went, he confident and she sagacious, until the day she told him that they were going to be three. It had clicked. What had clicked? "Oh," she said, "what's been pouring into me for months now. What you fetch up, Harry. It's worked. I have that within that passeth all understanding."

He dropped his beer glass into the middle of his plate, making the fried eggs and the cold ham bounce sideways. End of supper. He lost all appetite and almost thumped her face; but, for a machine gunner, he was not a violent man, just a vehement and quick-nerved one. He would rather have killed her than seen her pregnant, but in the end he cursed the factory that bound the book on wedded love, that made the bulb that was the diaphragm, that cooked the cocoa-butter pessary. Modern industry had let him down, he said, and here he was tending molten metal as if it were a suckling child.

"I'll be damned," he said.

"You'll be blest," she told him.

"I'll be working for ever."

"You'll be as soft as a brush once you see it."

"Bugger it," he said, tears seeping.

"Now, really. Using bad language is a poor welcome, poor thanks, Harry."

Already he could see it or imagine it. Slightly plumper, her face had smoothed out into an uncanny, voluptuous beauty, with smiles of creamy palpable depth and eye crinkles that told it all. She had come through, having converted her bias, her stratagem, into physical fact; she was no longer a woman whose only solace was in having made a decision she would not dare abandon. She was a farm. His physical desire increased and she received him nightly with almost visionary

236 · Paul West

abandon, sensing he was trying to knock the baby out of the tree. Truly, he was a man trying to couple with Kismet, to sap fate of its most insidious tricks. With his bad luck, he thought, he would end up creating twins; the chemistry of it eluded him, but he knew enough to know when women were running things from within while the poor sperm bearer plied his trade outside, gaining incessant relief but getting nowhere, just pumping his vital juices into the void called family.

Next thing, she had the piano brought from Number 7 to Number 17: brought home, as she pertly informed him, and its presence no longer calmed and ravished him. The piano was a premature child, occupying space that used to be his or neutral, surrounding him with acoustic ghosts as Hilly and her womb sat on the stool, their backs to him. She played with celebratory gusto, halting passersby as never before. Harry the warrior felt sick to his stomach, not just in couvade with Hilly, but because he had seen his life as an ingot that occasionally squirted outward. Now he was unmanned, opened up, no longer alone with magnificent horses named Heavenly Tureen, Barabbas's Badge, Mint Imperial, Jelly Minaret, Joskah, Moscowvane, and, of course, Araby. That exotic thicket of names had once enclosed him, never mind the money they won or lost; now, though, they all seemed less personal, less impudently familiar. Others had placed their seed and not got into this kind of trouble, so why had he gone wrong? He blamed Hilly now, for carelessness, for a special lewdness that stopped short of adultery but betrayed him in a subtler way with an offshoot of himself; she went to bed with his reflection and turned a loving couple into a family.

His shadow had failed him.

She belonged now to Sherwood Forest, the Derbyshire Dales, the nearby moors. She was no longer human.

Why, they had reserved themselves for each other in time of war, yearning and supposing, and here she was putting him second, as one whose work was done. He dreaded the thought of educating this child-to-be, should it turn out a boy, but to his credit he at least had the thought. Something of husbandry stirred within him: a glow-worm swatted by an uncaring hand, but continuing pale green.

Within a week he was boasting, the mangled revenant who could not be stopped, who had bided his time and then come home to his chosen bride. He now saw eight months as an unending taper: time trailing off into an invisible point. The only blot on the horizon, swelling fast as mines and factories closed (Staveley Coal and Iron Works included), was the coming ruin of everything, the panic away from the gold standard. It was summer 1929, and Harry in his anger wondered how the world could come to an end in the summer, with the harvest swollen on Earth's surface. It was no time to multiply, he decided; it was a good time to have another war; and he was right, although ten years ahead of history.

The coming of the Depression hindered Hilly not a jot, since she elected to teach music five days a week and soon had a dozen pupils, who became two dozen, all of whom knocked on the faded green front door and entered for grandiloquent scolding. Harry became accustomed to the plonk of the piano, once a daytime thing he never heard, now a small factory purring in the front room from six to nine every evening, as Hilly collected sixpences and shillings in an old potted-meat jar on which they depended.

Out of work, Harry became a grumbler, no more a gambler but a clever woodworker, sometimes cutting spills to light fires with, some-times clothespins. He tended the lettuces, pampered the radishes, kept the baby carrots covered with fine earth, and emerged as one who grew tomatoes to crimson bursting point and, on weekends, trudged to the River Moss or the lake in Renishaw Park with his smudgy pink permit to catch chub and dace, pike and trout, all of which, beheaded and cleaned, then dipped in flour, would have kept the economic wolf away. There was also, however, the lavish foison of Hilly's father's butcher's shop: They did not lack; indeed, they could have conducted their own black market had they been so disposed. Harry changed from revulsed agitator and spendthrift into him who, murmuring Gregorian chant, hunched at the lake's perimeter or, in the garden, sank his fingers into soil as into God's cheeks. He never lost his edge, but he aligned himself gravely with the inevitable while Hilly bulged, prattled, pounded music into unwilling disciples, and crossed off the months on the calendar.

Whatever went on in the world that had lost its metronome, it would not affect this child, groomed by her own viscera, spawn of a belated, sleepwalking reunion. She had never been happier, delighted to have to make do, cutting and sewing new clothes out of old ones. Her migraines increased in number, duration, and severity, and Dr. Sinclair blamed them on hormones. Somehow she found fresh energy in weariness, doing an algebra of fatigue, no longer the light sleeper she once was, while Harry read and radioed all night, climbing the stairs at dawn, his head full of the sounds of sacred Rome, his mind still attentive to John Buchan, Robert Louis Stevenson, Eric Linklater, Nat Gould and Jeffery Farnol.

The reader from Church Row was home to roost, and he dimly discerned now the fringe of a gentleman's life: workless, hourless, the whole of his being devoted to the tending of his appreciative soul, especially with regard to prose and music. He had begun to learn and recognize names, from Sibelius and Grieg to Bach and Elgar, on all of whom he doted, though on what would be called their popular works. He was a spy inhaling messages from ether, nodding at secret signs on paper, waiting for the next war to make industry's chimneys belch again. A man more gifted for idleness could not be found; he was the perfect exemplar of the at-rest society that limped around him, none of *them* dining on prose and melody's bananas. His main fantasy was that his blind eye knew the truth and could never be deceived, not after the trenches and the leaning Virgin of Albert. His other eye was for roguishness: tennis with Hilly and her brothers, a dog walked with Douglas, to whom he had become close (and Douglas's fiancée, Ruth, a Norwegian blown into Derbyshire by an ill wind and a poor map). Nowadays he read the newspaper twice lest he miss anything, but it was thin, there being no news, and he was glad when each morning, as high summer dwindled into chilly October, he lit the fire with it, watching disaster liquefy into flame, so accustomed by now to the to and fro of piano scales that his heart seemed to halt when *they* did and the sudden silence of the house become a scalded, bleached, unbreathable thing.

IT WAS easy for Hilly now. She felt she was being composed by some dense-minded, burly sonatist: music of a kind unknown, but to her as easy as scales. Everyone now had a role into which to fit and accept her; she had become ordinary to everyone save Harry, who knew she had gone beyond him, that too much of their life together had become irrevocable. On she taught, becoming more genial at her work, so much so that some of her pupils no longer trembled at the green door or on the mat within.

February, Harry said, observing that it was a poor month to be born in: windy, dismal, cold, cut short. A late baby would be into March before it knew it. Having maneuvered tenderly, and in agony, to get this far, Hilly felt she had taken on the forces of nature and triumphed. That it would only be demonstrably worth it after she had seen the child did not occur to her. A child was a child. A child of hers was a child of hers. If for some reason it came out deformed or unnatural, she would rethink all that tortuous gynecology. Even to get this far only to produce a monster would have gratified her somewhat; she wanted to be a mother more than she wanted to dote. Being a healthy mother-to-be also laid to rest a local notion that gifted or clever women, old or young, had miserable pregnancies and abominable confinements, as if nature were getting its own back on the mother for not being a draft horse. Grammar caused no abortions, she told herself, and manual flair at the pianoforte harelipped no infant. The intermittent illness of Dr. Sinclair, who never got paid, trudged up and down the ceiling of her life, coming, going, much reported on in the village, much scrutinized by other doctors, all with Scottish names: Crawford, McKellan, Macdonald. They came to see her instead of him, and this began to make her nervous. He heard, and made a house call in a state of honorable debility. She sensed then that she would never see him again, that he would never see the child she bore. She would have the baby at home, as was usual, surrounded by hot-water bottles, piles of starched white linen squashed flat, kerosene lamps, candles, and, if she were lucky, an artificial singer later to be known just as anthropomorphically as His Master's Voice. Handel's "Largo" would be right.

Harry would be over at Number 7 Market Street, curbed and fortified by Douglas and Thurrie, who were the most likely to be there. The Angel pub was nearest, with the Duke of York slightly farther, then, still within a fifty-yard radius, the Lion and Lamb, with, only a hundred yards away, the White Hart. Should he wish to smother his horror or his delight, he could do so with the brothers and a convenient bottle, or go afield to one of the pubs, leaning on the bar in shell-shocked abandonment, murmuring I never expected it to come to this. If I had known, I would have stayed on in Belgium or London, doing almost any menial job to keep from the patter of little feet. Puff, puff, on his pipe. Throw back the incinerating scotch. Let it all happen doors away, like a blood explosion, a woman blown up to release a red-hot fish into Christendom. He was stunned that a squirt so slight as his would create such a commotion: so much of the future, something so weighty as a person, someone likely to go on living and living until—at this needling juncture, Clive, so long suppressed, raised his voice in his mind's ear and tried to vent pleasure from the womb, but fell back, failing to breast that tape. He had much farther to go, and other fins to grow; but he heaved head upward at the mellow boom of Hilly's voice, heading a ball, heaving his skull against an ice shelf that turned out to be made of snow. Subsiding, he nonetheless made his presence felt. "Feel," Hilly said, clasping Harry's pipe hand against her belly. "It moved."

"It would," Harry said, shaken. "It's alive, isn't it?"

"It'd better not be dead after all this to-do."

"Sort of hard to get in touch with it, Hilly, and tell it to keep its chin up."

"Ever sarcastic, even in the tenderest moment," she said bitterly, mistakenly reproaching him, for this was his way: semiboisterous pedantry to keep the wild creatures of myth and medicine from his door. Something neat and miniaturist in Harry led him toward sterile and wound-up things, whereas the big blood floats and gossamer capillaries of the life force made him wondrous nervous. He loathed the finny undersides of fungi, the translucent peel of onions, the shaggy pit of the peach. He found nature overwhelming, sickening in its mindless profusion; whereas two glass blocks set on a table in a museum would be much the same a hundred years later, not subject to nature's idolatry of the germ. Such was Harry, the killer of old, happier to take a mouthful of light from a reading lamp than relish the wetness in a kiss. What saved him in this world was the *clop* of his cigarette case shutting, the fragrance of his first puff, the wad of money bedded down in his pocket, the pure Arctic fluff of a new pipe cleaner. Having been proven pulp himself, he wanted nothing near him soft or surging.

Sure enough, the day before Hilly threatened to give birth, Dr. Sinclair died, and she spared a tiny moment for his orphaned twins, Susie and Bobby. Harry kept on calming her as the sky choked up and snow began. It was a thick, dilatory snow, settling steady on a windless day, soon stopping such traffic as there was in this rural fastness. It was a snow like earplugs, he thought, muffling lines and smothering you with fresh-washed fleece. Other doctors would come and do Dr.

Sinclair's work. Locums, he had heard them called: locum tenentes, which meant they held the fort for someone else; the military overtone pleased him.

Hilly got through the night by talking to herself. Next day the two doctors Honeybone and Hardwick, whose names made him do his barroom smile and would have made him twirl the mustache he wore when in the army, made an effort to drive the seven miles from Sheffield in a clod-hopping convertible not fitted with chains. As they advanced or halted, they telephoned through to the butcher's shop, reporting, and then volunteer runners would leap through the drifts to yell however many miles the doctors were distant. Soon it was down to one, but Hilly was already in labor. Demoralized and quivery, Harry nonetheless figured the odds on the event, knowing that Honeybone and Hardwick would be in time, though how did he know such things? He knew them in the same way that made him pick a winner, or used to. Some tactless person from Number 7, perhaps Gerald White or Jim Webster, the one swishy, the other dour, had set a small stack of useful implements on a towel just inside Hilly's bedroom: some butcher knives, a bone saw, some twizzly skewers. Thank heaven, Harry thought, their foresight didn't extend to the humane killer. He swept up the jumble of steel and took it downstairs to the kitchen table, and then, upon a new thought, down the cellar steps to the stone slab on which the Sunday joint always sat.

Beginning to wail and guess, Hilly held hard to the hand of Mrs. Umpleby the midwife, almost hysterically explaining that a woman who has had all kinds of hospital work needs careful attention at a time like this. As far as Mrs. Umpleby could tell, Hilly was healthy, but Mrs. Umpleby was not a pianist. Things could explode. As it turned out, Hilly labored all day, all evening; the two doctors arrived at lunchtime and joined Harry in demolishing a huge and greasy pork pie that reminded Harry of Belgium, and a whole bottle of scotch. With the doctors present, Hilly did not care if they were drunk or not;

she believed in authority and knew now that nothing would dare to
go amiss. She slept, she tossed, she shrieked, she babbled, she cursed
Harry for getting her into such a pickle, while he airily told Honeybone and Hardwick "Women love it, really. There's pain, but it's the
thing they love to do. Who else, sir?" They laughed, then one of
them soft-shoed upstairs to see Hilly, and she nearly fawned on him,
asking his name several times and begging to be listened to by stetho-
scope.

Still healthy, she gave birth an hour later, at ten-thirty that night,
to a healthy, heavy boy with thick curly hair, and a blanched scar on
his back. The snow had stopped, having muffled the village, the pub
yard in which the doctors' car invisibly sat, and all roads in and out.
Hilly later told Lydia Fox and Norah Booth that it had been like
anesthesia; she had seen the flakes dance against the window as her son
slithered into the world. The weather had puffed, she said. The snow
had fleeced her. The doctors had been obliged to use forceps to
extract the boy's head: either his head was too big or she was too
small.

"Don't you believe it," she said to Mrs. Umpleby. "Children born
late in life have big heads and lots of brains."

"No pinheads here," the midwife said obligingly.

"No fear," Hilly said. "I'm hungry, would you believe it? A
sandwich, ham or tongue, would do very nicely. And a bottle of
stout." Thus began the eating binge she managed to sustain for twenty
years, as if, for the first time ever, her system or soul had relaxed and
then wanted to engulf the domain of edibles and potables, somehow
domesticating the external world. She had far too much milk, so they
gave her a breast reliever, a clinical-looking glass cup with a green
hooter bulb on its end: She applied it, made it snug, then squeezed,
venting air, sucking milk. She soon got the hang of it, thinking
blithely she was doing nothing by halves now. Small helpings, adrift
in the lower iconography of starvation, no longer figured in her list

of requests and demands. She chortled that she had to be milked. She adored becoming a mother at home; she could have what she wanted. Harry went outside and made a big snowball for her, set it on a plate, and went upstairs. She caressed it and then waved it away from her and the bulky child, whom they had agreed to call Clive, after numerous arguments in which Giles, George, Alfred, and Ken bit the dust. Clive would be Clive, not after Clive of India (though that would have chimed with Harry's soldierly metal), but because of Clive Hastilow in no-man's-land, the hearty, nonshaving young lieutenant from Warwickshire; he had taken Harry seriously, and now Harry commemorated him with pious seriousness. All Clives were Clive anyway.

After a week, young Clive had still not moved his bowels, as if pondering something so deeply (say arrival in the world of music and war), but the instant medical remedies were decided upon he relieved himself with a bang: announcing an arrival, performing a one-gun salute that kept Hilly chuckling for days. This was a child, she said, she already knew by heart. *He* would soon be calling for a sandwich, too.

IT WAS a good story to tell in afteryears, maybe even in the afterlife. The boy had been wondering if it were a good world to take a dump in; if not, go back into mother and improvise from there onward. It was the sort of thing Clive winced at when others told of it, but in secret he hugged the yarn to himself, detecting in it an obtuse radicalism his tutors would eventually discover and, after much anguish, give him credit for.

He was an original, even in diapers. He did not inherit his mother's pale-green-gray eyes, but blue ones, darker than his father's. Now, of course, with the dyke breached, Harry no longer tried to fend off the whole idea of progeny. He might have tried to restrict his offspring to one, but he no longer had the heart to resist Hilly's lunge into the future. He let what happen may, agreeably changing and wiping his little boy as if the child were a lily ported intact through many bombardments and brought home, a sempiternal souvenir held firmly against his body so their two hearts might match.

Harry was proud, but also crestfallen; his dreams of living it up, Belgian style, were doomed. His lecheries were bound to be mental now, staged during averted coitus with a woman who, having pushed her first child out, felt less sexual to him than she did before. Hilly was more metaphysical than ever, and he wished she were cheaper and more vulgar, more of a tart or a trollop, less interested in bringing up a baby than in new positions, unpermitted sensations. Harry the sensualist became Harry the sperm bearer, no sooner locked into her body than sloping off to hospital in Belgium, without saying a word, naturally, and willing to do so for the rest of his days, a climaxing backslider, a foreplay fugitive, a shuffler of images there in the darkness. Like ancient man in his cave, he yearned backward to the ravishing vision and repeated himself again and again in the part of his life that didn't matter, incongruously discovering in the middle of the sexual act the barbed-wire rules of nostalgia.

The gusher of memory, he found, has no core. Sampled, bottled, and even labeled, it keeps its deepest nature secret in a flux that pours behind fits of deliberate thought, behind tunings-in to this or that phase of a life he found it gross to call "lived," as if life were a hide and you cured it, or a trout and you fried it. Memory, Harry began to find, imaging sex while making love, was fraught with drift, seepage, and distracted languor. The periphery obtruded. The center blurred. Incidental music strayed to him from cowsheds, underground toilets and misshapen red buses plying between places whose names had gone and a makeshift sheet-and-clotheshorse tent, set up one summer in the nearby graveyard, within which a boy enacted rites, a fresh-plucked daisy in the meatus of his glans. The past murmured, hiccuped, and went limp. Some of it he could will back; some of it came unbidden, nuzzling at him. His heart twitched at a certain hue of stone, or the pile of a carpet under his naked heel electrified him. Sometimes he smelled the leathery aroma of a long-shut wardrobe, not his or Hilly's. Where had he been? Sometimes heartrending emotions announced themselves with a group of sparrows, two alarm clocks sitting on a mahogany tray, and the disjointed cantata of a donkey engine. Whose life had these fallen from?

He sensed that the expectation of something was always better than actually having it, which meant that the perfect life was all unbridled previousness, going nowhere. In his sexually absent and abstract way he kissed Hilly on the brow, cheek, mouth, chin, breasts, and navel, enchanting her; but he hardly knew who she was, or even whom else he wanted there in bed with him. If Wordsworth, whom she loved to quote, had really meant what he said about emotions recollected in tranquillity, then he, Harry, dealt in emotion prefigured. And why not? Life should not dwindle into mere snacking on the run, a hand-to-mouth scamper that chewed up what it could not taste and bolted its nectar. Dissatisfaction did not tell him how to live better.

He was still pondering this when, squinnying out with his one eye, he saw what he still did not believe: among not-quite-dry clothes, baby Kotch and two-year-old Clive lying side by side in a big laundry basket. Clive was uncommonly inert for a two-year-old, but he doted on the new life form that his sister was.

A blink from a half-blind man speeds calendars. The next time he saw them, "Ky" was trying to poke out his baby sister's huge blue eyes, but now Ky was three and Kotch was one.

Up they grew, aging a month every time he closed his eyes, taking strength and bulk from some tropic of increase not on the human scale. Out they had dribbled, and now they were like Germans advancing.

Harry closed his eyes. Too much of children dazzled him.

Hilly was already dozing, her main role in life fulfilled. No more Jessup's, no more twisting about in her insides to rectify whatever she had done to herself during the war, heaving beef around.

From the wood-turning factory over the wall at the bottom of the yard, Billy Emstock and Ken Frost had thrown packages of imitation cigarettes for the children to play with: wooden, square, and splintery, but contraband all the same, ten to a package and still warm from the lathe.

"Something's just come over," Clive would say to his mother as he raced to see what two bored workmen had made for them. Most of his booty went upstairs to the attic, where he secreted maps and plans in an oilskin pouch on a sooty ledge inside the chimney. He stayed there to avoid the smell of fried cheese in the kitchen.

Asking Harry, he heard this: "In Belgium, during the war, the ice cream was red. They mixed it with blood, my boy."

"Honest, Daddy?"

"What do you think? Now, tell me, why are lips red?" The boy was interested in everything, even the almost weightless ball of hair taken from a cow's stomach at Number 7, smooth and shiny as a piano lid. All the Fitzalan boys played with it, nervously.

"Do they lick themselves that much?" Clive said.

"With a rough tongue."

"It's like a memory," Clive told him, "a cow's pearl, a meadow oyster, Daddy."

When they went for a stroll together, Clive took his uncles too, parading through his head in a cortège of incompatible kinship. Unlike Uncle George who, when he entered the house, headed straight for the fire and crouched there, rubbing his hands together, hoping to produce a friction spark, these uncles seemed ready for humiliation. The youngest, Bert, had once again broken his mother's rules for good behavior, so she, tiny as she was, thrashed him with a wand of pale bamboo, then brought him round with beef sandwiches and strong mustard. Uncle Colin, the amateur pig killer, slunk abroad with his knives wrapped in dark-brown waxed paper. His nose oozed like a rubber tree. Uncle Henry slicked his hair by brushing it straight back after oiling it heavily, then built a frontal quiff by combing the top from left to right except for the salient inch, which plumped upward with a winning sheen. No, Clive decided, the Fitzalan uncles were different from the Moxon uncles. They were snootier. Only Douglas came home from cricket on Saturdays lanky and hollow-eyed, exhausted from a long day at bat.

To his father, Clive always seemed to be frowning. Does he frown all the time, Harry wondered, or only when I watch him? Perhaps I

am not seeing him straight. To him I am like something out of Robert
Louis Stevenson. No: Clive was doing his frequent roll call of uncles
and aunts. Having found Thurrie, who specialized in ruffling the top
curls of curly-haired little boys, Clive, oblivious of his sister, decided
that aunts clattered. Edith sang hymns in churches as well as at the
piano in selected homes: songs of exile, hubris, and barren infatua-
tion—to Clive, just songs, and too many. Nora of the moist hands and
periwinkle-blue eyes made exquisite pastry, even after she acquired a
colostomy bag. (On her deathbed she lingered long enough to stroke
a last piecrust.) To Clive, she was like a pretty, considerate bird.
Mabel, the henna-haired gambler and Harry's counterpart, stopped
the whole village when she went out walking; she was even more
beautiful than the three infamous Littlemoor sisters, Ella, Bella, and
Della, who linked arms and strode forward, much to Harry's delight
(he sometimes fell into step behind them merely to savor the quicken-
ing in his loins). To Clive, Mabel was a macaw, a bird he had never
seen but in pictures. Annie, Harry thought, frayed affably. Ivy grew
pinkly plump. Then Annie fattened out while Ivy grew emaciated.
Clive had no clear image of them.

So many children, Harry thought: All of them were Clive's aunts.
No wonder he misses one or two. How many of us children died?
How did we all come out of the same slender woman? Doris: Now,
who was she? Auntie Doris, Clive remembered, was Uncle Thurrie's
wife. About some of them there formed a mist, a mist his father
longed for, hating to have too many to worry about. Then, said Clive,
there was Ruth, Uncle Douglas's lady friend. Now, said Harry, there
is Ruth, who is too much woman for the likes of Douglas; she will
tax him to death. A woman of Belgian quality, I think.

Clive heeded aunts less than he did uncles; above all, he needed
images to counterpoint frogs inflated through straws in the anus,
which he had seen, and the rotting maggot-infested sheep down on
the Meadows, which he had heard about. The woman with the iron

foot, however, delighted him because he liked her gangrene smell and often took her hand to walk alongside her, mimicking her gait. He also took a zoologist's liking to old Alan with the billiard-ball lump atop his bald head, and Johnny Nettleship, whose curlicued mustache actually went up his nostrils into his nose, making a black bow for boys to mock and envy. Clive knew he was growing, but he could not feel it. Had he once been none? No years old?

To chew, he liked Nipits from Nettleship's shop: mentholated black pastilles he sometimes played tiddledywinks with. He rode Tom, the Fitzalans' newly acquired Great Dane, and chased Ruff, the Moxons' mongrel. He is a boy growing up, Harry told Hilly; we must not baby him too much. "He looks too pretty as it is. I'll have those curls shorn yet." He did, and Clive's head was anointed with brilliantine by Harry Sharman, who liked boys to be brisk and almost hairless. "Now you look more like a soldier," Harry Moxon said. "I'm not a bloody soldier," Clive wailed, "I'm my daddy's little lad."

Douglas, however, was not, nor was he any longer Hilly's constant burden : the blithest, the one most destined for a romantic and famous fate. Already too tall, too thin, burning his strength away, Douglas had been doomed as a teenager in spite of Hilly's feeding him up with soup, chops, and sausages, in total disregard of the needs of others. Reared on protein, he had become muscular and athletic, never needing like George to dangle in the living room from a harness attached to the ceiling. He seemed to be hunting black light, tuned in to a deathwatch the others knew nothing about. There'll be the devil to pay one day, Hilly would tell herself; Mother should never have had him. That was a long time ago, and now Hilly was saying the same thing about herself, fully equipped with two hostages to fortune of her own, newly linked to her own mother through late bearing. It was the family curse, taking so long to get to matters other women managed in their teens.

How long had it been since Douglas went off aboard the *Edinburgh*

Castle to South Africa as genius in residence to some enormous iron and steel works? Only months before, he had met his Ruth, daughter of Norwegian immigrants to Britain. Off he had gone, beribboned with honors, clanking with sports trophies and medals (for French and German, oddly enough), resolved to make a life out there and then send for Ruth. Or perhaps not: He left with his emotions regarding her on the cusp, poised between addiction and passionate friendship. In a way he had traveled in love rather than over the oceans; he had gone from one end of his state of mind to the other, an adventurer with a superior novelty at home, who saw in Africa only an accelerated career.

Douglas was lusciously trapped: unable to decide about Ruth until he had conquered Africa, yet unable to conquer Africa until he had Ruth by his side, talking Afrikaans. He had arrived in a workaday trance, fatigued by shipboard games, aware of but unattuned to huge stacks of railroad ties at the dockside, guarded by black men in pith helmets. His first Africa was garbled. One black with a long bone needle through his hair appeared to him as Christ with a misplaced nail. Greeting him in the hallway of his bungalow, a colleague-to-be had turned out in full military uniform: Sam Browne belt, revolver in holster, waterbottle, map case, and half a dozen lovingly polished medals. When Douglas made his way in a rickshaw-type vehicle drawn by one buffalo across a bridge flanked by lions on high plinths, he wondered briefly if the lions were real and how they could jump so high without getting breathless. It was the whites he noticed most of all, blacks not being allowed into view unless performing tasks. Men in blazers, with huge coats of arms over the breast pocket, mesmerized him as the heat poleaxed him, and he kept wondering how he was going to survive if he didn't go naked. He saw Dutch-looking gentlemen arranged along a brand-new locomotive as if they were all going to consummate a child's dream and set it into motion, becoming "engine drivers." There was the Africa he saw, of technocratic Afrikaans families like the Gerbers, who not only befriended him at once, but sonned and nephewed him too, pushing him toward their gorgeous daughter Wilhelmina. There was the Africa he had dreamed about, from huge papyrus swamps to sons of cannibals contemplating the Passion of the Redeemer done in photogravure. And there was the mirage, neither reality nor dream, something the climate had cooked into being: A servant girl sipped from a fountain on a patio, an apostolic prelate patted the top of a black orphan's head. Whatever was not in the rest of the world, Douglas decided, it was here. Africa was the land of quotient. He settled in like an ivory tusk sinking into wet sand, his only problem being Wilhelmina Gerber, who had developed for him a tactile voracity he tried to dodge, together with the weather, which by day thinned him out, turning him into one of the greediest water-drinkers they had ever seen. The trouble was that, nightly, Africa became cold; he spent each evening on a balcony or veranda in only a shirt and slacks, the former still wet from the day's sweat and therefore even more effective for cooling him down. He spent his evenings in a necessary shiver exposed to a chilly breeze, exposing the weak Fitzalan lungs to a new hazard. In only a couple of months he had contracted double pneumonia and died, his death less of an event than a mixture of myth and demented process, as if all along he had only been something decorative.

After the telegram, his mother never spoke another complete sentence. Hilly, reviling Africa, longing for Douglas, took Ruth in, thus enlivening Harry's private life and providing him with a gambling partner. It was as if the war, long over, had started again and reached out for new prey, snatching the handsome, thin six-footer to perform abominable experiments within the syrupy fug that hung over the military graveyards. Hilly wept and wept, victim to another view of war: It killed one for having spared another. Her father never again laid his cane alongside his cutlery at the dining table. George, who had been to Africa and come back, began to stoop, as of old. And Thurrie developed a permanently running eye, as if part of his body had decided on an individual tribute. Harry claimed that Douglas would not have died if he had spent the war years with Harry in Belgium and France. He had liked Douglas, found him the most welcoming, most flexible brother in the clan. Douglas was a greenhorn, Harry said, who should never have been allowed off on his own. For once, music helped Hilly not at all; it was as if her own child, before she had one, had died, having indeed been brought up by her ever since Victoria Fitzalan, half dead from bringing Douglas into the world, had lapsed into passivity and pain. Douglas took the heart of the family with him and buried it there in Africa within the neat stone borders of a grave covered with clean white pebbles. The photograph of that grave sat in full view in the center of everything, between the silver-backed brushes and the crystal candlesticks, in Hilly's marital bedroom, almost like a minified altar on the mantel, with the engulfing fireplace below, ready for ashes. Clive himself had grown up with an infallible sense that every family had lost one to Africa, a country that deserved God's wrath: slaughterer of the handsome, maimer of the young, despoiler of the weak and anemic. It was years before the unhinged Gerbers ceased writing letters and sending mementoes that had turned up in an old suitcase, the corner of a drawer. Eventually all of Douglas's stuff came back to his point of departure, tenderly bagged by Hilly, who wrapped everything in crackling brown paper as if consigning it to a funeral pyre.

From all this detritus, Clive received a box of enormous African butterflies that one day crumbled to dust, and a flimsy copy of Alexandre Dumas's *Histoire de mes bêtes,* a grammar-school text with Douglas's diffident scribbles in the margins. Again and again Clive pondered the disproportions of their lives: his father volunteered and maimed before he should ever have gone anywhere; Hilly prematurely made a proxy mother, thus making her late in having her own children; and Douglas, up like a dove, down like dropped carrion,

dead in his salad days. If Clive had had his way, his father would have
gone to Africa with Douglas; his mother would have devoted her life
to music, having no children at all; and he himself would have been
the fictional figment of another narrator, invoked and enabled, but
inaccessible, of no country, just the blissful cardboard-cutout over-
seer, the lover with no lips, the heartthrob with no EKG. A defaulter,
as military handbooks said.

Hilly would have no more children, Harry told himself, little
knowing that the mouth of her womb, angling away from eager
callers, had twisted far enough out of kilter to end conception. She
had fought her way into the valley of the shadow of fertility and
moved on, lugging two children and her burning grief with her.

The whole episode reminded Harry of war. Neat as an infant in its
packing, he said, there lay the shell, bomb, or death that had your
name on it, invisible but sure, and it was no use ducking or praying.
Perhaps the most adroit duckers managed to avoid one projectile, yet
merely walked into the path of somebody else's. Perhaps those who
bothered God most could deflect the trajectory an inch or two, but
the hot metal fragments spewed out over a wide area, so what was the
use? Douglas, he felt, after all his pondering, was the death the
Fitzalans owed the war.

Clive and Kotch would grow up not remembering Uncle Douglas,
though honoring his name, his title. Douglas's great reward, Hilly
said, was being able to see her children when they were tiny, since
they were in a way his siblings. Eventually Harry was able to muster
a hearty response to Douglas's death, arguing that he was an enormous
loss because there was nobody anywhere who could bat so well.
Death had got him out because no human could. It was a faint, jocular
response, appropriate only for the Harrys of the world, whose noses
death had tweaked and who, in return, had winked, with sulfuric,
ingratiated wit. The Douglases could die, and the Harrys sooner or
later swallowed the fact, wishing he had been a near miss like them-

selves. Events had now brought the voluptuous Ruth into Harry's cul-de-sac of boredom. She had the right foreign touch for him, behind golf bunkers, in elderberry lanes, in derelict barns; Douglas had been too much of an athlete to be much of a lover, always saying he was "shagged out," whereas Harry, numb at home, was a demon when released. They were soon gambling and shopping together, returning with presents for the children that drove Hilly wild. Clive and Kotch adored "Auntie" Ruth, who also found time to play with them and was not forever giving music lessons.

At first Ruth, the bereaved, moved in, taking the bus daily to teach school; this was second only to having Sister Binche on the premises with a full supply of Belgian decorations. Ruth was on the premises, but she went to the Fitzalans' to use the toilet. Then Ruth, urged on by some flaming rhetoric from Hilly, moved out.

"We don't," Hilly raged, "need your sludgy Norwegian diseases in a decent household. Here, sweeten your disposition with this." Hilly slung a pound bag of sugar after her, a blue one that fell into a puddle. Harry said he was going to leave too; you couldn't treat a guest like that.

"Guest," Hilly roared, at last free to vent wrath without restraint, since this was essentially a show closer, "she was no more guest than a cancer in somebody's innards. If she was a guest, then I'm a mincing machine. I damned well *am* a mincing machine. That's it. I am going to take these innocent little children out of the way of the likes of you. You didn't fight a war, you went sucking up to foreign trollops. What blinded you, my lad, was whorespit. Do you think I don't know what you were doing? Belgians, Norwegians. If I had that humane killer in my hand this minute, I'd knock a slot in your skull and have you skinned, you poor rotten stinking fumbler. You may have no morals, but you might develop a bit of common sense. Licking her chin while I slaved at that piano to make ends meet. You made different ends meet, didn't you? What you need is a year of Wordsworth to clean your head out. If she comes begging here again, dead Douglas or no dead Douglas, I'll be gone, and you'll never see me again as long as you live, or your children. So put that in your snoot and smoke it."

"You—" Harry began.

"Me? Don't you dare address me as *you*. My name is Hildred, and I won't have any shortening of it from now on. A little dignity wouldn't go amiss. Now, she's gone. You can have her, but you can't have both. Is that clear, sticky pants?"

When they rowed, or when Hilly let rip, Clive and Kotch began to wail and tremble, clutching first at her, then at him, feeling the earth quiver and float away. "Auntie" Ruth had been banished, for reasons unknown, and they divined around them a force, like death's majordomo, that removed loved ones without warning. How propitiate that?

After an hour or so, Hilly calmed down and the row culminated physically, with Harry embracing Hilly, who was all stiffness and aversion, nonetheless allowing herself to be held, and the two children clutching their legs. For solace, sometimes, Clive had crept into Ruth's bed, and had marveled at her smoldering body, the heavy bouquet of her sweat, and the feral grunts with which she populated sleep. Clearly this was a pagan woman from far away, bound to upset the locals, like a fjord overflowing into a cobweb.

Harry's final break with Ruth came in the local cinema—the Picture House—on a day that saw Bert, his youngest brother, accused of trying to steal the Red Cross collection box. His accuser was none other than Bernard Ditcher, now advanced to the status of Ruth's new gentleman friend. Harry arrived to find a motley crew of shamefaced locals surrounding Bert, harangued by Ditcher. A solitary policeman stood by, trying to take a statement, but the uproar was too strong.

With the simple, enormous dignity of the nearly dead, Harry marched up to them and began:

"No need to stand at attention, lads, this isn't a bloody parade ground, is it now? *Is* it?" His voice erupted and echoed against the slate in the walls. "Why don't you stand at ease? That's the ticket. Now, any of you that have no evidence to give, rules of order number 19 paragraph five A, can march away sharpish. We don't want you looking ragged, do we now? General Somebody might be looking. I have seen dead men's bollocks healthier than you lot. Now, who wants to send my brother to jail?" He seemed eleven feet tall, policeman and avenging angel in one, alternately cajoling and bawling while the stunned audience looked on, the film long ago having ceased to roll.

"Well now, step forward the accusers. I have a drink on the bar at the Lion awaiting me. In the old days, false accusers would be shot after first having their mouths jammed full with dead rat. Strapped to a wheel and left for the shrapnel to pick to bits. It's a bit milder these days, lads. Right now, who's first?"

Bernard Ditcher tried to begin. "I saw—"

"Sergeant Moxon here, sir. Will you kindly speak up, get your rotten little voice out of bed? Well? Don't interrupt. You saw him take it, you did. He was no doubt passing the box to the next person. I would. Wouldn't you? I thought so. But *you* read minds, of course, in between playing tiddledywinks with whatever form of life inhabits the front of your trousers. Let's see, Ditcher, late of the—Sunderland Fusiliers. What unit did you serve with, sir? Lost this eye myself serving with the good old Sherwood Foresters. Lincoln green. What, sir? Fusiliers? Army Service Corps? The Grenadier Guards? None of the above, you puckering powdered length of rotten bolony. Well, I must say, you're something to be proud of. You accused my young brother here—of touching the box. What a marvel of perception, sir. How do you know what his motives were? If he was going to steal it, and had made up his mind to do so, would he look any different from how he would look if he wasn't?"

"He'd look guilty," Ditcher said in the first available space.

"How dare you! Half the world looks guilty. You read faces, sir? Do you read palms and heels too? March out, Mister Ditcher, before I conscript you for corpse-washing in Belgium, Royal Edict Number 109. You may not have the flair, but you have two hands." He then spoke to the befuddled policeman. "Do you see any evidence of theft, sir? A gentleman wishes to prefer charges, inspired by his ability to read faces. We'd all be better off licking the slaughterhouse floor for nourishing bits of fat." Harry came smartly to attention. "Bert, go home now," he said, "and keep your head high as if you were marching to a promotion."

Nobody moved. The policeman closed his notebook with a flat clap. Bernard Ditcher opened his mouth, but said nothing, resorting to an adroit fumble. "Would you all," Harry barked, "please come to attention in the presence of the law?" They tried. Flattered, the policeman stiffened himself, chin high, his hand flat along the seam of his pants. "I must say," Harry said with imperious quietness, "you do look ragged. Stand up! Now, let's file out gently and let things get back to normal. Nothing happened here except an optical illusion seen by a professional civilian."

By sheer force of arms, as it were, Harry had quelled the incident, stern and handsome in the face of a rabble which now became a bunch of hangers-on, asking how many Germans had he killed. They bought him pints of beer at the Lion, and he went home pickled but proud.

FOR SOME reason Harry taught Clive how to salute, perhaps anticipating another war or just wanting the boy to appreciate him properly. Look the person being saluted *in the eye,* Harry told him, but only at the right distance. "You raise your hand smartly until the tip of your forefinger touches the lower part of your cap, or your forehead over your right eye, see." This was to show that you had no gun or dagger hidden in your hand. Americans saluted differently, he said, holding their hands edgewise, whereas the British opened the hand out flat. Also, he said, hold the salute for the right length of time; don't rush it, but don't linger over it, either. Hold it until the person saluted returns it, even if you feel frozen at the time and the blood drains away from your arm.

"Why," Clive asked him innocently, "can't you just wave? That might be friendlier."

"The aim of saluting," Harry answered, "is not to be friendly, but to be obedient, just as little boys are obedient to their fathers."

"Even when they misbehave," Clive said to tease him.

"Even then," Harry said gravely. "How would you like somebody to come at you with a gun or a knife? If they saluted, you'd see what was in their hand. If they didn't, you'd be on your guard."

Clive could see that, especially if you were one-eyed and surrounded by hostile Indians. "No," Harry said, "it wouldn't be any use with Indians. They have a different way of doing things." Well, Clive thought, puzzled, if *he* were trying to get at somebody with a weapon, he would do it in a place where saluting did not apply. Or he would open fire the instant he opened his hand to salute.

"Proper little spy," Harry said. "Next time there's a fuss at the Picture House, we'll send you to sort it out." Clive had heard about some to-do, but he took little interest in it, mostly for lack of enticing information. What had happened? he asked. Oh, Harry said, there was almost a scuffle. He'd told them to calm down, and that was that. No, "Auntie" Ruth had not been there, but her fancy man had. Had Uncle Douglas, Clive asked, been her fancy man too? "Or was it you?" No, Harry told him, he was Clive's father. A fancy man wasn't quite respectable. "What's that?" Clive asked, and Harry said "Doesn't salute properly," confusing the boy.

They carved wood together in a blizzard of shavings to make planes and galleons and submarines. The metal bits, the flanges and hinges, he himself shaped, his father humming through gentle catarrh. When they painted, at the same time sharing slices of apple clamped between their teeth during the tricky parts, Harry did the whites and reds, Clive the blues and the camouflage colors. Each left the other's areas bare. Harry threw balls for Clive to hit: balls of leather, rubber, wood, cork, and golf balls eviscerated, trailing parabolas of thin rubber ribbon all over the yard, unwound until the little ball of paint fell out and the golf ball was only a husk. Bat, pole, strip of floorboard, old tennis racket, Clive smote with them all. Swing. Wind-up. Wham. He never knew the right order in which the joys came, sometimes beginning with Wham.

"More, Daddy, more!" he'd cry, and Harry always could.

These were games of peace. "Don't close your eyes," Harry would say. "Watch the ball all the way in." Clive's nose bled. They swabbed it. Hilly came outside with a small towel sprinkled with eau de cologne, although in general she disapproved of things French and

Belgian. They played again. Then Harry's nose bled and Clive rode the elevator of his arms to dab it. Harry never tired until Clive did, and then they put everything away neatly, standing the bat in the corner by the door, rolling the ball of the day back into its drawer among buttons, tools, and sticks of sealing wax.

Clive joined Harry in a mud pit where he sat with three others, all in steel helmets except the corporal, whose hat was soft and had a floppy peak. Don't stay too long, he heard Hilly shouting. He sighted the Vickers as if it were the pencil in some short-legged, lethal pair of compasses. Bound in puttees, his father's legs looked bandaged and filthy. Clive's voice had almost broken, but, like the swan of Tuonela, wobbled about along the uneven line dividing life from death. Were there ancient Greeks who faked their age to join the colors?

Clive still knew, having been amply instructed when little, how to site a machine gun in the front line, siting it not on the parapet but behind the parados. Otherwise the site would be overrun, and the Huns would impale them on blood-wet bayonets. But what the parados was he could never remember, even after looking it up. He was destined never to remember. He promised to be good, the ever-ready son, to behave, to do his duty, the right thing at the right time.

What bothered him now was the knowledge that Harry loved him most when he was little and did not know that he loved Harry. That was why he was always volunteering to recover his father from some grave or other, tracking him into the midst of horrors that made Clive's teeth ache and narrowed his throat. He crawled after his father under the barbed wire while flares spluttered titanium white overhead and the enemy machine guns whipped and cracked. They got back by Verylight to see the grass along the parapet lift into the air as the bullets hit. Image of a ruined, deadlocked summer spent by a father and his boy. Hilly gave a rueful half shake of her head, reading his mind, knowing there was nothing to be done to revise Harry's monumental life. Then Clive reminded her how Harry and another soldier had greased a pig and let it loose in a Belgian dance hall. When they caught it, they dumped it into a well, and one of the Belgians who went down after it was bitten in the thigh. Told to read a book called *Somme Battle Stories,* but only nine, he thought the title was *Some Battle Stories,* selecting an indefinite plural over a singular river, a valley, a hell. How cheerily, he wondered, did his father fight? As if taking carp from a local lake with maggots or earthworms for bait? Or in steel-eyed aloofness, as when he hadn't slept well? Sometimes the Belgians fried eggs and ham for him. He always managed to find tobacco (dark shag) to stuff into the pipe—his badge of premature sagacity.

When the gun was really clean, and there was time for fun, his father hoisted Clive up at the smoky sky with a falsetto shout, and a rickety biplane hummed down. "One of ours, lads," the soldiers cried, and then pretended to fling young Clive at it as if to some aerial rendezvous of equals. Lofted thus, toward whichever sky, Clive smelled battle over the lettuces growing rank in the swollen summer yard, and, when they picked him up, into their dream at altitude, he never knew where he was, and hardly cared. They were all his father.

What had kept Harry going, so he told Hilly, was the dream that one day he would have a son; if he could persuade himself among all that carnage that he would have a son, and then imagine how that son would look, he was bound to come through. So he saw his future, as it were, through a child's eye, a child held out at arm's length like a talisman, held out as far away from the war as possible, a son to whom he would one day tell all, or even a daughter full of complicitous *ahs* who nonetheless slid away from him fast, into dolls and cookery, heedless of the names—Malines, Alost—which he and the son insisted on and mispronounced: *Maylinez* and *All Lost.* Dandelion yellow even more than poppies blurred the torn-up ground, and the seeds wafted through the burned-out villages. It was all Somewhere in Belgium, as the newspapers used to say with blatant secrecy. Thus his father, a knight called away from court and falconry to mortal tournament with the kaiser himself, pounded the kaiser into blood-red sludge and rode St. George's horse, a sprig of hawthorn between his teeth.

For Clive, the aspirant, there had always been, there still was, the sound in his head of his father talking, shouting even: grand confessional hero, getting into this character and that, as his mother sometimes did too. Again and again came that self-conscious war whoop as Harry launched his heir at the sky, and in passing Clive mussed his father's thick, brushed-back black hair, his little knee flicked Harry's trim sharp nose.

Small wonder his father wanted to spend the rest of his life listening to Grieg, one ear held firm against the wireless, the other one closed off with the palm of his hand. How did it go?

If he could envision a son, he could live.

So, to live, he had to marry Hildred.

If, looking ahead, Hildred might not want him, he was doomed.

Blinking the tears away, Clive tried to fix his mind on his father's face new-washed, his eyes unbandaged and exposed to the brightest lights: his father looking like a Greek statue.

Oh, there was light enough for Harry to shave by in later years, from the hissing and sometimes broken gas mantle in the bathroom, where he also took nearly invisible motes of shrapnel from under his top eyelid with a delicately shaved, pointed matchstick, while Clive thought of how, in Belgium, long after 1918, bodies and gun barrels, soup vats and the chassis of armored cars surfaced out of the earth's slow churning. "It's walking out, see," Harry would say as he slid the tiniest touch of what looked like oxide of metal on the back of his machine-gunner's hand. These hardly visible bits of German iron had no symbolic value for him and were just a nuisance, to be picked off as they showed up and laid gently to rest before he swept them to the linoleum with a minor sigh.

My father fishes in his eye, Clive used to think as he stood by him waiting to see the black speck leave the needle point of the match when Harry tapped the vein behind the knuckle. The eyelid would unroll to where it belonged. Clive used to dream that Robin Hood had a glass eye, or at least a head full of shrapnel splinters, and would rid himself of them by peering into a pool in Sherwood Forest. Breathing hard while his neatly manicured fingers groped and fished, Harry loomed in the gaslight, a pale man without an undershirt, and Clive saw on his father's back the white oval of a wound, big brother to the same scar on his own. Were all such things passed on, as a matter of honor? If so, such sons should be born with rearward vision too. The gaslight changed to a different, less comforting hiss, more of a taunt than a sigh. It was not hard, at such moments, to see his father as every bit a Sherwood Forester who burned trunks into charcoal. He *was* a St. George who rode a horse called Victory in a Grander National than *any,* since Harry, after all, was also just his dad, with a Worthington Pale Ale in his fist, and a Players Navy Cut cigarette perched unwet between his teeth.

Nobody joked about his dad. They all knew he had been and done the impossible. Reported Missing, Believed Killed, he had come home one day, walking slowly, with a patch over one eye: a man with no depth perception but, deep inside, the sense of having sat another examination and passed with flying colors.

LATER ON had come those other walks with his two children, always amid the light heaves of summer, Kotch and Clive trembling with pride that they had been allowed out with Harry in their exclusive charge. His left hand in Clive's (as they thought of it, although Clive's was in his, really), and his right in Kotch's (though really vice versa), Harry took his time, never knowing that, in little inbursts of vainglorious pride, Kotch and Clive now and then each closed an eye (the left) to harmonize with Harry, so that with him they veered gently to the left, "so that" here meaning both *to that purpose* and *with the result that*. Clive had often wondered what would happen if both children closed both eyes and trusted themselves to the one-eyed king in the middle. They never did so, but they took obtuse pride in walking wounded with Harry, sometimes while Hilly brought up the rear, keeping a keen gaze on whichever child was nearer the roadway.

After such outings, Clive felt the rigidity seep away from his body, as if he had been frozen: His whole frame worried that there was going to be an accident—a second German shell coming over, a bus mounting the curb and mashing them. When he was older, and yearning back to those walks, Clive told himself they were an elementary exercise; more to the point, he thought, was the act of stilling his body while seated or in fluent motion on his bicycle. He called this learning how to lie down dead, keeping a buttock, a hand, an eyelid without motion for twenty minutes, an hour, a day (what feckless presumption). Then he would know what death was like, and what the dead managed with devastating ease, never moving a muscle in years. Perhaps there were humans, such as Houdini, who could accomplish this feat, but all Clive ever achieved was an incorrigible twitch, a scream in the nerves that yelled *we're not dead yet*. How the dead lay still, flash-frozen by a quite unvengeful force that took sheep, water, children to its bosom with lethal equanimity.

This, Clive kept telling himself, is how the dead do it, quiverless and wholly arrested, with never a tremor of the lip betraying their true nature. As the earth shifted, he thought, of course tremors ran through them, or as the air in the coffin changed, or nature's other creatures bundled past, heedless of such gigantic prey trapped for ever in the final convulsive stretch of a throw that left one arm high and wafting, the ball long gone.

Give in to fate, Harry thought, and it will treat you only as badly as you deserve. Maimed a little, you will never be maimed more. But he had not reckoned with the slow seepage of maltreatment that humbled millions hour by hour. It was possible that nothing good would ever happen to him again, no matter how hard he pored over the doings of each day. One bright noon, walking in the woods between the Mill and the White Bridge, Harry and Clive made little pipes for themselves with matchsticks stuck into acorn cups, then marched sturdily ahead, mock-puffing and exchanging erudite comments about different tobaccos: how one burned your lip, how another had a hint of chicory, how yet another burned fast for having nitrate in it. Clive lazily picked a sheaf of bluebells, but tossed it away in the end as un-Harry-like. He wanted to impress him, not with book learning, but with soldierly virtuosity.

A faint, dreary wind blew all the way down from Scotland, announcing autumn's nearness, and Harry shivered, said "Back end, I think," and Clive nodded, knowing this was Harry's way of proclaiming the end of summer. Another lecture on saluting was just about due, not that Clive minded; he wanted to memorize and recite every town, casualty, advance, retreat; the names of the grocery stores, the churches, even the map coordinates, retrieving young Harry through maps and annals.

Back to business. Thirty paces was the correct saluting distance, wrist straight, thumb and fingers fused. Just doing this made little Clive wonder if his father had faked his age to enlist. Did he really riddle the sunset with machine-gun fire? Scissor the low cumulus until rain fell from it? Did he puncture the moon, aiming upward as if the gun were a theodolite? Did he ever reload? Did he ever have to? He never spoke of it, of inserting the brass tag end of the belt into the feed-block on the right-hand side of the gun. Then, Number One, his father took hold of the tag end and yanked it through, tugging back twice on the crank handle. How did Clive know all this? His father must have told of someone else's doing it, some other Number One, some other Number Two. Then they spotted a man in a white shirt, spying on them perhaps, but, curiously, moving back and forth in much the same position. They stopped and looked, hoping the man would go away, but, obscured by oaks and elms and yews, he stayed put, sometimes actually turning from them as if bored, at other times facing them full.

"He's watching us," Clive said.

"They do in these woods. The whole village keeps an eye on you if you go for a walk. God help those who come here to do a bit of quiet courting." Harry fidgeted. They walked forward and then up the slight incline, and there was the white-shirted man dangling from a rope, rotating slowly in and out of a tapering shaft of sun that burnished him, then left him pale. Harry sent Clive back to the path, but Clive did not budge. The man had evidently climbed the tree, gone along the bough he now hung from, and let himself fall some twelve feet. A good climb, Harry was thinking until he sprang to life and walked forward to check. The man was dead, but that was only the second thought in Harry's head. The first was that this was Bernard Ditcher, Bert's accuser from the other night—Ruth's fancy man, now gaping and goggling. Harry took his full weight and tried to hoist him.

But the head sagged strangled, the hands did not stir. Harry let him down again, amazed to have been able to lift him by the knees like that. He couldn't have been there long. Now Clive, unbidden, touched the dead man's shoes, tugged them as if to set them somewhere else, and administered a gentle push that set the body swinging back and forth, while Harry looked on in astonishment. A last ride, he thought, for Bernard. Before they left the scene, they had sent the body in a widish circuit of the clearing, mainly for fairground effect, not sadistic but experimental, just to see what else would happen. Bernard Ditcher gradually returned to the center, narrowing his orbits until he came to a swaying halt right in front of them: an accuser, a prop, no Sherwood Forester.

"Right, Bernard," Harry whispered, "they won't be calling you to the colors now, will they, you daft bugger?"

Then, realizing this was not the right idiom with which to leave one over whom he had already prevailed, Harry walked back, Clive watching him without daring to move. As he unpinned the veteran's badge from his lapel, Harry wondered what to say, unable now to banish the perverse thought that this man might have married Hilly if he, Harry, had been killed; and then he would have fathered a Clive. Harry pinned the badge on Ditcher with a sigh.

"You know, Bernard," he said in the undertone reserved for military secrets, "you'd have been better off with us in the trenches. By the time you got out, if you did, you'd have seen there is no novelty in death. None at all. It's commonplace, average stuff, death is. Even the best folk suffer from it. Good-bye, you can have the badge. It'll give you a bit of standing wherever you go." To Clive he said, with weary finality, "Once you get to know the dead, my lad, you see that they deserve as much room as the living. They have rights. The tendency is to think of them as only dead, see, but that's wrong: their being dead is the least thing about them, a bit of canary seed floating among all the other things. A dead person, even blown to bits, is still a person. To me, anyway." What was he doing, he wondered, telling such things to a fairly innocent child? It made no sense and would have angered Hilly, who thought he talked far too much about such things to an impressionable boy, turning him into a ghoul.

"Shall we salute him, Daddy?" It was the most appropriate thing Clive could think of to say. Erect on the path, and looking slightly uphill, they stood to attention and raised their hands, Harry musing on Ditcher's being no doubt the last man he would kill. They kept their hands in position for a full minute, then brought them smartly down. These were the drab gestures of eschatology, bringing neither peace nor pain to the recipient, who had never been known to return the salute, but healing to the giver, who had confronted death with tender etiquette.

Whenever Harry toured the woods now, hunting solace or the corrective of that special glade revisited, he had a sense that the birds were no longer singing, at least not to him: not that all of them were silent, just a few selected favorites upon whom he had always depended for a comfort between poignancy and frivolity. Where, for instance, were the small wrens that ran, mouselike, and were never seen to fly? They had short, rounded wings and fluffy plumage. Once there was a golden finch that delivered itself of four or five curt notes and responded most freely to his imitations. Its blue beak was often smeared with green juice from the seedpods it ate. He listened and heard neither, noting with a small agony the absence of what he had heard called the Rodrigues starling: a bit bigger than a blackbird, with white plumage, black trim, beak and feet bright yellow, and the call an incessant exultant warbling. It was a uniquely Derby bird, he thought, but it must have escaped; there used to be so many, to which he crooned when alone, loving the world.

Unable to abide desertion by these birds, Harry began to think of them as artificial, their songs made by a father and his boy walking through the woods with bird whistles to their mouths: little tin cylinders half full of spring water (father and boy had stopped at the Woody Nook), into which they blew through an attached straw. Sometimes no more than a bubbling or hissing came out, but sometimes a warble, a trill, thanks to an arrangement of holes in the cylinder. Was this bit of magic called a Bird Warbler, or what? Harry could not remember, but his memory transformed the dead-sounding wood into a make-believe aviary through which he and Clive sauntered with intent pouts. What they had in their mouths were acorn pipes no longer, at least according to Harry, a prudent and severe man who, alone in the house, would sometimes sit in front of the piano, its lid down, and plant his feet wide apart on top of two plates he set there to honor the gods of polish.

The fuss after the inquest had almost died down; Harry had got his badge back after having testified with a bad cold; and Ruth Lindstrom had returned to teaching after a few days off. Then, inspired or reminded, Pither Wetherby the chemist hanged himself in the hall of his own house for some petty deed of embezzlement; his wife entered and almost collided with his swaying body, its heels exactly above the doormat. Was the village, still remembering the war, having an attack of morbid self-punishment? There was no frenzy in the streets as there once had been during the war, but behind the scenes a ravening guilt began to keep men from their sleep, most of all those who had never been, as Harry put it, mustered to the colors. One young fellow roped himself to a gas lamp, but was cut down in time, and another, a young collier with a limp, allowed himself to drown quietly in Never Fear Dam, sucking into his lungs ounce after ounce of the green scum that curded the surface. He had *volunteered* and and been turned down. In the end, a little card the size of a bus ticket circulated in the pubs, composed by Harry and his cronies, counseling the men of the village not to take life too seriously, not in view of recent deaths. Such deaths, it read, were not necessarily manly, and those who considered them had best think again. Presumably they did; there were no more suicides, but for a while those walking in the woods looked nervously around them, hoping not to see a corpse swaying in the breeze.

"I swung him," Clive told Hilly, who shrieked at him to stop. "I swang him."

"English," she said. "At least get that right."

"Swing, swang, swung," Clive said, remembering he had not been afraid to touch the dead Ditcher. He didn't resist or moan, he didn't seem heavy or unwieldy, or smell. He just went the way you shoved him, and then came back, a mere corporeal offering aloft above the glade. Now Clive knew that nothing was going to frighten him ever, not even Hitler, who was brewing another war. They heard Neville Chamberlain make an ingratiating apology and the announcement of the state of war between England and Germany. That day, Clive and his sister walked down to the Mill and bought two bags of russet apples in case of rationing; it was the only thing to do at the end of a glorious summer. Perhaps, Hilly said to Harry, those men who killed themselves were afraid they'd be called up this time round. No, Harry scoffed, it was too long ago, 1918 wasn't 1939; though he could see that, if the whole village had the same sense of time as he and Hilly, it would have heeded only four or five years in the intervening twenty. Guilt eroded fast, but not as fast as time.

Harry was glad they would not need him this war, but he intended to take a fanatic's interest for the sheer sake of militant knowledge. He, who had lived history in a devourer's way, felt the old sick sucking of the inferno calling out to him again; it was all he knew. His God was Mars, and he wasn't ashamed of it, but he kept wondering why it was always the Germans, a nation he had been ready to respect: for cleanliness, linearity, courage, love of music. If he had to go, he would go, but only as an adviser to those dealing with red-hot ladles. Harry came to life, and when Clive stood in front of him a week before going to the Secondary School a mile away, all togged up in dark-blue and light-blue regalia, Harry caught himself feeling that old off-to-war elation. The boy had a big brown satchel that dangled too low against the back of his knees, so Harry tightened him up, knotted the tie harder, jammed the cap on more firmly, gave the shoes a flick with his hankie. It was almost as good as being in Belgium.

For the first time, Harry felt his life begin to take shape while moving away from him; these were the only children he would have, Hilly was the only wife, the newly regained job at Staveley the only one open to him. Life had closed in upon him, telling him things that heated his brain, so he tried not to think of them. All the choices not made plagued him. He had never peered at the part of Hilly from which the children came. He might have done so with a mirror; he might have investigated the underside of his scrotum, but he knew now he was never going to. At some point in the sexual onset of the first few years, Harry might have felt a sensation beyond sensation, something wholly unfamiliar, like a creamy nettle. It did not have to come, it was a matter of stonily hoping. The hope kept you going. Now he knew that, unless something electrified the pair of them, the linoleum of sameness would be their sexual lot.

Clive could only once smuggle the bloodstained copy of *Field Burial Service* into church in lieu of a prayerbook. When he brought it home he told Harry "They let you keep this because you'd been so brave." And Harry at once thought: In case I had to bury myself, rather. Only once would Clive be found skulking in the outdoor toilet because he hated going to Sunday School; he hid there until the ritual was approximately over, and walked into the house. Found out, Clive explained that he hated sitting on the cold floor, as they had to, and that was that. He spurned church, as Harry did, as Hilly almost did. They were a pagan trio, and Kotch was too little to care; or so they thought, little realizing that she had come to care, indeed, for prayers and communion rites, of which she saw less and less as the other three dropped the religious element from their lives. Only once, Harry saw, would Clive begin to use Harry's old kitbag to keep his toys in. Only once would those medals arrive by post, in a box that might have held condoms.

Harry smiled at the ambivalent face of fate, wondering if the new war was going to be interesting. Nothing had happened so far: no bombs, no reconnaissance planes, no sirens. Perhaps it would all be over in a twinkling; if not, they would soon be calling up the old brigade, the Old Contemptibles, to send them off again, glass eyes and all. The lack of certain bird songs kept him away from the woods, until the day he and Clive happened there upon the field of radio location devices and, perversely unpatriotic, tossed stones over the fence in high parabolas until they heard the sound of broken glass. They were telling the amassed authorities, the bosses, to go bugger themselves. If this device was there to pick up German bombers, it would pick up not quite so many now. The dead feel of the woods Harry now attributed to the war, wondering what else would soon lose its quality, its majestic savor: fishing, no doubt, or the Gregorian chant on the radio. Life never stayed put long; its essence was to squirm and alter, contorting the people it sustained.

When Grandma Victoria died of pneumonia, Hilly took Clive and Kotch to plant a last kiss on that cold, gaunt brow and to say, on instruction "Good-bye, Grandma." From that moment dated Clive's aversion to saying good-bye to anyone else; he could not stand so much frontal finality, unanswered and cold. Whereas Harry had schooled him in adjusting to the death of the soldier, the deaths of civilians wounded and appalled him.

AT LAST the question arose of Clive's learning to play the piano, which idea gave him the horrors; he had no desire, little as he was, to become one among the procession of tame bottoms that sat on the stool. He would have the knack, the flair, Hilly told herself without knowing why; but Clive did not want to share his mother. Indeed, he felt he was sharing her enough already. He knew, in any event, he was going to be an aircraft designer, and so was not going to become the son she wanted him to be.

Instead of piano, she taught him grammar from the age of four onward, with the result that he became a perfect monster, with nothing to say but a precisian's way of saying it. She taught him because he was there: nothing fancy in her reasoning. He was what she called a bird of restricted voice that sang not to announce its territory or its needs but to voice its pleasure in being alive. So there he was, leaned alongside her leg with his head at her knee as she read aloud to him the ghastly harmony of protasis and apodosis, as if that had anything to do with Hereward the Wake, the Saxon patriot who had held out in the Isle of Ely against William the Conqueror. He knew about Hereward, from Charles Kingsley's boys' book, almost before he could spell; she had read it aloud to him, to get him to sleep or wake up, it made no difference. He preferred Hereward to grammar, of course, but in the end grammar itself seemed almost dramatic or heroic and Hereward was the model of a grammatical man. He liked especially the idea that, because of William the Conqueror, as she explained it to him, many towns had French names and many of his schoolmates had French blood. Adventure was grammatical to him.

He loved pageantry, which was the reward for grammar. When he went to school, he went with a score of quotations bubbling off his little mouth as if he were some recitation machine from the lower depths, to be counted on one evil day to have books by heart, after all the books had burned. The classmate named Beecham, he found, was really Beauchamp, and the one called Beaver was really Belvoir. Where did he live? Exington, which surely, Hilly told him, must have been Aixenton, though she knew it was an Anglo-Saxon word from Roman times. Clive enjoyed this delicate transformation of his land-scape and its inhabitants, appreciating even that early in life what imagining could do.

It had not been his mother, then, he thought as he looked back on so verbal a boyhood, but language whose leg he had leaned upon, absently caressing it as he learned. Language was a woman, his mother was his muse, and language never turned its back on you provided you obeyed its rules. What, he wondered, looking back for her, did she say? Grammar was vocabulary's constabulary. Well, he reasoned in all the prime and post-prime of adulthood, if language would not betray you, neither would a mother. Verily: The antique word blew back to him from all those childhood readings with the piano stool behind him (in both senses). Wordsworth and Tennyson, Kingsley and Scott, were his true schoolmates. From them he went to school to study inferior forms of writing in primers written by hacks for pence. He had gone, he saw, from sirloin steak to sausage meat, so no wonder he grew up a little boy who scowled, knowing the learning was better at home, where the arts held sway. *His* mother was a pianist and a teacher of English; had read all the books in the creaking tall cupboard in the room that faced the street, where the piano sat. She sometimes painted in oils on cloth, sometimes on velvet, if she could find any, and he had seen the joy it brought her. He lived, Clive reminded himself (still shaking from the shock of having been born not long ago), on the brink of Lake Constance, by moonlight— Hereward the Wake's only grammatical lieutenant, but with a capacious future in the offing. It was as a small boy, he thought, that he had begun to fail his mother, and as a middle-aged woman that she had finally begun to forgive him: He played a few scales, and that was that; but still, he waited until his mid-twenties before writing books. The years between eight and twenty-five belonged to neither music nor prose.

Night after night, Harry, Kotch, and he heard the front door slam, the lock give its congealed crunch, and then, as she failed to emerge, the first notes of the "Moonlight." The three of them would creep to sit on the stairs outside her door, facing the overcoats on their pegs, while she cleared her head of amateurs' fumbles and thus reconsecrated herself to genius through perfect and stylish execution.

It was music's house, theirs, not just war's: Beethoven's, Chopin's, Liszt's. Harry, Kotch, and Clive functioned in there as subordinate shades to household gods of touch, expansiveness, and panache, to metronome and sustaining pedal. Doing his algebra or French homework in the dead of winter, whose clammy gusts whisked his slippered feet, or during the radiant, azure lulls of late summer when he began homework again with the aroma of harvest in his nose, Clive felt in and beyond the house a continuum of scales and chords—proof against all seasons, wars, changes of government, or health. On washdays, when Hilly hung linen on the clotheslines, he expected to find it emblazoned with treble or bass clefs from the mere touch of her hands as she set down the puncher which squeezed or punched the grime from the fabric into the tubful of battleship-gray suds. Chunky described her hands best, always wealed, scarred, and uncannily warm, worn down by housework, not arpeggios.

What had that life been like in Exington or Aixenton, or Aixenton-en-terre? Had that book he found in the back of the handkerchief drawer decided everything? *Married Love,* wasn't it, by Marie Stopes? Or had it been his father's favorite book, *The Impregnable Women,* which Harry read, or so Clive supposed, in hopes that the passage of the novel through his brain would inhibit the passage of his seed to where it would count? Had their love been a battle of the books, with Hilly on the quiet arranging to become pregnant, and Harry on the not-so-quiet sterilizing himself with Scottish prose? Again and again he fingered the weave of that choked-up life of theirs.

Perhaps he wanted to connect his parents on good bond paper. There was the male virgin that his father was, the female virgin that his mother was; but here was he, product of what used to be called defloration, and he wondered how many virgin men deflowered virgin women back in those old days. To him, creature of contrary imagination and some wrong information, first coitus was more like the *introduction* of a flower into a place where never before had flower sprouted. It had not occurred to him that a woman started with a bud or a bloom that had to be ravaged or dismembered. What a way to begin life, he thought. Sex had crept up on them like corroding peppermint; not to be spoken of, not to be prepared for. He could hardly guess at Hilly's first intimations of desire, brainwashed as she had been by that spinsterly mother who even cupped her hand over the tip of the teapot spout as she poured. Nor could he fathom well the hormones of Harry, from first stiffening to last fiasco. "I'm shut of all that rubbish," Harry had told him on his fortieth wedding anniversary, with almost desperate finality, like a man glad, a man hounded by hell.

Hilly thrived, he remembered that: buxom and accomplished, a woman of tides, postprandial dreams, and languorous gazes, while Harry stood tentatively by, a Noah whose ark had filled up while he yawned. Hilly must have felt untrue to certain idols of the maternal tribe, being pianist and governess, teacher and tutor first, while the whole village waited for her to get on with it. Her change of name was just a triviality of bookkeeping, and indeed Harry might properly have changed his name to hers: Hereward Fitzalan. He became her fourth brother, her third live one, living with her in nominal incest. If Harry's gift had always been for transfer, Hilly's had always been for transcendence: rising above not only the clamp of her parents' pragmatic love, the skivvying for George, Thurrie, and Douglas; the tilt of her womb; the barely discernible move up Market Street; the choked gamut of her essentially Victorian girlhood, but also the chronic anemia for which she endured a diet of raw liver. Again he saw her at forty, forty-five, releasing that winning, teenager's smile beneath a pair of keen, delicate green or gray eyes and above a jaw of silky, alert stubbornness, not as rounded a jaw as Harry's.

Quick now, he asked himself, did she voluptuously inhale the aroma of coffee, fresh ground or fresh pulverized? Of course she did. It was family ritual. The shiny tall crackling bags always sprang open with that dank, sweet stink coming out, like a soul that had been minced. What else did she do? She periodically took Kotch to hospital for radium treatment of a winy nevus on her left hand (Kotch being left-handed and therefore acutely aware of the blemish).

She spent, Clive recalled, exactly the same amount of money on each of her two children: a point of parental honor. And she refused to play the organ in the village church, for much the same reasons as she refused to play piano in the boardinghouse by the sea. Her life was an eclectic, juicy stew of most things undertaken, a few refused. She joined openness-to-experience with integrity-on-guard, refusing the organ in order to cherish the pianoforte; but determined to send her children beyond the village's orbit, to become her emissaries, satellites, takers of contingency samples, her robots even. She launched them, in her mind at least, as from an Alcatraz of class, history, and self-denial. She wanted the world to know she was there and had been cheated.

Yes, but what was her playing like? Clive trembled, knowing. It was never a mere translation from paper to keyboard, but an I'll-show-you bravura feat of performative zeal; she vented and honed a fearsome amount of nervous energy otherwise applied to hurling bags of sugar at Harry's head, after which she would storm out of the house, threatening to jump into one of the local dams. Brought back with flashlights, after the cry "Hilly's gone again!" she would calm down over a mug of Ovaltine or Horlicks, on which she would always blame the next day's headache. She usually went at night, when she had more time, although, Clive mused, if she'd had more time she would have gone in the daytime too. But then, he reasoned, had she had the time she would never have gone in the first place: being too busy was what drove her out. Having pupils to teach and two children to bring up was almost too much, and a layabout husband was the last straw. She threw the sugar, and the two children scooped it up in dessertspoons, blowing away the fluff and plucking out the hairs, the crumbs. This was why it always had an unrefined look, having been strewn and gathered. Their sugar always looked gray and secondhand.

THE OTHER three in the family soon became aware that they were living with a romantic, a woman who was prelude, fugue, and enigma variation all in one; a volcano inside a Dresden shepherdess. If any one of them winked wrong, or sniggered, or misintoned, the steeplechase wrath reserved for erring music pupils came their way instead, a shower of darts and brickbats, a ready-aim-fire onslaught of the complete denouncer, full of hysterical crescendos, tympanic accusations, jangling triangular rebuffs, and a special oral mode Clive could only call instrumental speechlessness, an aghast sostenuto induced by behavior so barbaric—Harry's sarcasms, Kotch's snatching a second slice of cake, Clive's burping—that no words could fit, but only the plucked, pulsing lips, the eyes paired in upward roll, the hand plastered histrionically against the temple. Hilly had begun to take after her highstrung mother, sometimes substituting frenzy for creative fulfillment. Without children and an almost unemployable war veteran for a husband, she would have been placid some of the time; much of it, even. But pressured she let rip, and they loved her for it, since she showed what could be done with a volatile temperament and a contrary world. She was operatic and eloquent, and she was never dull, not even when she calmed down after menopause. She could usually be roused, even in later years, by some feckless piece of obscenity, some colossal feat of rudeness. The recitatives of Hilly's indignation were really music of another kind. There were music lessons, Clive remembered in a fit of adoring indignation, from ten to noon, two to four, then from five to ten or even later: Year in, year out, to keep them fed and clad, and later on to supplement her children's university scholarships. In the profoundest sense she orchestrated their lives according to some score unseen by anyone else and loosely derided by envious ignoramuses for its refinement, culture, and gentility. Most found her stuck-up, but they didn't know a true intellectual snob when they met one. To Hilly, what was "decent" meant what fitted your gifts, what fostered and furthered them, what transformed them into artifacts of will as impersonal in the end as cave paintings or the medicine wheels of stones on the Canadian prairies, to all of which your own arrival and passing were incidental: You were here, or there, as a conduit for the miracle of human giftedness, and lucky to be thus equipped.

Hilly the Promethean-Victorian, offspring of small proprietors, made her acreage mental, her nest harmonic, her passions proxy. On she went, quietly manufacturing the heterodox antilife she had thought up, handmaking the children's clothes during the General Strike, in wartime giving piano lessons in exchange for black-market turkeys, ox tongues, and contraband pounds of butter. What was the good, her philosophy ran, of being in trade, as Jane Austen put it, if you didn't do a little bartering for the good of your dear ones? Always, she felt, music was worth food. So Harry and Clive and Kotch ate abundantly during the war; and they ate on the plane of emotion too. Hilly knew the horizon was an optical illusion intended for the children of those who could not see beyond. Behind Earth's curvature she sensed the curvature of occupied space.

As the war erupted, Clive went off to grammar school, somehow linking bloodshed with learning. The landscape turned itself inside out as people dug air-raid shelters, often only a hole reinforced with corrugated iron. In his back yard, a red-brick one appeared, far too small to accommodate the occupants of the four row houses, and Clive assumed the builders were counting on a few dying on the way to the shelter. Hilly shrugged in contempt and became an air raid warden, complete with steel helmet and official armband. Her job was to blow a whistle during raids and bang on doors when she saw light leaking through blacked-out windows. One pinpoint of light, she had been told, and she repeated it, was as large as a house from twenty thousand feet: a beacon to a marauding Heinkel or Dornier.

Harry and Clive made model planes, smoothing the wood with several degrees of sandpaper, then painting them accurately, after which they sat on the piano to be twanged to death. Harry did not need a war, but he didn't mind one; it gave him an interest in life, as he said, and he reveled in all the mistakes made by generals on both sides.

At first they hid under the cellar steps, where Kotch and Clive slept on the enormous box a pocket billiards table had arrived in (sign that the Depression was finally over), while Hilly and Harry sat up by the light of a candle, whispering about another war, one in which they had been apart. After a few nights in the dank red-brick structure, hunched in a rug on a chair, they came back to the cellar steps, sometimes all four crouching under the mahogany dining table. "If we have to go," Hilly declared "I want us all to go together," and nobody dared contradict her, even though the other three felt she was asking too much.

One night, as they were tucking into poached eggs on toast (one of Hilly's pupils paid for music in eggs), a screech seemed to come right down the chimney, and they all jumped beneath the table. The thump was a hundred yards away, but it might have been in the back garden. That was their closest bomb. After a while, they resumed their eggs on toast, legendary as a good air-raid meal; you could get it down in three minutes and, even as you headed for the shelter, cram the last mouthfuls in. It was the kind of food that collapsed, bizarrely in tune with crumbling houses and factories.

After a week or two of the Blitz, which was demolishing the steel city of Sheffield seven miles away, Harry and Clive would saunter out to watch the searchlights find the bombers, in their hands neat and firm brisket sandwiches, buttered so as not to slide. Up they looked and chewed, exclaiming as best they could, then devoutly examining the hole in the sandwich. Shrapnel made a light pattering sound around them and was hot to the hand; but no parachutes, bodies, or uniforms came out of the night sky. The most eerie sound of all was the alternating thrum of Nazi motors, wholly different from the steady bawl of the Rolls-Royce engines made in Derby not far away. Sometimes a searchlight touched the wing or fuselage of a bomber, but as quickly lost it, stabbing and hovering, sometimes going out altogether because an air gunner on high had fired down and blinded it. That, Clive thought, was pretty much what he and Harry had done in the woods, smashing the radio-location devices in that open field, just out of bloody-mindedness. One day, someone, something, would pay them back for doing so.

The nights were stealthy. Hilly neglected her duties as warden to look after Kotch or to make brisket sandwiches for the two males. That people in Sheffield were being blown to bits and roasted did not seem real; you couldn't hear anything, or smell it. Every night German squadrons came directly over them en route to the blazing target. The talk was of hundreds trapped in the dance-hall basement of the Grand Hotel, hoofing the war away until the fireball found them.

Riding to school on his bicycle each morning, Clive saw the sun of the burning city come up in the north: red molten metal brimming about on the horizon. Daytime raids sent the children into the huge air-raid shelters the school had built, where there was much grabbing of girls' underwear in the half-light and surreptitious jerking-off by the bigger boys, who could "fetch" in two minutes. Clive had the unusual vision of cream curd hidden in the spines of these heroes, gradually being sucked to the surface: fetched a long way and then slapped between hands into a million splattering brilliants, either to blind or to provoke a scream.

Only half of Clive's mind was on war, though; he doted on French, less on English. What he liked was foreignness, and he was even willing to traffic with grammar to get that authentic exotic flavor of life lived elsewhere. Tiny, he was "bushed" repeatedly, which meant being hurled into thorn bushes; he thought of French and somehow managed to put on a brave face, vowing vengeance on his tormentors. Hilly began to worry and encouraged him to come home for lunch, thus exposing him to daytime bombers, although she never thought of it. Home he came, scratched and disheveled—blooded, as Harry called it, although taking the names of the offenders himself, presumably for a military punishment to come: broken on the wheel or trussed and thrown into deep mud. Here, Hilly told herself, was a boy who needed a bit of mothering even though she had a full complement of music pupils.

Kotch would go to the same school in a year's time, to be defended by the same bullied little Francophile, as unaware of this chivalrous feat to come as of the sudden cessation of Goering's bombardments. Already, the Germans were behind Clive's defenses, ravaging his childhood, ruining his sleep, destroying perdurable cities he more or less idolized as big toys in concrete, where he loved to go and buy coffee, obechi wood (a balsa substitute), airplane glue, and foreign stamps. He could feel the fabric of life coming apart, the book from its jacket, its binding; he loved light, but light was suffocated by war, rammed back down the chimneys and blocked off at the windows. For the rest of his days he would be unable to sleep except in a pitch-dark room with the sound of an air conditioner if he could get it. Weekends he went to the top floor of the house, to the attic, and put on his military tunic: a brown blazer with a leather Sam Browne belt, a bus conductor's hat from a dress-up kit, and a pair of tin wings (a bombardier's) from a boys' magazine. Here he supervised air raids on aerial photographs of Germany torn from magazines, sighting through the pencil hole in a pair of compasses filched from school. He spoke in a pseudo-German, bombing the Nazis in their own jabber, concocting such phrases as *Eiger-schneider dasstagut und schnell der hafta schant*. He set Germany on fire, then doused it in gasoline and sulfuric acid. *His* war, he said, would soon be ended. When a plane went over, at least in his private world of war, it was always "One of ours."

AS THE DAYS passed, Clive began to panic, trapped as he was on the conveyor belt of his emotions with the demon of love cranking up the speed. His mother became a blur, a disintegration, a monumental effigy of all the wonderful or bizarre things she had done, all the fostering people she had been for a dozen years. Told about the boy who stood up in class at school and asked the teacher "Do we need to know this, Miss?" she observed mildly that it was always better to know something than to send it packing. "You never can tell," she said, "when you will want it. That was a silly boy. It wasn't *you*, was it?" It wasn't. When he was not well enough to ride back to school on his well-oiled Raleigh after coming home for lamb chops and rice pudding, she would seat herself by the fire and anesthetize him by clamping her always warm palm against his forehead while he sat on her lap. He was asleep in seconds while the wind screamed and the rain drummed, dreaming of being in his yellow cape and leggings, wheeling his bicycle up the steep hill to the school. She knew it was usually on such afternoons that he faltered and begged off; but, if he was only a little out of sorts, or improved as the afternoon wore on, she encouraged him to read some geography or a few geometrical theorems on the basis of *You might need to know that someday*. It never occurred to her that he was goofing off, and sometimes he really did need poulticing or a band of hot flannel, impregnated with camphor oil, wrapped around his throat. Once spared the trek to classes, he would usually unbidden begin to read a book, preferably fiction; and Kotch would have the same idea, which made the school suspicious, though siblings often went down with the same infection at the same time. The pair of them lay back in the velvet hammock of mother love while being argued about at school, and Hilly played the piano for them if there were no pupils (she took Wednesdays off halfway through her piano-teaching career) or read them stories from the big fat Kipling she had brought from her parents' home.

When he heaved into the enamel bowl, she held his forehead to save him from butting the rim. Much of his life, he felt, she had cupped her palm to keep him back from some collision or nightmare, but never to restrain him from a rightful goal. Upstairs, reading with his milk and biscuits beside him, he would wait patiently for her cry of *Oo-oo* from the bottom floor, signaling that it was time to go to sleep, and he was to answer her call with the same cry to show that he was all right. And Kotch too. So the evening hour often filled with *Oo-oo*'s, echoing and overlapping as if love had at last found a definitive voice. Then she would instruct them to be quiet and "save it up for tomorrow. We'll have a good *Oo-oo* then." He felt so secure in the enclosure of her devotion, almost like a unicorn within a fenced ring, bustling about and pretending to gallop away or at least toward a jump, but always falling back as her warm deterrents made themselves felt. Quietly deploring his untidiness, she repacked his schoolbag for him while he slept, caching the little books in the smaller outside pocket. She sharpened his pencils by inserting them into the globe of the world and twisting. She aired his underwear and shirt all night in front of the dying fire, or on the hot-water tank in the bathroom, on whose pipes bits of strontium nitrate from his chemistry set glowed beneath the night-glow cardboard skeleton that dangled from the cold-water cistern higher up. The simplicity of it all. Having wanted both him and his sister, she fussed them night and day. His father, meantime, oiled his tiny cap gun and made little lead weights to squeeze into the nose of paper gliders.

Shoveling memories to fill the chasm at his feet, Clive kept enlarging the photograph of Uncle Douglas's grave, dousing himself with his mother's eau de cologne, and surreptitiously smoking his father's cigarettes up in the attic with the window wide open while he poured test-tubes full of copper sulfate solution on passersby. Feverishly he took the plans of the next war, torn from some *Battle Illustrated*, folded them up into a waterproof tobacco pouch and hid them high in the fireplace. When he shot Mrs. Lewis, their neighbor, with his BB gun, Hilly chided Mrs. Lewis for getting into the line of fire, quite ignoring the fact that he filled her laundry on the line with mud and shot out the feet, the elbows, the genitals, sometimes with darts. When he wobbled into the front room with her regular cup of tea at 4:00 P.M. and caught her in mid-count or bang in the midst of chastisement's crescendo, he tried to make her laugh, but only got her fiercest stare and sometimes spilled most of the tea into the saucer, which meant he had to repeat the whole maneuver. She would never yell at *him* about music, he had seen to that. Addicted to the crisp, fragrant corners of loaves, he sometimes crept down the cellar steps and munched fearfully away in the dark, always found out, of course, and rebuked with a baker's smile. "One day," she said, "I'll bake a special loaf all of corners, and then you'll get a surprise, my lad, ferreting about in the dark down there. You won't know where to stop, but you'll know a loaf has only four corners." She looked with a dawdling smile on all the games he played with sealing wax, pen nibs (mating them), pincushions, safety pins, cookie cutters, Plasticine, and fresh-made dough, amused by her pet animal while she wound his mind up, except when his breath smelled of sherry or his room reeked of cigarette smoke. The bath was for motorboats. The big living-room table was for building float planes on (and homework). The sink was the well in which chemistry experiments took place. The gas was for

Bunsen burners, one of which melted a tripod Harry had made for him from brass (the soldered joints gave way). The fire was what set off little pellets of gunpowder. The cellar, and its steps, were the exclusive domain of Areemayhew, the capering red-and-yellow ogre that chased him back up the steps each time, making him slam the door and crash home the bolt. His, too, all string, all foreign coins, all matchboxes, all bottle tops, all paperclips, all milk-bottle tops, all broken toffee hammers, all nuts.

Remembering all this was like being born again a dozen times a second; he, Clive, was nothing but a heap of dawning pleasures. He recognized the delights of having been yearned for by a woman who had long thought herself sterile, or destined merely to teach scales. He was unsure when he had first known it, but to be born of Hilly was different from being "had" by any other mother. Hilly behaved as if she alone had discovered the notion of maternity; it had been intended for her and nobody else, so she embraced it with a lover's impetus, knowing that motherhood tested the hypothesis called love, mostly of the selfless kind. She believed in toys as well, each Christmas somehow managing to bestow on Clive and Kotch a pillowcase full of parcels except on such red-letter days as the one that brought a bright red railroad engine with pedals: He could sit in it and speed. All these gifts came from music, so it seemed to Clive, and of course made music all over again in her children's souls.

Could anything be farther from music than war? Not that music was not full of war; harmony had to have a context. But war had removed itself, and with it his father, to a separate place, while his mother and music had gone off on their own. Perhaps never would the pair of them—music and war, Hilly and Harry, speak again. He wondered about the helplessness of music, the dementia of war.

In his own schooldays, it had been Miss Garforth, a teacher of English, who first made Clive realize what music was. The class would assemble in the school dining hall, where a full-sized but defunct Rolls-Royce aero engine sat on its heavy wooden frame, distilling an aroma of machine oil, and then Avis Garforth would play Offenbach on the school radiogram, stalking about the room in severe concentration, her head held high, her arms folded, her feet slowly pavaning her to and fro, almost as if they belonged to a paddle steamer. Music fueled her inwardness; not that she seemed to walk in time to the music, *Orpheus in the Underworld;* rather, she tried to slow it down. Sometimes, she would already be marching around when they arrived, tiptoeing in so as not to disturb her, and he began to imagine her everywhere, a harmonic sleepwalker on the Yorkshire moors, on the Isle of Arran, Jesus-walking the North Sea, not the sibyl of music, like his mother, but music's policewoman. He remembered nothing of the grammar and literature she taught them (if any), but only her somewhat pulpy sternness of mien as she cruised through the dining hall to the strains of Offenbach. Later in life he realized she was an exceptionally attractive woman who, to flaunt her magnificent long legs and her tight sweater, walked right in front of them, day after day, and none of them realized it. She walked in aphrodisiac peace, weaving a spell in the teeth of the young, brooding on God alone knew what lascivious passage in her private life: a Scottish girl with blazing sapphire eyes. Why Offenbach, he wondered, who was frivolous in his music as well as fussily dapper in appearance (pince-nez and side whiskers)? Why did she never play *The Tales of Hoff-mann?* Miss Garforth must have been just the sort of person his father would have relished: the personification of exaggerated calm, some-thing he needed after he was twenty. What became of her and her thick, golden pinned-up hair? He almost felt as if he had spurned the love of his life. Clive calling Avis, chirped the radio of his mind. Anyway, didn't *avis* mean something in Latin? *Mavis* meant, he thought, "you prefer," and Mavis was a girl's name too. No, *avis* meant bird only, and Avis Garforth was a *rara,* never to be repeated on sea or land. She sauntered among the tables and chairs of his imagination, a permanently ambulant phantom, making him wonder, years later, what she had died of after having what kind of a life. Wedded to music, perhaps she married only Offenbach, had children only by proxy, and perhaps wished she had never left the distant northern island she came from.

"Dreaming again," Hildred chided. "You don't change much. I've seen that look on your face from the time you were four, when you first began to learn English properly. English put you to sleep, didn't it?"

"It woke me up, rather," he said. Language, the word his mother had not said, had awakened a dormant zone of his brain, making it quiver with piratical gusto, sending it far afield, and forever beyond the reach of pedantic taskmasters at the grammar school, to whom he seemed a lazy dreamer enthralled by only the names in geography, the faces in history, the shapes of the letters in algebra, the irregular verbs in French.

Did Avis Garforth have a soft, licking voice, ideal for Keats rather than Burns? Like his father, she marched; like his mother, she not only dwelt on music, she dwelt in it. She was the link he needed today, trying as he was to recapture his mother as a child even while looking at her with predatory affection, trying to recreate his father through her recollections because he had none of him, none of her. He needed a marching, musical personage into whom to burrow for memories small as sand grains, halting painfully every now and then to murmur, for either of them, if he had only known, if she . . . If they . . . It was no use. Pain was pain. His father should never have faked his age to get into the war. He should have hung around with the Fitzalan crew, just to see what turned up. His mother should never have come back from London. After her second trip, when she played the right music and afterward treated herself to some new underwear (a London trophy), she should have stayed on and sent for Harry. That would have changed their lives, Clive thought, instantly berating himself for yet another soppy daydream, acknowledging that their lives were lived, no longer subject to the interference of inventive sons. Indeed, come to think of it, the lived part of their lives was *safe* now. What a miracle. What unnerved him was the time they had remaining to them, and the thought of this kept the sweet side of him sour. There was nothing he could do that, by his standards, would be good enough for them, prompting the rapture non pareil.

Hilly sat in a room looking at fields, hearing her favorite music, waiting and wondering. On she sat, looking and waiting and wondering, almost voluptuously reliving her girlhood second by second with a host of "That was when"'s and "He'd no sooner arrived than"'s and "only a day later"'s. She made memory elastic, opening the pores of time, then she stretched the fabric for a second time, revealing new pores. On and on she toiled until all she had to look into was a single pore incapable of expansion, which swirled lazily like a top, the spinning colors on its cap the emotions she had felt over so many years, and somewhere in there, cold and underfed in the trenches, was his father, a little boy in a man's uniform: officially clad, hoping a shell would not land near him or that a sniper would not pot him when he went to the latrine at the back of the trench. Like a worm curling in a lettuce, he did his business and hurried back to stand on the duckboards that made up the trenches' floors, whereas the fire steps, a foot higher, were of earth only and therefore always sinking.

ONE DAY, however, soon after the pale-blue Messerschmitt-109 became an exhibit in the center of bombed-out Sheffield (a few coins bought him into the bloodstained seat), his world broke apart and then came together again in the weirdest way. Avis Garforth left and Ruth Lindstrom took her place, with never so much as a word indicating to Clive that she knew him, had once showered him and Kotch with superfluous gifts. She never called him by name, only by surname, as was the school way. Perhaps she got a perverse Norwegian thrill from saying Harry's surname so much. Her presence brought back Uncle Douglas's ghost, with a few grave-flowers sticking to the side of his mouth; straddling a huge Great Dane on the African veldt. Clive went upstairs to look at the photograph of Douglas's grave, like a breakfast tray loaded with pebbles.

Here was "Auntie" Ruth, playing Avis Garforth's music, and Clive thought the disharmony was as bad as the still-ongoing war. To have her back was one thing, but snubbing him another; he was certainly not going to learn music from *her*.

"If there's ever anything you want to talk about, man to man," Harry said gruffly, "just speak up, lad."

Oh, he would, Clive said, then asked, "What about, Daddy?"

"Girls, women, boys, men, cows, bulls, nanny goats and billy goats.

I haven't exactly been a shrinking violet, you know. Soldiers see more of the world than most."

"Oh," Clive said cannily, "you mean about the war."

"Private things," Harry said, wearying of this heroic euphemism, but unwilling to put the matter bluntly.

"You mean what I shouldn't ask Momoi about."

"That's a funny way of putting it. I suppose so. You're getting on, in long trousers, not in the Junior team any more. Almost a young man."

"You mean underwear," Clive said.

"Not in so many words."

"Would you like me to ask you something?"

"Well, no. . . . It depends."

Instead, Clive told him about the time, two years ago, when he went to camp with the school, and one day one of the big boys made him drink from a big bottle full of urine, kept in the tent.

"They forced you?"

"*He* did."

"Did you complain?"

Clive did not answer.

"I suppose it tasted bad."

"I pretended," Clive told him with grimacing solemnity, "it was pop."

"And it tasted bad."

"It tasted like death."

"A wise boy, so full of death."

"Learned from you, Daddy."

"So, if you learn nothing else, you will at least have learned that."

Clive nodded. "It's all right to smoke, then."

"Not if you want to chuck that ball at a hundred miles an hour."

"Seventy."

"A mild bump, then?"

"Eighty, then."

"A concussion. Good."

"A hundred miles an hour would kill, wouldn't it, Daddy?"

"Cure many a headache, boy. By when will you have worked up your top speed?"

"A year from now."

"Who will be target number one?"

"Mr. Lloyd. He held up my math exam and told the class he wanted to frame it. He was kidding. I nearly failed."

"His face?"

"His face. He plays cricket."

"And then what? Hospital, funeral, a headstone saying two plus two?"

"If he wasn't wearing a box I'd get him in the knackers."

Harry looked at his spellbound son, who planned revenge according to a strictly Old Testament code. The boy would be a soldier yet, he thought, certainly no pianist or monk. But you never knew; many a devotee of blood and ruction ended up a Wordsworth. He had seen it in the military. Many a tupper had become a mild husband with a list of predictable horses.

AS HARRY'S life settled down, unlike Hilly's (punctured by gall-bladder pains, prey to the hedonism of music), he realized his days were spent not in a succession of moments and acts, but in an ethos. Roy Fox, the boy next door, practiced his yodel every day. Fanny Lewis, next door the other way, walked her dog at the same hours while her husband coughed and chewed black twist tobacco. Every-one was slowly gravitating to some point, like a squadron of bombers edging in and out of view. He had begun to become receptive, a drinker-in of others' rigmaroles. He lived in the tropic of quiet grandstand, astounded to have fathered two smart children including a boy whose prowess at cricket was a marvel; apparently, Clive had just read in some book how to be good at it, and had obeyed.

"I always knew they'd turn out well," Harry said most evenings. Having given all for his country, as he saw it, his country had best start looking after him, and most of all look after his wife and children. Harry had an uncertain relationship with civilization and was not going to be urged back into partnership. There he was in the national honor roll, with stiff upper lip and single roving blue eye, flanked by the absconded God and the shell-shocked cretin. What he remem-bered how to do was his, and he treasured it—finding the Belgian border on a map, bringing home filched lengths of copper or brass rod, stood on end inside his socks; repairing shoes on the hearth rug with the last between his thighs and sweat pouring from his brow onto the leather he cut with a free hand as if carving a baguette. What he had forgotten, however, did not exist.

His worst moment was the night he wrote out the football coupon as usual, and began to ponder the line he and Hilly had agreed on before she went to bed. A punter had to predict the outcome of fourteen football matches, marking on the coupon a 1 for a home win, 2 for an away, X for a draw. It cost pence to gamble, but the winnings could be huge. This time, as he scanned the column of results, checking it against what he knew of the teams, he saw one forecast that was surely wrong, and changed it from a draw to a home win. By Saturday at six o'clock, when the news announcer on the radio read the results, mainly for football pools punters, he could not believe his ears. He and Hilly had thirteen right; the wrong one was the one he had changed, but Hilly was rapturous, thinking they had all fourteen; she knew the forecast line by heart, and her aural check told her she was a millionaire. Harry had always, in the space provided, signed his name, saying he did not wish any publicity in the event of a big win, and now he had signed it in vain. "Meddling," Hilly yelled. "Why can't you leave things alone? You know everything, don't you? Have you any idea how much you've cost us? Do you know how many hours of music teaching I'll have to do again? I won't say what I should say, because if I did you'd drop dead. Do you know what you are? You're a soft half-pennyworth, Harry Moxon. What you need is another war." Their second prize was a thousand pounds, but the first prize was almost a million.

"Oh, we'd have had to share it anyway," Harry blustered. "Imagine the humiliation of that."

"You," Hilly pounded, "are insane. There's never a day when I'd mind sharing a million with some cleverdick who at least sends in the correct line he and his wife have worked out together. You must be insane to think like that."

Harry remained drunk for a week, drastically imagining how it would have been to win the big prize, torturing himself with images of luxury picked up from the novels of Leslie Charteris and Eric Ambler, which he read at night. None of his failures on the horses had been as grievous as this, and his failure to leave well alone struck him as comparable to certain bungles in his war.

Eventually Hilly forgave him, since money was only muck, and he forgave himself because, as a devastated veteran, he did not always know what he was doing. Yes, it was an error in penmanship; he copied wrong. That was how they left it, wrote it off, knowing he would never again copy out their forecasts. They never won, though, in all the subsequent years of competition; the silver lining had flashed its face at them just once and had gone back to heaven snubbed. They continued to study the teams and juggle predictions even to the point of attempting a minor permutation. Once or twice, Clive and Kotch did a line or two and won a few shillings, but clearly gambling was not for them, and would not be permitted.

Harry continued to fix his mind on the war, admiring such new fighter bombers as Typhoons and Tempests as they came out, announced in the newspapers as the latest secret weapon. And he tried to interest himself in Hilly's holy code of mental or esthetic transcendence, and was aghast when Clive began to talk of scholarships, when and where and how to sit the examinations for them. The son who had begun by declaring his hunger to be an aircraft designer now spoke of a life devoted to Rousseau and Gide, Baudelaire and Apollinaire. What Hilly had forgone, her two children would retrieve. They would find the Grail, or the football-coupon prize, and bring it home to be roasted, served up with thick brown gravy, Yorkshire pudding, crisp and eggy, and the most crackly roasted potatoes in the world.

Off to the grammar school Hilly went, to interview the head mistress, Miss Roberts, the tiny wiry flame who had replaced Dr.

Walmsley, gassed in Harry's war and unable to do more than whisper and, occasionally, thrash a boy.

"It's by no means a sure thing, Mrs. Moxon," Miss Roberts said. "The competition is appropriately appalling, and I am not certain we have time enough in which to prepare him."

"Oh," Hilly said sternly, wishing the woman would call her Miss Fitzalan, "it will come from within. I know. I have gone this way myself. In the end it comes from within, as with all sacrificial animals."

Miss Roberts blinked, then smiled, having encountered someone as tart and articulate as herself. The boy was the same, incapable of conforming, but a little sparkler of ideas; the sister too. Sow's ear into—well, whatever would be would be.

"I'll drill him," she said. "He will do three extra hours of homework nightly."

"Miss Roberts," Hilly said, her face all radiant vindication, "we have struck a deal. He is yours as well as mine. Push him, before he maims anyone else on the cricket field. When he first came here he was bullied, but now he has become a terror, banned at the St. Peter's Club for bowling too fast."

"He and Moore," Miss Roberts said, "have terrorized almost all of the school's opponents. Why is he so good?"

"He gets it," Hilly said with sisterly pride, "from his Uncle Douglas, dead in Africa. A Netherthorpe boy. Clive bowls, though, whereas his Uncle Douglas used to bat."

"Bully for him," Miss Roberts said. "I'll teach him to enjoy French poetry. I mean, I'll make him regret it—"

"I caught the ambivalence, Miss Roberts," Hilly said, her eyes agleam. "They do say that felicitous and intended ambiguity is the graciousness of impetuous discourse."

"I can see where he gets it from. If he doesn't prevail, we can make a professional sportsman of him."

"No you don't," Hilly said, leaving. "I don't want him designing aeroplanes either."

"He won't," Miss Roberts chortled. "Ever. He *can't count.* Fear not, Mrs. Moxon. Arty or hearty, that will be him. And his sister too, I think."

Hilly left, musing on the politeness and wit of educated women when they got together, after having heard about one another for years, guessing and rehearsing. Miss Roberts had no music in her, but perhaps a hint of the poetic. Mrs. Moxon, Miss Roberts thought, should be doing my job and I could be off in St. Malo sunning. Is that boy university material? If not, why not?

"Two clever children," Harry bragged. "That's what I have. T.C.C. I have Tee Cee Cee. Lucky man I am, and that's the truth." When, at the kitchen table, he went through this little speech over the cheese and pickles, whoever was on his blind side mouthed T.C.C. for the others to read, and he never caught on that his jubilant oration, varying little from pub to house, was a cause of merriment. To T.C.C. his two children tactfully added A.C.M. and A.C.F., A Clever Mother and A Clever Father. Harry was happy, hoping his clever children would never need money from him. Music would pay, as was right. Harry was a gambler when he was flush and a voyeur when broke. His children he created *en passant,* less aware of their conception than of certain losers in his stable of racetrack horrors. He never owned a house or a horse or anything much except a bag of first-class chisels.

The grown-up Clive, peering back at the crucible in which his Oxford days had cooked and bloomed, felt a tear cruise through his system, seeking exit; knowing that Harry was always the innocent optimist, letting Hilly pull bills from his pockets so long as bills were there. He looked back on them both, the pair of them denied. With a lancing pang he refelt the twisted chemistry of a mother love that urged Kotch and himself, overmotivating them. He trundled back to how Harry and Hilly viewed their offspring, each knowing in a different way that Clive and his sister would crash through their respective paper targets and carom on beyond as overachievers obliviously bent on collecting trophies that would enact and augment both Hilly's passion for the perfect, Harry's casual bias toward the winner.

On a wholly different front, remembered by Clive with preposterous vividness, Mr. Lloyd came in to bat, settled down, and prepared to receive his first ball which, flung savagely at the mat covering the concrete, reared up at head level and, with lethal speed, converted his face into a mass of blood. Away he went, blotted with handkerchiefs, as the scorer wrote opposite his name: "Retired Hurt."

CLIVE COULD tell that Harry was working with bruised dreams, the original part of his life already over, the remainder not so much silence as neat small gestures of near submission: elaborately inscribing his name on the football coupon, almost a monk caught in the act of self-illuminating. All he inscribed he did with languorous precision as if this or that line of *1*'s, *2*'s, and *X*'s were his last. He no longer enjoyed Hilly's friends coming to see her for coffee and cookies, so they came during the week. He loved his newspaper, read with glasses bought at Woolworths: two portholes for a pessimist. *Rawshuss villians,* he liked to say. "The world is full of rawshuss villians," knowing he was mispronouncing but letting that flaw in his public-private demeanor stand for his disloyalty to society.

After filing some brass at work, and having got brass dust into the eyelets of his work boots, Harry had to spend several days at home with a terrible dermatitis of both legs, treated with penicillin by Dr. Crawford, who sat for hours boozing with him. Next thing, Harry had no skin on his legs, thanks to a weakness created in the trenches when he stood in all that water. "Ye're allergic, Harry," Crawford told him as he snipped away the festoons of skin. "To water, brass, and penicillin. Take your pick." At this time, Hilly discovered how dictatorial Harry could be, demanding of her a full accounting each time she went out: whom she talked to, whom she waved to, especially men. He timed her, imagining her progress up and down Market Street, jotting down times of arrival, checking her shopping basket to see if indeed she had been where she said she had. Because he never spoke with strangers now, he expected much the same of her, wishing her to say beforehand whom she planned to talk with. She should stick to that, he said, lest she cause him undue pain, making him wonder for hours.

Harry had come a long way from the freebooter who shacked up blind with Fabienne Binche and entrusted his erotic education to her, whoever she really was. What in a sense had broken him was the sudden lunge of his children into early adulthood, both at the same time—as Kotch, like all girls, was precocious. No longer could he push special little morsels to the side of his plate for the pair of them, like puppy dogs, to snap up. In the old days, when he returned from work, they had snuggled down on either side of him as he sat and ate the food Hilly had kept warm in the oven. He had felt grand as a public library then, a true paterfamilias, even when later he napped, and they sat together on one side of him, waiting him out until they could read the newspaper to him. Having read it all already, with the monocle he kept hidden at work, he found the news old but the reading an almost lyrical joy. Now the pair of them had vaulted away from him, aimed at something trickier than the pleasing of a father, that ancient obeisance, and he felt deprived, maimed, undone, almost like one of the old gods in Keats's "Hyperion" (Hilly's thought, confided at last to Clive, who winced and buried himself in *Le Bourgeois Gentilhomme*.)

To cheer Clive up, Hilly told him once again about the years of anemia, when she had to eat chopped liver, and of migraine: the saw-toothed dazzles and the ensuing headaches. One touch on her skull, she said, would make her want to vomit. What causes it? he asked, and she trotted out the explanations she knew, from cheese to milk and chocolate, beef to herring, eventually telling him again about the pneumonia, when her hair fell out and regrew as baby hair. "Someone who has been a creaking gate for so long," she said, "is not subject to time. I wore that collar to straighten out the nerves in my neck, otherwise my hands went numb, and you can't play with numb hands. And not to play is waste, isn't it?"

Gradually he was gathering his mother together, salvaging her from the episodic account he had always had, haphazard as an autograph album. Now he began to see a pattern, contrasting it with his father's. All along, he told himself, Hilly had been tinkered with and adjusted, a superb design from Boeing that always needed tiny tweaks to keep her going. So she had always flown with a hole in the wing covering somewhere: unalarmed, buoyant, expansive, knowing she was one of the enigmatic deity's best experiments, loaded with variants, of course, reaching all the way from Liszt to Britten. Clive felt his spine elongate as he pondered her. She would always be wiser than he, of course, but he was gaining slowly; Hilly was a hundred years ahead of him, but he was only twenty minutes behind. Something like that.

She had more to tell him than he had suspected: a hundred memories an hour once she warmed to the task—her memories of others' memories, thus summoning to her aid the pasts of the entire family. So he asked and asked, and she responded, mainly about her own girlhood, showing him the tassels and fringes she might add to the tale, but then detaching them. She simplified, perhaps out of benign impatience. It was her own childhood that began to take over now, a recessive diminution akin to that which, through age, thinned her back, her arms, her wrists. Never her legs, though, unblemished, those of a thirty-year-old woman. He had them too, wasted on a male.

What, then, he wondered, was most splendid about her? She had this synoptic, almost abstract gift for keeping the tubes of talent clear. A woman as disabusedly aware of her spectacular abilities as of her students' ineptitude, Hilly nonetheless registered in Clive's eyes as an example of brilliant nurture. An orchid who doubled as a gardener, she whipped every neuron in sight into shape and blew lovingly into the synapses. She overflowed with survivor skills, whereas Harry had only just survived.

Perhaps she knew she had made him into someone who would sell her down the river for one beautifully built sentence. Art was the extremism they had in common, even though their tastes differed. That he was a budding monster he was sure, and not only for bad behavior. It was as if some four-year-old had mastered laryngology by six and could hardly wait until twenty-five, when he would perform his first surgery. Momoi had planted a time bomb. Was Clive going to be jailed for some criminal excess or knighted for undercover services to the Empire? Get his throat cut in the East End of London or become a golden-throated movie star? If the future came at all, it was bound to have features, quality, Contents like a book; so long as there was a life, things were bound to happen in it, for good or ill. This made her nervous. How could you ever tell what a boy was going to be, how he was going to turn out? You lit the firework and stood back, all control gone. Her son was just so much raw flesh ascending.

She slid her mind back almost half a century, now and then embellishing to please him (she knew what he was after), but telling the truth much as she recalled it. "There was meat to deliver, to wrap. Bookkeeping." She scowled. "And your grandmother was none too well—she hadn't really been right since she had Douglas."

"And Daddy? Was he able to write?"

"Not as often as he should have done. And what he did write they censored. We never knew where he was. If he said, they blotted it out with tar or something nasty." She took a deep breath, whether to relax herself or to fortify her for the next bout he could not be sure.

"There were other young men sniffing around?"

"I wouldn't say 'sniff.' Presenting their compliments. I know you think that's funny, but that's how we used to talk, until the modern world 'improved' English."

"You worried about him? And Uncle George, Uncle Thurrie?"

"Did we? Of course we did. At first. Then we got used to their being away, as if they were at a very long cricket match, day after day. We got on with our lives. I made do with the piano. Come to think of it, *I* did. In a way, the piano always came first." Because, he told himself, it linked her to the incomprehensible ocean of harmony she was always trying to tell him about. Mere people sometimes got in the way; his mother had always been an extraterrestrial, he felt, never mind how lovely, winning, witty. She came from another bark, a different path. She survived because she did not count in earth years; and she had coped with Harry's being away amid the carnage by relaxing her judgment to the point at which he was no longer a citizen of music's dimension. Poor Harry, disenfranchised while living on bully beef and (when he was lucky) bacon and bread or delicate French pastries, all in tin pans red with blood and gray with spattered brains. From time to time, she remembered, an officer would arrive and tell them how many soldiers had been shot for desertion; or, for a more minor offense, had been lashed to a cannon wheel for several hours, exposed to whatever jagged metal happened to be coursing through the air.

"Did you imagine him?" he asked.

"Always," she said.

"Did he come through?"

"Once a week," she told him with unaffected pride. "We never abused the privilege. There were those who say they saw the angels of Mons, actually flying, you know, like Saint Joseph, high above the smoke and the mud, but I never did, and what came through was ordinary stuff—he'd want a bath, he'd say, or he'd just had some good bacon. It was never much, but when I played certain pieces of music I thought of him hard, until my teeth ached and my fingers began to tighten up, and I'd get some through. I could tell he was listening to music, I just could." Perhaps only childhood sweethearts achieved this psychic reciprocity. As if, evicted from Wordsworth's golden nursery, they still trailed clouds of glory that overlapped.

He envied her because she had seen *the fire* and spoke openly about it as if responding to someone who asked if she had ever been in Kew Gardens. When she answered, with a bit of genial flummery about her time at the Royal College of Music, she seemed to be talking in tongues about always having one part of her, the romantic one, on the very brink of transcendental fire, which could be found in a trench or a pit, a furnace or a piano stool (whose lid lifted, Clive recalled, replaced the silky asafetida fume of all those bottoms with the sourness of musty sheet music). She had seen it, and smelled it too: the ineffable echelon of all the minds in history talking or singing or chalking to themselves. Something like that. She had heard the race crying out for what was not there: the atheists' *Messiah*.

Then she was saying, as if summoned up from a thousand years away, "I hate to eat fish when I've cooked it. I can't explain. It puts me off. So I'll be happy with some canned salmon, and never you mind. Eat up."

Dense, radioactive material began to gather in Clive's head: the gist of his parents' lives transformed into abiding, severe images, a calculus where he had been eager to settle for arithmetic. Something dreadful was going to happen soon, he knew, otherwise such imagery would not be scalding and dominating his mind. His father, like some abyssal polar bear of absence, waited for the worst to happen, crashing down in the shape of a doomed airplane, or slid under the door, popped into the letterbox—a warrant of execution. Hilly still saw Harry moving at intolerable, angelic speed over the dunes and hills of France, his Lincoln green ticketed with scarlet felt tacked on with resin, his eyes closed and his hands in his armpits. Was he always going to be wounded? The future, so dreaded, was no part of God's mind, or anything like that, but more the buildup of aspiration over the ages, as if everyone had exhaled and this was the tenderness of all breath rising. It was the cosmic way of seeing your own breath. If so, why was it all so terrifying? What was coming, Clive wondered? Hilly had taught him that the imagination makes its own comfort: Imagination grew because there was nothing else save love, and love would not always do because it sometimes drove you mad.

It was important, she would explain, not to be distracted by all the rules of grammar or harmony, or names such as Tennyson or Handel, or concepts such as clause and fugue. All these were essential, but there was something else that perhaps only a witch doctor or a shaman might do justice to: the caramel in the universe, the sweetshop in the midst of all the efficient clockwork.

Grievous things, then, began happening so fast that Harry wondered what prolonged war they echoed. His father, once of military bearing and stern thinness, succumbed to tuberculosis, his lungs never recovering from the cave-in at his mine. Harry, who had seen so much death, found his father's demise a glacial spike. What had his father always said, about those who told well the tale of all their injuries? "All these scroungers never happen anything." Lazyboneses came to naught.

"You ought to live in a better climate," Harry had always said to him, "where you can get out more."

"Ay," his father responded, "I'll be going to a better climate one of these days." He knew the weight, the altitude, the coordinates of paradise. A man whose touch was that of a butterfly, he had been known to speak harshly to children, but only when they came too close to him, liable to do him harm, cause him pain. Harry kept looking for the irate enemy who had put paid to his father, Alfred, but there was no one; his death had no author. His mother died soon after, heaving up curds of blood and phlegm: the Spanish influenza, locals whispered, although Harry knew better. She had always been a fertile wisp of a woman, a baker of enormous loaves, a maker of sandwiches, someone who let Harry and his siblings do what they wanted, as to punish any one of them would disrupt the others and provoke *them* to mischief too. Of course, Harry had become a Fitzalan, which meant that deaths in his own family were fractionally remote. Had his father ever been a boy, his mother a girl? The pair of them carefree, unbreeding, uncommitted. Who made things necessary? Who decided that all adults should begin as children, all living things die, all of life be as baffling as an inkwell to a newt? Clive kept choking on the arbitrary, wishing there were another mode of human life altogether in which a Hilly would not say "Did you hear that scream in the wind?" or a cloud full of death waft over, making everyone nervous to the point of fleeing underground.

Things went more slowly with Hilly's father, the ample churchwarden and man-about-the-village who gave money away, as his wife remarked, as if it were celery. He slowly became vague and began to wet himself, getting on buses and, because he was charming and easygoing, being allowed to ride free to the end of the route, where the police usually picked him up and brought him home. Mrs. Anthony took him in, she being someone with a strong, unexploited vein of the supervisory. She kept him clean and, as far as possible, off the map; but he was a born wanderer, gregarious and ingratiating. The more he traveled, the more pleasant he became, as if wanderlust were a civilizing force. Some journeys took him fifteen miles. He had been known to try to shake hands with a whole busload of people before being willing to dismount. He died in his sleep, then lay in state in Hilly's front room, where the local parson tried to berate her for not taking better care of him, a confrontation that Clive himself terminated after he heard his mother weeping. In he punched, stern as Barabbas, told the cleric to go to hell. No parson darkened the Moxons' door from that day forth.

Their world was whistle-windy and empty, as Harry said, a kind of no-man's-land, like looking for Sunday's paper on Saturday. The indelicate paw of the cosmos had moved among them, tithing as usual. Thank goodness, Hilly thought, I have not gone blank, but I don't think I want too much more that's worth remembering. I no longer aspire to the impossible sum of everything recalled. In as eidetic a command as he could muster, Harry kept linking the joys of an afterlife to the joys of anticipation.

Lips daubed black, Clive haunted the night now with his schoolmates, making a mixture of lead pipes and lead soldiers, melted up in a saucepan on a vacant lot. The result was what they called a "brutal headgear," shaped like a chamber pot or a highwayman's tricorne. It depended on how much lead you had. They poured the molten lead into a mold made of wet sand and were soon wearing it, all the cares of the world on top of their skulls. 1944. A flurry of examinations began, then another and another; fifteen-year-old Clive was being squeezed like a lemon, pumped up like an inner tube. It was all education, into the midst of which, one afternoon at school, Avis Garforth returned, both her arms dangling useless by her side; she had been bombed or raped; no one quite knew, but she had only come to say good-bye. Miss Lindstrom told the boys and girls Miss Garforth was going to a sanitarium to recover (or to die). The demon lover Clive always imagined for her was nowhere to be seen, but a nurse in crackling starched whites awaited her in the women's staff room, ready to guide her away from nostalgia.

All Clive could see for it was to get out of the world called school, aided or not.

"We'll try to pay," Hilly said, "if he's bright enough."

"Better with a scholarship. Those who aren't bright shouldn't go." Harry was still a sergeant.

"Then," said Hilly, "*I'll* take care of him, and her, if we have to. They'll get where they deserve."

"If they do," Harry said, "I'll be the first to give them all my good wishes."

After that, Clive's parents seemed to live for ever, slumping gradually, but full of preposterous zip, getting to know everything in history and music, as if competing with him and Kotch. Harry seemed inexhaustibly humbled, a dried-out specimen of whom Hilly was proud. Diuretics had thinned him into an older boy who floated to work and back in clothes far too big for him, raving about the future of Germany, which he was glad to see destroyed. Hilly dealt in politics not at all, reserving her best energies for the piano, at which she both toiled and rejoiced, playing her same old favorites with a look of truculent finesse.

Clive read himself into a night owl's delirium, subsisting on wafers of sleep and cramming his days with the music of Harry James, Benny Goodman, Artie Shaw, Charlie Barnet, Count Basie and the rest of the swing herd.

He would never forget the expression on Harry's face when he showed him the general essay paper he had taken at Oxford, hoping to win a scholarship. It had been the third or fourth of some dozen examination papers otherwise concerned with English and French literature. *Write for three hours,* it said at the head of the paper, *on one of the following topics:*

1. Awe.
2. The Categorical Imperative.
3. Duns Scotus.

"Well," Clive said. "Which?"

"Duns Scotus," Harry told him.

"Why? Because you've heard of him?"

"I know who he was. Pointed paper hat, sent outside the school, or to stand in a corner."

"Gottim," Clive said.

"But of course," Hilly said airily, "and never mind those of us who know about philosophers, you wrote on awe."

"How did you know?" Clive asked, keeping his teeth together.

"Because I explained it to you when you were little," Hilly said. "It stands to sense. Awe is reverent looking. True modesty about being alive. Awe is wondering who really wrote Bach's music, Bach or—well, you know the rest."

On they all four chattered, looking at the other papers, Kotch admiring the questions on Baudelaire and Keats, Harry tapping his finger at the piece of Russian in the translation paper (on which Clive did the French), Hilly counting up the hours of writing, Clive re-counting takes of life in an Oxford college: blazing coal fires, dark-brown marmalade for breakfast, a personal servant called a scout who brought you hot water with a morning cup of tea. Porridge and Hegel, toast and Voltaire. It was the paradise Clive knew about in detail long before he went near it.

Now, though, it was not the exam that occupied him, but his mother's voice, like the instrument called *corno,* that doubled the soprano line in the first and last movements of Bach's *Wachet Auf!:* a silvery nodule twirling. Hilly's voice had become unnaturally high that day, almost stretched with strain by the sight of the papers and the surviving son.

Harry sighed belligerently and Hilly cackled at the music Clive liked, but he did not care: Long on flank, Harry James had a tall, deep tuxedo made from a snowfield and a trumpet aimed at heaven. This brash, automatic music was the tune of another continent, where decorum mattered little, and Clive determined to get there somehow, later on, after walking on water. Night after night the living-room table bulged high with Clive's and Kotch's books. The radio stayed off; the aroma of coffee became a constant, and Hilly played or taught, Harry grumbled and went for a beer, leaving them to it.

When a wire came for Clive saying he had won an award at Oxford, he felt like the ball-of-hair heirloom from the Fitzalans': light, already rising away, freed from gravity. How had he managed to do something so boundless? He did not care, and he came back from his first term at Oxford speaking la-di-da.

Kotch had a male friend to stay over, and Hilly found the condom on the bathroom washbasin. The uproar, Harry said, was worse than being in the trenches. Didn't Hilly know her daughter would have a warm bed? "Under our own roof," Hilly screamed. "Remember us?" Harry sighed. "*We* were married," she told him. "Oh well," he said, "it is the twentieth century after all."

Then both children were gone, and Hilly and Harry could hardly face each other, as if they had done something shameful, banishing them thus. The time of letters had begun: Hilly's long and exquisitely calligraphic, Harry's meticulous and terse, tucked in the envelopes like fortune cookies, forever warning Clive against women and gambling.

"They weren't ready for the outside world," Hilly said, almost keening.

"They've been ready some time."

"They're out of our hands now," Hilly said.

"Hands across the sea," Harry told her. "Cheer up."

"I'm glad we didn't have three."

"Not likely," Harry said.

"Two wars."

"Children don't go to war, woman."

"One day they'll have to."

"Then I'll go too. Damn those Jerries."

Before he went off to America, among gangsters as Hilly said, Clive signed on to do his national service in the RAF, because he liked planes. His parents looked the same the day he left from Southampton as when he returned, brown and nasal. It was at either of those points that he began to develop his abiding image of them in middle age: Hilly far from withering, buxom in cable-knit sweater and tight skirt, low heels, her brown hair twirled into unnecessary curls, her eyes taut and keen, her hands warmly worn; Harry in a soft subdued French silk tie, green pullover, suit of striped blue, his first shirt with an attached collar, cuffs that buttoned. They felt somehow reprieved, rejected, sloughed off, used. The long haul was over, and no other destiny showed up. "There's only work," Harry said. "We're at a loose end. I ought to go into politics. You ought to get back on the concert stage. It isn't over, it's just pausing. We'll last for ages yet. Two wars and here we are shining like two linnets, our children off our hands. Where'd you like to go, Missus?"

"Greece," Hilly said at once. "Athens, if you please. But never mind about me; Clive, already finished at Oxford, gone to America, into the Air Force when he comes back. What a life!"

"Oh, I don't know," Harry scoffed, "I've had better myself. He'll never get blown up by a shell at this rate. Where's the fun? As for you, my love, you'll be lucky to get to Belgium."

They did see Oxford, Hilly attentive and slow motion, Harry sarcastic and impatient. "All talk," he said. "Imagine, these fellows work about five hours a week and get paid for reading books. Mind you, that's what I'd do too, it's easier than killing in Flanders, and you get to keep your own bodies. If you see."

"No, I don't," Hilly snapped. "These places," she announced, "are devoted to *mind*. They're quiet for thinking in. The food is very skimpy. That's the very idea of a college."

"I bet the beer is thick," Harry said.

"They have no time for beer in these places," Hilly told him in valiant worship. "Don't you know what this place is?"

"Beer," Harry scoffed, "helps the mind to good ideas. Honest. Look at me, woman."

"I'm looking."

"Well?"

She said nothing, but gestured at the soft sward of the lawns, the ancient stone of the walls, the stained glass of certain ecclesiastical-looking windows, the gowns on students' backs, the decrepit bicycles parked next to the porter's lodge.

"This is Oxford, not the First World War, not the Great War, the war to end wars. This is where you have to come up with the idea that ends all other ideas."

"I bet," Harry said, all affronted worldliness, "they have some rare old times in college. All that energy, all that freedom to come and go."

"They have to be in by ten at night," Hilly said.

"Only to bloody well climb out again and raise Cain. I wouldn't mind going with them."

"For shame," she hissed, haughty but genial. "Cain has been raised so many times he's gone over the top, if you see my meaning."

"I never do," Harry said. "I'm not that educated. Just a bit of well-bred cannon fodder, me. I'd do it for fun, you see—climbing out of the college. I'm young enough, aren't I?"

Hilly pressed on. "Well, now we've seen Oxford, we can put it behind us. It isn't everything." And then, like a soprano hitting a hitherto unreached high note, she said, "I don't mean Cambridge, either. Other places. They sort of beckon a bit of you that isn't homeloving."

"Tomorrow the world," Harry whispered without a pause. "Don't you remember? That's what it sounds like to me. We'll have to draw back a bit, or they'll think Hitler's come again."

"Hitler?" Hilly was scouring history for the allusion, unable to detect in affable grandiosity and its tourist tinge any hint of world politics. "Oh, I didn't mean that, softie."

"Two clever children." Harry sighed. "What more do you want, woman?"

She was ready for him, as almost always. "What I want, Harry," she said with strict craving, "is all that time before 1914 back again. Time melting as toffee."

"Well," Harry said, "we'll work on it. You've had your own way in everything so far. Who'd object?"

CONSIDERING Harry's favorite foods—eggs, ham, chops, crisp-roasted beef—and mutton fat, just about anything fried or otherwise regreased—what happened to him should have come sooner. His clogged arteries had hardened, causing what Hilly called his "funny spells": brief periods of utter abstraction, during which he might have been reading exquisite poetry. He smiled a sauntering smile that nobody could change; he smiled it for ten or fifteen minutes, altogether severed from what he or others had been doing or saying. Then he came around, blinking hard and clearing his throat severely. In no time he could speak again, unaware of having done anything unusual; and if, by some chance, he had hold of any of them, they had to stay put in his iron clench until he recovered. Hilly, Kotch, and Clive soon realized that, during these spells, he could not stand up either; if standing, he would fall, limp as a polish rag, as good as blind.

One day, home alone, he toppled face first into the fire on the hearth, burning his mouth. Then he began to go out for a drink and come back much later than usual, disheveled and flushed. People found him several hundred yards away from 17 Market Street, going fast, and brought him home. Hilly and he would go to the pub, then she would leave after first entrusting Harry to someone reliable. When she went to collect him, truant schoolboy, her mind would be on the way her father had roamed by bus.

Harry complained, but he remembered none of his own wanderings and thought the family were having a bit of fun with him. Found lying in the road, seemingly unconscious, he at last took a battery of tests and found himself on extra diuretics to rid him of water. He continued to drift, fall, and black out. That was the end of his pub days, although he drank at home and was encouraged to do so since liquor dilated his blood vessels. He always added a note to Hilly's more effusive letters:

> Yes I've had a busy time with H, but managed to plod through, she is knocking about again and eating better, she had nothing her first week in bed and she soon flags without food. In fact she was getting me worried, and that was causing me more of my funny spells.

Hilly came and went, soared and plunged as usual, always recovering with a bemused smirk, whereas Harry sank and sank, unable to account for his doldrums, his first cough and runny nose in years, for which he blamed the fog and the wet, ultimately content to wrap things up in one of his most famous expressions: Fine day but dull so far.

He had rid himself of his tummy, so why wasn't he much better? Was there no reward for humbug? A pain in his calf often stranded him, but he knew he was a galloper no more. "Perhaps this warmer weather will help it, I wish it would go." There was no army behind him now, no horde of Sherwood Foresters, not even a lascivious memory of Belgium. It was all flowing away from him as he did his best to remain upright, as if preparing to give or take a salute. A cane helped, but he cursed it roundly. Stuck at the sit, he interrogated Hilly about her every move, stationing himself at the front-room window behind the aspidistra to check the street; his mood one of inquisitorial calm.

The pulse that began in the top of his heart was no longer reaching the ventricles beneath, which meant his congested blood vessels mattered no more because the blood was hardly reaching them anyway. He was fibrillating and gasping, often in a blistering temper as a man being scrunched through a needle's eye and emerging sapped, dizzy, palpitant, and almost done for. His head ached and his chest bounced. Some ill-adjusted dynamo was running inside his ribs, and the pills he took only made him dryer, fainter, sleepier. He would have loved a cannonade at this point to demolish him, to save Hilly trouble. He imagined himself fractionally more alive than he was, then dismissed himself, saying "He's no good," he will never be any good any more, not as a stroller or a lounger, a breather or a bouncer. All he could do was sit still and stare through the wall with his dwindling eye. Had he once been brisk? An arguer, a soldier, an essayist. Of course, but now, he told himself, you cannot make a pattern from all blanks, it never works that way. I am hunched over like that statue of a man thinking. I am Dunce Scotus. Got that right. I am always either propped up by two clever children or laid to rest by my pianist. She is forever out Chopining, as if I remembered how to eat. One pill makes me thin, another dizzy, another breathless, another lame, another runny-nosed, another restless, another makes my ears sing. If he could only make himself some carb-soda for his indigestion. Up he flailed, humming, caught at the cupboard's bottom lip to support himself, then fell, rolling, no longer caring who found him or sold him or trussed him up in a greasy sack and lowered him into the trench.

He survived another day, tersely bibbing straight scotch, approved by Dr. Crawford, who stood behind him shaking his head. Nothing was working any more. Out he burst, to shock them all: "I'm having a wonderful day. One of my better ones today." The scotch was talking, Crawford said. In the night, Hilly, the light sleeper, heard him take an unusual breath and let it out. He breathed again, "rawshuss," as he liked to say, and out it came, ragged and lost. He never inhaled again or knew that he had not. In that bed of the warrior felled, Hilly lay again only once, taking to the one Kotch had left behind when she married. Hilly blamed the bed, grateful as she was for his unconscious end at seventy-five, he who might have been killed at fifteen or, properly medicated and fitted with a pacemaker, gone on to a hundred. She remained sedated for a month, while Clive stamped ants to death with his foot and glared into the sun. It would be a long time before he saw that his parents had come into the world to use life a lot, not to make a little glancing contact, and, as such, were bulk users, helping themselves with both hands in spite of vicissitudes and injuries, until they had had enough, and cried bravely aloud for a full stop.

III

UFFINGHAM
The Fragility of
Euphoria

IN HE HAD GONE, on tiptoe, but he need not have bothered; she had been fast asleep in her chair with the television cut down to a quiet murmur. He sat on the couch opposite her, his back to the open window and the silver birch outside. He sat thus for some twenty minutes until she woke, stared at him, assimilated him into her dream or daydream, and went back to sleep, content with the image her doze had yielded. Then she looked at him again, aware but befuddled and at a loss to know why her dream kept perpetuating itself in the realm of the physical. He smiled and, without moving, opened his arms wide as if to enfold her by suction from where he sat. She told herself that people in dreams moved and smiled, oh yes. It was a delicious dream, just the sort of thing she had often wished would happen on a rainy day. Then he stood up and walked toward her, creating (alas) a moment of genuine terror. She would have recoiled, but the high back of her chair held her there for his advance as he spoke.

She tried to stand, but fell back too cramped. Now she knew. He was there, whisked over that slate-blue ocean while she slept soundly: a salmon above the waves, belted in, his stockinged feet in the felt holsters provided.

"Well, I'm blest," she said, using a word that otherwise appeared in her vocabulary as "blessed," meaning damned—"Close that blessed door." He did, smiling as he did so at the providence of a country that left small bags of potatoes inside the hallway for residents to buy at twenty P. apiece. He might have brought her a couple of bags on his way in, just to prove he knew how she lived here, humbly systematic, but he was too eager to be there, confronting her.

How strange, he thought; if the tree of life is a eucalyptus, then its koala is the returning prodigal son. Am *I* prodigal? I have to get to know the ropes all over again. Here she lives so casually, door wide open, wind blowing in, as if willing to let the universe have its way with her unimpeded, whereas in Exington, that dourer place, she locked herself in like a New Yorker, with two keys and three bolts, daring anyone just to try.

She had come here in a hurry, almost overnight, having suddenly announced that she was ready to move, it was time to go, she could not bear the thought of another winter in Exington. That had been last year, her true motivation having been that she had become the oldest woman in the village, a status (an honor?) she had no liking for, so here she was in her own apartment in Uffingham, in a residence for senior citizens who could still more or less look after themselves. Ninety-four, she was the fourth eldest in the little dormitorylike building. It was quieter, slower, much more social here than in Exington; more mannered, and wholly agricultural except for NATO jets that thundered overhead, waiting for a war to go to. She had been to Uffingham many times before, to stay with daughter Kotch and son-in-law Bernard, in whose home she had slept in every room, including (she boasted) the dining room; so she had friends in the village, admirers even, and what to Clive always seemed a profoundly useful following among the local doctors. People lived long here, she knew.

One day, after a short walk around the little quadrangle out back, Hilly and Clive came back through the main reception room. The door was banging and, while Clive tried to fix it, Hilly wandered over to the piano to contemplate the keyboard and was soon tapping out a melody. When she sat, she began to play bits of tunes she knew she could never forget, giving a wry grin as a finger refused to function or a hand held back. Clive sat down to listen, and soon found a small audience forming around him, of which Hilly was heedlessly aware, who sat in the deep and comfy chairs to hear her out. Word spread through the hallways that she was at long last doing it, that she had been doing it without even seeming to think about it, while her son was mending the door. No, not dry stuff, the sort of music with a tune to it, as she had always said. In they stole, nodding at friends and neighbors but transfixed by the wispy presence at the keyboard, playing now as if liberated from earth's gravity, her hands still too small for some combinations and arthritis making her miss certain notes—though she was the only one who noticed. She seemed elated in a stationary way, playing not to them but to some invincible presence behind the nondescript print of deer on the wall opposite her. Every now and then she stopped, dry-washed her hands, and resumed with fresh momentum, a young girl again playing her way to that first gold medal and the sheepskin from the Royal College.

In all, she played for some twenty minutes, a breezy anthology of Handel, Bach, Brahms, Schubert, Delius, Parry, Ireland, and Chopin, without however risking Liszt. She did not breathe heavily or tire, and someone, meaning well, began a short promenade that would bring a cup of tea to the piano, but then thought better of it; she did a complete detour behind the pianist's back without spilling a drop, sat down with the tea, and drank it, toasting the pianist with the empty cup. It was quite a day, with those arriving late coming straight into the lounge to see what the party was about. Clive noticed with jubilant awe how his mother, accustomed to performing, merely noted another audience; she wasn't building up to something now, she was doing what she had come to do. Classical impetus had never carried her this far in the last ten years, but it now carried her farther, as she astonished them with her rendition of Sigmund Romberg's *The Desert Song* and favorites from the 1930s when her two children were growing up to the sounds of a wind-up gramophone. The words of Adela Florence Cory Nicolson graced the air again with the pastoral nostalgia of imperial romance: "Pale hands I loved beside the Shalimar," otherwise known as "the Kashmiri Song," which even Clive's father, preferring a monks' chorus, did not spurn to sing as the steel needle scraped along the helix in the Bakelite record. She was revisiting the echo chambers of between-the-wars when carefully enunciated solemnity was the in thing; protestations could go slowly, and everyone, at least in a certain social class, wanted to be found both noble and genteel. Here she came, with another chorus of "One Alone," whose version by Anne Ziegler and Webster Booth had always melted her heart; but no, she surprised them all, making them wonder what she was doing, Had she made a mistake? It was no mistake, as he recognized, being something of a buff; she had all of a sudden broken into the "King Porter Stomp" as played by Jelly Roll Morton, a whole tract of her life suddenly exposed. He had no idea she knew it, still tenderly ribbing her about the days when he played his records of the big bands, and she had said "That isn't music," and had done scathing parodies of Woody Herman songs and Count Basie curlicues. Only the fact that Benny Goodman also played with the Budapest String Quartet saved him. Now, as she reached a comfortably familiar place in the number, she seemed to settle on her stool, smiling to herself as she half turned round to check his expression. When had she learned it? Had he himself provoked her into it? For how long had she been saving this up? Since '42 or thereabouts? She was awfully good in spite of her hands, swaying with the beat, being a genuine American, and setting the entire roomful into motion as she Jelly-Rolled her way through, then started off again, a born stomper finishing with something he should have known, but did not: "You Got to Be Modernistic," after the version by James P. Johnson, which went down less well. She was tiring, and she soon stood, left the room without heeding the applause, held erect by the genial Scots matron whom she called Heart of Midlothian.

After Hilly's concert, while triumph lay all about her, Clive had to put her back together again, the Heart of Midlothian having receded to her quarters with a big Calvinistic grin. First Hilly stood, then Clive raised her gently with his wrists beneath her armpits, which helped her spine to come straight again. As she dangled there, half giggling, half gasping, he heard her vertebrae realign themselves with the sound of a teething ring falling to a hard wooden floor, an odd patter of bones, light and fast. It was plain this maneuver relieved her, so, after slowly letting her down, he lifted her again and kept her up longer, draping her across his front but without any contact save under the armpits. "That was quite a show," he said, close to her ear, wanting to hug her without breaking her.

"It must be jelly 'cause jam don't shake like that," she chortled, evoking a Woody Herman favorite from his teens that she had especially mocked without quite dismissing it. The words must have been good, having stayed with her for almost half a century. "Four-five times," she said, calling up the ghost of yet another number: a number's numbers, by the same band. "*She* didn't hang around," his mother said, meaning Heart of Midlothian, the dear departed. "*She* has her duties," he told her, knowing that his mother had almost got out of hand. "I wish Kotch had heard it, seen it," he told her, wondering if his sister would believe it when he told her.

"I didn't do it for her," his mother said. "This was for you, seeing that you're over."

He had been "over" many times, but she had never greeted him like this before, or made him feel he had so much of her attention, pointed and copious. From her came the pungent aroma of wintergreen ointment, the one that burned the skin on her back but which, because it generated heat, gave her ease merely by distracting her nerves. The trouble was it never lasted long, any more than the armpit lifts or the wintergreen, so she took codeine, with which she had fallen in love some years ago, always tempted to overdose on it, telling him the sensation was "over the moon."

The skin of her face seemed out of place from exertion, flushed and pushed sideways, as now. There was a stutter in her gait, and she sometimes hovered in mid-step, waiting for the hinges of her knees to loosen or her sense of balance to return, but she had good legs in spite of the twinges that ran through them. On her right temple there was a black patch like a scab of something cancerous, but it never changed, it had been there for years, and she never picked at it—she was that strict with herself, although she would sometimes pluck at her lower lip, pulling it out of shape to indicate a world gone wrong. Now and then she would rub one eye, trying to remove the cataract that bleared her vision and prevented her from sewing or knitting, even doing the crossword, and this seemed to clear her sight for half an hour. With the far-from-clinical affection of a Vesalius caught napping, Clive looked at her veins, perfect for demonstration purposes: almost autonomous above the layer of bone and muscle, standing out in every branch, and reassuringly thick, full of pianist's coursing blood. She had no flesh on her these days, thanks to diuretics; her size was smaller than a petite, although in her day she had been an extra-large.

Clive had to be off the premises by nine, when they locked the front door; he could have had a key, but hadn't bothered to ask, thinking it just as well to get out of her hair by then, after having spent almost twelve hours there. It delighted her to have her son with her, but it was demanding, it required more naps during the execution or the savoring, and it took more out of him too, not used to having her quite so passive. Deep down, she was still mourning the loss of Edith, and she grieved as never about Harry or the some one hundred of her friends who had gone before. Another friend, an Uffingham woman, a former piano teacher too, had died about the same time as Edith, a woman with the inspired, almost unmeritable name of Tranquil Gaunt. He could see how his mother's mind trailed after these dear ones, like Wordsworth in reverse: Trailing clouds or skeins of glory, they journeyed away from her, pecking or nibbling their way outward, *awayward,* to some undeclared terminus, where they might never be found by those coming after. If there were to be music in the space of death, she had explained to him with her usual jocular fatalism, things would have to be better organized than that, or they would all be soloists, out of earshot of one another.

Such talk as this he found hard to handle because he realized he would tell her anything, be either Christian or Hindu, just to soothe her about disappearance, the ultimate fate of the soul and the mind, the nature of heaven, which she had assumed was clean and harmonic. Heaven was like the little garbage can whose lid connected to a pedal to save her from stooping; but she jammed the lid open all the time, to air it out. So too with heaven, then: It was aired out like a bathroom, or, like a bed, it was always aired, never damp, the sheets and comforter having been in the airing cupboard and its cozy fug since the universe began. How fiercely he hugged his pianist now, dreaming he was holding her tight, but holding on to her with almost vehement need, as if she were the force that would stave off her own undoing, as if she, protector and protected, would protect him too, as she always had, cupping his forehead in the palm of her hand, easing him back into sleep and serenity. "You always die a little, they say," she had told him when Tranquil Gaunt died, "and you do. But you never die enough to keep the pain away. It doesn't help to die a little. Your father knew that."

Clive could still measure time, though, since it was he, no one else, who annually addressed himself to his mother's renegade eyelash, the one that grew faster than the other, actually becoming an inch long in the course of a year and setting up, just out of focus, a visual obstacle that worried and fazed her. Scores of times she tried to smooth it away, out of the line of sight, but it persisted in going forward, an antenna, a feeler, of no use except to measure the year by. So when he came he put on his best magnifying glasses (the ones bought cheap at the drugstore), told her to close both eyes, and snipped the eyelash off. Sometimes it was as much as an inch and a half long. Sometimes he wet his thumb and forefinger, then gently trained the lash forward, moist and conspicuous, picking up sunlight like a pitot tube on a plane. For a year she had forged ahead, irritated, yet aware the eyelash was a portion of all that she was, a little tribe of aberrant cells that refused to toe the line, but sought her attention by blurring her vision every bit as much as the cataract in the other eye. One day, she had fantasized in his presence, it would be a foot long, something to hold and tug her with. Yes, a wife-leader, he thought. No, he'd told her, "it always gets clipped in time. You can count on me for that. A steady hand I still have, and a half decent eye." It was a little ritual of intimacy; he cherished doing it, and wished sometimes her entire body were burgeoning just as mightily.

Parts of his mother had longings: not that she willed any of this, as she had willed thousands of things in her time. No, this eyelash had a will of its own, slightly coarser *qua* hair than the other lashes, perhaps because it had to fend for itself more. She was rather proud of it, and he wondered, being interested in her at this level, if the secretest folds of her being included other such accelerated features. He asked his sister, but she knew nothing of exceptional toenails, say, and he was rather glad in the end to be the custodian of his mother's one singularity. He had just such an eyelash himself and trimmed it by dint of squinting and peering: dangerous, he sometimes thought, but fun to do. A piece of runaway self, he called it, inherited from her: a link. Properly positioned, with their long lashes uncut, she and he might actually embrace face to face and have their elongated single hairs lie alongside each other or, more bizarrely, actually meet end to end.

The very thought cheered him, flimsy as it was; it was what almost no one else had, or even wanted, so it was uniquely theirs, a family-failing to smile about, maybe just a touch ruefully, when falling asleep.

"Steady now," she always said as he prepared to clip, "no punctured eyeballs, please."

"No, missus, none of those."

"And don't pull on it."

"I won't."

"It drags my entire eyelid after it, you see."

"It won't, I promise."

"Then don't take all day. It's only a matter of—"

"Finished, Momoi. You're done until next year."

"I still wish I could do it for myself."

No, he told himself: Only I do that. He wondered how many people on the planet had the same problem, if not with eyelashes then with other, slightly misprogrammed hairs growing out of pylonidal cysts in some ill-judged place or other, as if all human beings were walking, palpitant revisions on the brink of change: they just never knew how close they were to being Cyclops, Elephant Men, or Hunchbacks of Notre Dame. It was encouraging, really, this possibility of the preposterous, likely (he hoped) to win a freakish alien an hospitable welcome on Planet Earth. One touch of the freakish makes the whole world kin, he thought. It doesn't have to be much: just an intimation of glitch will humble us all when we avert our gaze from the unsightly. We simply need to be reminded that only good luck makes us as handsome as we are, if we are, any of us.

"I'M STRAIGHT again," she told Kotch.

"You're done, are you?"

"I'm done, and it's nice to see straight."

"Well, unclouded," his sister said.

"That," Hilly agreed.

"I could always clip it every three months," Kotch said.

"No," Hilly said, half merrily, "I like to save it up for him to do. He needs something to occupy him when he's over here. Since he stopped working so much with pen and pad on that upturned tray."

"I bet," Kotch said, looking hard through the window into the direct sun, finally compelled to close her eyes. Clive was in the presence of heirlooms, shibboleths, household gods, and he sometimes felt inclined to say nothing, to let sharp-edged family prattle go its way without contributions from him. His sister did a thousand chores for his mother weekly and got less thanks. He wanted to cling to the few tasks that remained his to do, working each one into something enormously altruistic, worth entering into the Doomsday Book of the Fitzalans with a big fat E for eyelash. In the old days, his mother had saved up things to do for him, almost taking on too much for each day of a visit; but she did almost none of that now, so what remained between them of loving attentiveness was precious beyond cavil.

It had taken him much of a lifetime to do it, but Clive had taught himself to flinch less and less at the mindless persistence of the universe. Who if not a human was absurd for calling the universe absurd? He found it almost soothing to consider the bowling greens of Orion, its ballparks and star nurseries, its fjords and puys, there for the asking mind, without the least trace of self-deceit. He needed to think he was wonderful, not in the sense of self-congratulation, but of wonder at all humans, coaxed into shape from hosts of squabbling atoms. I am a wonder walking beneath wonders, he told himself; I happen to have fixed upon Orion, but anywhere I walked on the planet there would be some ravishing flock of stars immediately above me, not sheltering, but simply hovering in random apprehensibility. To live amidst the universe without thinking about it—why, that is to have Beethoven on the player and be afraid to turn it on. It is not a matter of saying thanks, or of cowering, or of registering the whole cosmos as a feat of physics and chemistry; it is merely a matter of feeling special, just as a winged insect might, its wings folded against its back and thinking, for a second, how like a human it looks, with a pair of snowshoes on its shoulders. Not so much the sense of wonder, rather the sense of ponder, that is what ails me, if ailment I have. If only I had enough of the volcanic alertness needed to realize that every second is a blue-chip miracle: She exists, therefore I gasp.

Two months after he had returned to the States, having embraced her through the wide-open window frame, on his way home from a conference, he stood in Dulles airport listening to an announcement about the 8:45 evening jumbo jet to London, sensing that something was wrong. That was Friday. Saturday morning, he called Kotch, who explained that Hilly had fallen off her stool and cracked a rib. She was in the hospital being X-rayed, but quite cheerful, sending him a message to mail her some extra postcards. She was also raising a tiny fuss about there being men in the ward, but the fog in her eyes had misled her. By Monday she had died in her sleep and been revived with paddles long enough to whisper to Kotch "I think I'm dying, I'm sorry," as if unable to quell some final cosmic prejudice, and Clive knew he was not in her class at all.

ABOUT THE AUTHOR

PAUL WEST has published a dozen novels, among them *Rat Man of Paris*, *The Very Rich Hours of Count von Stauffenberg*, *Gala*, *The Place in Flowers Where Pollen Rests* and *Lord Byron's Doctor*, which became a bestseller in France and was shortlisted for both the Médicis and Fémina prizes. His numerous works of nonfiction include the best-selling *Words for a Deaf Daughter* and *Portable People*, a collection of biographical sketches. His short stories have been collected under the title *The Universe, and Other Fictions*, and a new volume of criticism, *Sheer Fiction II*, was published recently. He is at work on a nonfiction book about living with illness.

Paul West is a Guggenheim Fellow, and has received the Arts and Letters Award from the American Academy and Institute of Arts and Letters, the Hazlett Award for Excellence in the Arts, and other honors. He was a judge for the 1990 National Book Award in Fiction. Educated at Oxford and Columbia universities, he is a Literary Lion of the New York Public Library.

ABOUT THE TYPE

This book was set in Bembo, a typeface based on an old-style Roman face that was used for Cardinal Bembo's tract *De Aetna* in 1495. Bembo was cut by Francisco Griffo in the early sixteenth century. The Lanston Monotype Machine Company of Philadelphia brought the well-proportioned letter forms of Bembo to the United States in the 1930s.